JIM ANTHONY
SUPER-DETECTIVE

I0553077

Airship 27 Productions

TM

Jim Anthony: Super-Detective, Volume Three
"The Mark of Terror"
© 2011 Joshua Reynolds

Published by Airship 27 Production
airship27hangar.com

Interior illustrations © 2011 Isaac "Bobit" Nacilla
Cover illustration © 2011 Jeff Herndon

Editor: Ron Fortier
Associate Editor: Ray Riethmeier
Production and design: Rob Davis.

ISBN: 978-1-953589-47-7

Printed in the United States of America

Second edition 2023

Jim Anthony Super-Detective
"The Mark of Terror"

by Joshua Reynolds

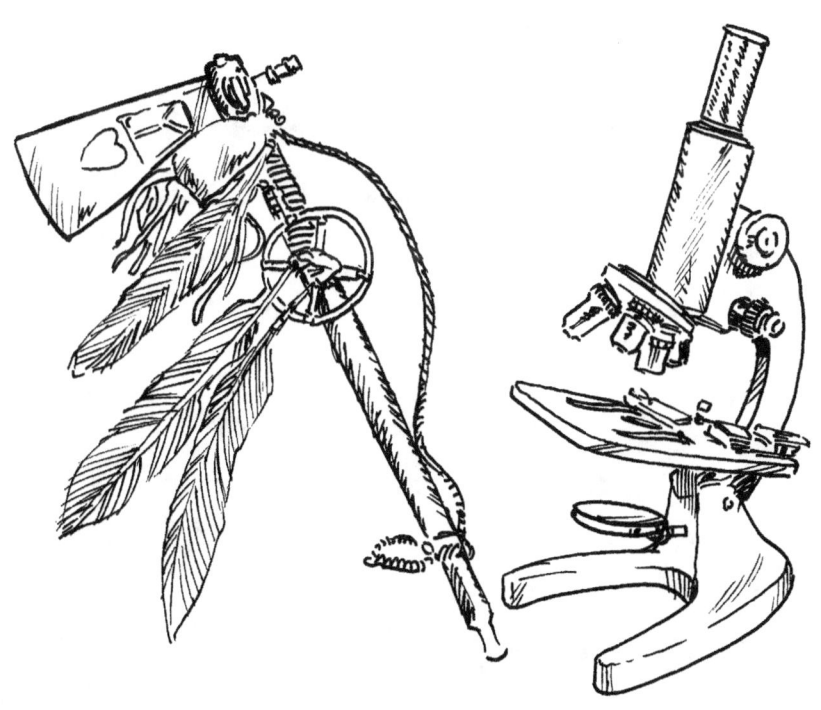

I.

London. 1931.

"You are quite the clever one, Mr. Anthony," Neville Soames said, reclining in his chair, a glass of wine balanced in one hand. Off to one side, a fire crackled cheerfully in the fireplace, driving back some of the shadows that shrouded the drawing room of the sumptuous Cheyne Walk flat. "Yes, quite clever. It's almost a shame that you have to die," he continued, drawing a pistol from where it had been hidden under his seat. The Webley's barrel gleamed in the light of the fire.

Jim Anthony, seated opposite his host, looked first at the pistol, then, deliberately, at the glass of wine in his own hand, then, finally, back up at Soames.

Soames chuckled. "Yes. You should feel quite honored. I sacrificed a delightful pinot noir in order to get rid of you, Mr. Anthony. We shall never see its like again."

"Poison," Jim said. Soames shrugged.

"Well, yes. You know by now that I'm a dab hand with various chemicals. Self-taught, mind."

"Why not just shoot me?"

"What would be the point in that? I'm a scientist after all." He gestured with the pistol. "It's my own personal concoction. Something special, just for you."

Jim ignored the compliment, twisted as it was, instead focusing his dark eyes on his host. Soames was a thin rapier of a man, with slicked back blonde hair and the face of a dissolute pharaoh. Anthony, in contrast, was tall and broad, his skin burnt bronze by a lifetime spent out of doors and his face was all sharp angles between the thatch of curly hair on top and the strong jaw opposite.

There was another difference between them, beyond the physiological. Soames was a murderer. And Jim Anthony was the world's foremost murderist.

As a hunter of criminals and killers he had achieved international repute, and, as the controller of one of America's foremost fortunes, he even had the pleasure of doing said hunting for free. Law enforcement agencies the world over had requested his help at one time or another and Anthony was only too glad to help.

Such was the case now. As 1930 gave way to 1931, fifteen men and women, members of London's exclusive Chelsea community and all attending the same New Year's Eve party, had collapsed, gone into convulsions and died. More, each one had died as the result of ingesting a different poison. Scotland Yard, at a loss to discover either culprit or motive, had inquired as to whether Jim was interested in lending them the benefit of his expertise. He had readily agreed.

And now it was looking as if that was the last thing he would ever do.

Soames watched him with a hot, eager gaze. "Honestly, this has been quite diverting. Imagine my excitement when I learned that the famous American detective, Jim Anthony, was hunting for me." His finger tapped the trigger.

"Glad to be of service," Jim said. He twitched, feeling a sudden, stabbing pain deep in his stomach. It struck like lightning, climbing his ribs, and curling around his spine. He took a breath.

"I actually feel quite invigorated," Soames said. "Whatever shall I do next?"

"Turn yourself in," Jim said, through gritted teeth. Soames blinked, then laughed.

"Why ever would I do such a thing?" Soames cocked his head. "Out of curiosity, how does it feel? The poison, I mean."

Jim leaned back in his seat. Thin rivulets of sweat rolled down his face as he fought to control his gag reflex. Eyes still on Soames, he forced a smile. "Take some and find out."

Soames hesitated, then leaned forward and tipped his wine onto the floor between them. "No. Not yet, at least. I have to refine it, you see."

"Is that why you killed them? Was it all just an experiment?" Jim said. Soames nodded.

"Of course. The mixture currently eating up your vitals is the result of the data I acquired on New Year's Eve. And your reaction will help me refine it further." Soames licked his lips. "The perfect poison. Odorless. Colorless. Tasteless. It could be water, but its potency is such that the merest drop can kill a grown man." He sat back and spread his hands. "So you see, any help you can give me will be appreciated greatly."

"Duly noted," Jim said. He bent double with a groan. His fingers sought his belt. Soames stood, face twisted into a gloating expression. The pistol hung by his side, apparently forgotten.

"Your stomach should have ruptured by now. Digestive acids will be flooding the crevices of your intestines. How does it feel?"

Jim gave a cry and fell forward, onto his hands and knees. Soames squatted. "Don't be coy, Mr. Anthony. Just tell me how you feel?" Then, more urgently, "Tell me!"

"I feel fine, actually," Jim said, looking up. Reaching out, he casually swatted the Webley from Soames' grip. As Soames jerked back in shock, Jim's fist flashed out, hammering into his belly.

Soames folded double and stumbled back, face going red. Jim rose to his feet with an almost feline grace. He tapped his belt buckle. "I took the opportunity to synthesize an antidote to your concoctions. Once I had the signature elements, the ones you included in every dose, it was easy enough to come up with a defense. I'll be sick to my stomach for a few days, though." A twinge rolled through him, and he winced. "Maybe a few weeks."

"You-you—" Soames gasped, his eyes the merest slits. With a hiss, he uncoiled, his fingers digging for Jim's face. Jim stepped back and grabbed the other man's wrists. Soames strained forward for a moment, his face a mask of hatred, then Jim's greater strength began to tell.

Jim hauled him forward abruptly and pivoted, driving Soames' face into the chair he'd just vacated. Chair and man toppled in a tangle. Jim stooped to scoop up the pistol.

"Detective Inspector Coutts will be here in a few minutes. I took the liberty of alerting him to my suspicions before you invited me for a nightcap."

Soames, on his feet, shrieked and lunged, something thin and sharp glittering in his hand. Jim spun as the tip of the poisoned blade tore through the sleeve of his shirt and he reflexively fired the Webley.

Soames stepped back, dropping the knife. He blinked, then looked down at the growing stain on the front of his coat. "Oh."

"Soames! Damn it!" Jim started forward even as Soames keeled over backwards, his head striking the floor with a dull thump.

Jim sank to his haunches and felt for a pulse. "Damn it," he said again. He hadn't wanted this. Soames had deserved to stand trial. The families of his victims had deserved to see him hang.

With two fingers he closed Soames' staring eyes and then rose to his feet. Outside, he could hear the wail of approaching sirens. Detective Inspector Coutts to the rescue. He looked down at Soames, wondering what had driven a man of such intellect to such perversity. Fifteen men and women, dead for what? To satisfy a deviant curiosity?

His eyes found those of a hideous mask mounted on Soames' wall. A triangular tongue jutted between opposing tusks, forming a terrible leer. Jim looked away.

How many like Soames had he seen in his career, he wondered. Malignant psyches driven by inhuman desires. He looked at the mask again, then stared into the fire for a moment, as if hoping that it held the answer. The sirens echoed loudly now. The police were right outside.

Jim went to greet them.

2.

New York. 1931. One month later.

Jim Anthony stepped down the stairs of the plane, bags dangling from one hand, his other holding his coat. He paused for a moment, taking in a whiff of the cold February air. He could smell the acrid scent of the New Jersey marshland mingling with the manmade odours of Newark Airport, and beyond them, the city.

It was good to be home.

A week in Monaco had been enough to flush the last effects of Soames' poisons out of his system, but New York beckoned, and Jim, ever the dutiful son, had answered.

While it was true that his business interests could run themselves, Jim wasn't the type to let other people make his money for him. There were decisions to be made, papers to be signed and deals to be negotiated.

A car was waiting on the tarmac, its driver slouched against the front bumper, arms crossed. Jim smiled as the man looked up, revealing a freckled face that could have been considered handsome three or four punches earlier.

"Tom. Good to see you again," Jim said, extending a hand. The big man took it, his scarred paw nearly enveloping Jim's own.

"Don't lie, Jimmy. There's far fairer sights to be seeing than this mug of mine," Tom Gentry said, his words ringing with a Gaelic lilt. The two men had grown up together, boyhood friends. No, more than friends. Almost brothers. The hulking Gentry had fought by Jim's side innumerable times, had taken beatings, blades and bullets meant for his friend, and Jim had done the same more than once.

"You didn't have to bring the Rolls, you know," Jim said. Tom chuckled and slapped a hand on the swell of the Rolls-Royce's hood.

"Hey, I wasn't there to help you with that Soames thing. Figured the least I could do was bring the fancy ride to take you home." Tom frowned. "I really am sorry about that Jimmy. I wish you had—"

"I know, Tom." Jim slid into the passenger seat. "I am perfectly capable of taking care of myself, you know."

"Now whatever gave you that idea, Jimmy?" Tom said, in mock surprise. Jim laughed and settled back in his seat as Tom took them away from the airport.

Jim dozed as they wound their way through the city towards home. He had lived in many places, the South West, for instance, and the Catskills, but New York was home. His father had called it the greatest city in the world, and Jim was hard pressed to find any flaw in that conclusion.

Thoughts of his father provoked a familiar brief flush of melancholy. The Black Mood of the Celts was only one of the many things he'd inherited from the man.

8

Shean Boru Anthony had been a giant of a man, both in body and mind. An adventurer and entrepreneur, he had built the company which now provided Jim with his idle lifestyle.

Granted, without the steadying influence of Jim's mother, Fawn, it was unlikely Shean would have accomplished half of what he did. The melancholy faded, replaced as quickly as it had come by something altogether lighter.

Jim looked at his hands, watching his muscles play beneath his deeply tanned skin. The latter was as much a gift from his mother as a result of too much time in the sun.

As a child, Jim's lullabies had been sung in Shoshoni and Gaelic, the birth languages of his parents. Where his father had been a black-bearded Irish madman, Fawn Johntom had been a woman of the Comanche. Where Shean Anthony had hurled himself at the throat of the world, Jim's mother had been calm to the point of stoicism. Practical. Still waters that ran as deep as the world was wide.

"*Cha bhi fios aire math an tobair gus an tràigh e,*" Jim murmured softly. An old saying of his father's…the value of the well is not known until it goes dry.

"Jimmy. We're here," Tom said, startling him out of his reverie. Jim looked up.

The Waldorf-Anthony Hotel rose above them, occupying the corner of Fifth Avenue like a titan of old. Built in 1897, then gradually enlarged until it had reached its current height of eighty-six floors, the Waldorf-Anthony was one of the greatest examples of modern structural engineering and one of the most expensive hotels on the East Coast.

It was also Jim's home in the city. He occupied the top three floors on a more or less permanent basis, staying mainly in the Penthouse.

Tom took the car into the underground garage, a feature known only to a select few of the hotel's more permanent residents, via the entrance on the corner. Jim had had a hand in designing the garage and the entrance both, just after he'd left the university. While architectural design wasn't something he counted among his talents, Jim felt he hadn't done too bad a job. The garage was a small thing, built around a descending spiral. As the Rolls maneuvered downwards, Jim leaned back.

"Is Dawkins here?"

Tom snorted. "Where else would he be?"

Like Tom, Dawkins had been with Jim practically forever, depending on how you judged such things. Ostensibly Jim's butler, more often than not he fell into roles as varied as medic and bodyguard.

While he presented the image of a traditional English gentleman's gentleman, Dawkins' lower class London accent and scarred features denoted a life not lived exclusively in the houses of the wealthy. Indeed, like both Tom and Jim himself, Dawkins was a veteran of the last great war, and others besides.

Too, he knew how to brew a refreshing cup of tea.

The Rolls settled into its usual space a few minutes later. Jim slid out, and Tom followed, both heading for the private elevator Jim had installed soon after the garage had been completed.

Tom closed the doors and twisted the knob. The elevator was an express, not stopping at any floors other than the top three, and it hummed as it rose.

"Feel good to be home?" Tom said.

"Always," Jim said. "England is a nice place to visit, but it's—"

"Too damp to live?" Tom said.

"I was going to say too orderly. They have their own ways of doing things, and they clash with mine, I think." Jim frowned. "Besides which, Soames' death has made me something of a persona non grata."

"What? But that lousy limey tried to drill you!" Tom was outraged. Jim made a calming gesture.

"Only after I provoked him. Sherlock Holmes might have gotten away with it, but I'm no Holmes," he said. "They wanted me to help find the killer, not usher him to the gallows." Jim shook his head. "I often underestimate the self-destructive urge of certain breeds of criminal."

"He was screwy is all," Tom said.

"Yeah." Jim smiled slightly as the elevator came to a halt. "Maybe so."

Dawkins was waiting for them as Tom pushed the elevator door open. Thin and wiry, he was dressed to the nines and carrying a tray, upon which a mug of tea sat steaming. Jim sniffed.

"Madame's mixture, sir. I thought you might like a taste of home upon your return," Dawkins said, brandishing the tray. Jim took the mug and sipped it with a twinge of nostalgia. His mother had been something of a chemical prodigy, mixing and matching disparate ingredients with a level of success that was statistically impossible. Dawkins had salvaged her recipes and herbal mixtures and clung to them the way a monk clung to scripture.

"Notice you didn't make me a cup," Tom grunted. Dawkins glanced at him, his carefully arched brow making his reply for him. Tom's eyes narrowed. Jim sighed and stepped between them, slapping the cup into Tom's hands.

"Here. Finish this for me. Anything happen while I was gone, Dawkins?" Jim said, stepping past the butler into the apartment.

The Penthouse was large, but cramped. The furniture had been selected less for taste and more for comfort. Peculiar iconography decorated the walls, jostling for space with framed photos, maps, and the odd painting that Jim had taken a fancy to. Pickman's "Subway Accident" shared a space with a cubist self-portrait by Campalans.

Jim found that the resulting clash of color and shape helped stimulate his thought processes.

The apartment spread out around the aleph of a curving stairwell that led to the roof. The kitchen, Dawkins' uncontested territory, was a slice of space separated from the main room by an island bar and a dress-maker's dummy studded with kitchen knives.

Large potted plants occupied the corners and flat spaces, stabbing some tropical vibrancy into the sterile art deco set-up. Familiar smells and sights seeped into Jim, easing the remaining tiny knots of tension he had carried over from England.

"I took the liberty of collecting the dailies for the past week, sir. Including the Daily Star."

"Morning and evening editions?" Jim said. The Daily Star was highly successful, as far as newspapers went, putting out two editions daily in every major American city. It also happened to belong, in its entirety, to Jim.

"Of course, sir." Dawkins managed to sound insulted without altering his voice in any fashion. Jim nodded.

"Excellent. And the Globe?"

"The Globe, the Times, and the Bugle, sir." Dawkins gestured to a neatly situated stack of newspapers sitting beside one of the overstuffed couches that looked out at the Penthouse balcony. "Though why you want the former is beyond me. It is little more than a yellow tabloid."

"Diversity is the spice of life," Jim said. "Any messages?"

"A Mr. Docker called for you."

"Pongo Docker?" Jim said, dredging a fleshy face up out of his memory. "I haven't seen him in more than a year. What did he want?"

"He declined to leave a message. Most sulfurously, I might add." Dawkins sniffed. Jim grinned.

"Sounds like Pongo. Not even a number where I can reach him, then?"

"No, sir."

"That sounds like him too. Any other messages?"

"A Jerome Smithback. He would like to take lunch, at your earliest convenience."

"Smithback? Hunh." Jim rubbed his chin.

"Know him, too, Jimmy?" Tom said, perching himself on the edge of the couch. He was about to take a sip of the tea when Dawkins swept it up and returned it to the kitchen. "Hey!"

"Not in the strictest sense." Jim stooped and scooped up an armful of newspapers. "Smithback was an acquaintance of my father's." Jim began to flip through the papers, scanning the front page of each, taking note of those things which caught his interest. A rash of disappearances in Red Hook. Missing children mostly, though a few adults as well. Jim frowned. "Why he'd want to have lunch with me, however, is a bit of a mystery."

"Business, maybe?" Tom said, staring longingly at the cup of tea. Dawkins carefully poured it back into a warming canister, ignoring Gentry's attentions. Jim glanced over an article detailing a gas explosion in a tenement in Harlem, leading to four dead and two missing.

"More than likely he wants me to invest in something," Jim said. "My father was an early investor of his. Helped him get started, actually." Jim continued flipping through the papers. Stories leapt out at him.

An explosion in Panama had claimed the lives of three employees of Morgan, Grenfell and Company. Two members of the Metropolitan Club had been killed in a car accident in upstate New York. A chemist in Vermont, working for Allied Chemical, had been caught in a chemical fire which had bleached his skin and boiled his brain. It was a season for accidents, it seemed.

A name caught his eye. Tupker. Alan Tupker. Jim stopped flipping and concentrated on the article. Tupker was an up and comer in the business world. Despite the tribulations rippling out of Black Tuesday, Tupker was renowned for remaining afloat. Everything 'Lucky Al' touched seemed to turn to gold. Or had, at any rate, prior to his throwing himself in front of train earlier in the month.

The picture accompanying the article was from better times, showing Tupker smiling with friends at the Cloud Club. Among the group, another familiar face caught Jim's eye.

Jerome Smithback.

"Hm." Jim folded the paper. "You know, I think I will take lunch with Mr. Smithback. Dawkins?"

"I have his number, yes, sir." Dawkins nodded and made for the phone. "I shall arrange it."

"The Cloud Club, I think." Jim examined the picture for a moment longer then folded the paper and tossed it aside. "Tomorrow."

3.

The next day.

Nearly nine-hundred feet above the corner of 42nd Street and Lexington Avenue sat the exclusive Cloud Club. Occupying the sixty-sixth, sixty-seventh and sixty-eighth floors of the newly built Chrysler Building, the Club played host to the elite of the Big Apple.

Business magnates and Hollywood stars mingled with politicians and old money blue-bloods amongst the polished granite columns and delicate etched glass sconces of the dining area. Wealth, celebrity and influence were all accepted forms of tender, and the average patron tended to have at least two of the three, and be hunting actively for the third.

At a table sitting beneath an impressive mural of Manhattan, two such patrons were coming to the end of what had been, up until that moment, a fairly civil conversation.

"Well. That's that, then." The speaker was an older man with the heavy frame of a born oligarch. Frowning, he thumped the table in front of him with the palm of one wide hand.

"Yes, I suppose it is. But that doesn't mean it has to ruin our lunch, Jerry," Jim Anthony said, smiling slightly. The older man's face flushed and he struck the table again, this time with a fist.

"Damn it, Anthony, I—"

"Jerome." Jim's voice was like a sun-baked stone—warm, but unyielding. Dark eyes flashed dangerously. "I have no interest in this scheme of yours."

"Scheme? It's no scheme!" Smithback blustered, his heavy features turning an unpleasant shade of purple. Jim braced the table as another blow rocked it.

"Stop taking it out on the table, please. I'd rather not have the bill for repairs added to my tab on top of that meal that you have, so far, not touched," he said. Smithback sank back into his chair for a moment, then rallied.

"Your father—"

"Wouldn't have had anything to do with such a plan either. Frankly, Jerome, I don't need the money. My current state of affairs is quite comfortable, I assure you," Jim said. He leaned back, draping his rangy frame over the chair and let his gaze travel towards the great windows which occupied the far wall. The windows of the Club sprang from floor to ceiling, unmarred by sill or lock. They were unblemished walls of glass looking out over the city. The view was wonderful, and one of the main reasons Jim chose to lunch at the Club on occasion.

"I can see that," Smithback grunted, eyeing Anthony's attire with distaste. In contrast to Smithback's carefully tailored business suit, Anthony wore clothing which could be, at best, classified as casual. Rough-woven cloth trousers covered

13

his long legs and narrow waist, and a dull colored sweatshirt hid his muscular arms and torso.

It was a constant wonder to Smithback how Anthony made it in to places like the Cloud Club dressed as he was. Force of personality, perhaps. Then, it could have been his status as owner of the successful Daily Star.

Or, maybe it was simply that Jim Anthony was the world's foremost manhunter. It wasn't the sort of hobby Smithback would've taken up but to each their own, he supposed. Privately, he figured it was the Comanche blood. Shean Anthony had married a woman of that tribe, despite the advice of his peers, and the barbaric savagery had obviously bred true in their son.

Jim smiled, ignoring the implied insult, and signaled the waiter for another cup of coffee. "Why did you even think of me?"

"A favor, Anthony, that's all." Smithback pushed his untouched plate aside with slightly more force than was necessary. "Your father fronted me my grubstake, way back when. I wanted to try and repay that debt. But, since you're not interested...."

"Not at all." Jim paused, then said. "Alan Tupker is dead."

He wasn't sure what he'd been expecting—surprise, perhaps. Acknowledgement. The news was several days old, after all. Instead, what Jim saw in Smithback's eyes was fear. Cold, naked fear. "Did Docker call you?" Smithback said.

"What?" Jim said. Before he could continue, a voice interrupted.

"Sirs."

Both Jim and Smithback looked up as a waiter hove into view, holding a silver tray balanced perfectly on long fingers. "Pardon the intrusion, sirs. Cards and drinks, compliments of the house."

Smithback grunted and took his drink and card without looking at the latter. It was a common way of doing business in the upper echelons of New York society. Interested in putting together a business deal? Send a card to the other party. Jim put his own drink aside and looked at his card, then at Smithback. "Silas Pender, inviting me for drinks. After the premiere tonight at the Roxy. Were you attending, Jerry?"

"That thing based on that limey play?" Smithback said, playing with his own card, but leaving it facedown. "Wasn't planning on it."

"Dracula. Based on a novel by Bram Stoker," Jim said. "It'll be a gas. Come see it, we'll go out afterwards. You, me and Pender."

"And?"

"We can talk." Jim shrugged. "Maybe Pongo Docker can come."

"Why would you think that?"

"You just mentioned him," Jim said. "Did he have anything to do with this? Maybe trying a different tack to get me involved?" Jim continued, thinking of Docker's call earlier.

Smithback said nothing, merely knocking back his drink. Jim shook his head. His suspicions, formerly only the smallest of things, flared to full burn.

"How many others are involved in this, Jerry? Beyond you and Tupker, I mean," Jim said, leaning forward. "And what about Tupker?"

"Just what I was going to ask."

Jim and Smithback turned, the latter visibly startled. A woman smiled pretti-ly, flashing white teeth, and leaned forward, pulling up a spare chair. "Catherine Kilkenny, from the Daily Globe. Do you gentlemen have time for a few questions?"

"I—" Smithback began. Jim knew from personal experience that Kilkenny was seven feet of professional barracuda crammed into the petite five foot and change frame of a pixie-ish young woman. He examined her as she focused her attentions on Smithback; she had short hair, cut into a bob, hidden beneath a cloche hat, and slim, straight limbs the color of vanilla. A fur lined coat completed the image of a bon vivant. But she was anything but.

"Perfect! So, how long have you been in favor of a lack of economic competition in international trade?" Kilkenny smiled again, pencil poised over her notepad.

"What?"

"The trade monopolies you're looking to establish? How does Jack Morgan feel about your attempts to push JP Morgan & Co. out of the international markets? What about South America?"

"How—" Smithback gaped at the woman. Jim hid a smile. It was rare to see Jerry Smithback at a complete loss for words.

"Do you think the recent death of Alan Tupker will impact your success in any way?"

"Tupker?" Smithback echoed, dumbfounded. Jim sat up.

"Who are you meeting today? A replacement? A new investor for your little scheme?" Kilkenny spoke quickly, firing questions like bullets. She glanced at Jim. "Jim Anthony! Howsabout that? Mind if I ask you a few questions, Mr. Anthony?"

Jim frowned. "Yes."

"Good. How do you respond to allegations that you're planning on a hostile takeover of Reid Enterprises?"

"First I've heard of them, to be honest." Jim pushed his plate away, suddenly no longer hungry. "What would your editor think of you interviewing the owner of a rival newspaper, Miss Kilkenny?"

"He'd be ecstatic. Story of the year. Why are you having lunch with Smithback here, Mr. Anthony? Business lunch, maybe?" She was already writing. Jim leaned back.

"No."

"No to lunch or no to business?"

"The latter," Jim said. Kilkenny snorted and switched her laser-glare to Smithback, who was caught rising from his seat.

"Right. What do you think of the rumors that you're trying to push Jack Morgan out of Panama?"

"I—"

"What about you, Mr. Anthony?"

"I don't," Jim said, sipping from his glass.

"You don't think?"

"Not about that, no," Jim said, pushing his chair back and standing. He tossed a few bills on the table. "Now, if you'll excuse us—"

The maître d' stationed at the entrance to the dining room coughed discreetly, and Kilkenny shot a glare at him.

"What?"

"Mademoiselle is not—ah—allowed up here unless she is zee guest of—" the man began, waxed mustaches trembling in indignation. Kilkenny snorted.

"Can it, Charlie. And that accent is atrocious." She pinned Jim in place with her pencil. "Just one more question, Mr. Anthony!"

"How long have you been on the Silk Stocking beat, Miss Kilkenny?" Jim said, hitting her with a question of his own as he waved off the fuming maître d'. Ordinarily, women weren't allowed in the Club, unless they were the guest of a member. That Kilkenny had gotten this far was a testament to her determination and guile. Smithback tossed Jim a grateful look as he took the full brunt of the reporter's attentions. "I thought your line was society gossip."

"Nose for news," Kilkenny said, tapping the tip of her nose with the end of her pencil. "And Smithback's Sinister Six is most definitely news."

"Sinister Six?"

"Alliteration plays beautifully in Peoria," Kilkenny said, at Jim's look.

Jim hesitated, unsure of how to continue, and looked over at the other man. "Jerry?"

Smithback's mouth opened and closed like that of a suffocating trout. He looked around wildly, the card that had been delivered to him clutched between his fingers. Jim reached towards him. "Jerry?" he said again.

Smithback screamed.

Kilkenny leapt back like a scalded cat as Smithback's suddenly flailing arms swept out, sending a passing waiter sprawling, and the maître d' scrambling back. Jim lunged, seeking to grab him. Smithback shrieked again, his normally deep voice spiraling up into a high-pitched whistle, and he swung around, catching Jim across the jaw with a wild blow.

Jim staggered, more out of surprise than any force in the blow. Smithback, his screams degenerating into a continual whine, sprang away from Jim and hurled himself towards the closest window.

Jim, acting on instinct and adrenaline, made a grab for the back of Smithback's coat. The carefully tailored seams gave way with a loud series of pops and Jim found himself holding only a torn rag.

Glass shattered in the next instant and, with a fading scream, Jerome Smithback made his exit from the Cloud Club, and the world!

Glass shattered in the next instant and Jerome Smithback made his exit from the Cloud Club, and the world!

4.

Jim stood in the remains of the shattered window, the wind surging around him as he stared down at the weaving serpents of pavement below. Somewhere at the bottom of the Chrysler Building lay Smithback's body, smashed beyond all recognition.

The police had arrived on the double, as was their wont when members of the Silk Stocking Society were involved.

What had happened? One minute, Smithback had been fine. The next-gone. Simply gone. The rapidity of the event had shaken Jim to his core.

Alan Tupker had died in a similar fashion, hadn't he? A train, rather than a window, but it had been an obvious suicide, sudden and unpredictable. Jim possessed an amazing clarity of memory, one that was the envy of statistical agencies the world over. Little details, gleaned from the Tupker article traipsed through his mind, parallel to the events of the past few minutes, as Jim automatically sought correlation. Someone coughed behind him, interrupting his stream of thought. Jim glanced over his shoulder. "Detective Healy," he said.

Detective Turkish Healy stomped towards Jim through the maze of tables, hands in the pockets of his trench coat, a shapeless homburg jammed onto his narrow head. He was followed by a bevy of uniformed police officers who trailed after him like disconsolate baby birds. At a gesture, they split up, joining the other officers in barking questions at witnesses and, in general, cluttering up the scene.

Healy had thin, sallow features and at the best of times looked like he was about to drop dead. Now was not the best of times. A scrawny hand flashed up, and a thin finger poked the air between them.

"Should have known you'd be here," he grunted. Jim took the comment in stride. "I heard about that thing in London, Anthony. About that nut, Soames. About how you shot him down cold."

"Self-defense, Detective," Jim said, face blank. The relationship between himself and Healy was, to be blunt, strained. Healy had the ear of the Commissioner, by virtue of marriage, and while that, in and of itself didn't make him a bad cop, he was jealous of his place in the city hierarchy.

He and Jim had gotten off on a bad foot in their first meeting, during the events surrounding the Emerald Horror incident. Things had been unpleasant ever since.

"Yeah. Yeah, that happens to you a lot, don't it? You defend yourself on a weekly basis, don't you?" Healy stepped closer, looking up at Jim. "How do I know this wasn't more of the same?"

"I assume because you've already questioned the other witnesses," Jim said, a trifle more sharply than he'd intended. Healy grunted.

"Yeah. Fine. What happened?"

18

"We were about to leave. Jerry, Mr. Smithback, seemed to suddenly lose his senses, and he—"

"Took a gainer out the window there," Healy finished for him. "No clue why, Anthony?" He fixed Jim with a gimlet stare. "You usually got a clue, at least."

"Not this time."

"Hnh. Imagine that." Healy stepped up beside Jim and stared down. "You were having lunch?"

"Yes. He was a friend of my father's." Jim leaned against the side of the window frame, arms crossed.

"Emphasis on 'was,'" Healy said.

Jim didn't react. Healy stepped back. "Don't leave town."

"Wouldn't dream of it," Jim said. Healy gave him a look. Jim pushed away from the window. "If we're finished…?"

"Yeah." Healy turned away. Jim took a last look at the window, then headed back to his table. The uniformed officers Healy had brought were busy questioning the other diners and the staff. Jim threaded through them and back to the table. He picked up Silas Pender's business card and slipped it into his pocket, wondering what Pender wanted to see him about. Then, he wondered whether Pender knew Smithback was dead yet. And if not, how would he react?

A flash of white on black caught his eye. Jim sank to his haunches and scooped up the offending object. The card that had been delivered to Smithback, tossed carelessly to the floor.

When Jim turned it over, a hideous face leered at him, blade-shaped tongue protruding between curving tusks. A stylized demon's maw was the only thing which occupied the surface of the card. A tingle of recognition stroked the edges of Jim's memory, but he couldn't recall as to where he'd seen the image before.

"Find something interesting?"

Jim turned, sliding the card into his pocket. Catherine Kilkenny stood behind him, head cocked. "What was that?" she said.

"What was what?" Jim said, sauntering towards the elevator, hands in his pockets. Kilkenny followed him. He glanced at her. "Shouldn't you be staying here? This is where your story is, isn't it?"

"Hardly. Since when is a banker throwing himself out a window news?"

"When it happens twice to the same group?" Jim said. Kilkenny smirked.

"You were listening. Can I ask you your opinion?"

"I'd prefer you didn't."

"Is it murder?"

Jim stopped. "Why would you say that?"

"Why wouldn't you?" Kilkenny shot back. "Two men dead, in similar circumstances, belonging to the same group. The pulps eat this stuff up, Mr. Anthony."

"This is real life," Jim said.

"Fair enough. Now, about Smithback," she said, following him, her pencil zipping across the page. "Can I quote you?"

"On what?"

"That you don't like to think about the rumors concerning his little consortium."

"I didn't say that," Jim said, heading for the elevator. "How did you even get in here, by the by? The Cloud Club doesn't admit women."

"And you're in favor of that?" Kilkenny dabbed her pencil on the tip of her tongue. "Would you say that you're not a fan of the Nineteenth Amendment?"

"I believe I simply asked a question. How you choose to interpret it isn't up to me," Jim said.

"Ooh, splitting hairs. What don't you want to say, Mr. Anthony?" The elevator arrived and the door clanked open. Jim stepped inside and Kilkenny barged on after him. "What about the reports of your love affair with—"

The elevator doors closed. Kilkenny sniffed and closed her notebook. "Finally."

Jim looked askance at her. A sinking sensation occurred somewhere in the vicinity of his stomach. "Finally what?"

"We're alone."

"Fred's here," Jim said, pointing to the elevator attendant. An older man of African ancestry, Fred smiled politely and tipped his hat. Kilkenny pulled a wad of bills out of her coat pocket and waved it at Fred.

"Fred can get off at the next floor."

"No, he can't," Jim said.

"Yes, he can," Fred said, taking the money and counting it. "I'm on my break."

"Fred, what about the elevator operator's code?" Jim said a trifle plaintively.

"Don't cover this. Sorry, Mr. Anthony," Fred said, without an iota of pity in his voice. The bell chimed and Fred hauled the door open. He tipped his hat again as he stepped off. "Mr. Anthony. Miss."

The door closed. Kilkenny looked at Jim, tapping her foot. "Well?"

"Well what?"

Kilkenny slapped him. Jim rocked back, then found himself slamming into the wall of the elevator as she leapt into his arms, her lips locked against his.

She pushed away from him after a moment, breathing a trifle heavily, then slapped him again, on the other cheek.

"Jackass," she said, straightening her hat.

"Ow," Jim said, rubbing his cheek. He twisted the knob near the door, setting the elevator to moving again.

"Ow nothing, buster. It's like slapping granite, so don't go looking for pity," Kilkenny said, rubbing her hand. "Elevator operator's code?"

"I gave it a shot," Jim said. "What's got you upset now?"

"You ditched me."

"Really? When?"

"Before Christmas! At the Sparkle Lounge!"

"Not on purpose," Jim said.

"Of course not! It's never on purpose," she said, gesticulating. "What was it this time? Bank robbery? Some fat cat get his purse cut?"

Jim avoided the question. "I think you did just fine without me. Whatever gossip you heard was all over the back pages of the Globe the next day. Is that what got you bumped up to the big leagues?"

"You've been reading the Globe then?"

"Pays to keep tabs on the competition," Jim said. "The Lounge revoked my invitation because of you, by the by."

"Serves you right. You know what today is, Jimmy?" she said.

"No?"

"Valentine's Day, Jimmy."

"Ah."

"You owe me," she said, poking him in the chest with a finger. "And don't you forget it."

"I never forget my debts," Jim said. The bell gave a ding, and Jim slid the door open. Cat slithered out past him and headed for the doors.

On the street, Jim watched Cat hail a cab, then, before she could protest, slid in beside her. She glanced at him, a smirk decorating her features.

"You following me now?"

"Merely satisfying my curiosity." Jim tapped her notepad. "The Globe continued to run with the story of Tupker's death after the facts had come in. Why?"

"Why don't you ask my editor?"

"I think I'll do just that."

Cat blinked. "What?"

"You're going to the Globe, right? To file your story?" Jim asked. Without waiting for a reply, he tapped the driver. "Daily Globe offices, please."

The taxi pulled away from the street with alacrity, leaving behind a storm of police lights and sirens. Jim glanced back. Jim watched as they slid a gurney into the back of an ambulance. Then, another car pulling out into traffic blocked his view.

He turned back around. Cat was glaring at him. "You can't do this. If Bushkin, my editor, figures out what we're doing together, he'll can me for certain!"

"Relax, we're just sharing a cab." Jim leaned back in his seat, hands behind his head. "No harm in that. Besides, I'm a known flirt."

"That's an understatement if I ever heard one," Cat said. "Besides which, what makes you think he's going to just let the owner of a rival paper wander in and snake our scoop?"

"My winning personality?"

Cat laughed. Jim shook his head. "Fine. I know Kelly Clayton. The owner? Went to school with him. Not to mention, got him out of quite a few jams. If your editor gives me any trouble, Clayton will straighten him out."

Cat whistled. "Rarified circles, Jimmy."

"Not as rare as one might expect." Jim glanced out the back window. "Hnh."

"What?"

Instead of replying, Jim leaned over the driver's shoulder. "I'll double the fare if you can lose that dark green Ford behind us and still get us where we're going."

"Dark green what now?" Cat turned in her seat. There was a sound like a car backfiring, and Jim wrenched her down, eliciting a yelp of surprise. "Jimmy, what—"

"Head down," Jim said. The cab took a sharp turn, tires screeching.

"Was that a gunshot?" the driver said, a strong Bronx accent coloring his words.

"I don't know," Jim said.

"'Cause it sure sounded like a damn gunshot!"

"Possibly. Think you can make sure it doesn't happen again?" Jim said, looking out the back window again, eyes narrowed. The Ford was three cars back and the passengers were only dim outlines. There were two of them. That much he could say for certain.

"Watch me, high-pockets," the driver said, spinning the wheel. The cab slid around a corner.

"What the hell is going on, Anthony?" Cat barked. Jim looked down at her.

"Somebody might, or might not, be shooting at us," he said with a smile.

"Might be? You don't know?"

"It's a possibility," Jim said.

"A possibility?" Cat's voice went up an octave. "Stop the cab! I want out!"

"Still ain't lost 'em," the driver said.

"Determined sorts. It's probably nothing," Jim said, directing the latter to Cat. The taxi shuddered suddenly as the dark-green Ford whipped out of line and bashed its front bumper into the taxi's rear. The cabbie began to curse as the Ford rammed them again.

"Nothing, hunh?" Cat said, hunkering down at Jim's gesture. "Some nothing."

"Maybe it was an accident," Jim said, twisting in his seat. The cab shook from a third impact. "Then, maybe not."

5.

Jim swatted the cabbie's shoulder. "I'm going out for some fresh air. Keep the cab steady, please."

"You ain't gonna do what I think you're gonna do!" the cabbie said.

"Depends on what you think I'm going to do," Jim said, before squeezing half way out the passenger window. He grabbed at the sign on top of the cab for support and thrust his other hand into his trouser pocket. No pistol meant he had to improvise.

He withdrew a handful of coins as the Ford swung after them, and rolled one, a quarter, between his thumb and forefinger. The cab wove in and out of traffic, leaving a trail of furiously honking horns in its wake. Jim nudged the tip of his thumb up under the edge of the coin and took aim at the Ford's windshield.

If he hadn't practiced on gophers and squirrels as a boy hunting for dinner, the shot would have been impossible. As it was, it was merely improbable.

The coin left the crook of his forefinger and sprang across the distance between the cab and the Ford, striking the windshield of the latter with enough force to crack the glass.

The driver of the Ford swerved instinctively, and the cab shot ahead, leaving it behind in the sea of traffic. Jim gave a jaunty wave, then eased himself back into the cab with a grunt of effort.

"What the hell do you call that?" Cat said. Jim shrugged.

"A quarter well-spent, at the very least."

"Hope you got more than that in them pockets of yours, pal," the cabbie said. "Somebody's got to pay for the damage to my hack, and I got a feeling those friends of yours ain't the generous types."

"I think I can cover it," Jim said, settling back in his seat. Cat snorted.

"Bet you got an account set aside just for this situation, hunh Jimmy?"

"Pays to be prepared, if that's what you're implying." Jim looked at her. "Now, the question is why they were after us in the first place?"

"Case of mistaken identity?" Cat said.

"Doubtful. You don't ram a car on a 'maybe.' Somebody was waiting for us." Jim scraped his fingers through his hair. "But why?"

"Think it has something to do with Smithback?" Cat had her pad open. "Be honest, Jimmy."

"No comment."

"I despise you," Cat said.

"Hey, mack," the cabbie said. "We're here. Now do me a favor and get out. Please."

The Daily Globe was a victim of the latest architectural frenzy, all long, pol-

23

ished angles and sharp edges. A statue of Atlas stood straining on an alcove mid-way up the building's length, and Jim felt a pang of sympathy roll across his own broad shoulders.

"Clayton's done well," he murmured as he paid the cabbie and tipped hand-somely to cover the damages. "That should cover it."

"No offense, but next time I see you, I ain't stopping," the cabbie said as he pulled away from the curb. Jim glanced back up at the building.

"Makes the Star offices look like a bit dodgy."

"Trust me, Jimmy, it's only skin deep," Cat said, moving towards the revolving door that led inside. "Place is still the same depressing tabloid it always was."

"Harsh words," he said, following her.

"I've been on the bottom of the stack for three years, Jimmy. It gives you a unique viewpoint." She looked at him. "You really need to do this?"

"If you're right, and there's a connection between Tupker and Smithback and these others, I want to know about it."

"Why?"

"Call it idle curiosity," Jim said.

"If I let you do this, you owe me."

"So you keep saying."

"Smithback. Tupker. They were the tip of the iceberg, Jimmy, and you damn well know it."

"Maybe so, but it's not exactly my stock in trade." Jim shook his head.

She blew a raspberry. "Bull. They were murdered."

Given what he suspected, Jim tacitly agreed, but refused to give her the satisfac-tion. "Healy is investigating."

"Healy is a dope. I want your promise you'll keep me up to date on things. You're planning to investigate, aren't you?"

"Maybe," Jim said. Kilkenny snorted.

"Of course you are. I caught sight of a business card earlier. Silas Pender wants to meet you." She dabbed her pencil on her tongue. "I want to come along."

"No, Cat," Jim said, folding his arms across his chest. Her eyes narrowed. Jim hesitated. Kilkenny's eyes were slits, her jaw set.

"What happened to honoring your debts?" she said.

Jim looked up at the ceiling of the car and sighed. "I'm meeting him tonight. At the Roxy. The Dracula premiere."

"I assume your invitation came with a 'plus one' attached?" she said.

"Yep."

"What time are you picking me up?" she said, smiling.

"I—" Jim shook his head. "Fine. But you have to promise to behave."

"Ha!" Cat said again. The elevator arrived then, and Jim gave up on any further verbal sparring as a bad deal.

Riding the elevator up, Cat made sure to stand as far away from Jim as possible, something he found slightly amusing.

The relationship between them had started in an elevator, after all. Jim recalled the scene—he and Cat trapped in an elevator during one of the so-called Balloon Buster's daring upper story robberies. Both of them had been heading up to a party at the Stratosphere Club; Cat for the paper and Jim for the under-the-table alcohol. With the arrival of the Balloon Buster, in his eponymous mode of transportation, the power to the building had been cut, including the generators that powered the elevators, trapping Jim and Cat between floors.

Things had progressed from there, as they were wont to do. Jim, thinking pleasant thoughts, watched Cat and surreptitiously admired her shape, the set of her hips, the way she tilted her head. She was vibrant, always moving, always doing something. He appreciated that kind of life in a woman. Too much so, at times.

Other faces swam to the surface of his thoughts...Josephine Balsamo, a lady both sinister and seductive. Irma Vep, as vicious as she was voluptuous. That odd Persson woman who'd first made love to him, then tried to stab him the next day. Catherine Kilkenny was a cut above that trio in the morals department, true, but still as invigorating in some ways.

It was the intelligence, Jim thought. Sharp like razors, cutting across obsolete opinion and forcing the minds of others into new contortions to keep up.

The porter pushed open the doors. "Bullpen, Ms. Kilkenny," he said.

"Thanks, Willy." Cat stepped out, her posture shifting as she turned up the wattage on her confidence. Jim followed her at an amble, hands in his pockets, taking in the offices of the Globe at a glance.

Reporters barked questions at one another or into telephones and paper flew, shifting from one pile to the next. A psychologist friend of Jim's had equated an active newsroom to an organic mind, the reporters carrying nerve impulses from one area to the next. Jim thought it was more akin to a bee hive, and about as dangerous, if you weren't careful.

He moved quickly, not quite following Cat as she marched determinedly towards her editor's office. He would give her a few minutes to soften the man up. Until then, he decided to keep his ears open for anything that might put him on the right path.

Mostly it was the usual newsroom chatter. Jim found an unobtrusive spot and let the flow of voices roll over him. His focus sharpened at intervals, catching things.

"...two dead in fire..."

"...so how did he get in? It was locked, right..."

"...definitely going down for it..."

"...she was with who..."

"...Panama disaster..."

"...Turkish ambassador dead at..."

"...telling you we've got him!"

Jim's eyes opened. Cat was in full crusading form, shaking her fists at her beleaguered editor. Jim sauntered towards the office. Now was as good a time as any.

"This is it, chief! Two men dead, tell me that ain't kismet!" Cat said. "If that no-good shyster won't play ball...."

"And which shyster would that be?" Jim said.

"None of your business," the editor, Bushkin, said. "Who are you?" He was a heavy man, with a doughy middle and a pate that gleamed like a newly waxed floor. A ragged chunk of cigar hung from his lips, smoldering gently.

"Anthony. Jim Anthony," Jim said, extending his hand. Bushkin looked at the hand as if it were a poisonous snake.

"Hell you say," he said, his eyes widening. Jim's face wasn't well-known, but his name more than made up for it.

"Afraid so," Jim said. "I'm sure Ms. Kilkenny has shared the news?" He sat on the edge of Bushkin's desk and flipped open the humidor that sat there. "Do you mind?"

"I—no. No. Help yourself," Bushkin said, taken aback. He looked at Cat. "Why is he here?"

"He's stalking me," Cat snapped. Jim silently applauded her acting skills.

"I noticed Ms. Kilkenny slipping out after the—ah—incident she no doubt just reported to you. She did the articles on Alan Tupker's death as well, didn't she?" Jim said as he snagged a match out of a bowl and lit the cigar.

"Maybe," Bushkin said.

"I want to take a look at any information you might have on that."

"The police already looked at our stuff," Bushkin said, eyes narrowing as he watched Jim puff on the cigar.

"But I'm not the police, am I?"

"Good point. No," Bushkin said. "The Daily Star hasn't exactly been burning up the rollers on this. You think we got something, don't you?"

"Possibly. Or perhaps I'm just curious."

"Yeah, curious like a fox." Bushkin sat back. He took his cigar out, examined it and tossed it into the waste paper basket beside his desk. "The publisher will skin me alive."

"No, he won't." Jim gestured with the cigar. "Clayton and I go quite a ways back. If you'd like to call him—"

"Chief," Cat began. Bushkin waved her to silence. He eyed Jim for a minute.

"What do we get?" he said.

"I'll turn over everything I find to you, should I discover something untoward." Jim puffed on the cigar. "I can go places your reporters can't. And if there is some scheme afoot, I can dog it out."

"And you won't give it to your own people?"

"I didn't say that," Jim said. "I simply said that I would turn anything interesting over to you."

"How do you know we have anything?"

"I don't. But a reporter might see something a police officer misses. And considering that Ms. Kilkenny is on a long leash—"

"Hey!" Cat said, face flushing.

"You're pretty sure we got something," Bushkin finished for him. He tapped his fingers on his desk, obviously mulling it over. "Tell the truth, I wasn't. Until now.

Looks like you got good instincts, Kilkenny."

"Gee whiz, thanks, Chief," Cat deadpanned. Bushkin grunted.

"I want an exclusive," he said.

"With me?" Jim said. Bushkin nodded.

"Yeah. I want you. After it's all over."

"Hardly appropriate," Jim said.

"Neither is letting you look at our files."

"True," Jim said. "Fine. And I assume you want me to liaise with Ms. Kilkenny throughout?"

Bushkin blinked, as if such a thought hadn't occurred to him. "Unh-yeah. Yeah, you stick to him like glue," he said, glaring at Kilkenny.

Cat saluted. "Roger-dodger."

"Then it's a date," Jim said, clapping his hands. Bushkin looked at him curiously.

"Yeah. Whatever you say. Cat, show him the files."

Cat led Jim out of the office. "Smoothly done, Mr. Anthony," she said without turning around.

"Always, Ms. Kilkenny. Always," Jim said.

6.

Conceived as the world's largest, not to mention finest, movie palace, the Roxy Theatre was known as 'the cathedral of the motion picture' for good reason.

Occupying a spot between Sixth and Seventh Avenues, the Roxy was a magnificent edifice, one designed to cast visitors into a state of stupefied awe.

For the most part, it succeeded.

Flashbulbs popped and questions pattered over the red carpet like rain. Hollywood's best and brightest were on hand for a first glimpse of what was being billed as 'the strangest love story of all.'

Kilkenny, sitting in the back of the Rolls-Royce as it pulled up to the curb, looked over at Jim. "Photographers."

"Worried about having your picture taken?" Jim said, fiddling with his tie. She frowned.

"Depends. If my editor knew I was stepping out with the owner of the Star—"

"Don't worry kitty-cat, they'll be focused on Gorgeous George there," the driver of the Rolls-Royce said, jerking a thumb at Anthony. Gentry turned to glance at them, his broad, freckled face split by a grin.

Cat laughed. "With a face like his, who wouldn't?"

"People with taste?" Tom said.

Jim snorted. "Circle the block. I'll sneak you in the back if you're interested in seeing the film."

"Nah," Tom said, waving a hand. "I got a steak dinner calling my name. You kids have fun. I'll be waiting on you."

"Your loss," Jim said, getting out and circling around the Rolls to open Cat's door. "Milady."

"Sir."

They walked up the red carpet, Jim waving as cameras flashed, and Cat endeavoring to hide her face. Despite Tom's assurances, the wrong picture getting in front of the right eyes could see her without a job and potentially blackballed, Jim knew. Oh sure, he could give her one, but she'd have lost all credibility by then. And what was a reporter without credibility?

So why then was she risking it? Was the story really that important?

"Yep," she said out loud.

Jim looked down, nonplussed. "What?"

"Nothing. Where's Pender?"

"No clue. I assume he's meeting me—"

"Us," she corrected.

"Us afterwards." Jim smiled as Cat frowned. Kilkenny had a number of fine

28

qualities. Patience wasn't among them. "Enjoy the film, Cat. There'll be plenty of time to light a fire under Silas after."

She sniffed. "Fine." She eyed him as they entered the Roxy. "Are you seriously considering throwing in with him and his cronies?"

"Not even remotely. I am curious as to what they're planning, though, just like you. And why it might have cost two men their lives." He looked thoughtful as they stepped into the large, columned rotunda that served as the Roxy's lobby. The Grand Foyer featured the world's largest oval rug, and, at least for tonight, the world's largest collection of celebrities. The crowd was a loud one, and familiar faces were plenty as Jim and Cat squeezed into the mass, looking for a quiet spot.

"So you are planning to investigate. The great Jim Anthony, Super-Detective," she began, but was interrupted.

"Jim Anthony?" a voice said.

They turned to see a slim blonde with pale blue eyes. Jim smiled. "Yes, Miss…?"

"Colquitt," the blonde said, extending a hand, which Jim took with seasoned grace, brushing his lips over her knuckles. Cat frowned.

"Colquitt. As in Senator Colquitt?" she said. The other woman nodded, smiling slightly.

"My father. Delores."

"Your father's name is Delores?" Cat said.

"Ah. No. I'm Delores," Delores said, blushing slightly. "I mean—"

"I know what you mean," Jim said gently. "We've met before, haven't we? At the last fundraiser for your father?"

"Yes. You auctioned off that strange egg."

"Elasmosaurus egg, actually," Jim said. "I found it in-"

"Catherine Kilkenny," Cat said, taking Delores' hand. "We've never met, but I'm sure Jimmy will rectify that, won't you, Jimmy?"

"I—" Jim began, looking back and forth between the two women. "Yes, of course. Forgive me. Ms. Kilkenny, Ms. Colquitt. Catherine is a reporter with the Daily Globe." Jim gestured. "And Ms. Colquitt is the executor of her father's philanthropic interests."

"Ah, the famous Colquitt Charities," Cat said. Delores nodded.

"And I've read your articles on the society scene with some interest, Ms. Kilkenny. I didn't know that you and—ah—Jimmy were an item."

"We're close," Cat said, entwining her arm with Jim's. Delores smiled.

"So I see. It was nice to see you again, Mr. Anthony. Ms. Kilkenny," she said. "I think I need to find my seat, though." Jim watched her weave her way back into the crowd, his eyes lingering on her legs. Cat smacked his arm.

"I'm your date, remember?"

"Hmm? Yes. Sorry," Jim said, looking down at her. "Funny to see her here."

"Is it?" Cat snorted. "I don't know why. There are quite a few celebrities here."

"Big event." Jim looked around. There was the star of the show, Bela Lugosi, resplendent in black, bending over the hand of his co-star, Helen Chandler. Photographers for the major papers, including his own, he was gratified to see, scurried at the fringes of the crowd, taking candid shots of famous profiles.

"You look like a cat in a room full of rocking chairs, Anthony," Kilkenny murmured. Jim smiled.

"Large crowds have never been a favorite of mine," he said. "Shall we find our seats?"

"By all means, let's."

They merged with the crowd as it moved into the auditorium. Jim kept an eye peeled for Pender, but hadn't yet caught sight of him.

Silas Pender was old money, New Amsterdam money. The exact opposite end of the spectrum from Smithback and Tupker. Both were self-made men. They took chances as a matter of course. But men like Pender didn't. Risk was an unknown country to them. They lived off accrued interest and centuries old business deals. So how had he come to be involved with the other two?

What had Cat called them? The Sinister Six. Only now they were more like the Frightful Four. A countdown by any other name....

Smithback had been desperate. And in Jim's experience, desperate men did dangerous things. He'd come, hoping that Pender could answer the growing number of questions he had. Hoping that maybe, just maybe, he could find what was going on, and whether one of his father's oldest associates had been up to his neck in something illicit. Something that had gotten him killed.

He didn't owe Smithback anything. Nor had he truly enjoyed the man's company. Not really. But Jim had failed to prevent his death. And that, frankly, rankled.

Thinking sour thoughts, Jim looked up as they entered the auditorium. It truly was a magnificent design. Spanish, he thought, in its style. Two tiers rose above the ground floor and swept back, giving the whole arrangement a curious tilted look.

"Seats?"

"What?" Jim looked down. Cat nudged him.

"Seats, Jimmy. Where we sitting?"

"Ah." Jim pulled the tickets out of his coat pocket and maneuvered Cat to the correct row on the ground floor. "Here we are."

"Y'know, I heard that Lugosi guy can't speak English," Cat said, as they sat. Jim snorted.

"I had lunch with him in London a year or two ago. He didn't have any difficulty then."

"Lunch with Lugosi. Hmmp. Sounds like an article I should write," Cat said, surveying the faces of those sitting around her. "I also heard Browning wanted Chaney in the lead."

"That would've been interesting. You've become quite the fount of celebrity gossip, Cat." Jim smiled. The lights fell as on the screen, the opening credits began to roll.

"I play to my strengths," she whispered, watching the screen. "God. Look at those eyes," she said, after a few minutes. Lugosi's burning eyes and jagged face occupied the screen. Jim settled back in his seat.

He'd been to see the play, once, in London. While the immediacy of the screen amplified Lugosi's already considerable charisma to a frightening degree, the film rolled on much as the play had, beat for beat, and Jim found his attention wandering.

So it was that he caught sight of Pender sitting above him, on the front row of the second tier. He was a thin crane of a man, with a New England jaw and a face that defined the term 'blue blood'. They had only met formally on a few occasions, at parties and the like. Pender had never been anything less than courteous, but Jim could tell that the man considered him an nouveau riche upstart. Silas's eyes were locked on the screen, and as Jim watched, Pender stood and reached into his coat.

The crack of the pistol split the ambiance of the theater like a roll of thunder. Pender screeched and fired again, aiming for Lugosi's great, grinning face.

Jim was up and out of his seat like a scalded cat. His mind was quicksilver, processing the scene before him instantly. There was no time to get upstairs in the traditional fashion, so alternate methods were required. He jumped up onto the back of his seat, but only for a moment. With a flex of nigh-superhuman muscles, he was hurtling upwards, arms stretched out before him.

Pender fired again, his voice rising to a banshee wail as people screamed and rose from their seats, moving away from him in a panic. Jim hit the front slope of the tier and scrabbled at the smooth surface for an instant before his fingers found purchase. Shoulder muscles rippling, he heaved himself back and up, flipping around to deposit his feet on the edge of the tier balcony.

Pender stood in front of him, eyes wide. He swung the pistol towards Jim, babbling incoherently. Jim sprang from his perch and straight into the other man. They crashed into the front row, Jim snagging the man's wrist as he pressed his other arm, elbow first, against Pender's windpipe.

Jim gave the man's wrist a gentle squeeze and Pender made a whine high in his throat as the pistol fell from his nerveless fingers. He thrashed wildly as Jim sought to calm him.

"Silas! It's me—damn it—Silas!" Jim tried to hold the man down. Pender howled, lips flecked with froth, and squirmed loose of Jim's grip. Jim staggered as a flailing arm caught him on the side of the head. As he stumbled back, Pender flew to his feet, his eyes bulging from their sockets, mouth agape in a silent scream.

Jim reached for him, but too late. With a sickening realization of what was to come, Jim watched as Silas Pender stiffened and then, like a puppet with its strings suddenly cut, fell sideways and off the tier towards the floor below!

7.

When the police arrived, Jim was already sitting on his haunches beside the body. Carefully, he checked each pocket, looking for anything that might provide him with a clue as to Pender's sudden turn.

Minutes after the man had fallen, Jim had reached the body. The auditorium had been cleared, with most of the crowd waiting in the lobby. The only other person still inside besides Jim was Cat.

"Guess I won't be getting to ask him any questions," she said, watching Jim work. He didn't turn.

"Earlier, when you were badgering—" Jim began.

"Interviewing."

"Interviewing Smithback, you mentioned something about trade monopolies." He felt something flat in the inside pocket of Pender's coat.

"Remember that business he was trying to interest you in earlier?" Cat said. "Yeah. Word is that he and a few others were engaged in some serious financial hanky-panky." Cat sat back, perched on the arm of a seat, her legs crossed.

"Yes," Jim said. When he didn't elaborate, Cat went on.

"Never was too sure what Smithback did, though."

"Commodities," Jim said. He pulled a thin white card out of Pender's pocket and held it up between two fingers. A familiar grotesque leer greeted him. Jim felt an instant shudder of revulsion.

It was the same card. Jim closed his hand around it, blocking the demonic grin from sight. Definitely not a coincidence.

"Awright! Step back," a voice barked as the auditorium doors were slammed open. Jim slid the card into his own pocket and stood smoothly.

"Anthony! Did you kill him?" Detective Healy snarled as he stomped down the aisle.

"No, but—" Jim said, prepared to continue. Healy snorted and the finger swung towards Cat.

"Did you kill him?"

"Hell, no," Cat said, fixing Healy with a hard stare. Healy grunted and his eyes filled with recognition.

"You're that Kilkenny dame, aren't you? From the Daily Globe?"

"And what if I am?"

"I don't need a reporter sniffing around my investigation!" Healy barked.

"She was my guest, Detective. She's hardly sniffing around," Jim said, stepping between them.

"Damn it. It's Valentine's Day, did you know that?" Healy said, looking at Jim. "You know what that means?"

32

"Anthony! Did you kill him?" Detective Healy snarled.

"I forgot to get you flowers?" Jim said.

"No!" Healy snapped. "Though that would have been nice. No, what it means is I had to leave my wife alone at what should have been our Valentine's Day dinner."

"Ouch," Cat said.

"Surely you're not blaming me," Jim began. Healy poked him in the chest.

"No. I'm not. I'm just sharing my misery. What happened?"

"I don't know," Jim said, looking down at the body. "He started shooting, and I made to stop him, but at the first opportunity he pitched himself off of the balcony."

"No help from you, huh?"

"Not this time," Jim said, eyes narrowed. Healy frowned. "You really don't like me, do you Detective?" Jim continued.

"Now why would you say that? I love you. You're my own personal albatross." Healy whirled, jamming his hands into his pockets. "Somebody call the goddamn meat wagon!" He turned back as one of the uniformed officers scurried out. "Tupker. What do you know about that?"

"Alan Tupker. I know he died recently," Jim said. Out of the corner of his eye he saw Cat straining forward to hear.

"You know how?"

"Suicide," Jim said. Healy was silent for a moment. Then, he grunted.

"He threw himself in front of a train."

"And Jerry Smithback threw himself out a window," Jim said. "I'm guessing the papers will call that a suicide as well."

"And, apparently, if what you're telling me is true, so was this poor bastard." Healy nudged the body with his foot. "Three suicides in just over a month. Two on the same damn day."

Jim cocked his head. "You sound suspicious, Healy."

"I was born suspicious." Healy swallowed, his Adam's Apple bobbing. "What do you think?"

"I take it I'm no longer a suspect?"

"Anthony," Healy said warningly.

"I want to look at the body. Tonight. Before you take it away," Jim said, crossing his arms. Healy looked as if he had bitten into a lemon. But then, he always looked that way.

"Fine. I want to be kept in the loop this time. Not like that damn Old Soldier business last year!" Healy growled. Jim nodded, remembering the case in question. The Old Soldier, whose identity was still a question mark, had been involved in the murders of a number of ex-army officers. Federal pressure had forced Healy off the case, but Jim had continued on, and finally caught the killer, bayonet in hand as it were.

The Old Soldier had shot himself, in the end. His body had fallen into the Hudson, and that had been the story of him, leaving Jim with only his scars to remember him by.

"We're doing it right this time," Healy continued. "I'm getting tired of cleaning up after you! I want a trial this time, not a visit to the coroner!" Jim didn't blink, but knew that, in a way, Healy was right. Many of Jim's cases ended the same way. Death delivered to the dealers of death, usually by their own hand. It bothered him, when he allowed himself to think about it, which wasn't often. He liked to concentrate on the lives saved rather than those lost. Soames' face floated to the surface of his mind, and he grimly pushed it back down. Lives saved.

"You'll be with me every step, Detective," Jim said, fingering the card in his pocket. "I can say that Pender looked panicked. Frightened out of his mind. Just like Smithback."

"He would be, falling like he did."

"No. Before that," Jim said. "He was quite literally insane with fear. It's the only reason I can think of for him to turn a pistol on a movie screen."

"I can think of a lot of reasons," Healy grumbled. He took off his hat and slapped it against his thigh. "Fine. I'll let you have the body. But only for fifteen minutes. And you'll let me know—"

"Everything," Jim said.

"What about you," Healy said, looking at Cat. "You got anything I need to know?"

"If I did, don't you think I'd have told you?" Cat said, smiling slightly. Healy grinned.

"Maybe. Or maybe you're saving it for tomorrow's edition of the Globe, hunh?"

Cat paled. "You wouldn't."

"Yeah. Sources played you wrong on that one. If you so much as breathe about this, I'll let your editor know who you were out with tonight." He looked meaningfully at Jim.

"You sonnuva—" Cat began, starting towards Healy. Jim caught her.

"I'll vouch for her, Detective."

"I bet you will," Healy said, slapping his hat back on his head. Men in white came down the aisle, carrying a stretcher between them. Healy intercepted them, and began barking orders to the uniformed officers. Jim took Cat's arm and maneuvered her towards the doors.

"I cannot believe that man!" she snapped, glaring over her shoulder at Healy. "I'll pillory him in the press!"

"And then he'll get you fired," Jim said. "Besides which, despite his manner, Healy is quite a fine detective."

"And Gengis Khan was faithful to his wife," Cat said tartly. She pulled her arm free of Jim's grip. "So what was it?"

"What was what?"

"Whatever you found, what was it? Was it the same thing you found before?"

Jim looked at her, eyebrow quirked. Cat sighed. "You found something, Jimmy, otherwise you wouldn't have been in such a hurry to get out of there, earlier."

Jim frowned. "I don't know yet. It might be something, it might be nothing."

"But you think it was something. Otherwise you wouldn't have snatched it." Cat peered at him. "What was it?"

"I…" Jim began. He stopped. "I don't know. Yet. Out."

"But—"

"Out. I'll fill you in later," he said, hoping to placate her. She stifled her protest and slipped out of the auditorium, shooting him a parting glare. Jim closed the doors and leaned into them, just for a moment, gathering his thoughts. Then he turned.

He picked up his jacket, where it lay momentarily forgotten across the back of a seat, and felt for a hidden seam across the inside back of the garment. Finding it, Jim pried apart the loose threads holding the seam closed, allowing a strip of leather to unfold and dangle.

A number of items were attached to the strip, items Jim had found useful again and again in his career. Healy watched Jim remove several of these and shook his head.

"You always carry a murder-kit around with you, Anthony?"

"Not always. But, invariably, when I'm dressed in my best, something untowards comes up. Murders at vicarages and country houses, on yachts and at fancy parties," Jim said, smiling slightly.

"If that's a joke, it's a bad one."

"Regrettably, it's not." Jim squatted beside Pender and laid out the tools he'd selected: a pair of thin forceps, a long scalpel sheathed in calfskin, and a small circular magnifying glass.

Jim took Pender's jaw in hand and twisted the man's head one way, then the other. His neck had snapped on impact with the floor, but Jim had a suspicion he'd been dead before he connected. He looked up at Healy.

"How much leeway can you give me?"

"Like what?" Healy took his omnipresent cigar out of his mouth. Jim mimed sliding the scalpel down Pender's chest. Healy jammed the cigar back in his mouth.

"No way. The city pays good money to the butcher-docs."

"What about the spirit of cooperation?" Jim said.

"Spirit of cooperation doesn't extend to you slicing and dicing him like a Chinatown meat-man!"

"Fine, fine." Jim replaced the scalpel and removed the magnifying glass. He bent onto all fours beside the body, examining it closely. Before Healy's incredulous eyes, Jim crawled around Pender's stiffening corpse, examining every inch of it.

After a few minutes of this, Healy said, "Well?"

Jim hopped to his feet, tossing the magnifying glass from hand to hand. "Yep. He's dead." Healy opened his mouth to reply, but Jim pressed on. "I suspect heart failure. I want to take another look at the body. Tomorrow. And Smithback's as well. Unless you've released it to the family?"

"Ain't no family," Healy grunted. "Fine. Tomorrow morning. Early. Before any of your lady friend's peers in the cockroach network crawl into the station."

"Perfect."

Jim replaced his tools and folded his coat over his arm as he left to look for Cat.

However, he was only a few feet from the auditorium doors when the hairs on his neck prickled. He stepped away from the crowd, his head going up like that of a wolf on the hunt. Nostrils flaring, Jim allowed his keenly honed senses to expand and fill the lobby.

Someone was watching him.

It was a peculiar thing, Jim's sixth sense. According to his grandfather, his mother had possessed it, or some variation thereof. A tingle that started small, at the base of the spine and flowed upwards, spreading through his muscles until it set the base of his skull aflame.

He had that sensation now. A voice said something to him, but he ignored it. There was someone—

There!

Eyes without a face burned into Jim's own, glaring at him from the protective screen of the crowd. Eyes that were like twin suns crackling with raw hate!

8.

The eyes belonged to a man dressed as an usher in a bright crimson jacket and black trousers. But earlier, at the Cloud Club, he had been dressed as a waiter. Among the many examples of his mental acuity, Jim's memory for faces was legendary. Even among the many incidentals who crossed his path, Jim could pinpoint with nearly perfect accuracy the when and where of their previous meetings.

The man stared hatefully at him, with eyes like the raw, red end of a lucifer's snapping tongue. He had been the one who had delivered the cards and drinks to his and Smithback's table. The same man who had quite possibly sent Jerry Smithback reeling into Death's embrace in some enigmatic fashion.

Perhaps it was merely coincidence that had brought him here tonight. Maybe he was moonlighting. Or maybe he was a murderer.

The moment lengthened, then abruptly snapped. The usher spun on his heel and sprinted for the stairs, shoving actors, actresses and the elite aside in a mad dash.

Jim, acting on instinct, broke into a run. There was no telling if the man he'd seen was actually involved, but his instincts screamed otherwise, and questions could wait for later.

He tossed his tuxedo jacket aside as he ran, letting it fall behind him, and kicked his shoes off with a skill born of practice. Jim bounded up the stairs two at a time, rebounding off the wall, avoiding the slower members of the crowd with animalistic ease.

The dark shape of the watcher wove through the crowd, then stopped on the top stair, turning, hand diving into his coat. Jim slipped sideways, grasping a pillar and swinging himself up onto the balustrade as an automatic blared a staccato warning to stay back.

The faux usher fired again, bullets plucking chunks from the wood as, bare-footed, Jim ran swiftly down the length of the balustrade, arms pumping. He had learned, in his youth, the benefits of bare feet in maintaining balance. The human foot was a meticulously designed bit of organic machinery, capable of clinging, thrusting, and balancing all within the same span of seconds. Shoes, in contrast, just got in the way.

Jim pounced from the balustrade, arms extended. The gunman stepped back, eyes widening slightly. He was a man of indeterminate years neither especially young looking, nor especially old, with a Mediterranean complexion. Jim crashed into him, grabbing for his wrist. He was surprised by the strength in the man's slender limbs; a strength seemingly equal to Jim's own.

Feet pounded up the stairs. The shots had summoned Healy and his boys in

38

blue. The momentary distraction allowed his opponent to drive his knee up into Jim's kidney. Jim grunted and staggered. The pistol whipped around, the black maw of the barrel lining up with his face.

Jim threw himself backwards. The automatic roared and the heat of its passage left a trail through the hairs on Jim's forearm as he twisted out of the way. He slammed into the balustrade, nearly falling over.

The gunman took the opportunity to turn his attentions to the police rushing up the stairs. Coolly, he aimed and pinked a patrolman, knocking the man around with a bloody sleeve. Healy and the others hit the stairs as celebrities fled or threw themselves down.

Then, whirling, he moved past a trio of paralyzed minor Hollywood starlets, heading for a side exit. Jim bounded after him, sending the women scattering at last.

"Hold it!" Jim bellowed, reaching out. The gunman spun, slapping aside Jim's grasping hand. Jim stumbled, shocked.

Beneath his blazing eyes, the man's face was suddenly that of a nightmare, a grinning, tusked maw, bifurcated by a jutting triangular tongue!

"What in—" Jim stepped back and that second's hesitation was all his prey needed to make his escape. He was out the door and gone. Jim hit the door moments later and charged down the stairs, trying to understand what he had seen. He caught the stair-rail and vaulted over, dropping a flight to land in a crouch just ahead of the gunman.

It had to be a mask. But it had seemed almost too organic for that. A shudder coiled through Jim's muscles as he rose from his crouch and swung a loose blow at the man's head.

The blow connected, and the gunman stumbled. Jim lashed out with a foot, pinning the man's gun-hand to the wall. Jim hit him again, hissing in pain as his knuckles connected with the strange half-mask.

With a grunt, the gunman shoved Jim aside. Desperate, Jim managed to swat the pistol out of the man's hand. It clattered to the ground and the gunman hit the door that exited onto the street.

As Jim skidded out onto the street in pursuit, the man was sliding into a car pulling away from the curb.

Even as the passenger door slammed shut, Jim snarled and pounded after it. He'd only indulged in this kind of chase a few times before, and never successfully. But that didn't mean he wouldn't try.

With a grunt, he leapt up onto the roof of a parked car and jumped from it to the one in front, clambering up over it and hurling himself to the next one in line as the black car, a 1929 Dodge, pulled out into traffic. Jim leapt sideways, landing half-on and half-off the roof of the Dodge. He hooked his fingers around the door-frame as the car peeled out, tires squealing.

Jim held on grimly as the car forced its way into the flow of traffic. It wasn't moving fast but the driver jerked the wheel, and Jim was whipped back and forth. The car scraped against another, sending up a spray of sparks. Jim turned his head to avoid the worst of it and tightened his grip.

A lean form rose up out of the passenger side window. Jim's prey faced him, hideous features too close for comfort. A hand came up, holding a new pistol to replace the one he'd lost and Jim felt a sudden shock from the passage of a bullet. He reacted instantly, grabbing the man's wrist and bending the pistol up and away.

"Not today chum!" Jim said. The man was silent. He hadn't spoken the entire time, not even a grunt of effort or pain. Jim felt the muscles in his wrist bunch as his opponent tried to force the Colt back down towards his face.

Eyes like hot marbles gleamed and Jim felt his soul shrivel just a fraction. The gun came down, even as Jim slid forward. The bark of the Colt was thunderous as it fired just over his shoulder. Jim let go of the door and dug his fingers into that horrid devil-grin. The man cried out then, for the first time, as the car suddenly fish-tailed and then Jim was flying through the air.

He hit the roof of another car and slid to the street. He grunted as he hit, the air rushing out of his lungs and a flare of pain dancing at the edges of his vision. Jim looked up as another car barreled towards him.

He leaped aside, but not quick enough. The car struck him a glancing blow, sending him spinning into the path of traffic. Muscles shrieking, Jim pushed himself straight up, and found himself thrown up across the hood of a car and into its windshield. Glass cracked, and then he was over its roof, flailing wildly.

Jim rolled across the street, his head ringing. Headlights approached, unstoppable. As Jim tried to gather his wits, the car bore down on him, horn shrieking. He hauled himself aside with only seconds to spare as the car sped past. Scrambling to his feet, he dove for the sidewalk and landed in an awkward crouch. Breathing heavily, he took a moment to regain his equilibrium.

Smithback hadn't committed suicide. Neither had Tupker. Or Pender. He was fairly certain of that now. Jim smiled slightly, and rubbed his ear, which was still ringing from the gunshot. Yes, he was fairly certain.

He looked down. Something dark hung from his grip. The half-mask. Jim held it up, examining it. It was made of metal, but almost rubbery in texture. Loose, rather than stiff.

Slowly, he stood, every joint aching. A mask. Why did they always wear masks? What kind of man wore a mask? Only one with something to hide.

Flashbulbs popped as the paparazzi found something even more exciting than celebrities to capture. Jim wondered what the headlines would look like.

"Holy Hell in a handbasket!" Cat said, pushing towards Jim through the crowd of onlookers that had gathered. "What the hell was that?"

"A mistake," Jim said, rubbing his shoulder. "One I'm going to regret tomorrow."

"Teach you to jump onto a moving car," Cat said.

"Sometimes it's worth it," Jim said, hefting the mask. "Look what I found."

"Hideous."

"Yes, it is, isn't it?" Jim said. He held the mask up to his face. Cat pushed it aside and looked up at him.

"Are you okay, Jimmy?" she said quietly.

Jim took her hand for a moment. "I've had worse nights."

"I haven't," Detective Healy snarled, forcing his way through the crowd with altogether less grace than Cat. "What the good goddamn were you playing at, Anthony?"

"Simply trying to apprehend a suspect, Detective," Jim said, stuffing the half-mask into his pocket. "Unfortunately, he got away."

"Really? After all that? I'm shocked. Shocked, I tell you," Healy said, tossing aside the bedraggled ruin of his cigar. "Did you accomplish anything useful with that little matinee idol display, Anthony?"

"Other than proving your suspicions, and mine, correct?"

"You got one of my men wounded, Anthony," Healy said, lighting a second cigar. He puffed on it until it turned an angry red. For a moment, Jim was reminded of the gunman's eyes. He pushed the thought away.

"I'm sorry," he said. And he was. He'd seen enough to know the wound hadn't been serious, but it grated on him nonetheless. Healy stared at him, as if judging his sincerity, then waved the apology away.

"Flesh wound. He'll enjoy the light duty. But don't do it again," the detective said. "So I was right, hunh?"

"Right as rain," Jim said. Healy grinned.

"Yeah. So, now what?"

9.

"So, dinner?" Cat said. The crowd had thinned out as the excitement faded. The press had faded quickly, chasing Healy from the scene. Jim had given the detective as much of a statement as he'd thought prudent.

"Not tonight, Cat." He turned as a Rolls pulled up to the street, the driver leaning on the horn. "There's Tom. Where can I drop you?" He held up a finger as her mouth opened. "Not the Globe."

"But—"

"No. You heard Healy. And remember our deal."

"Fine. Home, I guess." She glared at him sourly. "No dinner, no story. Some date you are, Jim Anthony!"

"This really wasn't my fault," he said as he opened the door for her. Gentry turned, leaning over the seat.

"Don't listen to him," he said, face flushed an even darker shade than normal. "I saw that, Jimmy! Took me forever to work my way through the traffic snarl you caused! What were you playing at with that stunt? *Chan eil saoi air nach laigh leon!*"

"I'm hardly a hero, Tom, and I've never claimed to be invincible."

"And another thing, where the hell is the rest of your tux? You know how much a good tux costs?" Tom continued, as if Jim hadn't spoken.

"Here it is," Cat said. She had Jim's coat folded over one arm, and held his shoes up. Jim gestured for her to get in.

"Well at least one of you kept your head," Tom said, turning back to the wheel. "Are you going to get in or not, Jimmy?"

Jim slid inside and pulled the door closed. He closed his eyes and sighed. "Home, Tom, please."

After extracting a promise from Cat to keep the night's exploits out from under her byline, they dropped her off at her apartment. As the Rolls pulled away, Tom said, "She's some gal, Jimmy."

"That meant as a compliment, Tom?" Jim asked, head tilted back, his eyes closed once more. Gentry laughed.

"You've done worse."

"Don't remind me."

"Sorry, Jimmy, that's part of the package." Tom squeezed the horn as a car pulled out in front of him. "Can't have you getting a swelled head, can we?"

"No danger there. Especially after tonight," Jim said, rubbing his aching arms. "Not exactly my finest showing, I must say."

"So what happened?"

"Someone committed murder, and tried to make it look otherwise." Jim massaged his temples. "The usual, in other words."

"That's why they pay you the big bucks, right?" Tom said, before sticking his head out the window and screaming imprecations at another driver. There weren't many cars out tonight, but enough to cause Tom's normally placid temper to bubble to the surface.

"They don't pay me anything, Tom. Remember?"

"Then that's why you pay me," Tom said. Jim could see his grin reflected in the windshield. "Who was it?"

"Pender."

"Damn," Tom said. "And Smithback this morning? We heading to the Penthouse?"

"The sooner, the better," Jim said. He pulled the mask out and examined it. It was light, and carefully crafted. This wasn't some dimestore mask, or even something created by a professional costumier, Jim concluded. It was something else entirely.

He turned it inside out. Thin tubes ran the length of it, leading to what could only be some form of filter inside the mouthpiece. Jim grunted.

"What?" Tom said.

"Oxygen tubes," Jim said. He looked up. "This thing is a gas mask. A grotesque one, to be sure, but it's a gas mask all the same."

"Why the hell would a guy be wearing a gas mask in the middle of New York?"

"Do you remember the Purple Gang?" Jim said meaningfully. Tom made what might have been a growl.

"Hell. Think they're connected?"

"Probably not."

"Thank the Virgin Mary for small favors," Gentry said.

"Don't thank her yet," Jim said, looking at the mask again. Then, he pulled out the card he'd found on Pender's body.

He had been correct in his initial reaction. The mask was the spitting image of the gargoyle leer on both this card and the one that had been delivered to Smithback. Jim rubbed his thumb over the embossed image. A memory tugged faintly at the edges of his consciousness. Where had he seen something like this before?

"Home again, home again," Tom said, taking the Rolls into the underground garage. Jim leaned over the seat.

"You contacted Dawkins?" he said.

"Yeah. He was more worried about the tux than you," Tom said. Jim snorted.

"Sounds like Dawkins," Jim said.

"Prissy limey," Tom grunted, a brogue creeping into his words. Jim laughed. He knew Tom didn't mean it. Not really. They left the car in its usual spot, and headed for the elevator.

"So. You think someone killed them fellows?" Tom said, hands in his pockets, as they rode upwards. Jim shook his head.

"Yes. But not directly, as I said. What I can't fathom is why."

"Does it matter?"

"Maybe not. But it usually helps with the who and the how." Jim loosened his bow tie. He felt confined in the elevator. Everything was too close. He pushed the feeling aside and concentrated on what he was saying. "I don't think this was the last one, unfortunately. Especially if Cat's information is to be believed."

The elevator buzzed then, causing Jim to flinch slightly. If Tom noticed, he gave no sign as he hauled the door open. Dawkins awaited them, impeccably dressed, one eyebrow quirked.

"Sir, I'll take your things," he said. Jim gratefully handed over his coat and shoes and began to strip off his shirt as he walked into the apartment. Tom headed for the kitchen, even as Jim stepped out of his trousers and stretched. Gleaming bronze skin stretched tight over impressive muscles as Jim strode towards the glass doors that led to the balcony. As Dawkins scooped up his discarded clothing, Jim stepped out onto the balcony, clad in nothing more than the linen loin cloth he wore beneath his clothing.

The cold wind crawled refreshingly across his skin, and he hopped up onto the edge of the balcony, luxuriating in the sensation.

Jim was no ascetic, no puritan, to deny himself certain pleasures. Wine, women and song were always welcome in moderate measure. But more than that, was the pure joy of being at one with the natural world. It was something his mother had taught him.

Jim stood, arms spread, back straight, and looked out over the city that sprawled beneath him—a shadow river pregnant with a million lights.

He breathed in the myriad scents, letting his senses stretch as his grandfather had taught him, letting his mind grow still like cool water. He opened his eyes. And nearly fell.

Jim's muscles locked as the city seemed to swirl beneath him. The darkness gathered like a hunting cat about to spring, and the rumble of distant traffic was the growl of some savage beast. Jim's heart hammered in its cage of bone and muscle and he felt weak. Terrified, in fact.

Vertigo clawed at him, and he clutched his head, nearly toppling from his perch. At the last second, his instincts kicked in, and Jim flipped himself backwards, landing heavily on all fours on the balcony.

Breathing heavily, he shook his head, trying to clear it. Adrenaline screamed through his system, flushing out the weakness that had momentarily afflicted him.

Still shaking, he stood. The city looked as it always had, and had taken no notice of his close call. Jim took a breath, then another.

"Sir?"

He whirled. Dawkins stepped back, eyes widening slightly. "Sir? Are you well?"

"I—yes. Yes, I'm fine, Dawkins, thank you," Jim said, running a hand through his hair. "Just fine. The items I brought—"

"I placed both that disgusting mask and that vile little card in your laboratory, sir, with the other one," Dawkins said. "Your tuxedo is heading straight for the cleaners."

"What would I do without you, Dawkins?"

"Starve, sir," the butler said, stepping aside as Jim came in out of the cold. Jim laughed, though it was a weak thing.

Dawkins held out a folded double-square of clothing, and Jim took it, dressing even as he moved towards the laboratory. Thin but tough linen pants and a steel gray sweater, his usual ensemble.

"Sir, Mr. Docker called again, as well," Dawkins said.

"Hnh. Did he leave a message this time?" Jim said, recalling that Cat had mentioned Docker's name in relation to Smithback.

"Only that he needed to see you at your earliest convenience," Dawkins said. Jim frowned.

"Nothing else?"

"No sir."

"Fine. Fine," Jim said, running his hands through his hair.

"Jimmy, you need some help?" Tom said, coming out of the kitchenette, drink in hand. Jim waved him away.

"No Tom. It's been a busy night, and I'll need you fresh tomorrow morning. I want to get to the morgue early."

"Just what every man wants to hear," Tom said.

Jim closed the door to the lab and leaned against it. A tremor ran through his muscles. Excess adrenaline from earlier, he knew. That was what it had been. What it had to be.

The laboratory was a model of the one he kept at the Tepee, his hidden retreat in the Catskills. Shelves of chemical solutions hung over sterile counters. A flat tray contained the latest university journals, as well as more esoteric scientific periodicals.

The mask sat on a model bust of a human head, leering at him. Jim ignored it and went to his work bench. He picked up the card and ran his fingers over it. There were any number of tests he could try, both chemical and physical, to see what the card was hiding. If it was hiding anything.

The card was the key, though. He knew it, even if he didn't know why. He had honed his instincts in this regard to a fine point, and he rarely questioned them anymore.

He tossed it down and set about getting to work. First, he turned on a bunsen burner and, clamping the card between two tongs, held it just shy of the flame. He rotated it slowly, looking for any hidden message that might have been revealed by the heat.

Disappointed, he sat back. He turned off the burner and cast his eyes toward the carefully organized racks of chemical substances that sat over the work bench.

He pulled down several and, using a syringe, he let a few droplets from each fall onto a different area of the card. Again, he found himself disappointed.

He leaned back, rubbing his chin. It was possible that he was approaching this from the wrong angle. Maybe there was no message on the card; rather, the card itself was the message.

"Simple," he hissed, suddenly angry with himself. He wasn't thinking clearly. He rubbed his shoulder and looked around.

The mask was gone. Jim froze, his hackles rising. The room seemed to spin as he lurched to his feet. Where was it? Where had it gone?

Something scraped across the tile of the floor. Jim spun, heart thudding, sweat beading on his skin.

Hate-filled eyes bore into his own and his throat was filled with a caustic reek as talons reached for him. Jim staggered back, wrenching open the hidden drawer in the work bench to reveal one of a number of specially-modified pistols he had hidden in out of the way spots in the Penthouse.

Jim snatched up the weapon and fired three times. Then, with a clatter of brass scales, the thing was upon him!

10.

Tom leapt to his feet even as the echo of the first shot faded and was replaced by the roar of the second. He tossed aside his drink and dragged the .38 revolver from the holster beneath his left arm even as he leapt over the edge of the couch and towards the door to Jim's lab.

"Jimmy!" he said, slamming his shoulder into the door. The lab doors were coated in a special sealant to make them leak-proof, though not quite airtight. Compound that with the structural reinforcement Jim had added in order to contain possible explosions, and the doors were the next best thing to unbreachable from the interior. From the exterior, however, it was a different story entirely.

Tom hit the doors like a bull at the charge, and they bent inward, if only slightly. "Dawkins! Get out here!" Tom snarled, hitting the doors again. This time they burst inward, nearly throwing him to the floor, something which proved fortuitous as Jim whirled, pistol in hand, and cracked off a shot, parting the air where Tom's head had been only seconds earlier!

"Jimmy, what—"

Jim screamed. It was less a cry of terror, and more the full-throated howl of a wild beast pushed to its limits. A savage shriek of berserkgang-proportions. As Tom got to his feet, his oldest friend attacked with a speed that would have quite possibly left another man dead.

Jim lashed out, cracking the barrel of his pistol across Tom's face and sending him staggering back out the doors. Tom managed to keep his feet under the force of the blow, but only barely.

"Jimmy! Jim, you gotta calm down!" Tom croaked. Jim snarled and smashed into him, digging iron fingers into Tom's throat.

Tom reacted instinctively, dropping his pistol and shoving both of his forearms up between Jim's own and forced Jim's hands away. They had fought many times, as boys and as men, but never like this. Tom rammed his knee into Jim's belly and pushed him back.

Jim made to dive on him again but Tom rolled aside. The hard wood floor cracked as Jim's fists struck it. He gave an inarticulate cry and launched a kick from his crouching position. The sole of his foot caught Tom on the hip, sending him flying to the ground.

"Damn it, Jimmy!" Tom said, sweeping his legs out and knocking Jim's out from under him. Jim hit the ground, none of his usual agility in evidence. It was as if his reaction times were slowed, his senses dimmed. Which was very likely the only reason Tom was still alive.

Jim rolled onto all fours and shook his head, as if trying to clear it. Tom didn't waste the opportunity. He launched himself at his friend and wrapped his long arms around him, trying to pin him. Jim flexed, breaking Tom's hold, and jerked his head, causing the back of his skull to connect with Tom's face. Tom stumbled, and Jim spun, planting a fist square in his belly and knocking him sprawling.

As Tom pulled himself upright, Jim reeled back and screamed again, clawing at his face. Tom watched in horror as his friend surged to his feet and turned towards the balcony doors.

Thoughts of the other deaths Jim had mentioned flooded Tom's mind. "No! God, no! Jimmy!" he said.

Then, suddenly, Dawkins was there. As Jim raged towards him, the butler avoided a wild punch and slapped his hand flat against Jim's chest. There was a snap, and a crackle and the stink of ozone filled the room.

Jim toppled, pale smoke rising from him. Dawkins looked down sorrowfully at Jim, then at Tom. "Up, Mr. Gentry. We need to get him to the couch."

"What did you do to him?" Tom said. Dawkins held up a hand, encased in a strange looking glove, with tubes and wires spilling off of it to connect to a leather harness studded with square-shaped electrical generators.

"I took the liberty of finding a better way than trying to trade blows with Master Anthony. I thought the glove of the Electric Phantom might provide the required assistance."

Gentry shook his head. "God bless Jim for being a pack rat."

"Indeed." Dawkins stooped and grabbed Jim's legs. "His arms, if you would."

Together, the two men maneuvered their employer and friend to the couch that Tom had only recently vacated. "What the hell happened to him?" Tom said, looking down at Jim's unconscious form.

"We shall simply wait for him to awaken and tell us," Dawkins said, removing the glove and harness. "I do hope the voltage wasn't as high as it appeared."

"Probably not," Tom said, rubbing his throat. "That thing was designed for flash more than fry. That Electric Phantom jackass was looking to scare people more than kill 'em."

"Though that didn't stop him in the end, did it?" Jim said, voice rusty, his eyes still closed. Tom and Dawkins leaned close, helping Jim to sit up.

"Take more than a lightning bolt to keep you down, hunh, Jimmy?" Tom said. Jim cracked one bloodshot eye.

"Maybe. But I wouldn't want to try it a second time," Jim said, gently probing the scorched patch on his sweater that now bore Dawkins' hand print.

Jim's vitality had been honed through a lifetime of rigorous exercise and endurance trials. He could shake off blows that would fell other men and ignore the poisons fatigue introduced into the human system for a long time by the standards of most modern athletes. He could even shake off the effects of an electrical zap such as the one Dawkins had delivered within a few minutes.

But the shock, combined with the drugs he now suspected to be in his system, had wrung him out like a wet kitten. Jim sat back, trying to ignore the ache that filled his muscles like cement in an oil drum.

He closed his eyes. Images rolled across the inside of his eyelids. Phantasmagoria the likes of which would have shaken the faith of William Blake surged up out of the darkness, but they were pale things now, all of the hideous reality drained from them by a divine thunderbolt. Jim smiled, sure that Dawkins would be quite offended if he said such out loud.

He took a breath, fighting to control the sluggish surge of adrenaline that insisted on pumping through him. Animal fear gnawed at the base of his brain, quieter now than before but still there. He opened his eyes, looking up at Tom's freckled features.

"Tom, I—" Jim began, coughing.

"Nothing, Jimmy. It was nothing," Tom said roughly. He traced the fading mark on his throat and cheek. "Barely a love tap."

Jim grunted. "I think I know what happened to Smithback and the others, though I'll have to confirm it."

"Confirm it when?" Tom said.

"Tomorrow." Jim levered himself up. He felt his heart slow. His system was finally flushing the poisons. The electric shock had helped, most likely. Dawkins put out a steadying hand, but Jim waved him away. "Dawkins. Get the protective gear out of my lab. Seal the card and the mask in Bakelite containers. Don't let them touch your bare skin."

"At once, sir," Dawkins said. Jim moved into a sitting position and rested his head in his hands. Tom brought him a drink, which he gratefully accepted.

"So. They were poisoned," Tom said, bluntly. Jim nodded.

"A very specific poison." He rubbed his chin. "I saw things...."

"What things?"

"Nothing important. A byproduct of heightened fear responses, provoked by the simplest of stimuli." Jim sat back. "A poison that instills fear, Tom. It literally scares its victim to death."

"And you think that's what did for them like Smithback?" Tom said, incredulous. "Somebody scared them?"

"Not just scared. Terrified, beyond all reason," Jim said, standing. "I couldn't think, Tom." He turned, staring at his friend. He tapped the side of his head. "I was so frightened that I literally couldn't think. All I could do was react to imaginary phantoms. And once my emotional threshold had been breached...well."

"Fight or flight. You tried to run," Tom said softly. Jim hesitated, then nodded.

"I tried to run," he said hoarsely.

"No shame in it, Jimmy," Tom said, putting a hand on Anthony's shoulder. "You weren't in your right head."

Jim's face was like stone. "When I was a boy, my grandfather would take me on vision-trips. Peyote rituals, held in isolated areas, with only the natural world to see. And Mephito, of course."

Tom frowned at the mention of Jim's maternal grandfather. Mephito, that wizened bundle of bones, who looked more like a sun-blackened skeleton than a man. Tom, like many men of his upbringing, was just two shades shy of superstitious, and Mephito pressed all of his buttons in that regard.

Half mystic and half mad, Mephito was the lone spot of the irrational in Jim Anthony's otherwise impervious fortress of logic and science. Thankfully, he was also not here at the moment, having opted to remain on the Sioux reservation with friends after their recent adventure out west with Captain Hazzard and his crew.

Tom breathed a silent prayer of thanks, then turned his attention back to Jim.

"Mephito would guide me then," Jim said, his eyes far away. "Talk me through it. He trained me, to do it myself. I still use it sometimes."

"Peyote?" Tom said, shocked. Jim gave him a crooked smile.

"Perfectly safe, Tom. Better than tobacco, at any rate."

Tom grimaced. "I know you think them things will kill me, but I ain't the only one who sneaks a cigarette now and then, Jimmy!"

Jim raised his hand to forestall the beginnings of an old argument. He knew what the experts said about tobacco's salutary effect on the human body, but his own research had shown the opposite. Getting Tom to believe that he was right wasn't the hard part, unfortunately. It was getting him to stop smoking that was the challenge. "I didn't say I wasn't guilty, Tom. Merely pointing out the difference." He dropped his hand. "The point is, I know how to control myself under the influence of strong hallucinogens. But this stuff ate through my defenses like acid. I was helpless. I can only imagine what it must have been like for poor Jerome."

Dawkins re-entered the room, carrying two Bakelite disks. Flat and circular, the disks were of Jim's own design and could range in size from roughly equivalent to the wheel from a Rolls-Royce to the size of a drink coaster. These two fell somewhere in between. Jim grimaced at the sight of them, but pressed on. "Thank you, Dawkins. There are any number of hallucinogens that could result in an attack similar to the one I experienced, but the severity...." He trailed off, shaking his head.

"This is something new, then?" Tom said.

"Or something old," Jim said. He blinked, then sat up. "That's it. No wonder I didn't see it. I was looking for a compound. Something created by man. But what if it wasn't created, but merely harvested?" He stood and took the disk containing the card from Dawkins. "Certain spores or fungi might have a similar effect."

"Still doesn't explain the mask," Tom said. He poked the sphere containing it. "Stuff obviously ain't airborne, right?"

"No. Too concentrated," Jim said. "Skin contact appears to be the trigger. A paste or gel, smeared on the card and absorbed through the victim's fingers. I only got a full dose because I handled two cards. As far as the mask goes, it's another layer to our mystery." He tapped the sphere. "I've seen this shape before. Somewhere."

"In your nightmares?" Tom said.

"Close. College," Jim said. "Maybe. Right now, though, the question is how did whatever is on this card get in contact with Smithback and the others? And, more importantly, why?"

The morning found Jim sitting on the couch, a nest of reference books and newspapers surrounding him. Tom and Dawkins had both retired not long after the incident, but Jim, despite his exertions, found himself unable to sleep.

As the weak light of a sad, gray dawn filtered through the windows and the balcony doors, Jim put aside the book he'd been reading and looked once more at the mask.

He'd found a number of potential culprits among his catalog of toxic substances, but none of them stood out. Hallucinogens had accompanied mankind out of the caves, and there were dozens to choose from, any number of which could be the origin of the paste on the card.

Still, something about the combination had sparked a nagging ghost of memory. He leaned forward, chin balanced on his fist. "Where have I seen you before?"

The mask didn't answer, for which he was grateful. Sighing, he stood and went to the balcony. Outside, the cold air cleared away the lingering traces of his lethargy. He'd trained himself to do without rest when necessary, but rarely had he ever been unable to sleep when he wanted to.

Leaning his weight on the rail, he went over the facts. Three men, all connected by ties of business, dead in apparent suicides. Those suicides were most likely the result of contact with a form of strong hallucinogen. And that hallucinogen had been delivered, at least in two cases, by a card.

Safe to say it had probably been delivered the same way in the other case as well. Business cards were a form of currency among the upper echelons of the business world. Jim himself had several dozen encased in a simple Rolodex in his study. Easy enough to slip a card into a pocket when the victim wasn't looking. Was that what had happened to Tupker and Pender? Or had they, like Smithback, had it delivered to them overtly?

But if that was the case, why the warning of the demonic illustration? Why not simply dose a normal business card? Why the dramatics?

Jim frowned. He knew why. It was a foolish question, given his experiences with such in the past. It was the fear. The card was indeed a warning of sorts. A gloating statement:'you will die.'

But as he'd said to Tom, the question was why. Why had Jerry Smithback, Alan Tupker and Silas Pender been targeted for assassination?

New York rose out of the wet morning mist like Atlantis rising from the depths, and Jim contemplated the sea of Twentieth Century ziggurats. There were times he regretted spending so much time here, away from the quiet, contemplative reaches of the Southwest or the brooding majesty of the mountains. At other times, he was struck by the alien beauty of the city.

51

Now was one of those times. Somewhere in that warren of concrete and steel was a murderer. Murderers, perhaps. And it was up to him to find them.

He knocked his knuckles on the rail and went back inside to wake up Tom. Dawkins was already in the kitchenette, preparing coffee. He sniffed in displeasure.

"Sleep is the ally of acuity, Mr. Anthony," he said. "I have prepared breakfast."

"No time to eat, Dawkins. I have an appointment to keep with Detective Healy." Jim snagged a cup of coffee and drained it in a searing gulp. "Is Tom awake?"

"I took the liberty of awakening Mr. Gentry before I came up."

"Dawkins, you are a wonder," Jim said. "Caffeinate Tom, please, while I shower."

Jim's attire was his usual working outfit, as Tom liked to call it. On top of the sweater, he added a tooled leather holster containing another of his modified .45 automatics. Unlike the other, this one was loaded with special mercy rounds. Despite his reputation, Jim preferred not to kill his opponents if possible.

A dark longshoreman's coat completed the ensemble. If Jim were any other man, he would blend in on the street, looking like nothing so much as one more dockside rough neck. But the combination of his striking features, his eyes and his skin made him hard to miss in a crowd.

Entering the kitchen again, Jim saw that Tom was on his second cup of coffee, and hurriedly wolfing down a slice of jam-slathered toast.

"When you're finished, Gentry, we have somewhere to be," Jim said. Tom swallowed and glared at Jim.

"The sun's barely up!"

"Crime doesn't sleep, Tom."

"Have you been listening to those cornball radio programs again? You ain't Captain Spectre and I ain't a Lightning Legionnaire."

Jim laughed and headed for the elevator, pausing only to scoop up one of the smaller of the Bakelite disks, the one containing the business card he'd recovered from Silas Pender's body. As he and Tom got onto the elevator, Jim said, "Dawkins. Move that mask into the safe in the laboratory. I doubt my friends from last night will lay siege to the building to get it back, but better safe than sorry."

"Even as you say, Mr. Anthony," Dawkins said.

In the underground lot, Tom headed for the Rolls, but Jim waved him off. "The Ford, Tom. I'll need the equipment in the back." Tom grimaced.

"Man, I hate that rolling lab. I'm always afraid if we hit a pothole, we'll get blown sky-high!"

Like each of the six automobiles Jim owned the Ford had been modified for a specific purpose. It was, in effect, a mobile crime lab, allowing Jim access to a variety of tools he considered necessary. While forensic pathology was still considered hokum by many official personalities, to Jim it was an art. Fingerprints, hair samples, dust and detritus could all paint for him a picture of a crime and potentially identify its committer.

"It's not like I have more than one or two volatile chemicals aboard, Tom. And

I almost never use them in transit," Jim said. "Besides, with the way you drive, I'd be surprised if a pothole registered as more than a blip!"

"You know, you could drive yourself," Tom said, getting behind the wheel. Jim laughed and slid into the back. As he settled himself, he pulled down the back of the seat beside him, turning it into a flat tray. Reaching up, he fumbled with a series of straps set across the roof of the car, and pulled down a flat steel box of instruments and a pair of black rubber gloves.

It was early, and traffic was light. "We're paying the cops a visit, right?" Tom said, putting the car on a heading for Little Italy, 240 Centre Street, and the headquarters of the New York Police Department.

"Please," Jim said, pulling on the rubber gloves. Carefully, he opened the container and plucked out the card. He opened the case and pulled out a thin scraper, a pair of tweezers and a set of microscopic slides. He gently scraped the surface of the card and deposited the clear substance that came loose onto one of the slides. He did this several more times, then re-sealed the card inside its disk and put it aside.

There was every chance that no residue would remain on Smithback's body. But another sample might provide insights into the origins of the poison.

"Tupker," Jim said, aloud.

"What?"

"Tom, I need you to do some digging for me," Jim said, eyeing the samples he'd taken. "While I'm busy here, I need you to find out where Alan Tupker was buried."

"Aw, geez—" Tom began.

"Relax, Tom, no exhumation will be necessary this time. I have a method for acquiring samples from the interred that I've been aching to try." Jim reached under his seat and pulled out a small strong box. Flipping it open, he pulled an extendable shelf up and out and perused the triple rack of test-tubes contained therein.

Each of the test-tubes contained a different reactive agent, specifically designed to help Jim identify various poisons. In his line, it had come in handy more than once. He had used a variant of the Poison Box, as Tom had dubbed it, to identify and devise an antidote to Neville Soames' particular concoction earlier in the year.

He pulled down the hidden shelf attached to the back of the seat in front of him and placed the box and its contents on the fitted space. Attaching stabilizers to keep the whole thing steady, Jim laid out one of the samples. Deftly plucking a test-tube from his repertoire, he dripped a bit on the sample.

The sample bubbled and hissed and began to seep a dark cloud. Jim's eyes widened and he slapped the top of the glass slide back in place before more than a whiff could escape.

"Jimmy, what the hell are you doing back there?"

"Satisfying my curiosity." Jim watched as the sample rapidly changed colors. "It's as I suspected."

"What?"

"This agent, whatever it is, bears a remarkable similarity to Aminita Muscaria."

"Which is?"

"A deadly poison and a strong hallucinogen. Grows practically everywhere." Jim held the sample up to the light. "Which, unfortunately isn't really going to make this investigation any easier."

"When are they ever easy?" Tom snorted. Jim replaced his equipment and set the samples into a padded container as Tom maneuvered the car through the streets of Little Italy.

The baroque palace that was the ultimate headquarters of the New York City Police Department rose up to the side of the Ford. Tom looked at Jim. "We're here."

"So I see," Jim said. "Remember, find out—"

"Where the fatcats are buried, right. Want me to pick you up?"

"No. I'll make it back on my own. It's a nice walk," Jim said, sliding out of the car. Tom shook his head.

"That's one way of putting it."

Jim laughed and slapped a palm on the roof, sending the Ford on its way. He turned.

Healy was waiting for him. The detective sat on the steps, hunched over, smoke streaming up around his face like a gray halo.

"Bright and early, Anthony," the detective said, dropping a cigarette onto the stairs and crushing it with his heel. He stood, almost reluctantly. "What a way to start the day."

"I thought you lived for solving crimes, Detective?" Jim said, striding towards him. Healy grunted.

"Not hardly. Body is downstairs in that meat-locker you recommended the Commissioner have installed." He turned and ambled up the stairs. "You got anything for me?"

"Poison."

Healy looked at him. Jim smiled. "The victims were poisoned. Dosed, rather. With a powerful hallucinogen."

"All of 'em?" Healy said. Jim shook his head.

"So I suspect. But I'm quite certain I'm right."

"Oh, well, if you're quite certain," Healy said sarcastically. "That's not good enough and you know it. Even if you are friends with the mayor."

"I know. Which is why I'm here to double-check my findings, Detective." Jim ran a hand through his hair. "So, the Commissioner did as I suggested?"

"We got bodies coming out our ears thanks to you!" Healy snapped. "What the hell good are frozen corpses gonna do me, huh?"

"The benefits of post-mortem pathology far outweigh the minor inconveniences."

"Nuts! Nuts to pathology and nuts to you!" Healy waved his arms in wide circles. "It ain't proper policing!"

"And I'm not a proper policeman, eh?" Jim said avoiding Healy's flailing arm. "Silly, me. I always thought an open mind would be of benefit to a detective."

"Well you thought wrong." Healy stopped at the door and turned. "An open mind is a sieve, Anthony. It loses as much as it takes in."

"Interesting way of putting it," Jim said. It was easy to take Healy's brutish façade at face value. In truth, the detective was a smart cookie. He had an instinctive grasp of crime that rivaled Jim's own. But change was not Healy's friend. And Jim, for better or worse, intended to change the way the New York Police Department did business. "A better way of phrasing it is that an open mind is more conducive to lateral thinking."

Healy snorted. "Lateral thinking. You said the same thing about that business with Arno Stark. I knew he'd murdered his secretary right off the bat!"

"Yes, but you didn't know why," Jim said. "And considering he was selling information concerning America's military infrastructure to foreign powers, it's a good thing we found out."

"None of which mattered in the end, because Stark blew himself up in that idiotic tin suit of his." Healy lit another cigarette. "Case closed. Your corpses await, Anthony."

"Trying to change the subject, Detective?"

"Better than standing out here in the cold arguing about it," Healy said, shivering slightly. "Inside."

Jim walked into the building, Healy trailing after him. Jim had arrived just as the night shift was giving way to the morning shift. Jim glanced at Healy. "Early morning or late night, Detective?"

"Does it matter?"

"Crime doesn't sleep?" Jim said. Healy glared at him. Jim stifled a laugh and followed the detective through the building. Everywhere, uniformed officers went about their business, some nodding to Jim. He had worked with many of them before. Healy frowned as Jim stopped to shake hands.

Minutes later they were downstairs in the newly-built morgue. Fashioned along the lines of similar facilities in certain hospitals, Jim was pleasantly surprised to find that the designer had obviously taken several of his own suggestions into consideration. Square drawers lined a wall, and the air was cool. He stripped off his coat and hung it up.

"Yeah, yeah, wipe that smug grin off your face," Healy said as Jim examined the room. He gestured with his cigarette. "First body is in the third drawer, middle row. Place is like a damn meat-locker."

"Which is where you used to keep the bodies, wasn't it?" Jim said, pulling out the indicated drawer. "Keeping it this cold ensures that the bodies don't decompose as rapidly." Silas Pender's rictus of terror grinned horribly up at Jim.

The shattered remains of Jerry Smithback were in the next drawer over. Jim pulled it out and fell silent, studying the body of his father's friend.

"Forgot to ask whether you knew him," Healy said, quietly. Jim nodded.

"Not well. Friend of my father's." He placed the box of samples carefully beside Pender's body and flipped it open. "I notice the presence of stitches on the torso. Did the investigating doctor determine what killed him?"

"Sudden heart failure. Figures it happened about the time he would have pitched over the side." Healy examined the smoldering tip of his cigarette. "So you're off the hook there."

"I assure you, I was on pins and needles." Jim retrieved one of the untouched samples and set it aside. He pulled out a small case from the box and retrieved a set of goggles, much like welders goggles.

"What the hell are those?" Healy said.

"Portable microscope," Jim said, putting the goggles on and twisting the small knobs set to either side of the eyepieces. "Same principle, just easier to use." He lifted Pender's hand. "Ha."

"What?"

"See this slight crystallization on his fingers?" Jim asked, twisting the hand so that Healy could see it.

"Yeah, so?"

"I'm willing to bet that if we warm it up a bit—" He turned. "Matches." He snapped his fingers. "Please."

Healy frowned, but tossed Jim a book of matches. Jim looked at it. "The Kit-Kat Club? Really, Detective?"

"Get to it, Anthony, I got places to be, murders to solve."

"Getting to it." Jim bent, lit a match, and waved it over Smithback's fingers. "Hope it's not flammable—ah." He blew out the match and used the opposite end to scrape a rough gel off of one finger. "There." He took an empty slide out of the case and scraped the substance onto it. Then, pulling off the goggles, he handed it to Healy. "Put them on."

"What? Why?"

"Put them on," Jim insisted. He grabbed one of the samples from earlier and handed it to Healy. "Look."

Healy squirmed for a moment, but put the goggles on and held up the two samples. "Huh."

"Exactly." Jim crossed his arms. Healy looked at him.

"Where'd you get the first sample?"

"Does it matter?" Jim said. Healy stripped off the goggles and tossed them at him. He held onto the samples, however.

"You bet your ass it does. Chain of evidence, Anthony. Where'd you get it?"

"Answer me a question first…did you find anything out of the ordinary on the first victim? Tupker?"

"Like what?" Healy said suspiciously.

Jim hesitated. Then, "A card. A business card."

"I—no. No. We didn't find anything like that."

"What the hell is going on down here?" someone bellowed.

12.

"Who the hell are you?" Healy snarled. The man, another detective by his dress, flashed a badge. He was tall and broad shouldered, with sharp features that seemed to change shape as the light caught him at different angles.

"Corrigan. DA's office. Who the hell is he and what the hell is he doing down here?" the newcomer barked.

Healy stepped between Jim and Corrigan, and gestured for the former to remain silent. "He's here 'cause I want him here. You, on the other hand—"

"And who are you?" Corrigan snapped.

"Healy."

Corrigan cocked his head. "That supposed to mean something to me?"

"Depends why you're down here," Healy said. Corrigan gestured to the body.

"I'm here for that. My case now."

"Bull pucky," Healy said lighting another cigarette. "No one told me."

"DA got to run everything by you now?" Corrigan pushed past Healy and stuck a finger in Jim's face. "Now who are you?" He glanced at the body and his eyes widened. "And what the hell are you doing to the body?" He whirled. "Where's the evidence, Healy? 'Cause if he's touched it—"

"I assure you that I've tampered with nothing, Mr.—ah—Corrigan, was it?" Jim said, turning to collect his equipment. Corrigan spun back and grabbed his arm.

"Leave that stuff there! You ain't taking nothing out of here!"

"Back off!" Healy said, grabbing for Corrigan's own arm. Something clinked as Healy's fingers closed on the man's forearm. "Hey, what gives?"

Corrigan's face changed, the bluster draining away, becoming something else entirely. Jim felt a flash of recognition as he looked into Corrigan's eyes in that moment. "You," Jim said. This man was no police officer, no representative of the DA's office! In fact, he was the same man Jim had fought earlier, the usher, the waiter, the murderer of Jerry Smithback and Silas Pender!

Jim's hand snapped out, scraping across Corrigan's face. The pale Irish skin was scraped clean, revealing a darker tint beneath. Some kind of grease paint!

Corrigan shoved Jim backwards, onto Smithback's corpse, his strength as incredible as before. Healy stumbled back in surprise as Corrigan turned and gestured. There was a pneumatic hiss and Healy staggered, yelping.

Jim surged up, grappling with Corrigan. "Who are you? Why did you kill Silas Pender?" Jim said, pressing his forearm to the man's throat and driving him backwards against the wall. A knee shot up, nearly connecting, but Jim used his free hand to slap it aside. He drove a fist into the man's gut and felt his knuckles connect with something hard and unyielding. His hand went momentarily numb.

Corrigan brought his palms together on either side of Jim's head, causing him to reel. As Jim stepped back, Corrigan thrust his hand forward. There was another hiss, but Jim caught his wrist and forced his hand aside as a burst of colored gas coiled towards the ceiling.

The design of the strange half-mask he'd confiscated the night before suddenly made sense to Jim. The poison on the card might not be airborne, but this man had other resources that were!

Jim swept his leg out, knocking Corrigan off of his feet. Corrigan slid down the wall, a snarl on his face. For a moment, he resembled the mask he'd worn the night before.

But before Jim could act on his momentary advantage, he was distracted by a cry of the purest horror. Healy, on his knees, was screaming. Jim turned towards the detective, concerned, and Corrigan lunged to his feet, his hand diving into his coat.

Jim threw himself aside as Corrigan drew a short-bladed sword from within his coat and sliced down. Jim rolled across the floor and bounded to his feet, pulling his pistol in one smooth motion. Corrigan chopped at him, and Jim fired. Metal rang on metal, and the man staggered.

Jim sidled towards Healy while keeping Corrigan covered. "Healy? Detective?"

Healy, his face in his hands, was still screaming, though it had tapered off in intensity. Jim grabbed his shoulder and shook him. Healy's hands dropped away, revealing a face that was stretched tight in terror. Jim gasped, and glared at Corrigan. "What did you do to him?"

"Nothing permanent," Corrigan said, all trace of New York washed from his voice. In its place was something liquid and guttural. Jim had a good ear for such things, yet could not pinpoint the origin of the accent. Corrigan paced forward, hesitating only when Jim raised the pistol.

"Next shot will be for your head, chum," Jim said harshly. "Who are you? Why were you at the Roxy last night? What's your connection to Silas Pender?"

"You ask many questions. Do you really expect answers?"

"No. I know better than that." Jim gestured with the pistol. "Drop the sword."

"I think not." Corrigan smiled. "In fact, I think you will drop your pistol."

"And why would I do that?"

"Because if you don't, I'll drop this." Corrigan reached into his coat again and pulled out what looked to be a glass sphere half the size of a baseball. It looked as if it were filled with a greenish gas.

Jim froze. "What—"

"Those samples you took, I assume they were samples; yes, give them to me. Now."

"Why did you kill Smithback? And the others?"

"The samples. Or you can join your friend in madness." Corrigan pointed his sword at Healy. The detective had collapsed onto his side and had curled into a loose ball. Jim felt a wrench of sympathy.

"I'm assuming it's a less concentrated dose than was on the cards," Jim said.

"Just enough to paralyze and disorient, not enough to kill."

"The samples," Corrigan said for a third time.

"And the card as well?" Jim said. Corrigan frowned. Jim smiled grimly. "Yes. I have it."

"I want it. Now!"

"Did you happen to give one to Alan Tupker as well?" Jim said. "Did he get a card slipped into his pocket at some point?" He cocked his head. "Was that why you were there? To retrieve the murder weapon?"

Jim realized that he'd hit the nail on the head, as Corrigan's face went through a variety of expressions over the next few seconds before settling on something approaching resignation. Jim knew then what was coming. He acted on instinct, twitching his pistol aside and firing—shattering the small globe Corrigan held!

Smoke spilled down his hand as the man gave a cry and stepped back. Jim fired again, but Corrigan was already moving, reaching into his coat once more. The mercy bullet plucked at his shoulder, spinning him around. Jim crashed into him with leonine ferocity, swiping the barrel of his pistol across Corrigan's wrist, sending the sword flying.

Corrigan bucked, and Jim found himself falling. The man had training of a kind, and similar to Jim's own. Jim hit the wall near the door and tumbled down. Corrigan grabbed Jim's case of samples and was running, heading up the stairs. Jim scrambled after him.

Corrigan entered the squad room at a run, Jim just on his heels. Police officers turned, eyes widening. Jim's hand caught the edge of Corrigan's coat. He hauled backwards, trying to stop the other man's headlong plunge. Corrigan shrugged out of the coat, revealing a leather harness covering his torso. Steel plates riveted to the front and back gave it the appearance of a crustacean's shell. A series of tiny glass globes dangled from it, as did an empty sheath. Corrigan, scowling, slid a duplicate to the mask he'd worn earlier over the lower half of his face.

"Stop him!" Jim said.

Corrigan ripped several globes free, shook them and tossed them in different directions. A horribly colored smoke spilled out of the shattered glass, spreading quickly through the station. Jim covered his mouth with his hand and charged through the smoke. His skin tingled, and he could taste the same iron bile he'd tasted in his lab the previous night.

Screams filled the air as he grabbed the straps of Corrigan's harness, trying to pull him close. Corrigan, teeth bared, wrapped his hands around Jim's face. There were twin hisses and then, madness!

Fears both old and new surged up from the depths of Jim's mind like the tendrils of an awakened kraken. He fell onto his hands and knees, gagging. Corrigan looked down at him, his features swirling, changing. A demon leered down at Jim, pointed tongue protruding between curved tusks. It said something, in a language that sounded familiar, but Jim couldn't focus enough to translate. Fear spurted through him, then was replaced by adrenaline.

Fight or flight. Just like earlier. His mind was awash in conflicting colors and sounds. Lights danced at the edge of his vision and the air stank of burning bodies. Jim rose to his feet with effort, his skin slick with sweat as the sound of his heart thundered in his ears. Corrigan's face was a slash of darkness split by silver teeth. Claws flared and Jim felt his skin part.

He lurched forward, driving his fists into the darkness, relishing the pain that shivered up his arms. Better pain than fear. Jim's legs struck something hard, and he lashed out.

A flash of silver again, and the meat of his shoulder parted beneath the horror's claws. Jim grabbed for it. His fingers scrabbled across its scales and snagged. With a ripple of muscle, he yanked hard, tearing away the obstruction.

The darkness flowed away suddenly and Jim pounded in pursuit. Bat-wings flapping, the nightmare thing careened through the corridors of Police Headquarters, heading for the rectangle of light that was the exit.

Jim leapt, terror and anger firing his muscles in equal measure. Glass shattered and Jim hit the steps with bone-jarring force. He rolled down the front stairs, grunting in pain, his head already clearing as the cold February air whipped over him. But it wasn't enough.

On all fours on the sidewalk, Jim could only shake his head as Corrigan raced towards a black car idling on the street. A door slammed and the car peeled away. Jim watched it go, arms trembling with effort, then, with a groan, he collapsed, his blood staining the snow crimson.

13.

"**W**ake up, Anthony."

Jim groaned as a hand cracked across his jaw. His eyes shot open and his hand flew up, seizing the throat of the shape looming over him.

Healy made strangling sounds as Jim sat up abruptly. Realizing who it was he had in his grip, Jim hastily released the detective. Pain flared in his arm and he clutched at it. His hand came away red.

"You look like you got cut to hell and back," Healy croaked, rubbing his throat. He was pale and shaky looking.

"You don't look much better," Jim said, getting to his feet, one palm pressed to his wounded arm. Blood dripped down his hand and left a thin trail as he walked back up the stairs. "How are—"

"Gas started dispersing a few minutes ago. Right after you broke the doors," Healy said gruffly. "A few injuries, but nothing too bad. Nobody thought to go for their gun, thank God."

"I should have anticipated this. Especially after last night," Jim said. Healy glared at him.

"Yeah." Then, "Did he use the same car?"

"Same car," Jim said. He looked at his shoulder. The wound was shallow, and the bleeding was tapering off some. "Same man."

"What the hell was that stuff?" Healy stripped off his tie and shoved it into his coat. He looked ill. So too did most of the police officers in the squad room. Broken glass and wood littered the floor, but Jim's attention was drawn immediately to the strange harness Corrigan had worn. It lay discarded on the floor, where Jim had thrown it in his delirium.

"It was what killed Jerome Smithback last night, only less concentrated, luckily," Jim said, squatting to scoop up the harness. The plates rattled softly as he turned it over in his hands. "Hnh."

"What?" Healy leaned over him.

"Oxygen tubes. Just like in the mask. No wonder he ran when I ripped it off." Jim showed the interior of the odd cuirass to Healy. Airtight sacks were pressed flat to the inside curve of the armor. "See? He was breathing stored oxygen the entire time." He flicked a clear, nigh invisible tube that stuck out from the top of the harness. "Incredible."

"Yeah. Incredible." Healy straightened and rubbed the back of his head. "Look, are there going to be any—any—"

"Lasting effects? No. I assume someone has called for a doctor?" Jim stood, still examining the harness. "Has downstairs aired out?"

"Yeah." Healy flapped his hand. "He stole your samples."

"Not all of them," Jim said. "And not the originals." He glanced at Healy. "How are you feeling, Detective?" he said, more softly. Healy frowned and looked away.

"I saw things." He stopped and shook his head. "I want this guy. Yesterday."

Jim nodded brusquely. "I'm working on it, Detective."

"Yeah," Healy said again. He turned and began barking orders to the shaken officers. Jim took the opportunity to head back downstairs.

In the morgue, Jim pulled off his sweater and checked his wounds. Light cuts across his chest and the deeper one in the meat of his shoulder were the extent of his injuries. He wondered what other weapons Corrigan had been carrying. The wounds were unlike anything left by any blade Jim was familiar with.

After disinfecting and binding his injuries with the help of a first aid kit he'd snagged from the squad room, Jim set to examining the strange sword Corrigan had left behind.

Jim hefted the weapon and balanced it on his palms. It resembled nothing so much as a Roman or Greek spatha, with a rounded crosspiece and a flat, leaf-shaped blade that bespoke its origins clearly.

Its age was apparent as well, as was the care that had been taken in its upkeep. His keen eyes picked out the marks of regular repairs and replacements. The edge possessed all the signs of having seen much use.

Jim swung it experimentally. It had good balance, and Corrigan, if that was indeed his name, though Jim rather doubted it, had seemed well-versed in its use.

"Curiouser and curiouser," Jim murmured. Setting the sword aside, he knelt and, once more wearing his experimental goggles, searched the floor for the pieces of the sphere he'd shot out of Corrigan's hand. His hands protected by his sweater, Jim carefully picked up a shard and examined it.

The shard caught the light oddly, as if it were shot through with flecks of metal. And the glass itself was thick and coarse, as if it had been hand-fired, rather than machine-made. There were the tell-tale squiggles of writing on it, though any meaning the symbols might have had were eliminated by the breaking of the sphere.

Jim wrapped a length of bandage around his fingers and gently wiped along the inside curve of the shard. As he'd suspected, the mixture inside hadn't been activated by his shot.

Upstairs, Corrigan had shaken the spheres before hurling them. Obviously, some sort of kinetic charge was necessary to fully activate the vile effects. Jim's bullet hadn't been enough to do more than partially stir it up.

Jim sat back on his heels, eyes narrowed in concentration. An ancient sword, that odd cuirass with its primitive—and it was primitive, despite the cleverness of its function—breathing mechanism, and now, hand-crafted chemical grenades. Not to mention whatever devices Corrigan had had hidden up his sleeves.

All of it seemed entirely too familiar. But where had he seen it before. He blinked. "Dear God. It can't be. It simply can't be—" He stood, his mind awhirl

"Curiouser and curiouser," Jim murmured.

with the implications of his realization.

Could it be? Was that what his subconscious had been trying to tell him all this time? Jim shook his head, feeling slightly sick. Perhaps it was just an after-effect of the gas.

He needed his library. And a second opinion.

Carefully, he gathered up the remaining shards and wrapped them and the spatha up in his sweater and slid on his coat. Bare-chested he left the morgue and went back upstairs. He gestured to Healy as he headed for the exit.

"Where are you going?" Healy said.

"For more information. We know we have an enemy. Now we need to know everything we can about him." Jim patted his bundled sweater. "Do you have anyone willing to drive me back to the Waldorf-Anthony?"

Healy turned and snagged a passing officer, ordering him to play chauffeur. Then he poked Jim in the chest with a rigid finger.

"Anything you find, you get back to me, got it?"

"Got it," Jim said sweeping two fingers against his head in salute. Healy waved him away and Jim followed the officer he'd designated to the motor pool.

"So what happened in there, sir?" the officer said, when they were out of earshot of the gruff detective. Jim looked at him.

"Simmons, isn't it? You made the call on the first Old Soldier murder, didn't you?"

The young man flushed. "Yessir. Still have bad dreams about that, so I do." Jim clapped a hand to his shoulder.

"You're not alone in that," he said. "You're just coming on duty?"

"Yessir. Guess I'm lucky in that." Simmons shook his head. "Looked like the boys had just seen the Devil Himself. Including Detective Healy. I haven't ever seen the man look frightened…."

"He had good reason to be." Jim fell silent as his earlier conclusions swooped back up to the forefront of his thoughts. Simmons, perhaps catching sight of his face, said nothing else.

The ride back to the Waldorf-Anthony seemed to take no time at all, so distracted was Jim. He barely remembered saying goodbye to Simmons.

The lobby was busy as always. Jim threaded his way through the crowd, ignoring the looks his bloodied, bare-chested state garnered him. He caught the private elevator to the Penthouse to find Dawkins waiting on him as he shoved the doors opened.

"Miss Kilkenny called for you, sir. Several times." Dawkins' raised eyebrow said what he thought about that. Jim sighed.

"If she calls again, tell her I'm otherwise engaged."

"Progress then, sir?" Dawkins said, helping him out of his coat. He clucked his tongue at the sight of the bandages. "Or a setback?"

"Both, perhaps. The phantom foe becomes more physical, but his motives remain ethereal." Jim patted his bundled sweater. "I need every book we have on ancient Greek and Roman engineering. Italian as well."

"Byzantine, sir?"

"Obviously, yes, thank you Dawkins." Jim hesitated. "And Leonardo."

"Da Vinci?" Dawkins frowned.

Jim nodded, his face grim. "Oh, yes. Yes, indeed."

Jim went to his lab, as Dawkins hurried to comply. He laid out the glass shards after donning a pair of rubber gloves and examined them under a microscope. Satisfied that his initial thoughts were correct, Jim set about determining the origins of the glass. Different methods of manufacture bore the stamp of origin, as distinctive as blood samples or human hairs.

Meanwhile, several small stacks of books grew around him. Dawkins, without having been asked, set a book on silica samples and glass manufacturing beside Jim's elbow. Jim grunted his thanks and flipped through the pages.

"Greece," he said, after a while. "Constantinople."

"Istanbul, sir," Dawkins said, setting a plate of fruit, cheese and dried meat beside Jim. Jim looked up.

"Yes, of course. Thank you, Dawkins." He chewed a slice of apple and held up a shard, letting it catch the light. "The glass matches similar samples from early Greek industry. And the silicates it's composed of—"

"Also betray its country of origin?" Dawkins said.

"Yes. Is Tom back yet?"

"Regrettably, I have not heard a peep from Mr. Gentry."

"Damn." Jim tossed the shard down. He moved the glass aside and pulled the harness towards himself. Like the mask, it was delicately engraved at points. It was no mass-produced chunk of metal, but something unique. The work of an artisan.

He snagged a book. Leonardo Da Vinci had, quite possibly, been the inventor to end all inventors. A mind like his only came along once in a millennium.

And the instruments before Jim had been products of that mind. The cuirass with its breathing tubes, the mask, the gas-globes, all were described in intricate detail in certain of Da Vinci's surviving notes. True, there was evidence of modification, but it was slight. And the age of the items in question, pointed towards these being, if not the originals, then close enough.

Jim sat back. He chose another book at random and flipped through it until a familiar image caught his eye. He tapped the pages in front of him with a single finger. "It's all Greek to me," he said. "Ha."

"Sir?" Dawkins said. Jim turned.

"Greek. The face on that card, the face of that mask, is Greek. A Greek demon, to be precise. Deimos." Jim's eyes narrowed. "Literally, dread. Or terror."

He picked up the sword and traced the hideous face engraved at the base of the blade.

"The mark of terror," Jim said, softly.

14.

An hour later, Jim sealed the sword and the harness away in his lab safe to await further study. The mask he placed into a specially constructed briefcase. As he clicked the locks in place, he heard Tom Gentry's voice. "Jimmy!"

Jim turned. "Tom. Just in time. Did you find anything?"

"Yeah. Found him. Buried up in Green-Wood. Family mausoleum, which figures." Tom crossed his arms. "What the hell happened with Healy? I swung by on my way back, saw ambulances, press, the whole shebang."

"We were paid a visit." Jim gestured to his wounded shoulder. "And not the good kind."

Tom whistled. "I'll say. Same guy?"

"Same guy." Jim pulled on a shirt Dawkins had left folded for him on the edge of the work bench, and then gingerly slid his shoulder holster on, wincing. "Luckily, the blow to my pride was the only serious injury. That's twice now our new friend has gotten the best of me."

"Let's not give him a third chance. What's the plan?"

"Evidence, Tom. As always."

"Green-Wood?" Tom said, frowning.

"Green-Wood." Jim checked his pistol. "As soon as possible. Then…" He looked at the briefcase. "Then, onto new avenues of research."

"Which means?"

"A visit to Empire State University, and a certain visiting professor," Jim said, tapping the side of his nose. "A friend of mine. Charles St. Cyprian, late of Old College, Oxford."

"Ah man. St. Cyprian? Guy's a—"

"Brilliant lecturer and an authority on the occult. Which this," he patted the briefcase, "certainly is."

Briefcase in hand, Jim led Tom out of the lab and towards the elevator. Dawkins handed him a replacement for his shredded coat, and a large satchel.

"The device, sir. Also, Ms. Kilkenny called again, sir. I told her that you were otherwise engaged, but, well…."

"But?" Jim said.

Dawkins' mouth flattened into a thin line. "I was treated to a burst of rather unladylike language."

"Ha!" Tom said. He slapped Dawkins on the shoulder. The butler glared at him, but only for a moment until his blank façade reasserted itself.

"Dawkins, your grace under fire never fails to astound me," Jim said. Dawkins nodded stiffly.

"Too, sir, Mr. Docker called again," he said.

"Again? Persistent. I'm not quite ready to see him yet, I don't think," Jim said. "Especially if he's involved in this. Not until I have more evidence."

"Building the cage before baiting the tiger, sir?" Dawkins said. Jim nodded.

"Perhaps. Though Docker has never been particularly ferocious."

Tom trailed after Jim as they got on the elevator and descended once more to the parking garage.

"So, why the cemetery if you already know what you need to know?" Tom said, as they left the elevator.

"I have nothing but supposition connecting the deaths of Smithback and Pender to Tupker," Jim said. "The gentleman at the morgue wasn't what I'd call very forthcoming. Until I'm certain, I won't be able to proceed."

"And if they're connected?"

"Then I'll know where to go from there," Jim said. "But until then…"

"You'll just ignore me?"

Jim and Tom turned, Tom's hand flashing towards the pistol holstered beneath his arm. Catherine Kilkenny lifted her hands.

"Don't shoot, Paddy. I ain't the Baron's man. Or woman, as the case may be," she said, grinning.

"How did you get down here, Cat?" Jim said. "This is a private garage!"

"Reporter," Kilkenny said, pointing at herself.

Jim sighed. "Cat, we were just on our way to run an important errand."

"Out to investigate something? Something having to do with the deaths of three prominent fatcats in suspicious circumstances?" Kilkenny sidled towards Jim. "Or was it something having to do with what went down at police headquarters this morning, hmmm?"

Jim frowned. "You couldn't wait for me to return your phone call?"

"Jimmy, when have I ever?" Kilkenny shook her head. "Nope. You were leaving me out. I could sense it. I bet that works on your other lady friends, hey?"

Tom snorted. His burgeoning laugh turned into a cough as Jim glared at him.

Kilkenny continued on, oblivious. "But me, I'm a different bag of cats," she said, sniffing. "Now, where are we going?"

"We," Jim gestured to Tom and himself. "Are going to Green-Wood Cemetery. You," he pointed at Kilkenny, "re going home."

"I disagree," Kilkenny said. "I feel like visiting the cemetery."

"Must you?"

"I must, I must," Kilkenny said, smiling prettily.

"Winsome glances aside, you could get in trouble for this," Jim said, switching tacks. "What we'll be doing isn't exactly legal."

"Too impatient to wait for permission?"

"Too aware of the imposed time limit, more like," Jim said. "Three men have already died. How many more might follow?"

"Offhand? Three." Kilkenny held up the appropriate number of fingers. Jim blinked.

"Three?"

"Three. Smithback's other three partners in whatever ugly little scheme he was cooking up."

"Hnh." Jim frowned. "And you're certain you know who they are?"

"Not exactly. More like I suspect," Kilkenny said. "I've been dogging this story for weeks, Jimmy, in my off-hours from the gossip page, even before Brushkin gave me the story. It's big."

"Big?"

"Ludlow Massacre big."

Jim grunted. "Fine."

"Does that mean I can come?"

"If you promise not to—" Jim paused, then threw a hand up in the air. "Oh why even bother?"

"Good question. Which car we taking?" Tom said.

Jim gestured. "The Rolls. It will provoke fewer questions."

"And it's armored, just in case, right?" Tom said.

"Just in case," Jim said.

"Greenwood Heights, here we come," Tom said, as he put the car in gear. The Green-Wood Cemetery resided in Brooklyn, though the main entrance was on Fifth Avenue. As Tom maneuvered the Rolls through the city streets, Kilkenny laid out what she knew.

"Jerry Smithback was seen in the company of five other men over the course of the past three months," she began. "Alan Tupker and Silas Pender you know about." She ticked off two fingers. "But there was also Pongo Docker, Samuel Harpootlian, and Oscar Gaines."

"Hmm. Docker I know," Jim said. "He's a wildcatter of the first order." He didn't mention Docker's constant calls or his prior relationship. No reason for Cat to know that yet. "Harpootlian?"

"He's a lawyer. Ran for DA a few years ago, been quiet since. He specializes in business law. Gaines is old money. Older than Pender's by a Dutch year. Got a house in the Silk Stocking district, but not much else."

"Not a fan of Society parties, then?" Jim said. Kilkenny smirked.

"You're one to talk. But yeah, basically, he's a hermit. Sources say he's the money man, helping secure capital for whatever the other five were planning. A real sinister six, like I said."

Jim sat back, eyes closed in thought. "Intentions aside, what could this group have to do with the gentleman who accosted me?" He rubbed his shoulder and winced.

"Depends on the gentleman, I suppose," Kilkenny said. She fiddled with the briefcase. "Speaking of which, what's in here?"

"An item of evidence. Please don't touch it," Jim said, pulling the briefcase away from her. Kilkenny stuck her tongue out. Jim studiously ignored the gesture and said, "What else have you found out?"

"Not much more than what I said. Why do you think I came to you?"

"You want me to let you tag along on the investigation," Jim said. "You know what Healy said."

Kilkenny nodded. "We've had this conversation before. Besides which, Healy doesn't want me reporting on the murder. Which I'm not. I'm reporting on the very real chance that there's a new Standard Oil monopoly in the works."

"Hardly that," Jim said. "The group, if it is a group, has—had—differing spheres of influence."

"But those spheres overlap," Kilkenny said.

"True, but do they overlap in the right ways?" Jim shook his head. It could simply be a coincidence. Three men killed by the same group for three different reasons. But, in his experience, coincidence rarely entered into cases such as this. "Maybe there is something in it after all."

"Ha!"

"But first, we establish evidence of a connection." Jim held up a finger. "Hence our trip."

"Which is over," Tom said. The Rolls came to a stop, engine clicking. "We're here."

"Excellent." Jim got out, Kilkenny scooting after him. He hefted the satchel Dawkins had given him. "Tom, can you wait with the car?"

"Definitely. This time it's all yours, Jimmy." Tom waved a hand. "I'll watch the car."

Jim nodded. "And the vault?"

"Old Circle," Tom said. "That's all I got."

"Easy enough." Jim glanced at Kilkenny. "Would you like to come watch me make forensic history?"

"No. But I do want to snoop," Kilkenny said. She fell into step with him as they headed for the looming gothic revival-style entryway into the cemetery.

They moved through the necropolis in silence, passing a few mourners. By and large, though, they appeared to have the graveyard to themselves. They moved up the Greenwood Street side in companionable silence.

It was rare that Jim found a woman like Kilkenny. He had little trouble attracting women in any case, but most of them were of the same type: society mayflies, with little on their mind beyond the next party or the next allowance.

But Catherine Kilkenny was different. A smart woman in a day and age when smart women could still be penalized. The ratification of the Nineteenth Amendment was over a decade old, but in some ways women still weren't considered fully paid-up members of society.

Then, as smart as she was, Cat could also be infinitely annoying in a variety of subtle ways. Thinking of that made him think of the young woman from the previous night. Delores. He smiled slightly. Delores Colquitt. Interesting young woman.

"So, what did happen? You're favoring your shoulder, and the word on the street says the cops look like they tried to wrestle Satan into a holding cell." Kilkenny didn't look at him, but her hand found his, interrupting his train of thought. Jim was quiet for a minute, wondering whether the gesture was genuine or a play for more information.

Cat was, in many ways, his match. His equal. Both of them were hungry for information, intent on discovering the truth, regardless of consequences or repercussions.

"I found something last night."

"That mask? Is that what's in the briefcase?"

"Yes, but I found something else," Jim said. "Something which might have been used to murder Tupker and Pender, as well as Smithback." He looked at her. "Someone came for it."

"The man you chased after last night," she said, face intent. Jim nodded.

"Possibly. Likely, in fact."

"And he got away." It wasn't a question. Jim didn't bother to answer. Kilkenny nodded as if he had.

"No wonder you don't want to talk about it." She patted his arm. "I—"

Jim's sixth sense hummed painfully at that moment. A bristle of warning that caused him to spin, carrying Cat to the ground as the sound of rifle-shot cracked the cemetery's silence!

15.

"Jimmy, what the hell?" Cat squawked as Jim crushed her to the ground.

"Stay down!" he said. He raised his head, scanning the area. They were too exposed. He needed to get them into cover, but without knowing where the shot had come from.

Another shot sounded. The bullet plucked the gravel nearby. Jim scooped up Cat and sprang to his feet, bounding for the cover of the nearest row of tombs.

Not stopping, Jim hit the closest mausoleum door with his good shoulder, snapping it open with a crash. He and Cat rolled across the floor, only coming to a stop when Jim's back connected with the far wall.

Jim was on his feet an instant later, his pistol in hand. He pressed himself against the edge of the door and peered around the corner. No further shots came.

"Strange," Jim said.

"What? You think?" Cat said, scrambling to her feet. "No, I get shot at all the time!"

"I'm sure you do," Jim said, without looking at her. Cat made a face.

"Why is it strange?" she said, scootching herself up against the wall.

"He's using a rifle."

"And? He used a pistol at the Roxy!"

"He used a pistol very well at the Roxy," Jim said. "And a sword, again, very well, at police headquarters."

"Did he?" Cat said. Jim looked at her, frowning.

"Yes, but you didn't hear it from me."

"Off the record, mum's the word, I swear," she said, raising a hand. "So why is this strange?"

"Because whoever is out there is a very bad shot," Jim said. He took another look, a bit longer this time. Nothing caught his eye.

"Maybe you're just good at getting out of the way," she said, wiping at the dirt on her dress. Jim shook his head.

"No one can outrun a bullet."

"I hear that there's a guy in the Midwest that can."

"No one but him," Jim corrected himself. "Certainly not me." He looked around. "No. Whoever is out there had plenty of time to get it right."

"Which means?"

"That he's not the same man who tried to kill me before." Jim holstered his pistol. He dropped the satchel he'd been carrying to the floor and opened it. "Luckily, however, he's done us a favor."

"Has he?"

"Yes. We're in the Tupker family vault," Jim said, retrieving a series of thin metal tubes from the bag. On the end of one a wicked point gleamed. Jim screwed one tube into the other with a quick motion, and hefted the contraption.

"What the heck is that?" Cat asked.

Jim began to scan the markers on the drawers set into the mausoleum wall. "A subtle way of checking the condition of a body without having to bother with exhumation. Came up with it myself. I've been dying for a reason to use it." Jim paused. "Probably not the best turn of phrase, considering the circumstances."

"No. Probably not." Cat rose to her feet. "Think he's gone?"

"Almost certainly. Unless he's the patient type." Jim found the drawer he was looking for and raised the tube. "Here we go."

"Alan Tupker?"

"Of course," Jim said, placing the sharp end of the device to the stone. It took him only a few seconds to calculate the required angle and pressure required to achieve his goal. The tube was diamond-tipped, and had a pneumatic pumping action. "Quiet please. I need to concentrate."

With a grunt, Jim pushed the tube down on the flat face of the drawer, penetrating the stone with a loud chunk! Holding the tube in place, he rotated the end slightly, eliciting a hiss, as if from an over-size syringe. Then he pulled it free, leaving only a smooth hole to mark the action.

"Wonderful. It worked," Jim said, carefully breaking down the contraption. Twisting off the end, he displayed a glass tube, filled with a dull-colored ichor.

"What the hell is that stuff?"

"You don't really want to know," Jim said, holding it up to the few dregs of light that entered through the open doorway. "But, if I'm right, it will prove that Tupker's death was a result of the same hallucinogen as the other two deaths."

"Wasn't Tupker hit by a train?" Cat asked. Jim nodded. "Then what were you sticking that tube in?"

"Again, you really don't want to know." Jim packed everything away. "I need to analyze this sample, however, to be sure of my hypothesis."

"Really?"

"No." Jim slung the satchel over his shoulder. "As I said before, I'm reasonably certain this all ties together. This is simply to satisfy Healy and his superiors." He held out a hand. "Shall we?"

"You sure?"

"Not in the least." Jim smiled. "Which is why I'll go first."

"And if you die?"

"Run." Jim pulled his pistol. "Run very quickly."

"That's terrible advice. I'm wearing heels."

Jim laughed and stepped out of the mausoleum, holding his pistol down by his leg. He waited for one heartbeat, two, three. No shot was forthcoming. As he'd suspected. He turned, waving Cat back into cover. "Stay here for a minute."

Dropping the satchel, Jim moved towards the point where the first shot had nearly caught them. The glint of a bullet caught his eye. The second shot. Split-second calculations danced in Jim's head.

He calculated the angle of the shot and followed it, moving swiftly through the tombs and headstones, alert for any sound. They'd only been in the mausoleum for ten minutes at most.

Most professional killers of his acquaintance would have pulled stakes and vanished immediately. But this man wasn't a professional. Which meant he might be waiting. The thought left a bad taste in his mouth.

Jim backtracked the shot, sniffing as the delicate stink of powder reached his nose. Bounding up onto a headstone, he looked down. Cigarette butts, distressed earth. Shoe prints. Jim hopped down and traced the tracks. Good shoes. Spent brass casings lay discarded.

Jim plucked one up. Standard ammunition for an M1903 Springfield. Jim had carried one in the Great War and he recognized it easily.

Who had known he was coming here? Other than Dawkins, or Tom, who? He paced, retracing his route. He'd told no one. Healy might have suspected. He spotted Cat peering out of the doorway.

Of course.

"Cat," he said, heading back. "Did you just happen to intercept us, or were you planning on coming here anyway?"

She hesitated visibly. Jim knew that look. She was trying to guess how much he knew, and how much he suspected.

"Why were you trying to get a hold of me earlier?" Jim said, snatching up his satchel. "There had to be a reason."

"Maybe I just wanted to check up on you," she said, sounding hurt. It didn't last. "I wanted to snoop."

"But before that?"

"I paid a visit to Harpootlian," she said. "Another one."

"The lawyer?" Jim said. "Another visit?"

"No, the baker. Yes, the lawyer," she said, crossing her arms. "He wasn't happy to see me. Either time."

"I suspect not." Jim rubbed the bridge of his nose. "The first time?"

"A day or so before I went after Smithback at the Cloud Club." Jim looked at her, eyebrows raised.

"I was following an old theory," she said defensively.

"Which was?"

She mumbled something. Jim frowned. "What?"

"I thought Tupker might have been faking his death." She waved away his astounded look. "What? Like you never had that happen."

"Never when the person in question was hit by a train, no," Jim said. "Were you serious?"

"Not really. I wanted to rile Harpootlian. He's the weak link. I've got photos of him going in and out of several notorious Bronx speakeasies. The photos didn't rile him so, y'know." She shrugged. "I was hoping he'd get mad enough to spill something."

"And the second time?"

"Come on! Three of his partners are dead!" Cat almost wailed, gesturing violently.

"You told him you were coming here?" Jim demanded. Cat shrugged.

"Maybe. I was hoping he'd get nervous and spill."

"And instead, he sent someone to kill you." Jim shook his head. Cat planted her hands on her hips.

"We don't know that!"

Jim snorted. "Did Harpootlian say anything of interest?"

"No." Cat frowned. "Not a damn thing. Which made me even more suspicious."

"I can see how it would. Have you approached either of the others?"

"Nope. That's why I came to see you, actually," she said. "You know Docker, wasn't that what you said?"

"Yes. Not well, but well enough." Jim turned and headed for where they'd left Tom and the car. "I suppose you want me to introduce you?"

"Well, you're going to talk to him anyway, right?"

"Eventually," Jim said. He slid his pistol back into its holster. "First, however, I need more information on what I'm facing."

"Meaning?"

"The University," Jim said. Cat blew out a breath.

"Well. That doesn't sound interesting."

"Hardly the sentiments one expects of a reporter," Jim said.

"I've got focus."

"Obviously." Jim stopped her. Cat looked at him, but said nothing. Jim cocked his head, listening. He looked back at Cat. "I want you to stay at the Penthouse tonight."

"What? No, I got—" Cat began.

"You've annoyed someone. They tried and failed to kill you."

"We don't know that they were here for me!"

"They tried and failed." Jim continued on, relentless. "You go nowhere without me, or Tom, or failing that, Dawkins."

Cat turned away. "Fine. But I want to see Docker!" She turned back, wagging a finger under Jim's nose. "And—AND—I want a chance to snoop around Smithback's place. His office, I mean."

Jim hesitated. His thoughts had been moving in a similar direction. And Catherine, despite her impatience, might possibly see something he'd missed.

The Rolls came into sight, Tom sitting on the hood, smoking a cigarette. Jim waved. Then, "We'll go there this evening. After hours."

"Breaking and entering?"

"Entering, anyway." Jim looked at her. "You have an objection?"

"I didn't object to the grave-robbing," she said. She smiled. "You take me to the nicest places, Jimmy."

16.

Empire State University occupied a site near Washington Square Park. As Universities went, it had a storied history, and great events were promised for the future.

Jim wasn't a product of its hallowed halls, instead spending his formative years at Harvard and Miskatonic, as well as a brief stint at Old College, Oxford.

It was at the latter that he'd first come into contact with Charles St. Cyprian. Being of the same age, they'd shared a class or two prior to the War, and the events surrounding their first meeting had been less than relaxing, involving as they did a stolen mummy. Jim had come away with a profound respect for the man, however.

St. Cyprian, as a visiting notable, had a tiny office overlooking the campus quadrangle. Jim found him there, staring out the window, chin resting on his interlaced fingers.

St. Cyprian's hair was prematurely silver save for the temples, which were a deep black. His hair was brushed back from a profoundly Mediterranean sort of face. He turned as Jim knocked on the door frame.

"Ah! Jim," he said, unfolding from his seat and extending a thin hand. As always, Jim couldn't help but examine the strange iron rings that adorned St. Cyprian's hand.

"Charles. You're looking well."

"For a man of my habits, you mean?" St. Cyprian smiled. "Flattery, thy name is Anthony."

"Hardly." Jim placed the briefcase on the desk, gently shoving aside a set of African fetish-statues. St. Cyprian snatched them out of the way and placed them with a number of others. Jim found himself momentarily mesmerized by a hideous South Seas idol that was all tentacles and rounded paunch.

"How is your assistant? Ms. Gallowglass?" Jim said innocently. "Ebe, I think her name was? A shame she couldn't accompany you."

"Ha!" St. Cyprian chuckled. "I'll tell her you said that. You made quite the impression on her the last time you were in London. So, what gift have you brought me this time old bean? You were quite evasive on the telephone," he said, rubbing his hands together. Jim smiled.

"More because I didn't quite know how to describe it than anything else." Jim opened the briefcase, revealing the half-mask in its Bakelite seal. He pulled it free and handed it to St. Cyprian, who examined it almost reverentially.

"Astounding."

"Yes?" Jim said.

"Greek, I believe." St. Cyprian looked up. "Pity the image is bifurcated, as it is."

"Would this help?" Jim gestured to the card he'd brought. St. Cyprian examined it in turn, his eyes lighting up.

"This looks like—"

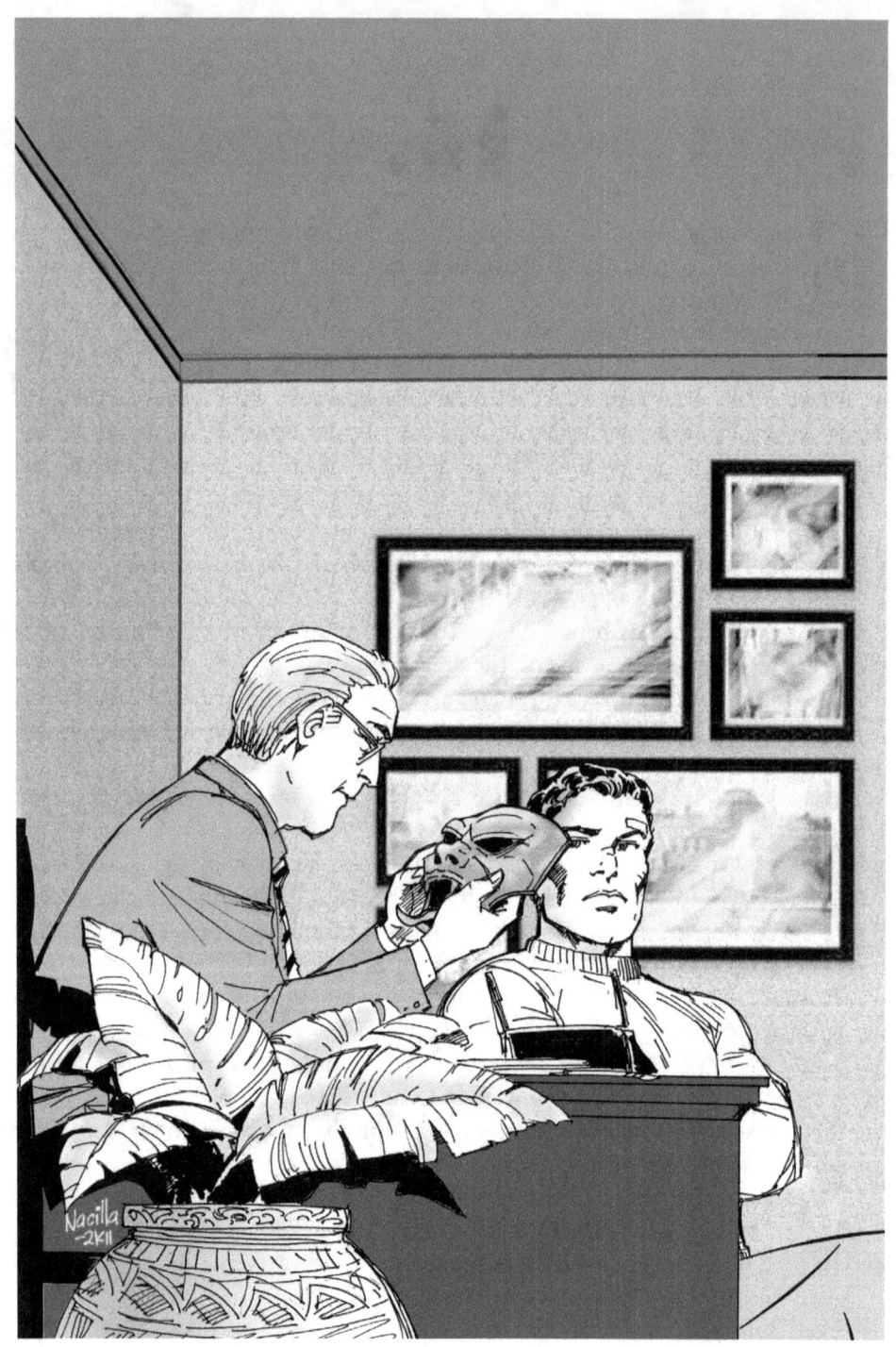

"Astounding," St. Cyprian said, examining it almost
reverentially.

"Deimos. God of dread," Jim said.

"Demi-god, actually. A minor avatar of Ares. His son, in some versions of the myth." St. Cyprian looked back at the mask. "Oxygen tubes?"

"Yes."

"Hmm." The man turned and pulled a series of thin monographs off the overstuffed bookshelf that occupied one wall of his office. "What have you gotten into, Jim?"

"The usual." Jim absently rubbed his wounded shoulder. It was slightly sore from the day's exertions, but otherwise he was suffering no ill-effects. "I took the mask off a gentleman who was doing his level best to do me in."

"Anything else?"

"A spatha," Jim said, gesturing. "About so long. Old. Well-used."

"You recognize the design of the mask, I take it?" St. Cyprian said, putting a book of Leonardo da Vinci's drawings on the desk and flipping it open. "The so-called Milanese Concepts. Military technology for his patron at the time."

"Including primitive chemical weapons," Jim said. St. Cyprian nodded.

"The Milanese Concepts are regarded in many circles as something of an urban myth. The plans were supposedly stolen right out from under Da Vinci's nose before he had a chance to do much more than build a prototype." St. Cyprian sat and gestured for Jim to do the same. "If what you've brought me is any indication, we may have found the thieves."

"Who are they?"

"Myths and half-truths." St. Cyprian waved a hand. "Two cults, that of Deimos and that of Phobos, were said to have been active in Greece from its earliest period until the fall of Constantinople in 1453. They vied with each other for control of, well, society, I suppose." He leaned forward. "Politics, religion, economics, the cults had members in every stratum of Greek society. Interestingly, they were divided along gender lines. The followers of Deimos were men, and Phobos, women."

"They sound less like cults than secret societies," Jim said. "Almost like the Bavarian Illuminati."

"Huh. To a degree, yes," the older man said. "Indeed, the foundations of that vile conference may in fact reside in one or the other of those groups. The end goal was the same. Control of society via calculated oppression. Though, in different doses. One group believed in swift, sudden actions, while the other practiced a more subtle, omnipresent pressure. All a matter of dogma, really." He shuddered slightly. "Ritual sacrifices, particularly of children, were a favorite of theirs."

"Fear and terror," Jim said. "The sudden and the subtle." He closed his eyes, thinking. "What happened?"

"The Ottomans," St. Cyprian said. "The cults were, and this is all hearsay, mind you, among the revolutionary groups that challenged Ottoman control of Greece. Like those other groups, they were supposedly annihilated."

"Obviously not."

"Isn't it more likely that someone else has co-opted the tools and methods of a long defunct group?"

"But for what purpose?" Jim rubbed his jaw. "No. This isn't some group of penny-ante gangsters who've gotten hold of some ancient technology. If they were modern criminals, they'd use modern means. No, this device, the sword, it all smacks of ritual." They sat silently for a moment, both men chewing over the problem. Then, St. Cyprian knocked on the desk with his knuckles.

"Jim, these groups were dangerous. Dangerous enough that the Janissaries were sent in to deal with them. Musket, sword and fire. If one of them is still active, here of all places, then you must step lightly." He tapped a finger against the Bakelite disk. "It was said that Constantine feared them. And that the Emperors of Byzantium considered their council. They influenced the evolution of the Mediterranean for centuries, if not Europe itself...."

"They've likely murdered three men. Tried to murder me. Historical precedent or not, I intend to see them in custody." Jim stood. "What else can you tell me, Charles?"

"Not much. I only know this much because of incidental studies I made while researching my last book." St. Cyprian stared at the mask. "They weren't afraid of collateral damage, Jim, but their goals tended to be small. If these are the same men, the same organization, then they're after something concrete." He looked at Jim. "You may need help."

"No. This is my responsibility," Jim said, swiping the air with the edge of his hand. "Besides, they've gotten on my nerves now."

St. Cyprian smiled. "Ha. Yes, I can see that. Be careful. I hate losing friends."

"I will. Thank you, Charles," Jim said, gathering his things. He shook St. Cyprian's hand and left the office, his mind shuffling facts like index cards. He headed for the stairs that led to the quad.

It made little sense on the face of it. Something was missing, some piece of information that would make the whole thing fit, like a child's puzzle.

So distracted was he, that he failed to notice the tingling of his senses until the gun was pressed to the small of his back and a voice said, "Mr. Anthony."

Jim stopped. "Mr. Corrigan."

"That is not my name."

"I rather guessed that. Care to share the real deal?"

"Call me...Metus."

Jim chuckled. "Cute. Latin for 'terror'. How creative. What do you want then, Metus?"

"Who were you talking to?"

"An expert in antiquities," Jim said quickly. "I told him nothing."

"Good. Give me the briefcase. And everything else you've stolen from us." The words were delivered flatly, with neither inflection nor accent. "They do not belong to you."

"You missed me at the cemetery," Jim said. "From our previous encounters, I assumed you'd be a better shot."

"Cemetery?" Metus paused. "What—"

"Never mind." Jim jerked his elbows back, catching Metus in the gut. The man staggered and Jim spun on his heel, cracking the briefcase across Metus' gunhand. The pistol went flying.

Metus stepped back, face contorting in something that might have been rage. He was much as Jim remembered him: dark, but bland looking. Certainly not ethnic in any regard. Jim hefted the case. "You want it? Come and get it."

Metus didn't answer. Instead, he gestured. Jim turned as a blow caught him on the shoulder. Two men closed on him silently. He knew they must have come up the stairs as he'd confronted Metus. His opponent had planned ahead.

"Yes. We know your capabilities, Mr. Anthony," Metus said, stooping to pick up his pistol. "We were surprised, at first, when you chose to involve yourself, but we adapt quickly. It is how we have survived."

Jim barely heard him, busy as he was fending off the snake-swift blows coming at him from two sides. The men weren't rent-a-thugs or bowery boys, despite the way they were dressed. They had been trained, and well. Some form of martial art that Jim didn't recognize. If he could find the pattern, he could unravel it easily enough.

A fist connected with his kidney, and Jim slid back, coughing. Then again, easy was just a word. Another blow landed on the side of his head. He blocked a third, catching it on his forearm, wincing as his wound flared in pain. As the man's arm slid past, Jim caught him in the jaw with an uppercut.

He put all of his strength into the blow, picking his opponent up off of his feet and knocking him backwards. As the man fell, his companion closed on Jim, wrapping his arms around him and wrenching him into the air. Jim gasped as he was slammed back into the wall hard enough to crack the plaster.

With a shake of his shoulders, Jim broke the hold and swept his hands up bringing them together on the man's ears. His opponent yelped and staggered, allowing Jim to grab him by his coat and ram his head into the wall with enough force to knock several pictures to the floor.

Jim let the unconscious body fall, and turned. Blood dripped down his arm in a thin stream and he clutched his shoulder.

Metus, surprisingly, had not taken the opportunity to leave. He held the briefcase against his leg and aimed the pistol at Jim.

"Mr. Anthony, you are a wonder to behold."

"Thanks," Jim grunted. "I suppose you intend to kill me?"

"Of course. We can't have a man of your talents interfering. But first, I require access to wherever you're keeping my sword." Metus gestured with the pistol. "And whatever other samples you may have taken."

"If you don't want people finding out who you are, you shouldn't be so damn sloppy," Jim said, inching forward. In that moment what he'd said to Cat before came back to haunt him. He wasn't fast enough to dodge a bullet. But he might be fast enough to reach Metus before the bullet could be fired.

"Perhaps." Metus raised the pistol. "And perhaps it might be more expedient to simply deal with you right here." Jim tensed to move, but even as he did so, he knew he wasn't going to be fast enough.

The pistol barked.

17.

Jim felt a momentary surprise as no bullet burst his heart. Instead, Metus gave a cry and spun. He stumbled against the wall, still clutching the briefcase.

Charles St. Cyprian advanced down the corridor, a British service revolver held extended before him. "Hello, Jim. Looks like you're having a spot of bother."

"Charles." Jim felt a sense of relief. "Careful, he's a tricky one."

"Do you ever deal with anything but?" St. Cyprian said, raising an eyebrow. He looked at Metus. "And you sir, drop the case."

"No." Metus pushed away from the wall. Despite all odds, he still held his pistol. "No."

"I insist."

"Charles!" Jim started towards Metus. A hand seized his ankle. He looked down as one of the men he'd thought unconscious tried to pull him off of his feet. Jim kicked him in the head, but the momentary distraction was enough for Metus to dodge past and head for the stairs, firing wildly, forcing Jim to tackle St. Cyprian to the floor. After a moment, Jim stood and helped his friend to his feet.

"He seemed in a hurry to get out of here," St. Cyprian said, brushing a speck off of his sleeve and eyeing a bullet hole in the wall. Jim crouched next to one of the men he'd downed.

"Not as much as he seemed. Those shots weren't as wild as they looked," he said, rolling the man over to display the bullet wound in the crown of his head. St. Cyprian hissed.

"Shot them both?"

"Unfortunately. Not as neat as a cyanide capsule, but just as effective." Jim stood. "And he got the mask back. They're damned determined to cover their tracks."

"They would be." St. Cyprian shook his head. "A secret society is only as effective as its veil of mystery."

"I'd say the veil has been stripped away," Jim said. "He was surprised."

"What?"

"When I mentioned the cemetery."

"What happened at the cemetery?" St. Cyprian said, looking bemused. Jim laughed.

"I was shot at."

"How many people are trying to kill you, Jim?" St. Cyprian said. "This time, I mean."

Jim laughed again. He went to the wall and traced the bullet holes, then looked at the floor. "No blood. Either he doesn't bleed, or...."

"My shot didn't penetrate. More armor?" St. Cyprian said. Jim frowned.

80

"Possibly."

"Divine intervention, then?"

"More your line than mine, don't you think?" Jim said. "Maybe you missed."

"Hardly."

Jim smiled. A quick call to the police summoned a meat-wagon for the bodies, and Healy to the scene. He and Jim traded glances as the detective stomped past towards St. Cyprian's office, but didn't speak. Healy was smart enough to recognize when Jim had the bit between his teeth and had no interest in interrupting him.

For his part, Jim had no inclination of hovering while Healy questioned St. Cyprian, amusing as it would be. He made his goodbyes and then his escape.

Jim left the building, feeling lighter than he should have. He'd survived death for the fourth time in half the number of days. Even if he'd lost half his evidence in the process, he felt he had a firmer grip on what was going on now. His instincts, which had become somewhat sluggish since the affair with Soames, were now firing energetically.

Hands in his pockets, he walked across the quadrangle, his mind working on multiple possibilities. One, whatever was going on was bigger than he'd first thought. Two, it was smaller. If it was the former then he was dealing with a conspiracy. If it was the latter, he was dealing with two that just happened to intersect. The methodology of each was unimportant.

Of course, there was always the third possibility, that nothing he'd seen so far was in any way the truth. That he was a blind man gripping an elephant's tail.

Jim stopped and looked up. The Washington Square Arch loomed overhead. He stared at it for a moment, admiring its curves. Architecture was a quiet passion of his. And the arch was a beautiful example of form and function.

It helped calm him. He stood and concentrated on expelling the excess adrenaline from his system. He needed to be calm. Collected. His eyes traced the arch as he thought, running over the dates and times, trying to piece together a linear scale of occurrence.

"Ah," he said, after a moment. "I've been stupid." He needed to get back to the Penthouse.

He'd sent Tom on, with Cat, after getting dropped off. The sun was an orange haze now. His belly gurgled, and Jim realized he hadn't eaten in some time. One more reason to get home as quickly as possible.

The walk back to the Penthouse was a brisk one. Jim moved down Fifth Avenue, whistling tunelessly. He picked out the car almost immediately, but only because he'd been looking for it. His hackles bristled and he fought the urge to glance over his shoulder. He couldn't be sure, of course, but there was little doubt.

Corrigan, or Metus, was obviously more competent than the run of the mill criminal. Capable of planning ahead. Was his flight from the University only a feint? A ruse to draw Jim out onto the street? Possibly. Only one way to find out.

Jim smiled and broke into a sprint. He dodged through pedestrians, bounding up onto the root of a street-light. The car, not black, Jim noticed, sped up, cutting in and out of traffic, pacing him like a shark in steel waters. It was definitely after him. He couldn't see through the windows, and he wondered if Metus was inside. At any moment, the windows might descend and the barrels of pistols or rifles might extend to sweep his position.

He waited, muscles tense. What had St. Cyprian said…they weren't afraid of collateral damage? Would that extend to attempting to gun him down in the middle of the street?

The car passed him and kept going, disappearing around a corner. Jim waited for one minute. Two. Then, satisfied, he hopped off of his perch and continued on, ignoring the pointed looks of several onlookers.

By the time he got to the Waldorf-Anthony, the car hadn't shown back up. He was oddly disappointed. Normally, in his experience, criminals ran. They didn't follow those hunting them. They tried to avoid him. To throw him off the scent.

Perhaps these men didn't think of themselves as criminals. Or, they weren't the men he was thinking of. He thought again of the cemetery as he passed through the lobby towards the elevator. In the Penthouse, Dawkins was waiting for him.

"Sir, Detective Healy called. He was quite incensed."

"So par for course then?" Jim said, stepping past Dawkins. "Cat?"

"Here." She was sitting on the couch facing the balcony, a glass of dark liquid in her hand. She shook it, causing the lonely cube of ice to rattle. "Jimmy. You know Prohibition is in effect, right?"

"Is it?" Jim said, going to pour himself a drink.

"I thought you were a man of the law," she said, taking a sip.

"I like to think of myself as a man of justice. The law can be bent or swayed. Justice cannot." Jim knocked back his drink, feeling it burn hot down into his belly. Cat laughed.

"That was almost poetic."

"Is Tom around?" Jim said.

"On the balcony, sir." Dawkins appeared at Jim's elbow and refilled his glass. Cat twisted in her seat, leaning across the back of the couch.

"We still stepping out tonight, Jimmy?"

"Of course." Jim headed for the balcony.

"When?"

"Soon."

"Soon when?"

"Soon," Jim said, stepping out onto the balcony and closing the door behind him. Tom leaned over the railing, smoke trailing from the cigarette clenched between his lips. He turned as Jim closed the door.

"We were followed. Just like you thought."

"Hnh." Jim looked out over the city and gently shook his glass. "Black car?"

"Nope."

"Dark green, maybe?"

"Bingo-bango," Tom said, tapping his nose.

Jim looked at his friend. "Could you identify the driver?"

Tom gave him a look. Jim held up his hand. "I was just asking. No matter. What do you think?"

"I think they were waiting on us to leave Green-Wood." Tom turned and leaned against the barrier, crossing his thick arms over his chest. "I didn't catch them at first because I was looking for those idiots in the black car."

"Who were also following us," Jim said, taking a drink.

Tom's eyes narrowed. "Something happen?"

"Our enemy has a name. Metus."

"Funny name," Tom said.

Jim nodded. "He accosted me at University. Wanted his property back," he said.

"And?"

"He got it."

"Jimmy—" Tom began.

Jim smiled and knocked back his drink. "Its okay, Tom. I'd learned all I could from what I had. St. Cyprian was very helpful."

"I'll bet." Tom grimaced. "Damned ju-ju man."

"Hardly that. Regardless, the visit was illuminating."

"Then you won't mind sharing, Jimmy," Cat said, standing in the doorway. Jim turned. She snapped her fingers. "C'mon. Gimme."

"It's a cult." Jim gestured and Tom pulled out his cigarette case. He offered one to Jim. Jim took it, and a book of matches. "A very old, and malignant, cult." Jim scraped a match to life and lit the cigarette between his lips. "They worship a god of fear."

"And that has what to do with the price of tea in China?" Cat said.

"Nothing. Other than the fact that we seem to have put ourselves at cross-purposes with this group, entirely by accident." Jim pointed the cigarette at her. "It's likely your fault, of course."

"My fault?" Cat said, eyes widening.

"When did you begin your investigation?"

"I—oh, hell." She looked away. "Hellfire." Jim nodded, his smile turning grim.

"Yes. It took me a while to put it together, but you said earlier that you'd been after this story for weeks. Think back, did you start investigating after Alan Tupker threw himself in front of a train…or before?"

Cat leaned back against the door, her fingers pressed to her temples. "God damn you, Jimmy," she breathed. Jim blinked, her sudden profanity startling him.

"Wait," he said quickly. "I didn't mean to imply you were involved."

"Oh can it, Anthony," she said, glaring at him. He nodded, offering her the cigarette. She took it and puffed on it until the tip turned cherry red.

"As I thought," Jim said. "You couldn't have known, Cat. And there's no proof. Merely a suspicion on my part."

"When was the last time your suspicions were wrong?"

"Nineteen twenty-seven," Jim said automatically. Cat puffed on the cigarette.

"So what does this mean?"

"It means that I now know that your investigation and mine are linked. Definitively." Jim hopped up on the railing, seating himself without apparent difficulty. "And tonight, we'll see how."

18.

Jerry Smithback had maintained offices in the Woolworth Building on Broadway. Constructed in 1913, it towered fifty-seven stories over the street. Since Smithback's death on the previous day, his offices had seen a parade of uniformed officers guarding the doors. At Jim's insistence, Healy had pulled the guard detail off for a period of a few hours, leaving the path clear to anyone willing to play cracksman.

Tom parked the Rolls and turned. "How we playing this?"

"Easy and breezy," Jim said, checking his pistol's ammunition clip. He smacked it home and holstered the weapon. "You keep a look-out. Healy said building security had been pulled off for the duration of the investigation, but we can't be sure."

"Better safe than sorry, yeah," Tom grunted, checking his own weapon. Jim looked at Cat.

"Do you have any idea what you're looking for?"

"Nope." Cat adjusted her hat. "But I've never let that stop me before."

The trio left the Rolls and headed for the front doors of the Woolworth Building, Jim pulling a thin case out of his coat as he led the way. Popping open the case, he revealed a number of thin tools.

"You weren't kidding about the breaking and entering, huh?" Cat said, looking up at the Gothic designs which coiled over the doorway. Jim bypassed the main revolving door and set himself in front of one of the smaller, traditional doors.

"I rarely kid," Jim said. He reached for the handle. "Huh."

"What?"

"It's unlocked," Jim said. Tom pushed past him.

"Right. I'll go first."

"Tom," Jim began. Tom shot him an exasperated look. Jim closed his mouth.

Tom opened the door and stepped into the lobby, pistol held low, head swiveling slowly. After a moment, he waved them inside. "Looks clear."

"Smithback's offices are on the thirtieth floor," Jim said, bounding towards the elevator. The lobby of the Woolworth Building was composed of a series of vaulting curves and glorious scrollwork. One of the most expensive buildings in American history, it dripped excess, with mosaics covering the ceiling and sculptures littering the corners.

As the elevator rattled upwards, Jim said, "We're not alone in here."

"In the elevator?" Tom said, looking up doubtfully.

"In the building," Jim clarified. "Someone beat us to it."

"Tell me you didn't plan for that," Cat said. Jim glanced at her.

"Not entirely. I thought it was a possibility, but I'd hoped we'd get here first."

"I drove as fast as I could," Tom said, mock-plaintively.

84

Jim snorted. "Metus, if it is him, is reacting much quicker than I'm used to. His actions smack of rote occurrence." He rubbed his shoulder, tracing the line of the bandage beneath his shirt. "He's following a plan."

"Seems like it's working so far," Tom said.

"Let's see what we can do to mess it up then, yes?" Jim watched the numbers over the door.

"And what if it's not this Metus?" Cat said. "What if it's whoever shot at me?"

"Then we can look forward to a pleasant evening's chat," Jim said. "And maybe a few answers."

The bell gave a ding and Tom opened the elevator doors. The corridor beyond was silent, but the lights were still on, as Healy had promised. Jim stepped out. His nostrils flared as he took in the smells of disinfectant and carpet shampoo. He paced down the length of the wall, the others just behind him.

"Smithback's office is just there," Jim said, gesturing. He eyed the hall beyond, not trusting the silence.

Tom patted his back. "Go with Kilkenny, Jimmy. I'll watch the hall and the elevator. Anyone comes up or down, you'll know it."

Jim nodded and stepped into the office. A large window looked out over Broadway. Jim wondered if Smithback had left it open a crack on the day of his death. Cat was already busy rifling through the unlocked drawers of a filing cabinet set in the corner.

"Desk is locked," she said, without turning around.

"Shall I open it then?"

"Only if you were serious about investigating," Cat said. Jim chuckled and bent to the task. Scratches on the lock caught his attention. He sank to his haunches and examined the drawers closely.

"These locks have been picked," Jim said softly. Cat closed the filing cabinet.

"And some of these files are empty." She turned. "You were right. Someone got here before us."

"But did they find what they were looking for?" Jim asked, dropping onto his back and reaching up under the desk. "My father had a desk like this. Only a hundred were made. Grupahs, they're called. My father bought this one for poor Jerry, I think, in better days."

"Handy fact," Cat said, sitting on the desk.

"Yes. It is." Jim pulled himself further under the desk. He felt along the edge, and grunted as he found what he was looking for. "As I hoped."

"What?"

"Secret panel." The desk trembled as Jim pried the panel free and slid back out from under it. He stood and proffered the panel, and its contents, to Cat. "See?"

"I see," Cat said, peering at it. "A notebook?"

"And a pistol." Jim hooked the trigger guard with a finger and lifted it. He sniffed the barrel. "Unfired." Cat picked up the notebook. Several items slid out.

"Passports?" she said. "Oh, Mr. Smithback. How unfortunate that you passed on before I could take you to task." She opened the notebook, flipping the pages.

Jim studied the passports. English, French, Turkish. That and the pistol made for compelling evidence as to Smithback's involvement in something unpleasant.

Cat made a disgusted sound and tossed the notebook aside. Jim put the passports down and picked up the notebook.

"It's gibberish," Cat said.

"It's in code." Jim skimmed a page. "A replacement cipher. Corresponding letters and numbers."

Cat leaned forward. "Can you break it?"

"Easily." Jim's mouth moved silently for a few minutes, then, "It's a record of his meetings for the past few months."

"Meetings with who?"

"Who do you think?" Jim closed the notebook with a snap. "Your instincts, it seems, were correct, Ms. Kilkenny."

"See? Reporter," she said, gesturing to herself. "So that's it then. We know that they're all linked now, which means there's definitely something hinky going on."

There was a thump from outside in the corridor. Jim's hand flashed up, silencing Cat.

"Tom?" Jim said.

Cat screamed. Jim spun as a shape filled the window behind him. Something grotesque leered through the glass, spear-like tongue jutting between curling tusks.

"Jimmy!" Cat said. Jim heard the hiss of the blade cutting the air even as he shoved Cat to the floor. Jim's palm caught the flat of the blade, deflecting the blow meant to cleave his skull into the edge of the desk. Hand numb, Jim stepped back, clawing for his pistol.

Two masked men crowded into the room, wearing the same strange, segmented armor Metus had worn earlier, over what looked like black silk shirts and trousers. Each wore a sword-belt and a rig holding several of the dangerous glass globes as well.

Jim knew at once that he and the others had interrupted a search in progress. He could only hope that Tom was still alive, and that he could ensure that Cat survived the next five minutes.

One of the men leapt up onto the desk and lunged, swinging his spatha down in a sharply angled arc. Jim leaned back, avoiding the blow, and fired his pistol. The mercy round glanced off the man's cuirass, causing him to hesitate. Jim closed with him, seizing his sword-arm by the wrist and cracking him across the skull with his Colt.

As his opponent slumped, stunned, Jim wrestled him into the path of his partner's sword blow. Steel glanced off of steel, scraping up a line of sparks. Jim's pistol cracked in triplicate, and the swordsman pitched backwards, skull creased. He crashed into a bookcase and slid down, covered in an avalanche of first editions.

Jim turned quickly towards the window, knowing that the third man was most likely already in position. He froze as a grim tableau confronted him.

Cat, her arms pinned and the tip of a spatha pressed to her throat, struggled ineffectually against her captor's grip. The face behind the mask wasn't Metus', but Jim recognized the look in his eyes regardless.

"Let her go and you can have the notebook," Jim said, carefully placing his pistol aside.

A patter of words issued from the gruesome facemask. It wasn't quite Greek. Something older, Jim thought. Thoughts for another time. He tensed.

"The notebook, and the chance to leave unmolested," Jim said, his voice calm. "Let her go."

The man stepped back, pulling Cat with him.

"Jimmy," she said, but the sword digging into her neck cut her off.

"Its okay Cat. It'll be okay." Jim stepped forward, hands held up. The man had his back pressed to the window. His eyes had gone flat.

Jim knew what was coming, and he knew his choices were limited. There was only one thing he could do, and it wasn't going to be pleasant.

The man's sword-arm tensed visibly, elbow rising. A trickle of blood slid down Cat's neck. Her eyes were wide and terrified.

The spatha slid forward, seeking flesh.

Jim leapt.

The window shattered as Jim, Cat and the man went backwards and out in a shower of glass!

19.

The city was a sea of lights rushing toward Jim as he plummeted downwards, his fingers ripping at his belt. Prepared for the shock of the fall, Jim already had the buckle undone even as they exited the cloud of glass.

Cat's pale face floated in front of him, mouth wide in a scream that was ripped away by the howling wind. Jim reached for her with his free hand. Iron fingers shot out and fastened around her wrist and, simultaneously, with one swift motion, he slashed out with the looped strap of his belt, hooking the horn of a scowling gargoyle and stopping their descent!

Jim grunted as a flash of pain cut through him, rippling up and down his shoulders and spine like fire. He fancied that he could hear his bones creaking under the weight. The muscles in his arm bulged and flexed as one-handed, he hauled himself up, tightening his grip on the belt's fibrous surface.

It was a composite thing, his belt, grown more than cut. Jim had taken samples of a rubbery fiber from a certain South Seas island and cultivated it at his Appalachian residence, the mountain environment being perfect for such things. Composed entirely of tightly woven strands of the fiber, the belt could just as easily choke a bear as it could hold up his trousers.

Cat's scream cut off abruptly and she and Jim swung back towards the building, then away. "Jimmy!" she said.

"Not now, Cat," Jim said hoarsely, trying by sheer force of will to keep his shoulders from becoming dislocated.

"But—" she said, fingers digging into his wrist.

"Hold on," he said, ignoring her. He looked up, trying to judge the best way to get them out of their predicament. He had designed his belt with similar situations in mind, and knew from past experience that it could comfortably hold close to three hundred pounds of weight for no less than five minutes.

So why was it beginning to fray?

"Jimmy!" Cat said. Something in her voice pulled Jim's attentions away from his calculations. He looked down, eyes widening slightly.

The man in black clung to Cat's leg like a remora, fingers around her ankle. He still held his spatha in his other hand and swung it wildly. He looked up at Jim, his eyes burning with the light of fanaticism.

"Ah," he said. That explained the fraying. "Cat, stay calm."

"Get him off of me!"

"Yes," Jim said, twisting around. "One moment."

"I don't have a moment!" Cat began to thrash. Jim grimaced as his wrist rotated with a sharp popping sound. With a growl, he swung his hips up and wrapped his legs around the gargoyle's neck.

"Stop thrashing or I'll let go!" he snapped.

"You wouldn't dare!"

"Try me!" Jim's coat seam popped with a sound like a gunshot as he hauled Cat and her passenger upwards one-handed. His temples thundered and he felt as if every vein in his upper body were about to explode from the strain. "Reach for the gargoyle!"

Cat stretched out a hand. The spatha hummed like a wasp and cut a gouge in the stone just beneath Jim's legs. He looked down.

The man in black had his feet stretched out towards a ledge. With a grunt, he swung himself, and by extension Cat, towards it, nearly pulling Jim from his perch. The stone made a grating sound. Jim's head whipped around and he saw the microscopic cracks beginning to form at the base of the gargoyle's horn.

"Damn it!" Adrenaline boosting his response, Jim yanked Cat up and slung her bodily upwards into an arc that carried her over the top of the gargoyle. The swordsman dropped lightly to the ledge as Cat landed on the gargoyle with a squawk.

Jim let go of the belt and dropped down onto the narrow ledge, facing the man in black. The lights of the city were reflected off the polished surface of the man's mask and he lunged smoothly, driving the spatha towards Jim's midsection.

Despite the awkwardness of his position, Jim's palms snapped around to catch the blade between them, the tip inches from his breastbone. "No. Not again," Jim said harshly. The man's eyes widened. Jim swung his arms out to the side and yanked the sword free of its owners' grip.

Spinning the sword around to grasp the handle, Jim assumed a fencer's stance. "Now. Talk."

The man said nothing, and instead looked up, towards Cat. Jim shuffled forward, the tip of the sword pressing lightly against his opponent's breastbone. "I said no," Jim said softly.

The man's harness jangled in the wind that curled around the Woolworth Building. His fingers twitched towards the glass spheres he still wore, but dropped. Jim nodded approvingly.

"Good choice. The wind is quite likely to simple blow it back in your face. There's no way down and no way up, save past me. You're trained. Athletic. But even you can't think to—"

The man jumped, fingers curled like claws, and slammed into Jim. The spatha went flying as Jim's arms windmilled and he and his attacker fell!

Jim grabbed his assailant's wrists as they fell from the ledge and slammed into the next one a few feet down. Cat's screams echoed in his ears. The ledge was only a few inches wide, not enough to accommodate two fully grown men. Jim felt a moment of vertigo as he found himself, or his top half at least, out over the abyss, wrestling with a madman.

More words spilled out of the man trying to strangle the life from him. Jim's knowledge of languages was first rate, but he only caught one word in three. But that one was death. He could fill in the blanks from there.

His back screamed as the ledge dug into it. Spots danced at the edge of his vision as the man's thumbs pressed down on his windpipe.

Every bruise and beating he'd taken over the past forty-eight hours seemed to be clamoring for his attentions. His wounded arm was going numb. Jim ignored it all. His fingers bent into the approximation of an eagle's talon and he drove it up into his opponent's belly. The armor bent under the impact. Flattening his fingers, Jim shoved, hard.

The man flew backwards, striking the stone, his head making a sound like snapping bone and he tumbled limply past Jim, spinning off into the ocean of lights like a leaf caught in an updraft.

Jim groaned as he sat up and pressed himself flat, away from the edge. Eyes closed, he fought to regain his equilibrium.

"Jimmy?" Cat called. Jim looked up. He could see her clinging to the gargoyle, leaning out slightly to look down. "You alive?"

"If I wasn't, were you expecting an answer?" Jim said.

"Funny. What the hell kind of stunt was that?"

"It worked, didn't it?"

"If you call us almost dying working, then yes!" Cat tightened her grip. "Get me off of here!"

"Coming, dear," Jim said, pushing himself back, then up. Carefully, his fingertips seeking out cracks or curling ornamentation, he scaled the distance between himself and Cat, doing his best to ignore the vertigo that still threatened at the edge of his consciousness.

He had climbed mountains for fun, but this was different. Somehow more threatening. He wouldn't be doing it again in a hurry.

Finally he made it to the gargoyle. Cat scooted back as Jim undid his belt. "The window is five feet above us. If you stretch, you can probably reach it."

"Stretch?" Cat's voice rose an octave.

Jim took a breath. "If you want to get inside anytime soon, yes." Using the belt as a grapple, he swung himself up onto the end of the gargoyle. "I'll do what I can to make it easier." Fingers working quickly, he pried off the rim of his buckle, revealing a sharpened edge.

"That thing Swiss army issue?" Cat said, smiling weakly. Jim said nothing. Cocking his arm, he swung the belt up, catching the sill of the broken window with the sharpened edge.

He handed the other end to Cat. "Climb. Quick."

"What? But, I—" She hesitated. Jim grabbed her hand and stuffed the end of the belt into it.

"Climb, Cat. This gargoyle isn't going to hold both of us. Not for long."

Face set, Cat began to climb, her legs kicking out. Jim noticed that she'd lost her shoes somewhere along the way. He held her steady for as long as he was able, then could only watch as she climbed the rest of the way.

Just as she was about to grab the ledge, a head popped out of the window. Cat screeched and the belt swung out as she leaned back in surprise.

Tom's hand shot out and grabbed hers. "Jesus, Mary and Joseph! What the heck are you doing out there?" he said.

"Oh, just hanging around," Cat said. Tom pulled her inside, then looked down at Jim.

"Jimmy, you need any help?"

"No. But if you could step back," Jim said. Tom's head vanished. Jim's legs bunched under him and then he was up, vaulting towards the window. Catching either side of the broken frame with his hands, he hauled himself in and slid down the wall to sit on the floor. Breathing heavily, he looked up at Tom and Cat. "Well. This has been productive."

"Says you. Getting chucked out a window doesn't rate high on my to-do list, Jimmy!" Cat snapped.

"Nor on mine, if we're being honest. But it keeps happening anyway," Jim said.

He stood, rubbing his aching shoulder. The unconscious forms of the other two men were gone. Jim looked at Tom, who had the grace to look sheepish.

"Quick suckers. One of 'em caught me on the side of the head before I knew what was going on."

Jim thumped his friend on the shoulder. "Think nothing of it, Tom. Luckily, they didn't bother to take the very thing they were looking for." He kicked at the square form of the notebook where it lay under the desk. Stooping, he scooped it up and brandished it. "And the very thing we need to get to the bottom of this whole sordid affair."

"You sound sure about that, Jimmy," Cat said. Jim looked at her.

"You know something? I believe I am."

20.

"The Hanseatic League," Jim said, sitting back on the couch. The notebook rested on his lap and he tilted his head up, processing what he had just read. Cat sat nearby, legs tucked up under her, a cup of coffee clutched in both hands. They had returned to the Penthouse after Jim had alerted the police to the altercation. He had also made a call to the only one of the three remaining members of Smithback's group he knew personally.

"The whosits?" Cat said.

"The Hanseatic League. An economic alliance of trading cities and prominent merchants that maintained a trade monopoly in the Baltic in—ah—"

"Thirteenth Century, sir," Dawkins said, handing Jim a cup of coffee and a pastrami sandwich from a certain all-night deli. "Or thereabouts."

"Thank you Dawkins," Jim said, gratefully taking a bite from the sandwich. "Smithback and the others were setting up their own version of the Hanse. Despite all of them having residences in the city, several of them maintained offices and interests elsewhere along the East Coast."

"So I was right," Cat said. She drained her cup and stood, wandering around the main room of the Penthouse. She gazed at the pictures that lined the walls and tapped one with a finger. "Is this your father?"

Jim looked up. "Yes. That was taken in Sumatra, I believe." He flipped through the notebook. "Or perhaps Mandalay."

"Traveling man?"

"You're the reporter, Cat, you tell me," Jim said. She turned.

"You know, in the months we've been dating, I don't think I've ever heard you talk about him."

"I talk about him often."

"No. You mention him often. That's different." Cat looked at another picture. "Your mother?"

"Possibly," Jim said.

"Yes. That's the missus," Dawkins murmured, sweeping past Cat. Cat smiled at the butler, then gently took the picture off the wall. She traced the woman's exotic features.

"She's lovely."

"She was, yes," Jim said, with the air of a man who wanted to talk about something, anything, else. "A six man monopoly, even these six men in particular, wouldn't have accomplished much. Smithback had little in the way of capitol. And Tupker…" Jim shook his head. "Someone had to be funding them."

"Pender? Gaines maybe?" Cat said, hanging the picture back in its place and returning to the couch. "The rumors mentioned them."

He tumbled limply past Jim, spinning off into the ocean
of lights like a leaf caught in an updraft.

Jim shook his head. "Neither had the sort of resources necessary for the operation Smithback's notebook describes." He closed the notebook. "Which perhaps explains the presence of our masked friends."

"Yeah?" Cat said, making herself comfortable.

"Yes. St. Cyprian mentioned that they were involved in more than just scaring people to death. Perhaps this sort of thing plays into their wheelhouse." Jim stood and stretched. Dawn was approaching swiftly, raw light creeping over the tops of the buildings. He looked back at Cat. She was snoring softly, eyes closed. Jim smiled and draped his discarded coat over her.

"When was the last time you yourself slept, sir?" Dawkins said.

"I'm feeling perfectly refreshed, Dawkins, thank you," Jim said. "Tom?"

"Asleep, sir." Dawkins' tone was faintly disapproving. Jim nodded and looked at Cat again.

"Well then. I guess it falls to me to press forward. Has Detective Healy called yet?"

"Yes sir. They have yet to find the body of the gentleman you tossed off the Woolworth Building," Dawkins said. "Healy was generally uncomplimentary in regards to your account, might I add."

Jim's smile tightened. "They must have retrieved the body."

"In light of recent events, I have taken the liberty of updating our security protocols," Dawkins said. "No one shall get in, or out, of the Waldorf-Anthony without you knowing about it, sir."

"Excellent. Has Pongo called again?"

"Not yet, sir."

Jim pondered this for a moment, then nodded to himself. "Fine. I suppose it's time I drop in for a visit, isn't it?"

"And what should I tell the others when they awaken?"

"That I'll meet them at the Cloud Club this afternoon for lunch. Make sure Tom wears a jacket," Jim said pointedly. "I can get away with a less than dapper ensemble, but he needs an edge to get past the concierge."

Jim was already on the elevator as Dawkins made his reply. His mind turned over the new information he'd gained and the new theories it brought to the fore.

If Metus and his people had been funding Smithback's group, why were they now eliminating them? Just because Cat had begun to investigate?

No. No, if it were that, it made more sense for Cat to die. Jim swallowed, unhappy to even consider the thought, but consider it he did. But she hadn't been a target, except at the cemetery. Possibly.

And what had that been about? An attempt to scare them off? Harpootlian's hand, perhaps?

What he knew about the lawyer would fit in a small envelope, something he would need to correct in the near future. Jim leaned forward, resting his head against the elevator doors. The only thing he hated about mysteries was the not knowing.

In the end, it all came down to the fact that three men were dead, for unknown reasons, due to the machinations of a group of fanatics. Somehow, those fanatics were tied in with the group whose numbers they were in the process of diminishing.

And if Jim wanted to prevent any further deaths, he was certain that he would have to act quickly. As he pulled the elevator doors open, a plan was already beginning to form in the recesses of his amazing mind. It was, on the surface, a simple one. One that any hunter would recognize with a smile of pleasure.

Jim passed out through the lobby of the Waldorf-Anthony and stepped out onto the street. A police radio car sat parked on the sidewalk, Healy sitting on the hood, lighting a cigarette.

"Anthony."

"Detective. Still missing a body?" Jim said. Healy gave him a glare.

"Yeah. Got an impact point, but nothing to scrape up." Healy tossed his spent match away. "Same as before."

"And what about the bodies from the University?" Jim asked.

Healy stood. "Both dead. Shot in the head. Perfect shots, mind." He sniffed.

Jim looked away. "He's a dangerous one," he said. "I assume you placed the bodies under guard, as I suggested?"

"Four of my best men. Nobody in or out without written orders from me," Healy said. "I don't want to lose any more evidence in this case."

Jim didn't flinch. "I have the remainder of the samples I took, as well as a few other odds and ends, safely locked away." He pointed upwards. Healy, who'd been to the Penthouse on several occasions, nodded.

"I hope so, for your sake." The detective exhaled a stream of smoke. "We're getting pressure to let this go. Some fancy pencil-neck has been raising cain with the Commissioner—"

"Samuel Harpootlian."

Healy blinked. "Yeah."

"One of Smithback's partners. Along with Tupker and Pender." Jim pounded a fist into his palm. "I think he tried to have an—ah—associate of mine killed yesterday."

"What?"

"Not important," Jim said. Healy's face went red.

"The hell it ain't!"

"It's not," Jim said. "Not right now. Someone is cleaning house, Detective, and with your help, I may just be able to prevent any more deaths."

Healy was silent for a moment. "We're being watched, you know."

He said it so bluntly that it took Jim a moment to process the content of his words. "How long?"

"Since before Simmons there parked us on your stoop," Healy said, nodding towards the uniformed officer sitting in the driver's seat.

Officer Simmons looked up from his paper, grinning. "They're still there, Detective."

"Of course they're still there," Healy snapped. "We're here, they're there." He looked at Jim. "Across the street. Three cars back. I was wondering whether you knew. Figured since you didn't mention it, you didn't."

Jim didn't turn, but merely flicked his eyes in the direction Healy's words indicated. The car had seen better days, as had the two men inside it. Caps and cheap jackets, with faces that hadn't seen the sharp end of a razor in several days. They didn't have the look of Metus' men. Jim wondered whether there was rifle sitting between them.

"Look like the guys from the cemetery?" Healy said.

"No clue. But I'd bet my life on it," Jim said. "I'd also bet that they're acting under orders from Harpootlian."

"Hunh." Healy casually leaned back against the police car. "Got any evidence to back up that particular assertion?"

"Circumstantial," Jim said. He stretched. "But I'm sure if we asked nicely, those two gentlemen across the street might tell us."

"You think you can make it before they peel out?" Healy said. Jim smiled.

"Are you giving odds?"

"Two to one."

"I'm in," Simmons said, folding his paper.

"Gambling's immoral, Simmons," Healy said.

"So's drinking, Detective, but I saw you taking a nip off that flask you hide in your coat."

"Shut up, Simmons," Healy said. He looked Jim up and down. "You packing?"

Jim shrugged out of his coat, displaying his shoulder holster. He handed the coat to Healy, who took it with ill-grace.

"Hopefully, I won't need it," Jim said. Then, with nary a preparatory twitch, Jim was up and over the hood of the police car, bounding towards the car and its startled occupants!

21.

The car's engine turned over with a roar. Jim bounded up onto the sidewalk, swung around a streetlight and landed on the hood of the car. Crouching, he hammered a fist into the windshield, shattering it. A second blow, delivered through the shattered window, caught the driver on the side of the jaw as the man reached for the pistol sitting between his legs on the seat.

The man in the passenger seat, curses dripping from his lips, hurled himself out of car. Jim stalked across the hood, launching himself at the man as he came to his feet.

They rolled across the street, the bleating of car horns marking their passage as morning traffic was delayed. Healy and Simmons sprinted out in opposite directions, holding up the morning commute as Jim swung his opponent to his feet. A knife flashed, and Jim's fingers snapped closed on his opponent's wrist. Kicking out, he caught the man's hip as he pulled on the wrist. There was a pop and the man screeched like a wounded animal as his arm went limp and the knife dropped from his fingers.

Divesting the man of the pistol in his coat pocket, Jim slammed him back against the car. "Good morning. You wouldn't happen to have an M1 rifle in the car anywhere, would you?"

"You sonnuva—" The man tried to swing up a fist, but Jim casually deflected the blow with his palm and gave the struggling gunman a gentle headbutt. The man's legs went limp and he slumped, blood streaming down his face.

Jim hefted him, keeping him on his feet. "Don't go lights-out on me just now, chum," he said, shaking him. "I find myself in sore need of answers."

"I—I ain't telling you nothing!"

"Double negative," Jim said. "I appear to have broken your nose. Let me fix that." Jim grabbed the man's nose and twisted, popping it straight. The man screamed and writhed. His eyes widened in shock and pain as Jim loomed over him. "Now, would you like me to fix that dislocated shoulder as well? Or do you feel like chatting?"

"I'll talk! I'll talk!"

"Wonderful. What were you doing here?"

"Waiting!" the man barked.

"For who? Me?"

"No! T-the dame. Kilkenny!"

Jim grunted. Then, "Who hired you?"

The man hesitated. Jim tapped his dislocated shoulder with a stiffened finger, eliciting a yelp. "All right! All right! It was—"

The bullet tore through his throat and cut the air above Jim's shoulder. Jim stumbled back as the weight of the newly made corpse flopped onto him. The driver of the car, jaw purpling, cursed loudly and took aim for another shot. Jim knew he wouldn't be as lucky a second time, but prepared to leap out of the way regardless.

A pistol snarled, but it wasn't the driver's. He shuddered and slumped. Jim spun. Healy moved towards him, service revolver extended, a thin query mark of smoke emerging from the barrel.

"You're welcome," he said.

Jim shook himself like a wounded bear. "I wish we'd been able to take him alive," he said, picking at the flecks of blood on his shirt.

Healy holstered his pistol. "Again, you're welcome."

"Thank you," Jim said, crouching beside the body. Swiftly, he searched the pockets of the coat and trousers, looking for anything that would confirm his suspicions. All he found was a wad of bills, rolled tight. Jim let the wad bounce on his palm, then threw it to Healy. "They weren't waiting for me."

"Then who?" Healy's eyes narrowed. "The dame." His face twisted into a snarl. "That Kilkenny dame! I knew she was gonna be trouble!"

"I won't argue that point," Jim said, rising to his feet. "But this isn't her fault." He looked at Healy. "In fact, it's quite helpful."

"You call two dead men helpful?" Healy said, gesturing. Jim frowned.

"Only in that they illuminate a path to getting to the bottom of things once and for all." He ran a hand through his hair. "I need you to meet me at the Cloud Club this afternoon."

"Me?"

"The police," Jim said. "Six men at least. Ring Dawkins. Have him provide you with the contents of Cabinet Seven."

"Cabinet Seven?" Healy said, looking off-balance. Jim nodded, jaw set.

"The pieces are all in place. If I'm right, there are two more deaths planned. And it's up to us to prevent them."

"You know who's behind it?"

"Not for certain. But I intend to find out. Now, I need to talk to a man about a monopoly."

"Anthony, wait," Healy began, but Jim was already moving, sliding back into his coat. He hated leaving Healy with the burden of cleaning up the third crime scene in half as many days, but needs must when the Devil drove.

Metus had reacted so quickly before, why was he stalling now? Unless he wasn't stalling, but circling, the way a lion did when it couldn't be sure of a kill. Of the six men involved in this economic conspiracy Cat had discovered, three had been public figures—Smithback, Pender and Tupker. Which left Docker, Harpootlian and Gaines. Pongo Docker was notorious for never being in one spot long enough to register. Gaines was a virtual hermit and Harpootlian…Jim's lips quirked. Harpootlian was attempting to stifle the police investigation, and by extension, Anthony's own. Which did not speak well of his involvement. One of the remaining men had hired thugs to kill Cat, most likely due to her snooping.

All of the evidence, circumstantial as it was, pointed to Harpootlian. The lawyer who had been instrumental in arranging the conspiracy was now, perhaps, knocking his partners out of the way, with the help of a band of fanatics.

But what was the connection there? Why was the Cult of Deimos even involved? No matter which way he approached that question, he couldn't make any headway. They were the wildcards in this affair.

Jim hated wildcards.

Pongo Docker's New York residence wasn't far away. He maintained apartments in the Shandor Building at 55 Central Park West for his infrequent visits to New York. Jim caught a cab at the corner and reached the apartment well before midday.

Jim flashed a few bills to get past the doorman, then hit the stairs. Pongo lived on the top floor, but there was no guarantee that he was in. He hadn't responded to any of Jim's calls, which wasn't in itself strange, as there was every chance he was still out west, overseeing his drilling operations. In a way, Jim hoped he was. He didn't relish the thought of putting anyone in harm's way, but it was necessary for what he was planning.

Pongo's door was open already when Jim got there. His hackles prickled, his sixth sense screaming a warning. Jim pulled his pistol and, thumb on the hammer, gently pushed open the door.

The apartment beyond was dark. The shades were pulled and the lights were out. The smell of spoiled food reached Jim's nose. He stepped through the doorway, head swiveling, eyes narrowed.

His eyes were better than those of the average man, but with little light to aid him, Jim could see nothing but dim shapes. His nostrils flared as he tried to classify and dismiss the odors in the air. Past the rank stench of the uneaten food was the bitter, illegal tang of spilled alcohol and the sharp, corrosive odor of cordite.

A gun had been fired here, and recently. Jim went to the far wall and pulled the blinds up, unleashing a flood of sunlight into the apartment.

In the light, the front room looked as if a hurricane had gone through it. Jim, pistol still in hand, wandered through the room. Empty bottles and discarded clothes cluttered the corners. A row of bullet holes stitched the wall near the bedroom.

It was small as apartments went, but Pongo was known to pride himself on his utilitarianism. Using the barrel of his pistol, Jim tossed aside a crumpled newspaper. A bevy of papers fluttered to the floor like a flock of frightened quail.

Jim holstered his pistol and crouched, going through the papers slowly. There were plans for slant drilling operations against the other major wildcatters in Docker's territory, and expansion plans for Western Africa, especially in relation to the Colony and Protectorate of Nigeria. There was also a list of English contacts, including one familiar name.

Soames. Neville Soames. Jim felt as if a surge of electricity had flashed through him. His mind reeled, recalling the strange mask in Soames' study that had so captured his attention. The mask that was, for all intents and purposes, the duplicate of the image he'd seen on the cards that had dealt subtle death to Jerry Smithback and Silas Pender!

It couldn't be...could it? Jim shook himself. He'd put Soames' gruesome experiments down to a mad urge, solitary and rotten. But what if it were something else?

What if his urge to create the perfect poison had not been a personal obsession alone, but part of someone else's mandate? He thought again of the strange glass spheres that Metus had employed. Of the hallucinogen on the business cards. And then, finally, he considered the havoc that Soames would have unleashed with those delivery systems.

Docker's money, flowing into Soames' pocket, funding God alone knew what. But connected by more than money.

Jim stood, slowly. How big was the Cult of Deimos? How far did its tendrils spread? Were these men, men he'd thought he'd known to some degree, part of it?

What if they weren't victims, but instead accomplices? Jim put a hand to his head, his mouth suddenly dry. And if they were, who else might be?

"Stop it," he said suddenly, startling himself. He shook his head. Foolish to think of such things. Considering Metus' seeming desperation to hide knowledge of the group from anyone else, it was entirely possible that no one knew anything.

Jim's nostrils flared. The reek of alcohol grew stronger. And something else... gun oil! Something scraped on the fibrous carpet.

Jim threw himself to the floor as a revolver snarled!

22.

As the leaden missile plucked a furrow through the thick carpet, Jim hit the floor shoulder first and rolled to his feet, spinning with lupine quickness. Coming upright, he was already moving towards his target.

With a growl, Jim was upon the gunman, driving him backwards through sheer weight and momentum until they crashed into the wall, dislodging pictures and toppling a bookshelf in the process.

The pistol flew out of the man's hand as Jim crushed his wrist in an iron grip. The man gave a strangled yelp as Jim pressed the edge of his forearm against the man's windpipe and pressed him to the wall.

"Now then chum," Jim said, then stopped. "Pongo?"

"Juh—Jimmy?" Jim's captive said, clawing at the arm that held him. Pongo Docker had seen better days. What had formerly been a ruddy countenance was now pale and flabby. Dark circles clung to the underside of his red-rimmed eyes like basalt weights and his breath reeked of too much illicit alcohol and not enough food.

"Pongo, you just tried to shoot me." Jim lowered Docker to the floor. Pongo shook his head.

"No, I didn't. There was a-a thief. Saw him." His words slurred at the edges, and Jim stepped back to avoid the worst of his effluvium. "Bastard."

"Not the first time I've been accused of that," Jim said, helping Docker to sit down. He crouched in front of the drunken wildcatter and placed his hands to either side of the man's head.

In his wild and heedless youth, Jim had had occasion to spend some time in Tibet. He hadn't learned much while there, but a monk—a Westerner, funnily enough, named Dumont—had taught him a few useful tricks. One of those was a way of sobering someone up quickly.

Jim wiggled his fingers, then swiftly pressed a number of pressure points on Docker's head and neck. The effect was instantaneous. Docker gave a grunt and stiffened, his eyes rolling up in his head. The smell of sour mash grew stronger as beads of pure alcoholic sweat popped into existence on his skin and dripped away. He crumpled forward into Jim's waiting arms.

"Uh. What? Anthony?" Docker looked up at Jim, eyes widening. "What are you doing here?"

"Coming to see you. You haven't been returning my calls, Pongo. Considering the situation, I wanted to know why."

"Situation?"

"Jerry is dead. Tupker and Pender as well. But then you knew that, didn't you?" Jim gestured at the newspapers strewn across the floor. Pongo blinked.

101

"No!" He hesitated. "I don't know what you're talking about."

"Stop trying to take the bunk, Pongo." Jim shook him slightly. "What's going on?"

"I said I don't know what you're talking about!" Pongo shoved Jim back and stood. He swayed for a moment, then took hold of himself. "Jerry came to see you?"

"Yes." Jim stood, crossing his arms.

Docker licked his lips. "It's all gone wrong. All of it."

"What has?"

Docker didn't speak. His head hung low. He gestured aimlessly. "I don't—I can't—"

"Pongo, how long have you been in town?"

"Since—ah—what day is it?" Jim told him. Docker rocked back on his heels. "A week. Came back right after poor Alan died."

"Was murdered," Jim corrected. Docker squeezed his eyes shut, but said nothing. Jim looked around. "You've been hiding, haven't you?"

"I want a lawyer," Docker said.

"I'm not the police, Pongo. I thought we were friends." Jim reached for the other man, but Docker stumbled back, falling onto the couch. "I wondered who had suggested me to Jerry. It didn't seem like his kind of thing, not considering the effort he made to distance himself from my father after he got started."

Jim looked around the room. "You suspected something. But you didn't bother to warn anyone, did you?"

"I couldn't. They wouldn't have believed me," Docker said, quietly. "I wouldn't have believed me."

"You heard about Soames, didn't you? About what he was up to." Jim snatched up a handful of papers. "Learned that your money was being used, in part, to fund his crimes."

"Not just him." Docker looked up. "The Chittagong Rebellion. That was my money too. The murder of Jake Lingle, in Chicago."

Jim froze. He had been asked to look into the Lingle murder, but he'd been too wrapped up in the Blue Ghost affair at the time. "Yours?"

"Pender. He didn't know," he said, before Jim could ask. "Didn't even suspect. None of them did, but me." He leaned back and rubbed his palms across his face in slow, circular motions. "Judge Crater," he continued. He saw Jim's expression and essayed a weak smile. "I saw in the paper that you thought he'd skedaddled with a mistress."

"All of the evidence—"

"Faked. Crater was in on it, whatever 'it' was. But he began to develop a conscience, as near as I can figure. So he had to go." Docker swallowed. "A military junta in Peru. Another in Argentina. Whipping up the Kurds in Persia."

"A blow to their old enemies, the Turks," Jim said. Docker looked at him in confusion.

"What?"

"The Cult of Deimos."

"The who?" Docker shook his head and held up a hand. "Never mind. They got the R101 too," he said, continuing on.

"The airship crash?" Jim said. "Why?"

"Who knows? Not me!" Docker barked, swatting a bottle off of the couch. He looked at Jim. "None of it makes any sense to me Jimmy! None of it! Why would they care who's in charge in Brazil? But that was them too!" His words were picking up speed. "Why do they care that we're going through one of the greatest economic crises that has ever faced a nation? But they do! They do, Jimmy!"

Docker stood and began to pace. "Jake paralysis? Jamaican ginger poisoning?" He spun. "That bastard Soames was behind that, I'm certain of it, especially after reading about your punch-up with him."

"How did you find out all of this, Pongo," Jim said slowly. He held out his hands, as if to confine Docker's mad pacing. "And how is it that the others are dead, but not you?"

"I know when a man is trying to kill me, Jimmy," Docker said. "You get a tremble in the cat line." He tapped his chest. "They ain't killed me yet, because it don't matter what I know." His eyes blazed. "They were always planning to kill me, you see. Whoever the hell they are."

"The others—"

"Same thing. They intended to kill all of us. Once they had their damnable claws into our finances, our investments." He laughed. "But I hid out. Kept 'em guessing where I was when all the time I was right here."

Realization hit Jim like the blow of a hammer. The phone calls hadn't been about business. Docker had been trying to contact him out of fear for his life! "You were hoping that I'd investigate!"

"Damn straight," Docker said. "When Tupker bought it, when I figured out what was what, I figured that if we got you involved, we might just survive." He looked around the apartment, then back at Jim. "What the hell took you so long?"

Jim laughed. Gesturing to his shoulder, he said, "Well, I've been busy, Pongo."

"Who are they, Jimmy? Who are these bastards? Have you figured it out yet?" Docker said. He stood and stretched, and wandered towards the door.

"Somewhat. Have you ever had any dealings with a man called Metus, Pongo? Or Corrigan?"

"I know an Abernathy Metus. Funny name." Docker closed the still-open apartment door and scooped up a spread of what appeared to be mail, judging by the profusion of stamps. "Works for a legal associate of mine."

"Samuel Harpootlian," Jim said.

Docker nodded. "He's a clerk."

"A clerk?" Jim scratched his jaw. Then, changing tacks, he said, "Why did you get involved in this dodge, Pongo?"

Docker stopped shuffling the mail. He didn't look at Jim. "Money, Jimmy. Why else?"

"That can't have been it, Pongo."

"All that matters." Docker crumpled his mail in his hands. "If I'd known…." He trailed off. A rectangle of white fluttered from the papers and envelopes in his grip. Docker looked down. "Huh." He stooped.

Jim lunged, seizing Docker's wrist. He halted the man's hand inches from the card laying facedown on the carpet. "Don't!" Jim said.

"What?"

"Don't touch it. Your door was open when I got here. Does your doorman habitually deliver your mail?" Jim said intently. Docker looked at him blankly.

"He's never—oh." He looked down at the papers in his hand, then dropped them as if they were burning embers.

Jim pushed him back, then squatted. Carefully, he used one envelope to scoop up the card and flip it over. Deimos' leering face stared up at him.

"What the hell is that?" Docker hissed.

"The mark of Deimos," Jim said harshly. "Don't touch it, whatever you do." He snapped his fingers. "Get me a handkerchief or a rag. Something. The thicker, the better."

Docker hastened to obey and quickly returned with a faded scrap of cloth that had seen so many coats of oil that it had become a dingy gray. Jim folded it and gingerly scooped up the card. Wrapping it in the cloth, he slit open an envelope with a thumbnail and a dropped the card inside, cloth and all. Then he folded it and stuffed it into his coat pocket.

"Jimmy, what was that? Why were you so worried about it?"

"Nothing less than terror in handy card form, Pongo. It was the murder-weapon in the deaths of Smithback and the others."

"Who are these guys?" Docker said, clutching his chest. "What have we gotten into?" He looked at Jim, his face sagging into incomprehension.

Jim patted his pocket. "That's what I intend to find out. With your help, of course."

23.

The Cloud Club was busy when Jim and Docker walked in. Docker hesitated in the doorway, hands clenching uselessly. Jim looked at him. "Steady, pal. Everything is squared up. You have nothing to worry about, Pongo."

"So you say."

"I do," Jim said. Docker looked at him.

"So why don't I feel any better about this?"

"Common sense?" Jim gestured towards a waiter. "Table for four? Reservation should be under Anthony?"

"Yes sir. One of your guests has already arrived," the mâitre 'd said, indicating their path with a sweep of his hands. Jim led the way, his keen gaze sweeping over the restaurant, looking for familiar faces.

Cat waved from a table in the corner. Tom sat across from her, his features tense. The big Gael flashed a gesture, which Jim knew meant that Tom had successfully followed his instructions.

He caught sight of Healy, lounging near the doorway, smoking a dog-end cigar and gazing serenely over the top of a newspaper. Not the Star, Jim noted. Healy's attention was all for the lunchtime crowd, and he didn't seem to notice Jim's arrival.

"This is a bad idea," Docker muttered. "What makes you think Sammy is even going to show up?"

"In fact, I'm counting on his absence," Jim said. "If he is, as I suspect, behind recent events, then he won't show up. Instead, he'll make an attempt to finish what he's started."

"Kill me and Oscar," Docker finished. "You're using me as bait, Jimmy, and I don't appreciate it!"

"Do you think that I do?" Jim said, not looking at him. "If so, you're dead wrong."

"Bad choice of words, Jimmy!"

"Yes," Jim said. He stopped. "If you want to run back to your burrow, Pongo, I won't stop you."

"I don't run," Docker said, jaw set. "I'm just saying that I don't—"

"I know what you're saying. And I know why you're saying it. But we have few options here, Pongo," Jim said. "I've been playing to their rules since this started and I'm tired of it. Damn tired."

"Jimmy, maybe it would be better if we did this some other time."

"No. We're here. Gaines is here. And we end this today." Jim sliced the air with a rigid palm.

"Why do you even suspect the shark to begin with?" Docker said.

"Because, he set up your deal didn't he? Introduced you to each other? Brokered the deals that allowed your finances to be used for various purposes." Jim stopped as they reached the table. "And he's been trying to halt the investigation."

"With good reason, I should say," a thin, crane-like individual said, unfolding from his seat. "Samuel Harpootlian, Mr. Anthony. I would say that I'm looking forward to lunch, but then I'd be lying."

Jim's mind whirred, switching tracks with a smoothness that surprised him. "Mr. Harpootlian." He extended his hand. Harpootlian looked at it, then at Docker.

"Mr. Docker. I've been trying to get hold of you for several days now."

"I just bet you have," Docker said. The lawyer looked at him oddly, then switched his attentions back to Jim.

"When I got Mr. Docker's call, I was, of course, curious." Harpootlian sat. "I've heard of you, Mr. Anthony."

"Have you?" Jim said, pulling out his own chair. Harpootlian nodded.

"Oh, yes. Beyond the usual gossip, mind. That affair in London earlier in the year?" Harpootlian smiled thinly. "A good lawyer could tear your explanation to shreds, Mr. Anthony."

"No doubt," Jim said. "You haven't heard from Oscar Gaines, by chance, have you?" He gestured to Docker. "Pongo gave him a call, and he said he'd be here."

"No. Haven't seen a whiff." Harpootlian frowned. "Any particular reason you've invited us here?"

"Maybe I'm reconsidering Jerry Smithback's offer," Jim said. Harpootlian blinked.

"What offer? And why should I care?"

Jim took Smithback's notebook out of his coat pocket and placed it on the table. Splaying his fingers across it, Jim locked eyes with the lawyer. "Alan Tupker. Silas Pender. Jerome Smithback. Oscar Gaines. Pongo Docker. And you."

"Did you invite me to lunch just to recite a list of names at me?" Harpootlian said, shifting in his seat. Jim flipped the notebook open.

"This was Jerry Smithback's. He was a bit anal-retentive, to borrow a phrase from Freud." Jim smiled mirthlessly. "He kept records of everything."

"Somebody's diary? This is what you want me to look at?" Harpootlian smirked and picked up his drink. "Would you like me to calculate the likelihood of it being taken seriously as evidence in a court case?"

"No. I merely wanted you to know that I had it," Jim said. He tapped a page with his forefinger. "And that you were mentioned in it."

Harpootlian paused, his glass halfway to his lips. Deliberately, he took his drink and then set the glass aside. "I wouldn't know about that."

"Are you sure?" Jim pressed. "Because it seems like you might."

"Are you accusing me of something?"

Jim leaned back, draping his arm over the back of the chair. "I intended to," he said.

"But now?"

"Still planning on it. Just not in the same way." Jim smiled, baring his teeth.

"You've been trying to get the official investigation into the deaths of your fellows stopped."

"I didn't say I knew them!" Harpootlian said quickly. Jim waved this aside.

"Nonetheless, you've been more than appropriately interested, haven't you?"

Harpootlian was silent for a moment. Then, "If you must know, I've been re-tained by the Pender estate to bring certain unwarranted investigations to a halt, yes."

"I thought you said you weren't affiliated with them."

"I'm not. Only with the Pender estate."

"Then why have you been trying to get in contact with Mr. Docker here?" Jim said. Harpootlian looked quickly at Docker, then back to Jim.

"I might, and I stress might, have learned through certain sources that Mr. Docker and Mr. Pender shared business interests—"

"You sonnuva—" Docker started to his feet, but Jim held him in his place.

"Interests also shared by the others I mentioned, including yourself." Jim point-ed a finger at the lawyer. "Interests that are highly suspect, especially in regard to current international law."

"I give you that the interests were, shall we say, suspect, but not my involve-ment." Harpootlian folded his hands.

"But you were involved?"

"Not in the least," Harpootlian said. Jim sat back.

"Why did you send someone to kill Catherine Kilkenny?"

"Who? The reporter?" Harpootlian raised an eyebrow. Jim was silent. Harpootlian shifted in his chair, obviously uncomfortable beneath Jim's steady gaze. "Fine. I'll play along." He spread his hands on the table, splaying his fin-gers. "Say, for instance, that a certain busybody stumbled onto something she, or he, shouldn't have. And in an attempt to convince them of the futility of further snooping, certain—ah—overzealous methods were employed."

"Overzealous?" Jim said. "Is that what you call it?" He could feel the slow burn of his anger building. Harpootlian smirked.

"Regardless, it's all theory anyway. And I notice that Ms. Kilkenny is still on this side of the River Styx," he said, gesturing idly towards the table where Kilkenny sat. "Thus, if some attempt were made, it obviously failed."

"And if it hadn't?"

"But it did." Harpootlian's smirk faded. "I have a question of my own…why are you interested?"

"Jerry Smithback was an acquaintance. As is Mr. Docker." Jim leaned forward. "I believe that you are lying to me, Mr. Harpootlian."

"Oh?"

"Yes. You're quite good at eye contact, but you have difficulty controlling the pitch of your voice."

"Oh, come on." Harpootlian made a dismissive gesture.

"Your body language exudes tension," Jim continued. Harpootlian froze. "In short, the signs of a liar."

"I'm paid to lie, Mr. Anthony. But no one is paying me to have lunch with you and to listen to these accusations. My reputation is unassailable." Harpootlian took a last sip of his drink and rose to his feet. Jim rose with him.

"If you leave this club, Mr. Harpootlian, there are several members of New York's finest waiting to take you into custody. And, as you yourself pointed out, a representative of the Fourth Estate here in the form of Ms. Kilkenny to document the whole incident. What will that do to your reputation, I wonder?"

Harpootlian stopped. Turning, his face was screwed up in a grimace. "This is uncalled for."

"Maybe. Maybe not." Jim leaned forward, balancing himself on his knuckles. "But that's not for you to judge."

"What do you want, Mr. Anthony?" Harpootlian said, sitting once more. "No games. What do you want?"

"The truth," Jim said. Harpootlian looked at Docker.

"Why not ask your friend there?"

"Because it was your idea," Jim said, tapping the notebook again. "Wasn't it?"

"I can't claim all the credit, no. I'm just a lawyer, Mr. Anthony. A business lawyer at that." Harpootlian smiled bitterly. "I just drew up the appropriate documents."

"You did more than that, shyster!" Docker snapped. "You brought us all in!"

"Not on my own recognizance, I assure you," Harpootlian said, ignoring Docker and focusing on Jim. "We all had our parts to play, as I'm sure you know, Mr. Anthony."

Jim flipped through the notebook, glancing between it and the lawyer. "I hear a 'but' coming, Mr. Harpootlian."

"Indeed." Harpootlian's smile could have cored an apple. "I notice Mr. Gaines isn't here. You mentioned that his presence was requested earlier."

Jim frowned. "Are you saying that Gaines hired you?"

"I'm not saying anything of the sort, Mr. Anthony. Merely noting his absence." Jim looked at Docker. "Pongo?"

"I—I don't know Jimmy. It was this shark who approached me about the whole thing," Docker said, glaring at Harpootlian. "Gaines has the cash…he and Pender were the money-men."

"Pender was broke," Jim said. Harpootlian nodded slowly. "He was there as a pointman, to sniff out new opportunities, to network. Smithback had the contacts in the investment sector. Tupker had contacts in the service industry and retail sectors. You, Pongo, had your connections in the oil industry. Harpootlian put together your paperwork. And Gaines provided the capital." Jim looked back and forth between the two men. "But the question is, who came to who first?" Jim rubbed the bridge of his nose. "It was Gaines wasn't it? He hired you, didn't he, Mr. Harpootlian?"

"I'd rather not comment," Harpootlian said smoothly.

"Who is Abernathy Metus?" Jim said.

"Who?" Harpootlian said, looking confused. As he leaned forward, the sound

"Mr. Docker. I've been trying to get hold of you for several days now."

"I just bet you have," Docker said.

of glass cracking filled the air. Jim pushed his chair back and saw shards of glass glittering on the floor beneath the table. A dark, sin—colored mist crawled across the floor. Jim shot to his feet with alacrity.

"Tom! Detective!" he said even as his hand darted into his coat pocket.

"Jimmy, what—" Docker said, eyes wide. Jim didn't reply, instead pulling out a small, specially designed gas mask and slapping it to his face.

More glass shattered and more smoke boiled out from under the tables of unaware diners. Soon, screams followed as the hallucinogenic gas took effect on the patrons of the Cloud Club!

24.

Smoke filled the Cloud Club, wreathing the pillars in a crawling bank of pure chaos. Jim, wearing his modified gas mask, was protected from the effects of the cloud, but others weren't so lucky.

Businessmen and politicians and bankers were screaming and running pell-mell in all directions, stumbling around in blind panic as the gas seeped into their lungs and filled their heads with nightmare visions. Jim could sympathize. He wished he'd been able to have the club emptied of all non-essential personnel, but they'd been necessary to complete the illusion.

Bait for the trap.

It was a cold thought, Jim knew. A hard one, as bright and sharp as crystal. But it was necessary. He rose to his feet, frozen for a moment as he tried to consider the best course of action.

The gas was a vomit-colored pea soup, thick and light devouring as it spread quickly in the confines of the restaurant. Jim felt his pores prickle as it enveloped him and he hoped to God that it wasn't able to seep into the skin in this state. Nothing he'd seen before had provided evidence for such, but there was still too much he didn't know about it.

Granted, now wasn't the time to try to learn. Jim snapped out an arm and caught a screaming banker from hitting the wall in a delirious panic. Hefting the screeching man, Jim slung him gently into the decorative ferns, hoping the plants would cushion the impact. Jim looked down at the table.

Harpootlian seemed paralyzed by fear, staring straight upward, his body as rigid as a board. Docker was huddled on the floor, a strong man reverted to a state of near-infancy by the cloud of terror.

Both men were obviously affected. Jim cursed himself silently, knowing then that he'd miscalculated. He'd suspected Harpootlian, even after he'd shown up. And maybe the lawyer was responsible for the attempt on Cat's life, but not for this...after all, what kind of madman would allow himself to be exposed to mind-numbing terror simply to hide his involvement?

"Jimmy! What's going on?"

Jim turned as Tom, Cat and Healy, all wearing similar masks to Jim's own, hurried forward, Healy and Tom with their pistols out. Other police officers, dressed in plainclothes and wearing masks, were in evidence as well. Only five of them, however, for Jim had only had a handful of masks prepared.

He had devised the masks, which were smaller, more compact versions of those used to varying success in the Great War, during his scuffle with the Purple Gang, who had used an all-purpose anesthetic to render their robberies easier to carry out. Now they would serve to keep Healy and his men moving amidst the fear-gas, or so Jim hoped.

"Just what I suspected might happen, Tom! Our ghoulish fear-mongering friends are making an attempt on Pongo's life!"

"And the shyster?" Healy said, looking around a trifle wildly, obviously recalling what the gas had done to him last time he'd encountered it. Jim gestured, swiping a clutching tendril of gas away.

"See for yourself. I think I may have been mistaken, Detective!"

"Hearing that makes it all worth it, Anthony," Healy said. "We've got to get these people outta here."

"No disagreements here. I'll see if I can manage Pongo and Harpootlian…" Jim began, but then his attentions were drawn across the room, eyes narrowing as he tried to pierce the smoke.

Under Healy's barked direction, the police officers were trying, with little success, to control the panicking crowd and funnel them safely out of the line of fire and towards the doors. But coming the opposite way, threading through the crowd, moving like sharks in shallow waters, came at least six figures wearing what Jim was coming to think of as the raiment of Deimos; hideous masks and armored carapaces beneath suit coats and over dining room attire.

Jim knew that they had been planted throughout the dining room, even as Healy's men had been. Or perhaps scattered throughout the Club's other rooms, judging by their angle of entry. He'd planned for this, luckily. If they could capture the assassins, even just one, they might be able to get to the bottom of things. It was the whole reason behind his arrangement of the meeting here. He'd gleaned from his previous encounters and from St. Cyprian's information that they wouldn't be able to resist coming for Docker once they learned that he still lived. And once Jim knew which of the surviving conspirators had tipped them off, he would be able to strike off the serpent's head, so to speak.

One of the new arrivals, carrying a Thompson machine gun, rattled off a burst as he caught sight of Jim.

Jim, reflexes undulled, shoved Tom into Cat, forcing both of them to the side and upended the thick table over himself like a giant oval shield, allowing the polished wood surface to absorb the fiery hornets of death that raged towards him.

Still holding the legs of the table, Jim charged forward, wood splinters falling over him like a painful rain. He crashed into the gunman, driving him backwards into the wall with a thunderous crack!

A spatha looped out, slicing a canyon across the back of Jim's coat, but drawing no blood. He spun, grabbing the wrist of the hand holding the blade and jerked its owner forward. Driving his elbow up into the gap between the man's mask and his carapace, Jim knocked him sprawling.

The cultist he'd hit with the table shoved it aside and brought his weapon up again, holding down the trigger and spraying the room. Jim threw himself flat as the fusillade cut the air over his head. Scrambling to the side, he drew his own pistol and bobbed to his feet. He fired as he rose, catching the gunman in the hand, forcing him to drop the Thompson with a muffled curse.

Two more bullets struck the cultist, pitching him sideways. Jim nodded to Tom, who was already swinging his Colt around towards another target. Jim bounded back towards Docker and the lawyer. He needed to ensure their safety. Already one of the masked men had reached the table and had drawn a spatha, which he was preparing to bring down on Harpootlian's skull.

Jim jumped up onto a table and launched himself at the swordsman, tackling him aside. The sword went flying as they crashed into another table, which shattered beneath their combined weight. Gloved fingers sought Jim's windpipe with deadly intent, but he brought both fists down on the man's face, knocking the mask askew and rendering him unconscious.

Jim rose, swinging his pistol around. He fired, catching another swordsman in the knee. The man stumbled and tripped over Docker. Jim, satisfied that both men were out of immediate danger, scanned the room for his companions.

Healy and two officers were trading shots with a masked man crouched behind a table. Tom had another in a tight grip, one arm locked around his throat and the other pinning the man's gun arm at an awkward angle. Cat was nowhere to be seen. Jim hoped she had enough sense to stay out of the way.

He heard a metallic 'click' and twisted aside instinctively as a pop-knife skidded just past his ribs. The man on the ground, eyes blazing, mask hanging loose, clambered to his feet and swiped at Jim again. Froth bubbled at the corners of his mouth as he lunged awkwardly, crashing into Jim and bearing him backwards.

Even through the filter in his mask, Jim could smell the pungent aroma issuing from the maddened man's mouth. Poison of some type, obviously. Jim backpedaled and the man stumbled, slumping, the knife falling from his hand.

Metus had shot his own men earlier to prevent them from falling into police hands. And they'd retrieved the body of the man who'd fallen from the ledge of the Woolworth Building. He should have expected that they would have methods of ensuring their own demise.

Arms suddenly snapped around Jim, hauling him out of his thoughts and from his feet with one brutal tug and tossing him aside like a rag-doll. He hit the floor and sprang to his feet without hesitation, just as a fist pistoned towards his jaw. Jim slapped the blow aside, then was forced to do the same to a second. The man he'd shot in the knee was up and looking to tussle. The man moved gingerly, his leg obviously hampered by Jim's shot, but there was nothing wrong with his arms.

His blows came fast and hard and Jim once again reflected on the obvious training these men possessed. He grunted as a lucky blow danced over his guard and across his temple, staggering him.

Jim dropped into a crouch and kicked out, aiming for the man's wounded knee. He was rewarded with a sharp crack and a grunt of pain. The cultist fell onto all fours, but was up again a moment later, catching Jim about the middle and carrying him backwards in a rush.

Jim smashed his fists down onto the back of the cultist's neck even as his spine connected with the glass of the large window that looked out over the city. The window that Jerome Smithback had crashed through not more than a day before.

The crack was loud, like a gunshot. And then Jim was moving back, falling through a cloud of stinging splinters, his opponent's arms still wrapped around him!

Flinging a hand out, Jim latched on to the edge of the window, halting his plunge. A fist hammered into his kidney and forced a groan between his clenched teeth. Jim brought his elbow down on the cultist, forcing him to loosen his grip. Another blow sent Jim swinging out, his steely grip the only thing keeping him from falling to his death.

Desperate, Jim grabbed the man's cuirass and yanked him forward, pitching him out of the window and placing him at Jim's mercy. His opponent dangled, clutching at Jim's wrist.

"Stop struggling! I can pull you up!" Jim said. The edge of the window seemed slippery in his grip and his jaw clenched as he fought to retain his hold. His much-abused shoulder began to shriek silently, spitting fire up and down his arm, but Jim ignored it.

The cultist went limp. Jim breathed a sigh of relief. "Finally. Someone is seeing sense. Now hang on."

The knife flashed out from its hidden sheath in the man's coat and swiped across Jim's wrist, lightly scoring the skin. The damage done was no more than that of a paper cut, but the shock of it caused Jim's hold to loosen just enough for the cultist to kick his way free and plummet downwards, his eyes never leaving Jim's.

Jim watched him fall, a sick sense of revelation settling over him. He knew now that no matter what he did, he would not be taking prisoners. Not from this group.

"Damn it," he said. Then, louder, "Damn it!"

25.

Jim pulled himself back in through the shattered window and leaned against the wall, clutching his injured arm. The sword-wound was bleeding again, and his skin felt flushed. He needed rest. Somehow, he thought that it was unlikely that he was going to get the time.

At least the hallucinogen was streaming out through the shattered window, clearing the restaurant. That was one problem he didn't have to worry about taking care of. It wasn't much, but at this point, Jim was willing to take what he could get.

"You okay, Jimmy?" Tom said, approaching him. Jim plucked off his mask and tossed it to his friend.

"Sore and tired. Did we manage to capture any of them?"

"Not a one. Bastards got foamy and died, or just got plain shot. I don't think they intended to get out of here alive."

"It's looking more and more like that, yes. Did we have any casualties?"

Tom's face grew grim. "Yeah. One."

"Damn." Jim closed his eyes for a moment. "Who?"

"The shark. Harpootlian."

Jim's eyes popped open. "What?"

"One of the masks got after them when you were hanging out the window," Tom said, hiking a thumb over his shoulder. "It happened so damn quick, by the time I got there the lawyer was dead and Docker was—ah—"

"What?"

"Well, see for yourself," Tom said, stepping aside. Jim hurried towards the table. Harpootlian had fallen from his chair and lay sprawled on the ground, a small .22 caliber pistol near one hand. A knife was buried in his eye, the hilt jutting upwards like some obscene decoration.

Docker lay a rough foot from where he had before, curled in a ball, blood pooling beneath him. Jim crouched beside him and was relieved to see that he still lived. "What happened?" he said, looking up.

"Looks like the shark shot him in the confusion," Healy said, taking off his mask and tossing it aside. "Figure whoever drove that knife into him probably got out of the way just as the gun went off. It caught Docker, though."

"How could it? He was on the floor," Jim said idly. He ripped one of Docker's trouser legs off and pressed it to the wound, blocking the flow of blood. "Someone needs to come hold this until we get a first-aid kit up here."

"Why can't you do it?"

"Oscar Gaines, Detective," Jim said. "He's the remaining member of this group still at large."

"Wait, I can send a couple of guys with you," Healy said, eyes lighting up. Jim cut him off.

"No time. He's the last one. He knew we were here but he didn't show up. What does that tell you?"

"That he's our guy?"

"We can but hope," Jim said, as one of Healy's men took his place. He rose, wiping his hands with a discarded napkin. "We're fast running out of options otherwise. Keep a guard on Pongo. Two, if you can spare them."

"Three, if you count me," Healy said, reloading his service revolver. "Don't worry, Anthony, I know how to do my damn job."

"Well, that's one of us then," Jim said mock-cheerfully. Then, more seriously, "Be careful, Detective. They were willing to lose half a dozen men to kill just two."

"Crazy don't mean unbeatable, Anthony."

"No. It just means it won't be easy." Jim tossed the pink-stained napkin onto a table. "You'll need to send men to Harpootlian's offices as well."

"Yeah?"

"Yes. We'll need his papers…anything pertaining to his activities with this group. Investments, injunctions, lawsuits, legal paperwork of any stripe. It may help to create a trail back to our phantom opponents."

"Makes sense," Healy said. "You think they'll try to destroy that stuff?"

"I think whoever you send should be armed and ready for anything," Jim said and headed for the exit. Tom and Cat caught up with him.

"Well, that was certainly exciting," Cat said. "Where to next, Jimmy?"

"For you? Home." Jim snagged a passing cop and prodded Cat towards him. "Officer? Be so kind as to see that Ms. Kilkenny makes it back to the Waldorf-Anthony in one piece, please."

The officer nodded, taking Cat's arm in a gentle but firm grip. "Come along, Miss."

Cat's foot stomped down, eliciting a yelp from the officer. As he hopped backwards, she cut Jim off, and crossed her arms. "Dirty pool. Where you go, I go, Jimmy. Remember our deal?"

"Cat, now is not the time," Jim said, grabbing her arms and pulling her out of earshot. "Not now. It's gone too far."

"Too far? Jimmy, I've been pitched out a window, shot at and almost run down in front of my own damn newspaper!" She gave a cold grin and jabbed a finger into his chest. "You're a smart guy, Anthony. But don't let it go to your head. Now, would you rather I go with you? Or alone?"

Jim hesitated. Looking down at the small woman in his grip he was once again struck by the intensity of her personality. A firebrand, his father would have called her. A woman not willing to back down, regardless of the circumstances. Surrendering to the impulse, Jim pulled her close, his lips seizing hers in a hungry embrace that sent fireworks rattling off in the deep recesses of his mind and soul. She melted into him, her nails digging into the flesh of his arms.

Far too quickly, Jim pulled away, swallowing down his desire. "I have to go."

"We have to go," she gasped. "Where are we going?"

"Gaines," Jim said, turning away. "It might be dangerous."

"And the past couple of days haven't been?"

"Point." Jim headed for the doors, Cat trailing behind him. Tom smirked at them both. As Cat approached, he doffed his cap with aplomb and swept it aside in a dandified bow.

"Milady is accompanying us then?" Tom said, in his best approximation of Dawkins' voice. Cat laughed. Jim, shaking his head, moved quickly past.

"Come on, both of you. We're running against time here."

"Yeah? So what's the score then?" Tom said.

"That's the problem…it's not my clock," Jim said. "We've been on the back foot since day one. All we can do now is try to catch up and hope it all shakes out okay."

"Optimistic," Tom said.

"Realistic," Cat corrected. "I scooped this up, by the by," she continued, handing Jim the notebook. "Figured we might need it."

Jim took the book gratefully as they climbed aboard the elevator. Blood stained the cover and Jim brushed at it distractedly. "Gaines has a house on Fifth Avenue. Not far. I doubt he'll be there, but if we're lucky, he won't have left yet."

"They won't know that their boys failed," Tom said. "Which begs the question, would they even bother waiting on the poor bastards?"

"If only to learn what happened. Metus doesn't strike me as a man to leave things half done. There are bodies and equipment in the possession of the police; things he'll be eager to either destroy or reclaim." Jim sighed. "No. No, he won't leave the city."

"You hope," Cat said. Jim looked at her. Then, he smiled half-heartedly.

"I hope," he said. He flipped through the notebook. "Harpootlian said that he'd been hired by Gaines. That Gaines had directed him to contact the others."

"Hunh. Thought he was a hermit," Cat said, stroking her chin. "Think this Metus guy is working for him?"

"I don't know." Jim hesitated. "He has to be getting his orders from somewhere."

"Maybe he's talking to God," Tom said, half-jokingly.

"Maybe he is," Jim said. They all fell silent as the elevator plunged downwards.

Downstairs, Jim and Cat waited as Tom brought the car around. "I still think you should wait at the Penthouse with Dawkins," Jim said.

"And I think you should lay off," Cat said. She sniffed. "This is my ticket out of the gossip ghetto, Jimmy. No more yellow journalism for me!"

"Is it worth your life?" Jim said, intently. Cat looked at him, then burst out laughing.

"Ain't you sweet!"

Jim snorted. "Fine. Maybe I deserved that, but still…." He trailed off.

Cat patted his arm. "This is who I am, Jimmy. I'm not some wilting damsel for you to coddle."

"Who said anything about coddling? I just want to make sure you don't get perforated before we get some time to ourselves," Jim said, flashing his teeth in a smile. Before Cat could reply, Tom pulled up.

The drive to Gaines' home was quick. Thanks to Smithback's notebook and Cat's earlier investigations, they knew the exact address. Jim had Tom park a little ways down the street. Cat made to follow him out of the Rolls, but Jim shut the door on her.

"Stay here."

"But—"

"No. Stay. Here." Jim looked at Tom. "Circle the block. Keep your eyes open. If worse comes to worst, alert Healy."

"I ain't leaving you Jimmy," Tom protested.

"I'm not asking you to. I'm asking you to go get reinforcements with which to more effectively rescue me," Jim said, smiling. "And don't let her out of the car," he continued, switching his gaze to Cat once more. She went red and opened her mouth to reply, but Tom pulled away from the sidewalk before so much as a curse could fly from her lips.

Jim watched them turn the corner, then started up the street himself. The house sat on the corner, a square thing possessed by the spirit of the gothic revival. Heavy curtains blocked the windows.

Looking at the house, Jim felt a chill creep up his spine. He let his senses spread and roam, but felt nothing beyond a twinge of apprehension.

If he were Oscar Gaines, he would have left New York as soon as possible. Win or lose, there was little to gain by staying.

Then, if Gaines were truly behind things, as Harpootlian had implied, then maybe this was just what he wanted. Jim hesitated, wondering if there was another way to go about things.

The movement of the upstairs curtains drew his eye. Jim looked up, knowing even as he did so that someone was watching him. Was it Gaines? No way to tell.

Deciding that there was no other option now save to do the thing as quickly as possible, Jim drew his pistol, checked that he had a full clip, and headed for the door. Subtlety, while seemingly called for in situations such as this, would be a waste of time. Direct was better. He was hopeful that the element of surprise would be enough to even whatever odds were stacked against him.

Jim glanced up and down the street as he climbed the steps towards the door. Then, taking a breath, he lashed out with a foot, kicking in the door with one swift motion.

Stepping over the threshold, Jim felt the floor give slightly in a spongy fashion. His senses prickled in warning, but too late. With a sharp series of cracks, the floor beneath his feet gave way!

26.

With a growl worthy of any beast of the veldt, Jim launched himself forward even as the floor gave way. Hitting solid wood shoulder first, he rolled to his feet just in time to witness the floor boards in front of the door split and tumble.

Rubbing his shoulder, Jim crouched beside the hole. The wound he'd received was still throbbing despite the unguent he'd slathered on it in the car before rebinding it. The unguent, one part jellied rattlesnake venom and one part secret ingredient, was an old family tradition, one his grandfather had passed along to him the first time Jim had found himself on the wrong end of a bullet.

Yet while it aided his own enormous recuperative abilities, it did not provide a sop to the pain. Especially considering the exertion he'd been involved in these past few days.

So, massaging his shoulder, Jim hunkered down in front of the hole and traced the edges with his fingers. The wood was not rotten, as he'd originally assumed. Instead, it had been sawn nearly clean through. Someone had set a trap for the first person unlucky enough to walk through the door!

At the bottom of the small hole, no more than a few feet down, was an even more grisly discovery: a series of sharp implements, jutting upward like the fangs of some demented subterranean beast. Shards of jagged glass and splinters of roughly shorn wood for the most part. Jim stood, looking around the entrance hall.

Where there was one trap, there was bound to be more. Suspicions began to crystallize. But still, it didn't feel right. Why would Gaines remain here? And if he wasn't here, who had Jim seen at the window?

The stink of strange spices filled the air as Jim moved slowly down the hall. Following his nose, Jim came to what he assumed was the sitting room. His gut churned as he saw what had been done to it.

In his life, Jim had seen many strange sights, many things that so-called civilized men might consider hideous in their archaic beauty. Strange relics of bygone times where modern standards of artistry and design had no place. All of it he could appreciate on its own terms. Beauty is as beauty does, as his father had said.

But what he saw in that room was nothing less than a desecration. Strange metal tripods sat haphazardly around the room, the odor of heavy incense emanating from their flared maws. Bowls of rotting fruit and meat were scattered at different spots, offerings of some kind. Signs and sigils of unknown origin had been drawn and carved into the stripped surfaces of the walls and floor. Over the remains of two toppled shelves, a large brass shield had been hung on the wall.

Jim stared at it, entranced by the Deimos' grinning face emblazoned on the surface of the shield. It seemed to speak to him, that face, with a vast hollow voice that echoed up out of time's black heart.

He reached out, his fingers caressing the metal. It was not cold, as he'd expected, but warm. Almost like flesh. Jim's skin crawled. The empty eyes of Deimos stared down at him, looking through him. Jim stepped back, feeling slightly nauseous.

On the floor, beneath the shield, was a spatter of dried blood. More spatters dotted the floorboards here and there. Evidence of weeks of sacrifices.

Suddenly, he recalled the newspaper articles he'd noticed earlier...the missing children in Red Hook. And what had St. Cyprian said? 'The fear of children'....

"Oh, God," Jim croaked, sickened. What atrocities had been committed in this room, he wondered. He could almost see the faces of the dead, swirling around him, bleeding through the walls, mouths open in mute agony. Ethereal hands groped for him, plucking at his clothing, begging for help that would never come.

"No."

He closed his eyes, feeling the familiar tingle of drug-induced panic clawing at the edges of his reason. He felt greasy, as if the air were thick with some unseen substance. Backing away from the wall and its hideous decoration, Jim made his way carefully out of the room.

In the hall, his heartbeat slowed. He was reminded of the sensation he felt upon leaving his grandfather's sweat lodge. A sense of relief, as if some massive pressure had been lifted from him.

"The braziers," he murmured. "No wonder ...." It seemed the cult did more than use fear as a weapon. It appeared to be central to their very existence. No wonder they displayed no concept of their own mortality. He could only imagine what being exposed to the substance, whatever its origins, on a regular basis would do to their biological and psychological functions.

"Nothing good," he said, more to break the inhuman stillness of the house than any compelling need to speak. Suddenly, the whole house seemed threatening, a predatory presence, like he'd felt once before in the den of a mountain lion that he'd hunted as a young man.

Overhead, a board creaked. Jim's head snapped up, and he suddenly recalled why he'd come in the first place. He turned towards the stairs, bounding up them two at a time.

The stairs creaked beneath his weight, and a vision of the deadfall in front of the door filled his head. Jim, hand on the banister, swung himself up to the landing with a grunt. Turning, he examined the stairs. True to his suspicions, his keen gaze caught the telltale marks of tampering. Shuddering slightly, he turned away from the stairs.

A door closed, quietly. Instantly on alert, Jim padded forward, following the noise, pistol in hand. He knew that it was obviously a trap. Someone had turned Oscar Gaines' family home into a weapon. Whether he was the intended target or not, he was here now, in the belly of the beast.

He stopped as he came to the edge of a rug that extended down the hall to a door that was open just a crack. Jim hesitated, then sank to his haunches and threw back the edge of the rug, revealing yet another deadfall. Unoriginal, but in the event of the police storming the house, it was a method of ensuring casualties and paranoid caution in the invaders.

A play for time, in other words.

Frowning, Jim slid around the hole, creeping along the wall towards the door. Why would they need to play for time? All of Jim's encounters with Metus and his crew to this point implied an organization that was intent on keeping its secrets to itself.

Was this just a backup plan, just in case things unraveled to a certain point? Or was it something else? Jim had dealt with masters of misdirection before, the devil Fantomas of Paris, for one. A hooded monster whose plans were never what they seemed and who spun webs within webs. Jim had nearly lost his life that time; indeed, he had come closer that time than in many times since.

What if his initial conclusions were correct? What if Metus was following through with some monstrous ineffable plan, of which Jim was only aware of this, the final phase?

Pushing those thoughts aside, Jim reached the door and carefully pushed it inward. He felt a tension in the hinges, and craned his neck around, looking up.

A shotgun was mounted just above the door, a string connecting its trigger to the door. Jim stared up at the double barrels and raised his pistol. He fired, taking out the chock that held the shotgun in its position. The weapon fell and Jim caught it, keeping the barrel aimed away from himself. Holstering his pistol, Jim stepped into the room, shotgun held at the ready.

The room was large and full of books. Free-standing shelves occupied most of the free space and the walls had been converted into still more shelves. It was a bibliophile's paradise, with sagging stacks of books occupying odd corners and out of the way spots.

Jim moved through the shelves quietly, his senses strained to the utmost. He caught no sound, no hint of movement beyond his own.

The books on the shelves were old, most of them. Leather bound volumes, shipping charts and log books and account records. Mixed among them were works by Cervantes and Poe and other, more esoteric artists. A good deal of those that weren't fiction or some form of record book seemed to deal with the history of the Mediterranean. Warning bells flared in Jim's mind.

The chair sat in front of the large window that looked out over the street. Jim stopped. Judging by the curtains, this was the window he'd seen the figure at earlier.

A hand dangled over the edge of the chair. Jim stepped closer, finger on the trigger. Reaching out, he took hold of the chair and jerked it around with a burst of strength, scraping the polished wood of the floor.

A dead man grinned up at him, skin tight and graying on his skull. Jim stepped back, coughing as the smell hit him full force. Bags of incense had been draped across the body, but this close they were less than effective in killing the stink of decomposition. Hemp ropes bound the body to the chair at the wrists and ankles.

Controlling his gag reflex, Jim set aside the shotgun and took hold of the dead man's jaw. Carefully, he twisted it from one side to the other, checking for wounds. There were none. However, in the sunlight dripping through the half-parted curtains, Jim saw that something glistened on the man's desiccated lips.

Jim stepped around the chair and ripped the curtains down with a flick of his wrist. He squatted, looking up into the face of the man he assumed was Oscar Gaines, and wondered how much he had suffered when someone, Metus, most likely, had smeared the fear-jelly on his lips and tied him to a chair clad in nothing but a dressing gown, leaving him to drown in his own terror.

Jim looked at the window again, wondering what Gaines had seen, as he stared through the window and boiled in his own terror. What nightmares had flown at him through that rounded panel of glass? Which one had, at the last, killed him?

For that was surely what had happened, considering all of the evidence at hand. The only question now was how long had Gaines been dead?

From the rate of decomposition, and the insect life suffusing his flesh, Jim knew that the answer wasn't the one he wanted. Gaines had been dead at least a week, perhaps more. Far longer than the others, save perhaps Tupker.

Which meant that the likelihood of Gaines being the mastermind behind things was growing slimmer with every second.

In what was becoming a far too familiar action, Jim cursed himself for his blindness. It had all been too neat, hadn't it? Facts lined up like dominos, dropping into his hands and propelling him along to this spot, where the proverbial rug was pulled out from under him.

Docker. It had always been Docker. He should have known when Harpootlian had displayed no knowledge of Metus; knowledge that Docker had mentioned he had.

Had Docker contacted Gaines? Or had Gaines done the contacting, then been betrayed? Who had Metus been working for, if anyone?

Jim reached out to search the corpse's dressing gown for anything useful. As his fingers spread the edges of the gown, something wobbled into view and tumbled out, crashing to the floor.

Jim tensed instinctively, ready for a burst of fear gas. Instead, there was a terrible flash of light and a thunderous explosion that blasted him backwards, straight out the window!

27.

Jim flew backwards, smashing through the window and plummeting down the slope of the roof. He crashed to a halt, scattering broken shingles, and rolled towards the edge, his mind sluggish and his body unresponsive.

As he swept over the edge, he forced a hand out, grabbing the gutter. It peeled away, slowing his descent enough to prevent him from crashing into the lawn below. Instead, he dropped into an awkward crouch, head ringing. His clothes were smoldering, the edges charred. He shrugged out of his coat, which had thankfully absorbed the brunt of the blast, and stumbled away from the house.

The upper story was wreathed in an unpleasant looking blue flame. Something about it sparked a memory in Jim's rattled skull, of another of Da Vinci's inventions, a crude incendiary device.

His wounded arm had gone numb, and there was a trickle of blood running down his face from a cut somewhere near his hairline. Jim's vision went for a moment, causing him to nearly pitch to the ground.

He regained his balance, spinning around. It was only for that reason that he saw the pair of men approaching him, Thompsons clutched in their hands. A black car idled on the side of the street.

The Thompsons opened up, playing a familiar Chicago melody. The ground around Jim's feet sputtered and tore as he forced himself to move. He darted for the only available cover, which was, unfortunately, the burning house.

The duo followed him, firing as they came, obviously unconcerned about the attentions of any neighbors. Then, why would they be?

Jim scrambled up onto the porch and crashed through the door, knocking it from its hinges. It fell across the maw of the deadfall, and Jim rolled into the house. Tendrils of smoke were already creeping down the stairs and the heat was growing oppressive. Jim pulled himself into a sitting position just beside the door, and yanked his pistol free of the holster.

It wasn't going to do him much good, but it was all he had. Blinking blood out of his eyes, Jim craned his neck to peer around the door frame. A Thompson roared and wooden splinters flew. Jim replied in kind, firing blind.

The Thompsons fell silent suddenly.

"Mr. Anthony?" a voice called out. Jim recognized it immediately: Metus. "Mr. Anthony, are you still with us?"

"Oh yes," Jim called back. "Tip-top and in fighting trim."

"Ha," Metus said. "Somehow I doubt that. It is past time for us to end this affair, Mr. Anthony."

"Couldn't agree more!" Jim checked the clip of his automatic. "If you surrender now, I'll do my best to ensure a fair trial."

122

Jim slid around the hole, creeping along the wall
towards the door.

"You have a sense of humor. It serves you well. It is unfortunate that things must come to this."

"You don't sound all that unhappy," Jim said, slapping the half-empty clip back into place. "Then, you could be hiding it. An Austrian gentleman by the name of Freud had a lot to say about that kind of thing."

A Thompson opened up and Jim hunched forward as more splinters and crumbled spackling rained down on him. "Something I said?" he called out.

"Merely reminding you that humor has its place, Mr. Anthony." Jim heard the steps leading up to the porch creak. "In other times, our people found new blood amongst the ranks of the enemy. Among the Turks and the Romans we found many recruits. Men who knew the face of terror for what it is."

"And what is that?"

"It is the face of change, Mr. Anthony. The face of evolution itself, red in tooth and claw," Metus said. Jim stood slowly, then swung around the door frame, his pistol extended. Metus didn't so much as blink as the barrel lined up with the bridge of his nose. He wasn't wearing his mask.

"Abernathy?" Jim said. Metus chuckled.

"Ah." A thin smile crept across his bland features. "I have many names, Mr. Anthony. I wear them like hats."

"You worked as a clerk for Samuel Harpootlian," Jim said. "Keeping tabs on things?"

"Perhaps I am a clerk, Mr. Anthony."

"Hardly. I'm betting that if you weren't wearing gloves, the only calluses I'd see on your hands would be from gripping a sword. No typewriter toughened fingertips, or old paper cuts." Jim cocked his head, peering over Metus' shoulder. The two men were standing at opposite angles, with Metus ready to cut him in half if he so much as twitched. "Do a condemned man a favor and explain things?"

"Are you condemned?" Metus said, spreading his hands. "It doesn't have to end this way."

"No?"

"No. As I said, we have often recruited from the ranks of our bitterest foes. Terror is a sudden thing, Mr. Anthony. A bellicose, roaring hurricane that sweeps down and burns the world behind it. It turns old allegiances to ashes and allows new loyalties to grow in their place."

"Sounds like a sales pitch," Jim said. Metus' smile flickered.

"Perhaps it is. Dead wood must be burned clean in order to allow new growth to occur. Thus it is with societies."

"Interesting theory. You should write a book."

"I have," Metus said. Jim grunted in surprise. Metus brought his hands together. "There are more ways than the obvious to set a fire. But fires and the elements that create an effective flame cost money."

"Now I know it's a sales pitch," Jim said.

"I'm selling nothing. Rather, I am giving you everything," Metus said, holding out a hand and closing it into a fist. "The power to control the destiny of nations,

Mr. Anthony."

"Is that what you offered to Gaines?"

"Perhaps."

"What about Docker? Harpootlian?"

"Our beneficence knows no bounds."

"And yet you killed them anyway," Jim said. Metus smiled.

"We all serve in our own capacity, each to his own measure."

"Even with your death?"

"It is all the same."

"Not even close." Jim's finger tapped the trigger of his pistol. "Not to me. You murdered those men, and for what?"

"I told you," Metus said, inching back. "The good of society."

"Whose society? Yours?"

"Ours is the only one that counts, Mr. Anthony," Metus said. Jim's mouth tightened.

"What about the others? The children?"

Metus paused. Jim continued. "Dead children. I found the bones. Does Deimos feed on the innocent as well as the guilty?"

"All lives are his to use or dispose of," Metus said. "I can see that my words are wasted on you. You have not yet felt full terror, despite my best efforts."

"Full terror? Enough to drive me insane, you mean." Jim's smile was hard. "Worse monsters than you have tried, chum. I'm still here, mind intact."

"But what of your body?" Metus said, then, with a sinuous lunge, he hurled himself aside, yelling, "Kill him!"

Jim cursed and fired, but not quickly enough as the Thompsons bellowed, shredding the porch around him. He was forced backwards, into the burning house. The fire had finally reached the first level, and as he stepped back inside, heat swept over him, nearly knocking him from his feet.

He heard popping sounds, and realized that the contents of the incense braziers in the sitting room were exploding. He wondered what would get him first, the poisonous gases the fire had released to mingle with the smoke or the flames themselves.

Coughing, Jim headed towards the back of the house, hoping to find another way out. The ceiling groaned, and orange light bled through the cracks as the boards above his head warped and blackened.

Smoke filled the hall as he made his way towards where he assumed the kitchen to be. Most of these old houses followed the same design pattern. He hoped that Gaines hadn't made an alteration to the scheme.

Behind him, he heard glass shatter as the heat caused the windows to explode out of their frames. Hand over his mouth, he pressed on.

The back door rose before him out of the smoke and Jim took it down with one kick as the heat clawed at him. A machine gun chattered agitatedly, driving him backwards. He fell onto the tiled floor, snarling.

Of course Metus would have positioned men at the back. Of course! Jim staggered to his feet, his lungs heaving, trying to drag in clean oxygen. There was little to be had. Bits of burning material dropped down onto him in a steady drizzle. Smoke boiled around him, marring his vision and crippling his other senses.

He could hear voices outside, but not what they said. More gunfire. He couldn't worry about that now, though. Blind, deaf and choking, Jim knew he wouldn't last long if he made another try for the outside. Which left only one direction.

Down.

Eyes burning with tears, he swung around, looking for the entrance to the wine cellar. Gaines had to have one. Every house in the district had one. With a growl of triumph, Jim saw it and stumbled forward, his fingers fumbling with the latch. The metal was hot enough to blister his fingers, but he ignored it and yanked the door open.

He tumbled down the stairs, his clothes smoldering. The floor of the cellar was dirt, as with most older houses, and the walls were cold stone. So long as the stone of the ceiling held up, he might just make it.

Still coughing, Jim began to examine the walls, looking for another way out. New York had been built over the bones of New Amsterdam, and many houses had roots dating from that time; roots which had bolt- holes, in case of attack. As swiftly as he was able, he ran his hands over the roughly stacked stone of the walls, ignoring the smoke that was creeping beneath the bottom of the cellar door.

As he went, he muttered a soft hymn in Comanche, one his mother had taught him as a child. It was a nonsense song and a subconscious thing, a sign that the stress was taking its toll on him.

However, the liquid trill of his mother's language helped calm his racing mind. Combined with the breathing exercises he'd learned in Tibet, Jim managed to push the atavistic panic that came with being trapped in an inferno from his mind.

Then, beneath his probing fingers, a series of bricks gave way. They tumbled inward, into a hidden tunnel. Jim breathed a sigh of relief and pushed harder, causing the ancient mortar to crumble further. He stepped through the rain of bricks and dust and into a dank, narrow scar of earth that arched back only a few feet. Less a tunnel than a slope, it angled upwards. Rotted wooden steps had been wedged into the dirt and Jim took them gingerly. A wooden platform had been set over the opening to hide it.

Jim struck it with his palms. Dirt shifted down, dropping into his face and hair. It had been buried, but not packed down. Just enough to protect it from the elements. Jim tensed his muscles and struck upwards again. The skin of his knuckles split as he punched through the wood with both fists and drove his arms shoulder deep into the dirt.

Then he began to climb, burrowing upwards blindly. His fingers breached the skin of the earth after an eon of torturous seconds and light fell upon him. Jim clawed his way up and out, kneeling on the edge of the pit.

Gaines' house had gone up completely, becoming a roaring firestorm. The sirens of approaching police cars and fire engines split the air.

Jim got to his feet and turned, only to find himself staring up into the barrel of a pistol!

28.

"**J**immy?" Tom said, jaw dropping. He lowered his pistol and swept Jim into a bone crushing hug. Jim patted his friend on the back weakly.

"Tom? Tommy! Can't—breathe—"

"Aw, geez," Tom said, releasing Jim. "I thought you were dead," he continued.

Jim nodded. "I know. I almost was. If it hadn't been for that escape tunnel …." He trailed off. "Where's Cat?"

"Safe. I parked the car down the street, near the cops. She's in a sea of blue, Jimmy. No worries. What the hell happened?"

"Three guesses. The first two don't count," Jim said. He coughed again, leaning forward, his hands on his knees. Tom patted him on the back.

"By the time we got around the block, the house was already burning. When we stopped there was a black car parked up the street. Must have taken off not long after I got to the back of the house. Guess that was them?"

"Yes," Jim said, straightening. "They were waiting to see if I was coming out. They must think I'm dead."

"Is that good?"

"It's not bad," Jim said. He looked down at his hands, which were cracked and bleeding.

Tom cursed. "Jimmy, we need to get you to the hospital!"

"I was just thinking the same thing," Jim said, scuffing blood off of his cheek. "Let's go."

With Tom supporting him, Jim made his way through the cordon being set up at the end of the street by the police. The officers, recognizing Jim, gave them no trouble as Tom helped him into the back of the Rolls.

Of Catherine Kilkenny, however, there was no sign. Jim looked at Tom. "Tom? I thought you said you left her here?"

"I did! Right here!" Tom said, then, with a curse, he swept his cap off of his head and tossed it down. Uttering foul Gaelic oaths, Tom grabbed the nearest policeman. "The dame! Where'd she go?"

"She said something about having to catch a plane," the cop said, prying Tom's hands off. "Nabbed a taxi right after you ran towards the house."

"A plane?" Tom swung around to look at Jim. "What the hell was she talking about?"

"I have a sneaking suspicion. We need to get to the hospital, Tom. Now," Jim said.

As Tom drove, Jim began to outline his theory. "It all makes a horrid sort of sense, I suppose. Judging by his library, at least what I saw of it, Gaines had an interest in the history of the Mediterranean, as well as the occult. He must have taken a trip at some point and made contact with the Cult of Deimos. Maybe he invited them back here to set up shop, or maybe they invited themselves.

"Regardless, when they got here, they set about doing what they always do."

"Which was?" Tom said, swerving through traffic, his fist connecting with the horn.

"They looked for funding. Money for the cult coffers. But not to make themselves wealthy. No, they used money itself as a weapon. A lance-stroke into the heart of civilization. The papers Docker showed me, the entries in Smithback's notebook, even the detritus of Gaines' library all told the same story, just from different angles. The cult used the money of powerful men to gnaw at the edges of society, supporting terrorists, murderers and monsters of all stripes. They engineered disasters and insurrections." Jim shook his head. "A monstrous, ineffable scheme that has been in play for centuries."

"Why? I mean, what for? Just to cause trouble?"

"Just to cause terror, Tom. Terror," Jim said, making a fist. "They are spreading their unholy gospel, my friend. Missionaries of hate and murder, they spread the influence of their abominable deity across the world with the help of a few greedy, ignorant fools. Or perhaps not so ignorant."

"You're talking about the shyster, aren't you? Harpootlian?" Tom said. Jim shook his head.

"No. I wish I was. Gaines may have brought them here, willingly or not, but someone else has been using them to his own advantage."

"But if it wasn't the lawyer, who was it?"

"Pongo," Jim said brusquely. Tom fell silent. "It had to have been Pongo. He implicated the others in order to throw suspicion off of himself. I began to suspect when he sobered up so quickly after I confronted him. But why would he go to such lengths to involve me?"

"Maybe he really wants your help?"

"Or maybe he thought to scare them from their track. To use me to keep them at bay." Jim sat back, rubbing his shoulder gingerly. "No. No, I caught him out, without realizing it, so relieved was I to see him alive." He sighed. "He investigated what was going on for his own purposes, not to ferret out trouble. Maybe he himself was behind the creation of that group, after making contact with Gaines' guests." Jim pounded a fist into his palm. "Maybe it was blackmail material. Maybe he wanted to protect himself from being dealt with in a similar fashion to the others, but he was in on it regardless. It was Docker's earlier phone call, when I was setting my trap that cemented his guilt in my mind."

"Yeah?" Tom said.

"If Gaines was already dead, who did Pongo talk to?" Jim said harshly. "Maybe the cult, or at least its representatives here in New York, decided to work with a more dynamic individual in pursuit of their goals. Gaines was old money, old ideas. But Docker is a new breed. A Twentieth Century man, with Twentieth Century talents."

"Hell, Jimmy. You think he faked getting plugged at the Cloud Club?"

"Maybe. Or maybe Harpootlian didn't die as easily as we thought." Jim closed his eyes and massaged his temples. "If we're lucky, we can ask Docker when we get to the hospital."

"And if we ain't?" Tom said. "Lucky, I mean."

"Then it's up to Cat to tell us where they're going," Jim said.

"You think you know where she was going?"

"Of course. She's following the black car," Jim said. "It was optimistic to think she'd sit back and be content to watch. No, I'd wager my fortune that she hared off after Metus and his cronies."

Tom whistled. "Wondered why you weren't more worried."

"Oh, I'm worried," Jim said softly. "Very worried. I assume you gave her a gun?"

Tom grunted. Jim smiled thinly. "Of course you did. Real bullets as well, I expect. Did she wheedle it out of you, or did you offer?"

"She told me she could shoot!"

"I expect she can. Full of talents, that woman." Jim settled back, his head throbbing. "Nothing for it now…" he said, then trailed off as exhaustion finally overcame him.

Still, Jim did not sleep. Not entirely. Instead he fell into a complex state of what he'd come to call 'hypermeditation'. It was a trick he'd learned, not in Tibet, but in the pueblos of the Navajo in the American Southwest.

Head tilted back, Jim allowed his body to go limp against the plush seats, letting the pent-up aggression and the dregs of the adrenaline that had thus far sustained him flood out. He pushed all complex thought aside in favor of soothing emptiness; an emptiness which encouraged his incredible metabolism to spring into overdrive.

While his physiology was less superhuman than some had made it out to be, it was still far past that of even the hardiest athletes. And thanks to the complicated mental processes he had stamped onto the very meat of his brain via constant repetition and practice, he could push past the natural limits imposed on the human frame. The trickle of blood from the slash on his brow slowed to a drizzle, then stopped entirely, already beginning to clot and scab. His shoulder, slightly inflamed, began to leak pus and serum, cleaning itself in the process.

All of the aches and pains Jim had accumulated over the course of the past few days, the strained muscles, bruised ligaments and battered joints, were flushed from his system as he descended deeper and deeper into his own mind. In the twenty minutes it took Tom to get them to the uptown hospital where Docker was being seen to, Jim's body had had the equivalent of three days bed rest.

"Jimmy?"

Jim's eyes popped open. Tom was looking at him over the back of the seat. "We're here. Looks like something is going on. New York's Finest are all over, running around like chickens with their heads cut off."

"Damn." Jim sat up and slid out of the car. "Keep the engine running. I have a feeling we won't be here long."

Without waiting for a reply, Jim was already heading for the entrance. A police officer tried to stop him until he caught sight of Jim's face. Then he fell into stride beside him and escorted him upstairs.

"Anthony!" Healy barked, as he caught sight of Jim. "You look like hell!"

"Nice to see you too, Detective," Jim said. He caught a passing nurse by the arm. "Gauze, please? And burn ointment, if there's any to be had. Doctor Brownlee will vouch for me."

As the nurse rushed to complete his request, Jim turned back to Healy. The detective looked ill-used and angry, more so than usual. "What's wrong?"

"The evidence." Healy bit the end of the word off.

"What about it?"

"It's gone. All of it."

"All of it?" Jim was momentarily taken aback. Healy gave a snarl.

"Every blasted bit of it! Gone! Ka-put!" He swept his hat off and crushed it between his hands. "Some jackass signed it out of evidence with a faked court order!"

"How do you know it was fake?" Jim said. The nurse returned, carrying a tray with gauze, ointment and a needle and thread. As she held up a mirror, Jim gently cleaned the wound on his head and then sewed it shut.

"It was old. Like something someone had gotten out of the trash and re-typed it!"

"Like, say, a legal clerk?" Jim said as he snipped off the excess thread. "Of course. What about the evidence from the Cloud Club?"

"The truck went missing," Healy snapped. "Can't raise it on the radio. Got cars out looking, but I'm betting it's in the river."

"Hopefully your drivers, at least, are safe. What about Harpootlian's offices?"

"There we're steady. For now." Healy tried to get his hat back into shape. "I got a half dozen men there. And another three at Smithback's offices. The DA's getting a writ to let us confiscate everything we can lay hands on, including everything in your buddy Docker's apartment."

Jim nodded, putting ointment on his hands. When he finished, he allowed the nurse to bandage them, leaving his fingers free. "Speaking of Docker," he said.

Healy's face flushed. Jim watched a vein in his head throb, then said, "He's gone, isn't he?"

"I had two men watching the door. Apparently they watched him walk out!" Healy said, turning to direct his last words to the two shame-faced looking officers standing nearby. "Or were you two idiots too busy flirting with the nurses?"

"It doesn't matter, Detective. What's done is done," Jim said quickly, taking pity on the two men. "I assume that's what the hubbub was about when I came in? You're looking?"

"Got the whole hospital cordoned off, but I'm betting he's already gone," Healy said. "Witnesses say they saw a black car waiting at the back entrance."

"Of course." Jim frowned. Healy shook his head.

"He's in the wind, Anthony. And we've got no clue where he's going …."

"I wouldn't say that, Detective. In fact, I think I have a pretty good idea."

"What?" Healy blinked. Jim flexed his bandaged hands.

"I said, I think I know where he's going. The airfield. A private one, near Newark. I have a plane there myself."

"Of course you do," Healy grumbled. "What about it?"

"So does Docker. He's smart enough to know you'll be looking for him. He and his accomplices will be looking to get out of the country as quickly as possible now that they've done what they came here to do."

"And that was?"

"I don't know. Not yet. But I think we should go ask, don't you?"

"I knew there was a reason I tolerated you, Anthony," Healy said. He slapped his hat back on his head. "What are we waiting for?"

29.

The Rolls-Royce sped through the city streets, followed by a half-dozen police cars, sirens screeching. In the front passenger's seat, Jim checked the clip of the oddly-shaped pistol in his hand. It had a thick barrel and a drum-shaped clip, making it resemble nothing so much as a shrunken Thompson machine gun.

"Thirty alternating rounds. Mercy, knockout, and solid," Jim said, as Tom wrenched the wheel this way and that. "One pistol for each of us. Breathing masks as well. And bullet-proof vests." He slapped the bag he'd taken out of the trunk before they'd set out. "Keep the mask on, no matter what. And the vest as well."

"I hate that damn thing," Tom grumbled. "Makes me feel all bound up."

"Good. That means it's doing its job." Jim smiled. "Wear it. Try not to get shot. Again."

"Once. One time!"

"Twice," Jim corrected. Tom spared him a glare, before returning his attentions back to the street.

"Fine, twice. You think Kilkenny is okay?"

"If she's as a good a reporter as she claims, yes." Jim wrestled his vest on and fastened the straps. "I should have expected that she'd hold some bit of information back for herself. She's too much the journalist to give away everything."

"You saying she knew what they were up to?" Tom said incredulously. Jim shook his head.

"No. But she knew that Docker had a private plane. And Cat can put two and two together as easily, easier, I'd say, as anyone. When she saw that Gaines' house was up in flames, she probably assumed that he was dead. Leaving Docker as the only survivor. And if someone you knew were the only survivor of a criminal conspiracy, what would you suspect?"

"That he was probably behind it," Tom said, nodding. "Ha! You think she's gone to confront him?"

"I don't honestly know," Jim said, with slight reluctance. "I'm hoping she's just gone to watch. But if not, all the more reason for us to get there as soon as possible!"

"Working on it, Jimmy!" Tom said, stamping on the gas. Jim hoped Healy had alerted the airport personnel that they were coming. Any delays on their part could mean the difference between arriving just in time or far too late. And if it was the latter, the chance of Cat being hurt in some fashion increased exponentially.

Jim pushed aside the statistics with a silent growl. The airfield came into sight, just beyond a light fence that ran along the driver's side of the road. Jim pointed.

"There's the private airfield."

"So how do we get in?" Tom said. "Do we gotta call someone?"

"Pull off the road. Here." Jim gestured. Tom obliged and the police escort followed suit. Healy was out and about even as Jim stepped towards the fence.

"What the hell are you playing at?" Healy snarled. "We got to get in there!"

"They'll be waiting," Jim said, bluntly. "Do you want another punch-up? Or do you want this handled clean?"

"Both," Healy said, straight-faced. Jim snorted.

"I'm going in first. I need to see whether or not Cat, Ms. Kilkenny I mean, is snooping around, and if so, I need to get her out of the line of fire." He pointed at Healy. "You, on the other hand, need to cover the exits from the airfield, and be ready to go in when I say. And not before."

"So you're in charge now, huh?" Healy said with a smile. "Fine, we'll play it that way. Go do your thing. We'll wait for you." Healy extended a hand.

Jim hesitated a moment, then took it. "Thank you."

"Don't mention it. Really."

Jim looked at Tom. "Stay with Healy. I'll be back before you know it."

"But—" Tom began.

"No. I need someone here I can trust. Just in case." Tom glanced at the police, then back at Tom. "Twenty minutes. Just like Montenegro."

"Hell with that. That was one of the times I got shot."

Jim smiled, turned and vaulted up the fence, barely seeming to touch it before he was landing on the other side. He had left his pistol in the car, but had brought his war-knife.

He swept it out as he loped towards the distant hangars, finding its weight comforting. The knife had been a gift from his grandfather upon Jim's ascendance to manhood, and he'd put it to necessary, if ugly, use many times.

Now, he stabbed the blade into the ground to dull the sheen, then padded forward, weaving amongst the buildings of the airfield.

He stopped short as the sound of gravel crunching beneath boot-heels reached him. Jim crouched in the shadows, waiting to see whether the approaching feet belonged to a security guard or someone altogether less innocent.

It proved to be the latter. The man was clad in black, and wearing a heavy coat. He clasped a shotgun in his hands. Jim caught the dull glint of armor and heard the rattle of glass. He moved swiftly, reversing his knife and sweeping off the man's hat with his free hand. As the guard turned, Jim thumped him with the heavy horn haft of the knife. The man's eyes crossed and he fell backwards. Jim snagged him and lowered him gently to the ground.

He dragged him into the shadow of an unused hangar and bound him with the straps of his armor. Jim shrugged on the man's coat and snatched his mask, placing it over his lower jaw. He left the glass globes where they lay, not wanting to risk contact with them. He took the shotgun, however, thinking it might be necessary. Especially if Cat had gotten herself into trouble.

With the coat, hat and mask, Jim thought he stood a good chance of passing for the sentry at a distance. The disguise wouldn't hold up forever, though. He would need to be quick; find Cat and get out, before the shooting started.

Jim moved back the way the sentry had come, cradling the shotgun in the crook of his arm, his eyes picking out the forms of other sentries here and there. He felt their eyes flicker over him and then away, his muscles inadvertently tensing every time. One or two were on the roofs of hangars. Others waited behind makeshift barricades. None of them spoke to him, for which he was grateful, but their positioning bespoke of preparation.

Granted, it could have been business as normal amongst this group, but somehow he doubted it. No, Metus was preparing for the worst. The airfield was a killing ground. But only if the invading force came via the usual channels. Jim stopped and turned. The fence line was unguarded. He filed that fact away and continued on.

He found the security force for the airfield a few minutes later. The bodies had been stacked like wood behind a hangar, throats cut and clothing removed. Jim paused, memorizing the pale, stiff faces and added to the mental tab he was keeping in Metus' name.

In his youth, he wouldn't have hesitated to kill a man like Metus. But the War had taught Jim Anthony mercy. Where every day was a blood-soaked nightmare, one soon yearned not to add to the butcher's list. Metus would hang, or fry, or rot in prison as the State of New York decided, and Jim was well glad to bear none of that responsibility.

He moved on, and caught sight of a number of barricades being set up around a brightly colored hangar. A stylized wild cat was emblazoned on the sloping roof of the building, and Jim recognized it as Docker's. The men took little notice of him, but Jim watched them out of the corner of his eye, taking note of their numbers and weapons.

His skin crawled beneath his borrowed coat as he passed close to the barricade. All it would take is one look, a little too close, and he would be facing an army. Not odds he relished.

Carefully, he moved around the building, trying to act as inconspicuous as possible. At the back, a number of crates and oil drums were stacked. Jim climbed them quickly, peering in through the hangar's back window.

Men were gathered around a plane, speaking softly among themselves. Docker stood among them, silent and pale, clutching himself. Jim tried to find Metus, but couldn't spot him.

Something rattled above him. He looked up, then swallowed the curse that had sprung unbidden to his lips. Above him, crawling awkwardly up the sheet metal roof of the hangar, was Catherine Kilkenny, a camera dangling from around her neck.

As Jim watched, shocked, Cat reached a section of the roof where a section of sheet was loose. She shifted the camera around and Jim recognized it as the subminiature camera he kept stowed in his Rolls-Royce. Cat was working it like a professional, and she snapped shot after shot of the gathering in the hangar.

Unfortunately, she did not see the two forms creeping towards her. But Jim did. He hauled himself up onto the roof and scampered upwards, hand over hand. Cat heard his approach and turned, her eyes widening.

"Oh shi—"

Jim slung the shotgun like a boomerang, catching one of the creepers across the face and sending him rolling down the roof with a loud clatter. The second leaped over Cat and drew his spatha. Jim tore off his coat and snapped it around his forearm as a makeshift shield just in time. Even so, the sword cut through the material with enough force to numb Jim's arm, only stopping when it became snagged. Jim pulled his arm back, yanking the spatha out of the cultist's grip.

Jim slid forward, the metal roof creaking beneath his feet, and drove a fist into the killer's side, where the armor gapped. The man staggered with a grunt. Jim took advantage of his opponent's disorientation and cracked his elbow into the man's forehead.

A dagger ripped up, skittering off of his borrowed mask. Jim stumbled, nearly losing his balance. He drew his own knife and stepped back, falling into a knife-fighting stance. His opponent dropped into a similar crouch.

"J—Jimmy?" Cat said, getting to her feet.

"Cat, I'm not going to ask how you even got up here. Just get down. Head for the fence-line," Jim said, without looking at her.

"But—"

"Now!" Jim said, as the cultist lunged. The knife sliced through his shirt. Jim could hear shouts below. Cat was moving slowly. The knife came in again, this time drawing a thin drizzle of blood from his hand. Out of the corner of his eye, Cat stumbled, fell, and began to slide down the roof. He turned as the knife dug for his kidney.

Jim swayed aside and his instincts took over. He looped an arm around the man's throat and slammed his knife up through a gap in the armor, angling for his opponent's heart. Jim let the body fall as he moved towards Cat, sliding after her. But not fast enough. Not close enough.

"Grab my hand!" he said, uselessly.

"Jimmy!" Cat yelped. And then she was over and gone. Jim halted his slide, digging his fingers into the metal, terror sweeping over him. Moving towards the edge, his mind conjured images of the worst, images which he swiftly quashed. It wasn't that far to the ground. At the worst, a concussion. Maybe a broken limb, if she landed wrong.

She was fine. She had to be fine. Jim stopped inches from the edge. From below, he heard voices. Slowly, cautiously, he peered over.

Cat lay on the ground. Around her, the servants of Deimos stood. Jim counted silently, praying. Then he saw her lips part and her chest rise and fall.

Just unconscious. Relief flooded him.

"It's the reporter!" Docker said, stumping forward. "The one following Anthony around."

"Then he must not be far behind," Metus said, following him. He turned, looking up. Jim froze, knowing there was no way the man below could see him. And yet—

"Maybe. Or maybe she came on her own," Docker said, squatting. He brushed his fingers through her hair, then reached into her coat. "Hunh." He pulled out the pistol Tom had given her, his eyes narrowing.

Metus spun and began relaying orders to his men. He looked down at Docker. "Kill her."

"No, we might need her," Docker said.

"Why?"

"Bargaining chip," Docker said. Metus snorted.

"We need no such thing."

"Better to have it and not need it, than need it and not have it." Docker gestured with the pistol. Metus stared at him, and Jim tensed, preparing to spring down among them. Then, the cultist shrugged.

"Fine. She can die later." He gestured and two of his men hauled Cat to her feet. "Get her to the plane." He looked at Docker. "You as well. We leave in twenty minutes."

Twenty minutes. Jim closed his eyes, thinking fast. He looked up, gauging the distance between the roof he was on and the next. Backing up the slope of the roof, he stood and ran, hurtling across the gap and landing with barely a sound. He charged up the slope, his knife in hand, heading for the sentries that might prove troublesome for Healy's bunch. They couldn't afford to be slowed down. Not with Cat's life at stake.

He bounded from hangar to hangar, trying to ignore the sense that he was abandoning Cat. But he needed to get to Healy and Tom. He couldn't save her on his own. Too many variables. Too many chances for failure. He couldn't afford that. Cat couldn't afford that.

Jim's thoughts flashed across the surface of his mind like lightning in a bottle. Calculating angles and avenues of attack, discarding them even as he bounded between buildings with ape-like agility.

On the third roof, he clocked a sentry, driving the pommel of his knife across the back of the man's skull with perhaps a touch more force than necessary. Jim was moving even as the body slumped. He didn't bother to check for a pulse. The sense of the last dregs of sand dribbling through the waist of an hourglass hung over him, forcing him to move faster. There was no time.

The second guard almost caught sight of him, but Jim swung around, sliding down on him, driving his heels into the cultist's chest. The man fell without a sound, tumbling to the ground. Jim didn't wait to see whether he got up. No time.

On the last hangar, he swept the rifle from the sentry's grip as the cultist whirled, and cracked the butt of the weapon against the man's temple. Breathing roughly, Jim crouched over the body, taking a moment to control his breathing.

Three men, out of the game, in less than ten minutes. He rose and dropped off the edge of the hangar.

He kept low as he raced across the field, heading back for the fence. Crashing into it, he visibly spooked the police there, and as he dropped down onto the other side, a bevy of weapons were aimed in his direction.

Jim rose to his feet, hands spread. "Time to go," he said.

30.

"**W**ell?" Healy said. Alone among the gathered police, he hadn't budged at Jim's sudden appearance.

"We have to move, now," Jim said, stripping off the borrowed mask and tossing it aside. He squatted and drove his knife into the ground, cleaning it. This done, he stood and sheathed it. "They've got her."

"Who? Kilkenny? They're welcome to her," Healy said. Jim's hand snapped out, grabbing a handful of Healy's shirt. A red haze suffused his mind. Anger at Healy, for his insensitivity. At himself, for failing Cat. At Metus for the deaths to his name. He hefted the detective up into the air, and bared his teeth.

"Let me go!" Healy said, grabbing at Jim's wrist. Jim's response was to lift him higher. Healy's cheap shoes were a foot above the ground before anyone else could react.

"Jim! Jimmy!" Tom yelped, grabbing him. "Put him down! We got no time for this."

Jim hesitated, then dropped Healy, who plopped onto his rear on the ground. Several officers moved forward, but Healy waved them back. "I'm fine. Landed on my pride." Healy peered at Jim, who blew out a noisy breath. "That's another I owe you, Anthony."

"Add it to the list," Jim grated. "Men on the roofs of the hangars. I got most of them, but they might have noticed by now. They're ready for us. Do your men still have the equipment I loaned you?"

"Every man jack." Healy jammed a cigarette between his lips. "What's the plan?"

"We go in. Follow us, we'll take the brunt. The Rolls is armored."

Healy nodded and turned. "Everyone back in the cars. We got some heads to bust! Move!"

"Thanks," Jim said, watching Healy move away.

Tom nodded. "Think nothing of it, Jimmy. Besides, like I said, no time." He gestured to the car. "Get in."

Tom pulled onto the road. "Now what? Which way are we going? Any ideas—"

Jim grabbed the wheel and shoved it around, throwing the car into a half-moon spin and sending it crashing through the fence and onto the airfield.

"Or we just do it that way. Okay," Tom said, taking hold of the wheel once more. "Could have just said, Jimmy."

"Sorry, Tom. Time is of the essence, as you said." Jim gestured. "Keep going straight. If I recall correctly, Docker's hangar is at the end of this row." He glanced over his shoulder. The police were doggedly following. Jim could practically hear Healy's curses. He grinned.

No gunfire dogged them as they sped down the row. The hangar at the end was abuzz with activity as the Rolls swept towards it. Men in masks were running back and forth, putting the finishing touches on the impromptu barricade to protect the runway extending from the hangar. A plane was already taxiing out, propellers spinning sluggishly.

Bullets struck the hood of the Rolls and the strengthened glass of the windshield, creating a spider web of cracks. "Guess they were waiting for us," Tom said. "Just like you said."

"How about that," Jim said. "Go straight through. No stopping."

"No stopping?"

"We need to break up that barricade, otherwise Healy and the others will be stuck slugging it out with whatever suicidal killers Metus leaves behind." Jim hefted a heavy pistol and switched off the safety. "And I need to get to that plane."

"Going to be tough," Tom said. Jim fitted his gas mask about his face.

"That's what I pay you for. Remember your mask." Jim crouched in his seat. Tom spun the wheel, slinging the car sideways into the makeshift barricade, even as Jim tumbled out of his open door.

Pistol spitting fire, Jim sprang to his feet as the oil drums and wooden crates set up as part of the barricade tumbled down around him. Men in masks rushed towards Jim, and spathas cut the air. He stepped aside, avoiding one blow, and drove the heel of his hand into the bridge of its owner's nose. The man dropped like a stone. Jim spun on his heel, firing short, controlled bursts.

A quick count, and Jim saw that there were no more than a half-dozen of the fanatical killers in evidence. He put another one down with a well-placed shot, sending the man spinning.

The police were already taking up positions. Tom, his vest in place and his mask fitted to his face, stepped through the hole in the barricade, firing his own pistol. A cultist staggered, Tom's shots singing off of his cuirass. The big Irishman grabbed the man by his gorget and spun him into the side of the Rolls hard enough to dent it.

Healy, standing on the running board of a car, lifted a Thompson in one hand and sprayed the area with a steady stream of bullets and curses as his driver carried them through the hole Jim and Tom had made. The detective hopped off, kicked a chunk of crate out of his way and emptied the Thompson's drum, sending cultists scrambling for cover.

Glass shattered on the ground as fear-globes were hurled. Jim, in his mask, ignored the gas, knowing it would disperse quickly out in the open as it was. He concentrated on heading for the plane, which was rolling forward quickly. Jim ejected the clip from his pistol and slapped a smaller one in place. Taking careful aim at the back of the plane, he fired. Then he sped up, trying to reach the front of the plane. If he could damage an engine, or even get inside, he might be able to prevent it from taking off. But just in case, the round he'd fired would prove useful.

Jim was under the wing now, keeping pace with the plane. The door on the side was flung open. Cat's wide-eyed face appeared, an arm wrapped around her throat and a pistol pressed to her temple.

"Now!" Jim said, as the cultist lunged.

"Jimmy! You know how this goes, I expect!" Docker bellowed, loud enough to be heard over the plane's engines. "Back off or the lady gets it!"

"Pongo! This is idiotic! What makes you think you can get away?" Jim shouted in reply.

Docker said nothing, merely shoving his gun tighter against Cat's head. Jim couldn't hear her whimper, but he recognized the look in her eyes. And that look was something he couldn't bear.

Jim stopped moving. He stepped back, hands spread. His pistol fell to the ground. Docker's eyes widened.

"Good move, Jimmy! Good move!"

A few moments later, Docker shoved Cat out of the plane, even as it rushed down the runway. She stumbled down the tarmac, arms flailing wildly until finally she lay still. Jim raced forward, reaching Cat even as she sat up.

"You idiot! He's getting away! They're getting away!" she snapped.

"No, they're not." Jim untied the ropes that bound her wrists. "Not for long anyway. I attached a tracking dart to the plane."

"A tracking dart?"

"I like to plan ahead," Jim said, helping her to her feet. "Unlike some people. What were you thinking, going off alone like that?"

"I was thinking that it'd be a great opportunity for an interview," Cat said snidely. "Seriously, Jimmy? You have to ask?" Jim looked at her and she sighed. "Fine. I'm sorry I didn't tell you, but I needed to know I was right."

"About?"

"Docker. I pegged him from the start," she said. "As soon as I saw the smoke, I knew I was right. It was all too pat, Jimmy. Too clean. If he really had needed your help, he would've—"

"Come to me directly, yes, I know. I suspected as well," Jim said, taking her hand and pulling her into the cover of a parked car. "I thought we were sharing information, Cat."

"So did I," she said. "But you didn't mention your suspicions either."

"Point." Jim peered around the front of the car. A bullet spanged off the chrome and he jerked his head back. "And you knew that he'd be needing to leave as quickly as possible."

"Which meant either a plane or a boat. Docker was the only one who owned either." Cat said, pulling the loose ropes from her wrists and hurling them aside. "Journalist, Jimmy. Remember?" She sighed and crossed her arms. "I figured he was trying to get away from you *and* those religious nuts. Like maybe he'd double-crossed them to handle his pals."

"Only it turned out that he was working with them instead. Which is why you should have waited for me!"

"What, and let Healy send me home? No, thanks!"

"Did he say anything to you? Docker, I mean. Did he mention where they might be going?"

"It was all Greek to me, Jimmy. They were speaking some funny language."

Jim surged to his feet and extended an arm. A running man connected with the rigid limb and dropped heavily, gagging. Jim fell onto him, shoving his fingers into the man's mouth, but too late. Jim sat back with a cry of disgust as foam billowed at the corners of the man's mouth and he jerked in his death throes.

"Damn. Tom?" Jim said.

Tom hurried towards him. "Jimmy, did you find her?"

"I'm right here, you great Irish loon," Cat said, pulling herself up. "Was that you shooting at us?"

"I never," Tom said. "The plane just took off, Jimmy. Did you manage to get one of those tracking-thingies onto it?"

"Got it. If you'll get the plane ready, I'll get the tracker out of the Rolls," Jim said, looking down at the body. He shook his head. "What a waste."

Tom moved to comply, even as Healy arrived, smoking pistol still clenched in one hand. "They put up a good fight," he said.

"They've had practice. But for once, we moved too quickly for them." Jim looked back at the runway. "Unfortunately, it still wasn't quick enough."

"Yeah. I saw that. We got any clue where they're going?"

"No. But I intend to follow them, so it's a moot point."

"You intend to what?" Healy's jaw sagged as an engine coughed to life and rolled out of a hangar further up the row. Tom waved from the pilot's seat.

The plane was a Sopwith Camel, almost twenty years out of date, but lovingly maintained. Its propellers sputtered and then picked up speed.

"What the hell is that?" Healy said.

"My ride. I brought it back from the War. Cost quite a bit, but I had a sentimental attachment to it, you could say." Jim went to the Rolls and opened the trunk. He rummaged through the gear strapped inside and pulled out a device shaped like a radio-receiver. Jim turned it on, and smiled. "Excellent. It works."

Jim looked at Healy and Cat. "Detective, if you could see to Ms. Kilkenny's safety, I'd be obliged. Cat, it's a two-seater, so don't even ask. I'll be back!" Jim turned and sprinted for the plane before either could reply. He pulled himself up into the spotter's seat even as Tom took them out onto the runway.

"Into the wild blue yonder, Jimmy?" Tom said.

"Where else?" Jim said. "Up, up and away."

31.

The Sopwith cut through the air like a bird in flight, rising up over Newark and falling into line on the trail of the other plane.

"Just stay on this heading. They're moving out over the Atlantic," Jim said, leaning forward to be heard over the shriek of the slipstream. He patted the radio-receiver on his lap. "With the tracer, we can track them anywhere."

"I admit Jimmy, when you came up with that thing, I was skeptical," Tom said. "But it'll come in handy. The sun is setting," he continued, pointing towards the horizon. The sun was descending into the ocean in a brilliant display of raw color.

"Can you fly this thing at night?" Jim said.

"I can fly anything, anytime, Jimmy! You know that."

"Just making sure, pal," Jim said.

"So, how we playing this?" Tom shouted back. "Try and make 'em land, or what?"

"I was thinking something more creative," Jim said.

"It better not be what I think you're thinking," Tom said. "Because that didn't work so well in Marseille."

"We're not in Marseille, Tom."

"No, we're over the Atlantic Ocean, or we soon will be! Less chance of a handy tree breaking your fall, Jimmy!"

"True, but we don't have enough fuel to keep pace with them forever, and I refuse to let them escape!" Jim pounded a fist on the side of the Camel. "Not after everything we've been through. I want answers, and Docker is going to give them to me!"

"Don't have to tell me twice, Jimmy, but still—"

"When we spot them, get as close as possible," Jim said, his tone brooking no argument. "I'll do the rest."

"Fine, but don't come crying to me when you fall off!"

"If I fall off I won't be able to come crying to you, Tom," Jim said, smiling slightly.

The geography of the Upper New York Bay passed below. Jim could see Staten Island coming up. The shape of the Statue of Liberty loomed in the distance, and Jim fought down an impulse to salute.

Docker's private plane was a powerful thing, but he couldn't be intending to make the trans-Atlantic flight in it. No, there had to be another reason. A boat perhaps? Waiting just off of the Northeastern shore of Staten Island, hiding in plain sight in the harbor?

Yes, Jim decided. A boat. A fishing vessel, or a merchantman. That was what he'd do. A boat bound for some Asian port, carrying its passengers out of American or European jurisdiction.

142

Some minutes later, the bulky shape of Pongo Docker's private plane came into sight. It was flying low, and Jim motioned for Tom to get above and alongside, if possible.

It was a tricky maneuver he had planned, but if it worked, he'd have the element of surprise on his side. If it didn't—well, he wouldn't be worried about it for long.

Regardless of the danger, Jim realized that it was very likely his only chance to wrap up this whole fiasco in a satisfactory manner. They had enough evidence to look into the business dealings of Docker's consortium, but that wouldn't go far. They could freeze Docker's assets, even ruin him financially, but that wasn't the same as punishing the murderers of Smithback, Tupker, Pender, Harpootlian and Gaines with good, old-fashioned American justice.

And, though he was loath to admit it, even to himself, Jim was just petty enough to want to tangle with Metus one more time. The leader of the Cult of Deimos had bested him at every encounter they'd had. It was going to be immensely satisfying to see him behind bars.

"Jimmy! If you're going to try and pull off this stunt of yours, you need to be getting ready!" Tom said, pulling Jim from his thoughts. Jim looked over the side as Tom banked slightly to the right, putting them slightly ahead of the Prohaska six-seater that was carrying Docker and his accomplice to God alone knew where.

The stocky-bodied twin-engine Polish aircraft was one of only a few dozen available for purchase. Jim had considered buying one himself, but decided that the relatively low-altitude plane was an extravagance. It was designed for comfort rather than speed, something Jim now intended to take advantage of.

Swiftly, he doffed his bulletproof vest and shoes, discarding everything but the clothes he wore and the breathing mask hanging from his neck. He placed that over his mouth and nose and pulled the straps tight.

Then, taking a deep breath, Jim lifted himself from his seat and took hold of the base of the top wing of the Sopwith. Slowly, slowly, Jim stepped out onto the wing, fighting to maintain his balance against the wind, even as Ormer Locklear had taught him during the War.

Granted, Locklear had died two years later, but Jim was certain that that had simply been bad luck. He swung himself along, moving towards the tip of the wing closest to the Prohaska. It wouldn't be long before they were noticed.

Braced against the wind, his hands clutching the sponsons to either side of him, Jim glanced over his shoulder at Tom. Tom nodded and thrust the control stick forward, forcing the Sopwith ahead and above the Prohaska.

Jim closed his eyes, trying to control the thunder of his own heart. He counted to five, then let go of the wing.

He fell forward for only a moment before the wind caught him and hurled him back, tumbling head over heels over the wing of the other plane. Fingers like curled iron hooks crashed against the material of the wing, puncturing it, as Jim held on for dear life, wrestling himself from the wind's clutches and onto the Prohaska's wing. The plane dipped slightly at the addition of his weight.

Tom peeled away, curving back and around, falling in behind. Jim, pressed flat to the surface of the wing, began to haul himself hand over hand towards the body of the plane. His shirt, already ripped in places, was shredded by the wind and pulled loose from his muscular frame.

Reaching the end of the wing, Jim gripped its edge and swung himself beneath it, planting his bare feet against the side of the plane itself. He swung back, then forward, kicking the door to the passenger compartment with his full weight.

The door buckled under the weight, and on the next swing, Jim was able to slide his fingers between the edge of the door and the frame. Hanging from the wing by one hand, bare feet planted to either side, Jim's shoulders bunched like a clump of steel cable. The door popped loose with a howl of tortured metal, then went shooting past him, ripped free of its hinges.

Papers and debris swirled around Jim as he lunged inside, the cabin depressurizing instantly. Two men were waiting for him, one with a pistol that snapped and snarled. Jim ducked beneath the shot, snatching aside the man's wrist and driving his fist into the gunman's belly. The cultist dropped to his knees, coughing, and his face met Jim's knee coming up.

The second cultist came in high with a thin blade knife, something old and Italian, driving towards the top of Jim's skull. Jim weaved to the side, letting the blade pass over his shoulder, and grabbed the man's arm with both of his, bringing his shoulder up against the trapped elbow. Bone snapped like brittle candy, and the man screamed. Jim swung him around by his broken arm and drove him face first into a seat.

Standing over the two men, Jim eyed the remaining occupants of the passenger compartment. "Pongo," he said. "Fancy meeting you here."

"J-Jimmy? How—" Docker gabbled, half-rising from his seat. Metus, sitting across the aisle from him, gave a bark of laughter that was stolen by the wind whipping through the compartment.

"Excellent. Excellent!" He rose and shoved Docker back into his seat. "How I hoped that we wouldn't leave it at that. How I hoped that the fire hadn't done for you. When Docker mentioned seeing you at the airfield, I scarcely credited him."

"Happy to be of service," Jim said, falling into a fighting stance, fingers spread, legs braced. "Give it up, boys. One way or another, you're done. And your scheme, whatever it was, with you!"

"No!" Docker rose, thrusting his pistol towards Jim. "No, I fought too hard for this! You don't understand!"

"Silence, Docker," Metus said.

"Explain it to me, Pongo," Jim said. "Explain to me how you can work with a man like this, knowing what he and those like him have done!" He looked from one man to the other. "Was it you from the start? Was it Gaines? Have you accomplished anything other than a waste of life?"

"Life itself is wasted unless given in service to something greater, Mr. Anthony," Metus said, silencing Docker with a gesture. "You should know that better than anyone."

"Pretend I don't," Jim said. "Explain it to me."

Metus began to unbutton the coat he wore. "Change and growth are violent things, Mr. Anthony. Born of war and horror. We follow that horror, guide it to where it will do the most good. The Mark of Deimos can mean the difference between stagnation and evolution." The coat fell to the floor, revealing the strange cuirass that Metus wore. It wasn't the crab-shell thing that Jim had come to associate with the group; instead it was a single chest plate dotted with numerous holes in the shape of a demon's face. And beyond those holes, something that wept and smoked.

"We seek to guide the world to Paradise, to Aaru, to the Fortunate Isle, to the Elysian Fields and the House of Song, Mr. Anthony. But such nirvana is only accomplished through the purging of all that is wicked."

Metus stretched bare arms, revealing intricate tattoos that crawled from his wrists to his shoulders and beneath his chest-plate. "And the wicked may only be purged through terror, Mr. Anthony. Through the sword of dread."

"You're insane," Jim said. Metus nodded.

"Yes. For only the mad may walk with God. Every faith says so." He held out a hand. "I ask you again, Mr. Anthony. Give me your hand. Join us. With your wealth, your influence, we could spread the Gospel of Terror from sea to sea. We could drown the world in blood and skim the worthy from the froth."

Jim felt light-headed. The face on Metus' chest seemed to grimace and snarl. The thin trail of smoke rising from the odd holes widened and swirled around him, pulled by the wind. On Metus' arms, the tattoos seemed to undulate and coil. Jim stepped back, gripping the seats to steady himself. Even with the aid of his breath-mask, he felt ill. Sick to his stomach. Sparks danced across the line of his vision, twisting and writhing, forming into nightmare shapes that tried to catch his attention.

"Join us. Join the Sons of Terror, and aid us in our father's holy work," Metus said softly, drawing closer to Jim, his eyes seeming to glow with purpose. "We will make this world better, Mr. Anthony. We will stay the waters of entropy and say, 'this far and no further.'"

Gorgons and ghosts clutched at Jim with unearthly talons. He knew they weren't there, but he could feel them all the same. Metus reached through the tangle of phantoms, his fingers stretching towards Jim's face.

"No," Jim said, his hand shooting out to grab the neckline of the chest-plate. At the same second, he lashed out with a foot, catching Metus on the hip. The chest-plate came away with a snapping sound as its straps broke. Metus' bare chest, a motley assortment of tattoos just like his arms, was revealed. Jim hurled the chest-plate out of the open door of the plane.

Metus staggered back, his bland features twisting in rage. "You fool!"

"I'll make the world better on my own terms, thanks," Jim said hoarsely. He knew he was lucky that the combination of the wind and his mask had prevented him from feeling the worst of the effects of that strange aegis. "And I'll start by bringing you both in."

Jim was suddenly hurled backwards as the plane went into an dive! Plastered against the pilot's compartment, Jim ripped aside the curtain and saw the pilot slumped over the controls, mouth covered in poisonous foam. And beyond the windscreen, the ocean rose up to meet the plummeting plane!

32.

Metus laughed as he hung onto the seats.

"Did you honestly think we were going to fly to freedom, Mr. Anthony? That we would not know that you would have men waiting for us at every airfield within the fuel-range of this plane?"

"I didn't figure that meant you were going to commit suicide, no," Jim said, twisting around to glare up at Metus.

"What you call suicide, I call sacrifice!" Metus crowed, releasing his hold and crashing into Jim. Fingers sought Jim's throat. Jim grabbed the other man's wrists. "We will die together, Mr. Anthony, both of us for our causes, both of us for the greater glory of Deimos!"

"Oh, shut up!" Jim snapped, ramming his head into Metus' face. The man reeled back, clutching his face. Jim knew he'd only have a few moments in which to act. As Metus stumbled away, Jim dove for the controls, hoping to pull the plane out of its death-dive!

An arm snaked around his throat, halting him mere inches from his goal. "Oh, no, Mr. Anthony! Today is Deimos' Day! Today you die!" Metus wrapped the fingers of his other hand into Jim's hair and hauled his head back. "And you die without knowing what any of this was about!"

"No!"

The bullet caught Metus on the side of the skull, spattering blood across the windshield. His grip slackened and Jim shoved him backwards instinctively. Metus flailed, twirling towards the open door and only just stopped himself from flying out, gripping either side of the doorway, his eyes glassy.

Jim grabbed the control lever and jerked the plane up out of its dive, hurling the Prohaska upwards into the darkening sky. Then he turned.

"Pongo?" he said.

Docker, pistol clutched in one trembling hand, pulled himself along the aisle. He kept the gun aimed at Metus. "I don't want to die, Jimmy. Not for anything. I'd rather rot in jail until I've got a beard to my shins than face the worm."

"Pongo, give me the pistol," Jim said, reaching towards the man he'd once called friend. Docker stepped back, swinging the pistol wildly.

"No! I've got to finish him, Jimmy! If we don't, he'll just come back!" Docker said. "You've got to protect me from them! I'll tell you everything, if you just help me!"

"No!" Metus snarled, throwing out his long arms and grabbing Docker by the throat. Even as Jim rushed to intervene, the pistol roared once, twice, and then a final time.

Metus staggered back, eyes wide, but he didn't release his hold on Docker. Jim lunged, but not far enough as Metus fell back, out of the plane, and pulled the screaming Docker with him!

Jim threw himself forward, reaching out, knowing it was useless even as he did it. Docker's screams were swallowed up by the wind and the rumble of the night ocean. Jim took a moment to mourn the man he'd known, before he'd become someone else entirely.

Then, Jim was up and shoving the body out of the pilot's chair. The fuel tanks were almost empty. Metus hadn't been lying about not intending to make it. Jim set the plane on a course for Staten Island and crossed his fingers.

It took another two hours for anyone to find him. The Prohaska, no puddle-jumper, had dug into the soft beach at a cock-eyed angle, and water lapped around the base of one wing. Jim stood nearby, waiting, his arms crossed.

As the boats from the mainland approached, he stared out at the ocean, wondering if there was any point in dragging the area. He was reasonably certain that Metus was dead, even as all of the men he'd brought to New York from wherever were. And poor Pongo with him.

And for what? He still wasn't sure. The money? Had this been merely a foraging operation? A way of restocking the coffers and covering the tracks of a strange, secretive society that seemed to thrive on death and fear?

Or was it something more?

Metus had seemed intimately familiar with Jim, with who he was. Had that simply been the knowledge of an enemy cultivated by a seasoned warrior? Maybe something Docker had told them? Or was it something more intimate?

Jim couldn't help feeling that his path had crossed that of the followers of Deimos more than once prior to this week. Prior, even, to his confrontation earlier in the year with the poisoner, Soames.

Pongo's notes certainly seemed to imply such. That Jim had, without knowing it, been engaged in foiling the activities of these madmen for some time. Perhaps they had decided to take a more active part because of that.

Had all of this been simply one more move in a long game that he was playing, albeit unawares? And if so…who was winning this shadow tournament?

"Anthony! What the hell happened?" Healy was the first man off the Harbor Patrol boat. "Where are they?"

"Gone," Jim said.

"Gone? What do you mean 'gone'?" Healy barked.

"I mean gone, Detective," Jim said. "Docker is dead. They're all dead."

"Hrm." Healy took off his hat and turned to look at the water. Officers swarmed over the downed plane. "Your pal Gentry made it back okay. Just."

"I assumed so."

"Yeah." Healy looked at him. "We've got a lot of bodies and a story straight out of the pulps to go with 'em."

"Does seem that way, doesn't it?" Jim said. He shook himself. "I tried to stop it."

"I know," Healy said. Jim looked at him in some surprise. Healy shrugged.

"I saw you try and save that stooge at the Cloud Club, Anthony, remember?"

147

The detective looked up. "Get out of here. I'll let you know if we find anything." Healy coughed into his fist. "Oh, and about earlier…."

"Yes?"

"I'm sorry."

Jim opened his mouth to speak, then closed it and trotted towards the boats. At the city harbor, Tom was waiting with Cat. As Jim climbed up onto the dock, she rushed towards him. Jim opened his arms, but Cat stopped just short.

"What happened?" she said. "Leave out no detail, Anthony, or I'll make you rue the day! Gimme the skinny!"

Jim lowered his arms. "Yes, I survived. No, no, Cat, don't worry. I'm fine."

"Of course you're fine," she said. "Now spill!"

"Later," Jim said, pulling her close. Cat resisted for a moment, then came willingly. Jim heard the sound of a pencil scratching across paper. "Are you writing while we share an intimate moment?"

"No?"

"Okay. Later. I'll tell you everything." Jim stepped back. Tom stepped forward and the two men clasped hands.

"I admit, I didn't think that stunt would work, Jimmy."

"It almost didn't," Jim said.

"Docker?" Tom said softly.

Jim shook his head. "I couldn't save him."

"I'm sorry Jimmy."

"He made his choice," Jim said. He looked back at Cat. "By the by, next time you get caught, I'm not rescuing you."

"Who asked you to? That story could have made my career! A Pulitzer, at the very least! Reporter Uncovers Ancient Conspiracy!" Cat gestured. "I could have written my own ticket with that kind of scoop."

"You could also have been dead," Jim said.

"But I'm not," Cat said. She smiled. "Thanks to you." She stepped forward, locking her arms around the back of his neck and pressing her lips full against his. The kiss held for several moments, until a cough from Tom caused Cat to step back. She gently chucked Jim on the chin.

"Go take five, wild-man. I've got to get a write-up on what the boys in blue are doing now that everything is over or Bushkin will skin me alive."

"Breakfast, then?" Jim said.

"Who knows, Jimmy? This story ain't gonna put itself to bed!" she said over her shoulder as she started towards the boat that had brought Jim back. "Hey! You! Harbor guy! What's it gonna take for a gal to get a lift?" she shouted.

"Woman ain't nothing but trouble," Tom said, lighting a cigarette.

Jim smiled. "She is, isn't she?"

"Still. She hasn't tried to kill you."

"Yes," Jim said.

"Yet," Tom said, flicking his spent match away. "Ready to go, Jimmy?"

"Ready to collapse, more like," Jim said.

The ride back to the Waldorf-Anthony was quiet. Jim didn't mind, as the silence gave him time to collect his thoughts on the events of the past few days.

At the penthouse, Dawkins was waiting, as always. Tom slumped off to sleep, and Dawkins, observant as always, retired, leaving his employer alone on the balcony.

Jim looked out over the city and breathed a silent sigh of relief that not even the faintest trace of vertigo colored his senses. Dawkins had left the morning mail on the balcony table, and Jim idly flipped through it.

A white card slid out of the pile of envelopes. The mark of terror grinned up at him.

Jim looked up without touching it, his breath coiling around his head like a halo in the moonlight. His hands clenched into fists, then relaxed.

"No. No, I don't think so," he said out loud. Maybe it had been delivered earlier. Maybe not.

But it didn't matter, in the end. If he was a participant in some twisted game, then he would win. Even if he had to cheat.

Jim smiled, and it was the smile of a tiger on the prowl, suddenly alerted to the presence of fresh game in its territory.

Whether they had intended for it to be so, or not, the cult of Deimos had caught his attention. And now, Jim Anthony, Super-Detective, was on the case and one way or another, he'd bring them to heel.

He could do no less.

The End

ABOUT OUR CREATORS

AUTHOR:

JOSHUA M. REYNOLDS is a freelance writer of moderate skill and exceptional confidence. He has written a bit, and some of it was even published. For money. By real people. His work has appeared in anthologies such as Cthulhu Unbound 2, and in periodicals such as Innsmouth Free Press.

Feel free to stop by his blog, [http://joshuamreynolds.blogspot.com/] and cast aspersions on his character.

INTERIOR ILLUSTRATOR:

ISAAC "BOBIT" NACILLA is a Filipino freelance illustrator/artist. He has various illustration projects in his name ranging from character designs, children's books illustration, comic strips and editorial cartoons. Although an upstart in comic art and spot illustration, his long experience in various other projects has helped prepare him to produce quality illustrations for books. He takes inspiration from the works of great comic artists whom he considers as his influences namely John Byrne, Jim Lee, Erik Larsen, Rudy Nebres, Nestor Redondo and Whilce Portacio. For samples of his works kindly visit www.guhitkamay.multiply.com

COVER ARTIST:

JEFF HERNDON is a freelance artist located in Fort Collins, Colorado. Drawing inspiration from the movies he loved as a kid, he puts his imagination to work with every stroke. He studied the figure, design and composition but is happiest when all three come together in illustration. Bringing both imagination and realism to the canvas, Jeff has a knack for bringing characters to life.

Jeff has been drawing since he was a small child and has been an avid painter since college. He does not discriminate when it comes to materials, he's versatile in almost any medium. He devotes his time to a variety of projects. Whether it's designing creatures, costumes or covers above all things, Jeff is a story teller.

Besides painting his days away, he spends as much time as possible with his sweetheart and their fish.

Check out more of Jeff's work at www.JeffHerndon.com.

JIM ANTHONY SUPER-DETECTIVE

Airship 27 Productions is thrilled to present the all new adventures of one of pulpdom's most cherished two-fisted action heroes, Jim Anthony Super-Detective. Half Irish, half Comanche and all American, Jim Anthony is the near perfect human being in both physical strength and superior mental intellect. He's a scientific genius with degrees in all the major fields. Operating from his penthouse suite, which also houses his private research laboratory, he ventures forth into the world at large as a champion of justice, a modern knight righting wrongs and defending the helpless.

Follow the "super-detective's" all-new adventures in these volumes written by today's best New Pulp Authors.

PULSE-POUNDING PULP EXCITEMENT
from AIRSHIP 27:

This is just a small sampling of the thrilling tales available from Airship 27 and its award-winning bullpen of the best New Pulp writers and artists. Set in the era in which they were created and in the same non-stop-action style, here are the characters that thrilled a generation in all-new stories alongside new creations cast in the same mold!

"Airship 27...should be remembered for finally closing the gap between pulps and slicks and giving pulp heroes and archetypes the polish they always deserved." –William Maynard ("The Terror of Fu Manchu.")

www.ingramcontent.com/pod-product-compliance
Lightning Source LLC
Chambersburg PA
CBHW071919220626
47052CB00002B/427

The cycle of Xhól

Book 1
The Merchant of Death

by
Cécile Chabot

translated by
Cécile Chabot & Anna Doherty

IN WHICH THE AUTHOR IS TOLD A STORY

ONE NIGHT, IN A forsaken inn of Alta Verapaz, a man of a certain age approached my table as I was finishing my meal and asked in ceremonial Spanish if he could speak to me. I looked him over and liked what I saw: the awkward smile revealing a gold inlay in his left incisor, the well-worn hat kneaded by nervous fingers and the proud and intelligent gaze, despite the shyness. From his faded shirt to his rubber boots, nothing set him apart from the locals. I pushed away the plate on which some black beans in a thick sauce were congealing, and invited him to have a drink. He sat down with dignity and, instead of alcohol, he ordered coffee. That is how, one evening at the end of the rainy season, I became acquainted with Don Pepe.

After a few minutes of conversation about the weather (no worse than usual) and family (his), he came to the purpose of his visit.

'I hear that you are looking for caves?'

'Yes, indeed.'

'And that you are interested in relics? In pottery shards?'

I let him take his time, knowing full well that it would serve no purpose to hurry him to get to the point.

'But most of those found in entrance porches are broken.'

'Yes,' I answered cautiously.

'Would you be interested if I took you to a place where there are unbroken ones?'

'A place where looters haven't been?'

'Yes, a site that nobody knows about,' he replied with confidence. 'Just me.'

'How can that be?'

'Well, it is far away, in the forest. When I gather chicle, I go as far as possible to avoid trouble with my neighbours, two young lads who are too strong for me. So, I go deep into the forest, over there in the hills,' he said, gesturing vaguely towards the east. 'And one day, I came across this cave.'

'What cave?'

'A cave that nobody knows. It has no name. There is no community out there, you know. It is very far from everything.'

'How far?'

'Well,' replied my new friend, 'at least a five-hour walk from the end of the dirt road.'

'The end of the road?'

'Yes, the one that goes to Rinconcito, then to the Gomez lands. It stops at the edge of a lagoon where the cattle are brought to drink. After that, one walks. Five hours. Maybe more,' he added, casting a puzzled glance at me.

'Five hours. Maybe more,' I pondered, sizing up the rake-thin man. Better to plan for eight, if not more.

'Yes, that's interesting. But how can we go there if it's so far from everything?'

'We could take the bus as far as Rinconcito and walk from there,' answered Don Pepe.

'It will take us one day to get there and back. Probably two, if I want to spend a little time there exploring this cave. Is that all right with you?' I asked. 'By the way, what is the cave like?' I added with fatalistic resignation.

I had learned over the last weeks that all the caves that were suggested to me were 'big, very big' and that they were all bound to go 'deep, very deep'. Except that, when I arrived at the said 'cave', it often turned out to be, at best, a rock shelter a few metres long or at worst a narrow tunnel filled with spiders that could only have been used by a tepezcuintl*, and a tepezcuintl not too particular about its lodgings at that. After three weeks of this little game, I had learned that caution was a useful virtue.

Don Pepe was different, and not just on the question of alcohol (I later learned why he didn't care for rum). He gave me exact details about the height of the entrance porch, its width, the large chamber inside, and the small passage that branched off the left wall. He seemed to see the cave unfold before his eyes while he was talking to me, to remember the path. He could not have made all that up. He must have seen it. In any case, it was the most precise and promising description I'd heard during this prospecting campaign. It had to be checked out.

That is how, the next morning at five o'clock, Don Pepe and I met again in front of the church and waited for the first microbus to Rinconcito. Taking advantage of the fact that we were still alone, I gave him one hundred and fifty quetzals as his first-day wage and confirmed that he would receive the same amount per additional day spent guiding me.

Many hours of bussing and walking later, we arrived late in the afternoon in front of an entrance porch leading to the promised treasures: a large chamber, shards of pottery, even whole pieces encrusted in calcite. I drew several sketches, took pictures, and left everything in place.

---

* Tepezcuintl or *Cuniculus Paca*: common rodent of Central America, sometimes confused with its cousin, the agouti.

We then went out of the cave and, given the late hour, decided to sleep under the porch. Don Pepe was surprised, surprised that I didn't touch anything, surprised that I didn't want to take the pottery away. In front of the small fire on which we heated the leftover stew, packed for me by the cook at the inn, we had a lengthy discussion, about these relics from another time, my contacts with some archaeologists to whom I would communicate this discovery, looters, and the harshness of the times that transformed them all into the gravediggers of their own culture. That night, I discovered, underneath the uneducated chiclero, a layer of infinite sadness for this past that he did not understand, which was disappearing under the assaults of looters, collectors, and the forest, that devourer of ruins. We talked for several hours, and then we each wrapped ourselves in our blanket.

This conversation stayed with me for a long time, and I can only suppose that it stayed with Don Pepe too because, when I came back the following year, he welcomed me with a broad smile and said he had a surprise for me. I asked him whether it was another cave.

'No,' he answered, his eternal coffee in front of him, 'better'.

'Better?'

'Yes, I convinced someone to talk to you.'

'Who is that?' I asked.

'My aunt.'

'Your aunt?' I replied, unable to disguise my surprise.

'How could he have a still living aunt?' I thought, while I quickly tried to do some mental calculations.

'Yes, my father's older sister. We live long in our family,' he continued, with a slight smile at my surprised look. 'I told her about the cave from last year,' he went on, with a grave face. 'She liked it. She liked that you left everything in its place. She thought a lot over the winter and when we were told that you were back——'

'You were told?'

'Yes, what do you think? It wasn't two hours from the moment you got off the San José bus before the whole village knew. And so, my aunt would like to see you.'

That was how Don Pepe took me to his aunt, and he stayed for the entire conversation, translating a large portion of it because his aunt was not comfortable with Spanish and preferred to express herself in K'iche'.

What Don Pepe's aunt told me so was stupefying that I stopped prospecting. That year, I just returned day after day to the little smoky cabin and, in the dancing shadows of the fire, listened to the calm voice of Don Pepe translating the stories of an old lady, shrivelled up like a badly preserved mummy. Hunched over the sturdy notebook bound in grey canvas in which I kept my prospection notes, I transcribed her story.

I was mesmerised by the sing-song voice speaking in an unknown language and listened as she told me what she had learned from her aunt before her, tales which, according to the family tradition, dated back to 'before'—before their arrival in this valley, before the arrival of the Spanish, before the new religion—from a time when the first woman of the family had heard these tales from the mouth of her uncle, her uncle the painter.

I took notes at top speed in the short time at my disposal for this expedition (I had to be back in Belgium by the end of the month), seizing this extraordinary opportunity. And rightly so because the following year when I returned to the little village lost in Alta Verapaz, I learned that the Bocay family had left, that they had moved away; Don Pepe, his sister, and the children had all left for nobody knew where. Some said La Democracia, others Nueva Jerusalem or even Guatemala la Ciudad, following the youngest son who had found some work there. They were all sure of one thing: the aunt was already dead by the time they left, from a bad cold that had seized her at the end of the rainy season and turned into pneumonia.

All that was left of my encounter with Don Pepe's aunt were these hastily transcribed pages. At that time, I thought no more about it and continued with the expedition (I was not alone that year, and we were able to explore some of the caves I had recorded in previous years).

It was not until many years later, moving out for the third time since, that I came across a sturdy notebook bound in grey canvas abandoned at the bottom of a box. On the verge of throwing it away, I held back and began to leaf through the dog-eared notebook. I forgot about moving, sat down on the floor in the middle of the half-empty room, and began to read. A voice rang from the distant past, a hesitant voice, a voice hardened with age, singing in K'iche'. As soon as I landed in my new flat, I got my computer out and began to compile the story the name of which struck me as obvious: *The Cycle of Xhól*, from the name of that distant ancestor, first to tell the tale to his niece (Itzel?).

In copying those notes, I realised that, during my first, hasty transcription, I must have made some mistakes or misunderstood certain passages, or Don Pepe himself might have incorrectly translated certain K'iche' terms into Spanish. Too many years have gone by now for me to have any hope of finding him again. Therefore, I have done my best to address these omissions or errors to allow for a fluid and, I hope, pleasant read.

Cécile Chabot
Brussels, November 2012

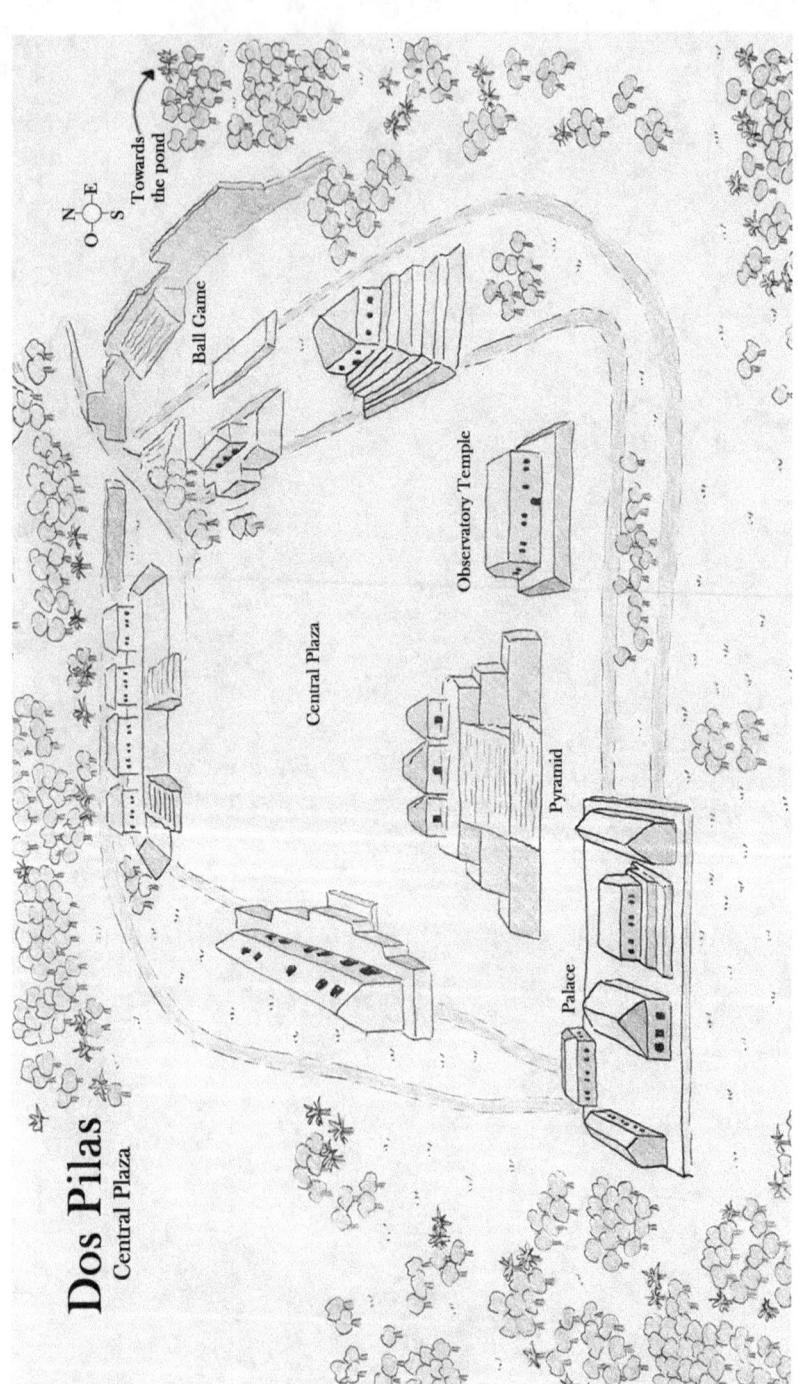

Dos Pilas
Central Plaza

N
O E
S

Towards the pond

Ball Game

Observatory Temple

Central Plaza

Pyramid

Palace

The Merchant of Death

CHAPTER ONE
9.12.6.17.13 - 6 TZEC 1 BEN
(17 May 679 AD)

THE AJAW* CAME FIRST, the noble B'alaj Chan K'awill. Tall, imposing, he was displaying all the insignia of his newly regained royal dignity: the elaborate feather headdress in shimmering shades of blue and green, and the heavy jade ornaments in the hair, on the ears, on the ceremonial cloak, and again on the wrists, the ankles, and the chest.

Head held high, impassive, he moved slowly, clutching in his right hand the sceptre-axe, symbol of

---

* Ajaw: the reigning lord, the sovereign.

his sovereign power. Then came the priests, reduced for the occasion to the role of mere assistants, the full college led by Thirteen Jaguar, solemn and straight-backed despite his age. The Ajaw's family followed next: his eldest daughter, Six Sky, and the lady of Itzán, his second wife, accompanied by the two sons that she had borne him. Behind came the nobles of minor lineage and the throng of warriors and servants. The procession left the palace and headed for the central plaza, around which the entire population of the town was gathered to admire their lord who had finally returned.

The Ajaw had just come back from his five-year exile in Calakmul. He had first made the most urgent decisions and sorted out the day-to-day government of the city. Today, he would regain full control. The Ajaw would leave no one in doubt about his royal status, thought Xhól, who was admiring the ceremony from an angle of the sculpted staircase. The position he had been given allowed him to see the whole ceremony. But was this not as it should be, since he was the one who had sculpted the stela? He had, of course, followed the instructions of the lord and the priests when it came to the subject of his sculptures: the Ajaw himself, in all his glory, the Cauac monster, the representation of the sky and the underworld. Yes, he had followed their instructions, but he was the one who had sculpted it, repeated Xhól to himself with pride. Alone, because his old master had died during the Ajaw's exile. Carrying out the work on his own, it had taken him months.

And that work was completed today with the erection of the stela, of which he was so proud.

The return of the Ajaw had restored the natural order of things, prefiguring a new cycle of abundance for the painters, sculptors, musicians, and artists of all kinds who lived at court. Had not he, Xhól, already received this order for the stela to be erected today, as well as the grave responsibility of finishing the painting of several temple panels, neglected since the defeat against Tikal and the flight of the Ajaw? A new era of prosperity, yes. But would this be a new era of peace? That was less sure. Xhól could not imagine how the rivalry between Dos Pilas and Tikal could ever come to an end. Even if, by some miracle, peace was to be had with Tikal, what would then be the attitude of Calakmul, their current ally? It seemed clear to him that they could not help having to choose between two enemies. Which was the best option: a close enemy like Tikal or a distant one like Calakmul?

The Ajaw had already given an answer to that question, at a time long before his birth, a time about which the elders did not speak freely, a time about which Xhól knew very little. On deciphering the stela marking the foundation of Dos Pilas, he had received confirmation that the Ajaw had been placed at the head of the new settlement by his father, the then reigning lord of Tikal. For one katun[*] after the foundation of the city, the Ajaw had loyally

---

[*] Katun: a division of time made of twenty 'tuns' (or 360-day long 'years'), roughly twenty year.

held Dos Pilas on behalf of the great mother city. One day, when Xhól was still a small child, the Ajaw had suddenly turned away from Tikal to become a vassal of Calakmul, the eternal rival. The result of what dealings, of what defeat? That, Xhól did not know: nobody among the elders spoke of it, not even in low tones. Since then, they had always been at war with Tikal.

Xhól's attention returned to the ceremony. That was just like him, forever losing himself in his thoughts to the point of no longer seeing what was before his eyes! This is what allowed him to see the sculptures before they ever took shape in stone, but how much trouble had it also caused him.

The Ajaw had now arrived at the chosen location, where a hole had been dug the day before by labourers. Acting on my own orders, thought Xhól with renewed satisfaction. The stela, lying backwards close to the hole, was just waiting to be raised up and then swivelled into the hole, where it would stand up straight. But before that, the Ajaw had to consecrate it. A priest approached the Ajaw carrying the cup of offerings in his two hands, eager to perform well. He was positioned at an angle where Xhól could not make out his face, but it had to be Ah Chuen B'alam. Such a servile attitude coupled with such an ardent desire to shine on an important occasion only belonged to him, decided Xhól.

Now, he was missing some of the action. There were too many people in front of him. By raising himself a little on the tips of his toes, he caught a glimpse of the Ajaw taking nine pearls of jade, one after the other, and dropping them with reverence into the cavity. Then followed the precious shells that came from the shores of the faraway sea, again nine in number, and finally the water lilies. A priest might explain to him the precise signification of the whole thing... if he were ever brave enough to ask. The Ajaw stepped back a few paces and made a sign. The labourers got to work. The first two, kneeling on both sides, maintained the base of the stone, while a third one threw a noose of rope over the head of the stela and tightened it there, then repeated the operation with a second rope. The four remaining labourers, the most vigorous, positioned in front of the stela, began to pull the rope that the one at the head threw at them while their two kneeling mates held the base of the massive stone. Slowly, it began to rise. May they not let go! thought Xhól in alarm. What if they damage it? But no, the stone, once in motion, drew a lovely arc and stood up. When it began to lean dangerously forwards, the man who had steered the head grasped the second rope and pulled it back, calling out other servants to assist him. Now balanced between the two ropes—one rope at the front, the other at the back—the stela was pushed with great difficulty into the cavity, crushing the offerings that had been laid there as it sunk into it. When the stela was in place, the Ajaw made a sign of approval, and the ropes were untied.

The Ajaw in all his majesty turned away from the stela and headed towards the area located to the east of the central plaza where the festivities were to continue. Just behind him came Thirteen Jaguar, the oldest among the priests, then the other members of the procession. Xhól, still on the first steps of the sculpted staircase, stared at the old priest: how old could he be? Not only was he the oldest priest, he was also the oldest man in the community. Nobody could recall his birth or his parents. He was the last of a generation. Despite old age and a sleepless night spent preparing the ceremony, the man still stood up straight. Some whispered that he was immortal!

But it is true that everyone here is relatively young, reflected Xhól. Not many of our men are more than three katuns old: the wars have seen to that. The oldest now are of the Ajaw's age, who himself arrived in the city as a child. These are now old enough to see their own sons entering adulthood. There were no survivors from the high priest's generation, who was already old when he arrived at Dos Pilas to attend, instruct, and guide the sovereign, still a mere child then, and who seemed to hang onto life effortlessly while so many children, young women, and warriors were taken in the continuous and changing flow of life and death.

Despite his age—he must have been close to eighty—the high priest was still there, still faithful to his lord, and still ready to contain the ambitions of the other priests, thought Xhól, seeing how Thirteen Jaguar purposefully overrode the conniving Ah Chuen B'alam.

The central plaza emptied, and Xhól followed the general movement. He had better stay around, he thought with a sigh. He hardly enjoyed these festivities: his twisted leg and his shoulder prevented him from playing ball or holding a weapon. As a rule, he did not mind, but on a day like today, a day when he could not work at what he was proud of, he was once again conscious of his differences. Especially when the young, able-bodied warriors made comments to each other about his crab-like gait. He would make a show of patience and stay, appear to enjoy himself, even if it was not the case. He knew well that it would count against him if he isolated himself too much. He needed the goodwill of his neighbours, of the young warriors, of the priests and the nobles, even though everyone despised him a little for his handicap, even if he was the only member of the new generation to have learned to write the history of the city in stone or paint it onto its walls.

Xhól let himself go with the flow of spectators and took place on one of the high terraces above the left-hand marker. He wanted a good view of the game and to be seen by everyone as well, at least for a while. Two groups of young warriors formed, one led by the Ajaw's elder son, the noble Itzamnaaj B'alam, a boy of around ten years old who would one day become their lord, the other by Itzamnaaj K'awill, the younger son born in exile.

The youngest of the priests threw the ball to mark the beginning of the game. Xhól scanned the spectators seated in the terrace opposite to him.

In the centre, above the marker, sat the Ajaw with his second wife, the lady of Itzán, and the noble Six Sky, born from his first marriage. Six Sky, a young girl barely out of childhood, sat with dignity, erect and haughty, not deigning to grant him a glance nor a smile, and yet he was her old childhood companion.

Today she was playing the role of the lord's daughter. Why blame her? It was her duty, her position, her destiny. Tomorrow, she might again become the little girl with the smile that made a cleft in her round chin, her hair flying freely instead of being plaited with ornaments like today, the little girl from before the exile, the little girl he preferred. In this, too, his opinion differed from that of the rest of the community, thought Xhól as he overheard Shield of Jade, a young warrior of his own age, and already a head taller than him, talk with his cousin.

'How pretty the lord's daughter is today! Do you think we might have a chance?'

The cousin took a quick look at the young girl opposite them and answered.

'No way, mate! The Ajaw would be mad if he didn't use her to strengthen our relations with Calakmul, or even further away, over there in the north.' 'She won't be staying here much longer anyway.' he added, following the ball with his eyes.

Xhól could only approve, even if it hurt him. Yes, the part of the daughter of the reigning lord was to consolidate her father's diplomacy through a marriage that was advantageous for her native city. She would soon leave. And this morning during the ball game, she too seemed conscious that her past was evaporating little by little behind her, soon to be replaced by a still uncertain future. Was she sad? Impossible to know considering the manner in which she avoided catching his eye. Perhaps in that case, yes, a little sad. But not that much! She also liked being there, adorned and displaying her rank. He could see it in her sparkling eyes when one of her half-brothers made a particularly successful throw. Yes, she was proud of her family, her lineage, her position. She was turning her back on childhood today, fully accepting the destiny of reigning lady that would one day be hers.

Xhól could not take it any more. After the ball game—the Ajaw's elder son won—after the feast, after the generous distribution of pulque, after the singing, after the dancing, he had had enough. Now, he could slip away without fear; most of the participants were too inebriated to notice his absence. He just had to rid himself of a staggering Shield of Jade, who leaned heavily on his shoulder—the good one, thankfully—talking gibberish about how he was not to go as they had not finished emptying their jugs. He extricated himself gently, sat him down against a column, and told him that he was, in fact, going to get fresh jugs. He did not need to look back to know that the young warrior, under the influence of the drink, was now sleeping where he had left him. Peace, serenity, silence, that's what he wanted, needed, thought Xhól, as he moved away from the feast, limping even more than usual.

On the northern path that he needed to take to get back to the family enclosure, he noticed a troop of men approaching. He stopped short: was it possible? Them! He hurried towards the little group. Yes, it was indeed the merchant Pek, who had left seven uinals* before, followed by heavily laden slaves. And all this time they had thought he was dead!

Xhól greeted master Pek with the courtesy required for someone of his rank. Was he not the richest merchant in Dos Pilas and one of the most-listened to of the Ajaw's advisors? From the clearing between two dwellings in which they stood, they could hear the hubbub of the feast taking place on the central plaza. It did not escape the merchant's notice.

'What is happening?' the merchant asked, right after the usual politeness. 'What are you celebrating?'

Xhól explained in a few words. Master Pek listened to him carefully, asking short questions about what had happened in his absence.

'Has there been a new attack from Tikal? How are the Ajaw and the noble lady of Itzán?'

The man didn't say anything about himself, noticed Xhól. After a pause, Xhól finally dared to ask.

'Why did you stay away for so long?'

Master Pek stiffened.

'Of that, I will talk only before the Ajaw,' the merchant let out with a sneer.

---

* Uinal: period of twenty days.

'It will hardly be possible today,' replied Xhól. 'It would be best for you to join the feast and put off all serious business until tomorrow.'

Xhól went back towards the central plaza with the little group and brought master Pek before the Ajaw. The lady was on his left. She had insisted that her sons remain with her, even if the two boys would have preferred to join the group of young warriors. To his right, the daughter fated to a political marriage, proud in her ceremonial robes, watched Xhól draw nearer with curiosity and something bordering disdain. What was he doing before them at such a moment?

The music stopped. The guests straightened and stopped dancing or talking upon seeing Xhól cross the space in front of the dais, bow down before the Ajaw, and declare that there was somebody there whose unexpected arrival would certainly give the lord great pleasure. At these words, master Pek stepped out of the shadows and came forward into the light of the torches surrounding the platform on which the Ajaw and his family sat.

Once he had completed his duty, Xhól retired into the shadows and observed the scene with interest. The Ajaw stood up without allowing his surprise to show and took two steps forward to welcome the traveller. The ceremonial sceptre in hand, the headdress and the heavy ear ornaments weighing upon a head that did not droop under the weight, he demanded with a glance the homage that was his due. Master Pek got the message as plain as spoken and placed one knee to the ground to salute his lord and pronounce the words of tribute. A slight smile played on the Ajaw's lips. Satisfied, he suggested that master Pek enjoy the end of the feast with his family, adding that he would grant him an audience first thing the next morning. With these words, he went back to his place on the seat covered in jaguar skins, the insignia of his royal rank. Master Pek stood up, looked around for his family, and immediately headed towards his wife. Her face had assumed a livid hue on seeing her husband's approach. Xhól was surprised at first but then understood. The rumour was that, prior to his departure, master Pek had been giving his wife a hard time. She had seemed to enjoy her independence during his absence. She managed the slaves well and succeeded in keeping the family's fields in perfect condition. She had even had time for her weaves, which now seemed more handsome, more complex. Quiet, thought Xhól—quiet, there was nothing like the sound of quiet for creating.

Xhól finally managed to slip away, and went back to the enclosure belonging to his sister and brother-in-law with whom he lived. They were staying late this time; the children were having such fun! He couldn't blame them. Tomorrow he would start to work early, painting a panel of the small temple on the central plaza. For that, he would need a clear state of mind. It would be the most visible panel, the one that would attract the most attention and the most comments. It was up to him to prove that he was as good as his old master, One Snake, dead just a few months; that there would be no need to bring in another more capable painter from another city. Away from the feast, the night was calm, and dark too, due to the waning moon. He breathed in the fresh air deeply and told himself that it was good to be alive, and above all to be alone. No one to wonder at his oblique gait. No one to point out that he was slow. No one to interrupt his thoughts. And he wanted to think. To think about that panel. Once again, he had been given the gist of it: an offering of prisoners to the triumphant Ajaw. Beyond that, it was up to him to imagine the scene and position the characters. It was also up to him to ask himself many questions. Such as how could he introduce a little colour into the scene, which would be flat and lifeless if he only used ochre for the robes of the nobles and white for the loincloths of the prisoners.

So many questions, questions of prime importance to him, questions that he could discuss with no one. His sister was merry, friendly, and a good weaver, but certainly not an artist. She wouldn't understand his concerns. His brother-in-law? Although he was a good potter, he wouldn't understand either. They both thought that it was a great honour for him to be in charge of carrying out these paintings, but neither one could understand. Understand that things did not pop into his head already made. Well, they did, sometimes... but not often. Most of the time, he had to sit in front of the panel, force himself to begin—a detail here, a floral decoration there—and then inspiration would come.

However, when he was still at the stage of drawing a first outline of a painting, the main characters and their signification, he was faced with a thousand questions; a thousand questions that he had to resolve before beginning, and he could share his concerns with no one. It was at times like these that he felt the loss of his old master most acutely. There was no one left to share his art with or turn to in time of confusion. It weighed upon him.

The only one who seemed to show some benevolence towards him was Thirteen Jaguar, the high priest, who would sometimes stop in front of the new panel. Xhól would see the shadow of a hooked nose appear on the wall, as elongated and emaciated as its owner, and the voice of the old man would pull him out of his thoughts. At first, he had wanted to get up and bow before the priest, but Thirteen Jaguar had ordered him to stay where he was, to keep on painting. Feeling the attentive priest behind him without being subjected to the piercing gaze that was enough to paralyse him, Xhól had gradually grown bold enough to dare to ask some of his questions. The young man and the priest, just as interested, had begun to share their thoughts.

Oh, it rarely was for more than a few minutes at a time, but these few minutes were precious to Xhól. They gave him greater confidence in what was suitable, the errors to avoid. That was the advantage of working on the central plaza. The disadvantage was the incessant comings and goings, the shouts, the laughter, and the unhelpful remarks, such as

'Oh, that's beautiful!' He knew it was beautiful! If that was all they had to say, they had better let him work in silence! Yes, he would to take full advantage of the next morning to work in peace for a few hours. Everybody would still be asleep when the sun would come up. With any luck, it might last for an hour or two, seeing how much had been drunk that evening.

Lost in his thoughts, Xhól moved further and further away from the central plaza, crossed the small irrigation channels, followed one path, then another leading around enclosures, each surrounded by hedges. He first headed north then east to where his brother-in-law's homestead was located. Under the zapote* marking the entrance to the family enclosure, he turned left and headed towards the shed serving as his lodgings. That was his request, not theirs, feeling more comfortable a little apart. To lie down was a delight. Such a long day did not do any good to his shoulder, and his back was hurting—it did not bode well for the morrow.

---

* Zapote: fruit tree found throughout Central America.

CHAPTER 2
A DISCOVERY

THERE WAS INDEED A rich reward to be reaped in not drinking, thought Xhól with glee. Since early morning, he had been busy painting a mural on the side of the small observatory temple—with nobody in sight. No noise on the central plaza, no noise coming from the palace of the Ajaw, no movements, no incessant shouts that he had to force himself to purge from his consciousness. He had never worked so well as that morning. A good reason to appreciate festivals, maybe.

He slightly shifted his knees, stiff from immobility, and felt a surge of pain strike through him. He had to find a better position! His already twisted back could no longer take the bent position towards the bottom of the mural that he had imposed upon himself from the beginning of the day's work. Absorbed as he was by the details of the hem of a coat and then by the kneeling prisoners, he hadn't felt the passage of time or the onslaught of pain.

Now, it was time to get up, in stages—first unfold the left leg, then the right, massage the ankles next, get the articulations in the feet moving, lean against the wall, and finally get up, little by little, with no sudden jolts. This is what he had learned to do. His old master had told him that these cramps, these pains, would happen to anybody who painted. That it was not down to his shoulder or his twisted foot. It was their sacrifice: the lords shed their blood, the painters and the sculptors made their own bones crack—and it was no less painful!

After rising up, Xhól took a few faltering steps, holding onto the wall of the temple. Leaning against the lintel of the door—one that he had sculpted, he reminded himself with pride—the young painter looked around the central plaza. He could only see one frail, old woman on her way to get water. Nobody else. He still had a good hour of quiet work ahead of him. As he turned back to his work, Xhól froze. Who was that walking along the path from the cave of bats? Who was there so early in the morning? And why?

It didn't take him long to guess, even at this distance, even without making out the face——it was that bizarre sensation of seeing his own self reflected the way that others saw him. It was the same limp, the same brusque movement of the hip, the same twisted shoulder that automatically positioned itself to counterbalance to the left. It was the only other cripple in Dos Pilas. He too had survived the illness that had struck fifteen years ago, taking several young children at the time. Yes, it was One Hunter, his 'other self,' as he was wont to label the young man. What was One Hunter doing there? An interesting question, but a question that could wait. For the moment, what mattered most was to get this snake right! The perfect movement, the perfect curve eluded him——as often.

He was less talented at painting animals than people, and he knew it. What did his old master say about that? 'Think of them as men; give them a personality, a soul; imagine they are one of your neighbours.' If this snake was one of his neighbours, then who would it be? he wondered as he contemplated the mural. 'The priest Ah Chuen B'alam!' he exclaimed with a broad smile. Yes, the man was a perfect fit: smooth, soft-tongued——but deadly to those who displeased him——insinuating himself into the Ajaw's favours, fanning for attention... and positioning himself as the indispensable successor to Thirteen Jaguar, the high priest who was getting old. Yes, he was the man! Xhól got back to work with more enthusiasm——he was going to get his snake right!

A new morning, a new start for the Ajaw's authority—shaken by the exile to Calakmul. A new cycle for the city, thought Thirteen Jaguar. A new cycle, yes, but of this one, I will not see the end. Was that not the natural order of things? Growth and decline. Ascension towards maturity and descent towards death followed each other in an eternal and endless cycle. These days, he was giving more and more thoughts to the subject, more and more time too. Meditating allowed him to see things clearly, finally; to understand the teachings he had received a long time ago. On the other hand, he ought to keep a firmer hand upon the young priests and the novices. He sighed. In any case, this morning his duty was to attend the council of the Ajaw.

Thirteen Jaguar entered the room, bowed in front of the Ajaw, and headed towards his usual seat to the right of his lord. The Ajaw, hieratic, majestic, stood on the platform covered with jaguar skins, as though there had not been a five-year hiatus, as though he had always been there, as though his reign had never been interrupted.

The old priest approved of his lord: yes, that was the right attitude to adopt. And the ceremony of the day before had been the right thing to do, too. The Ajaw had demonstrated his determination to regain his power with a firm hand, which was good. His two sons were still so young! Too many nobles had hoped that the occupation of Tikal would last, benefitting them. They had to be brought to heel if he wanted to give his line a chance to continue.

Once the merchant arrived, they would see where everybody stood. Things would get interesting. First, because the noble Eighteen Puma could not stand Pek and would do all he could to discredit him, thought Thirteen Jaguar as he watched the arrogant and chiselled face of the warrior appear in the doorway. Being from a noble line, and the cousin of the lord was no guarantee of intelligence. He would not shed any tears for that one if he were to hear of his being killed on the battlefield—or taken prisoner, which amounted to the same thing.

The Ajaw had welcomed each one with a solemn nod of the head. He had once again taken care of his appearance for this audience: the ear ornaments, the headdress, the ceremonial jade axe; all the insignia of power were again on display to indicate in a dazzling way who was the true ruler. Even if the noble Eighteen Puma did not like it. Even if he had harboured ambitions of supplanting his cousin. Even if some members of the council had at one time appeared to lend an ear to his whispers about how little glory there was in preserving a lord who had been in exile for so long. Despite the influence of Eighteen Puma, these men had not known how to, or had not wanted to question the incontrovertible right of the Ajaw to retain his rank on his return from exile.

It would have been a curse for the city had the noble Eighteen Puma succeeded, thought Thirteen Jaguar. Nobody's life would have been safe, not even his. Especially not his. He was under no illusions:

the noble Eighteen Puma knew perfectly well that he had scant regard for him.

The curtain masking the door rose again, and one after another, the members of the Ajaw's council came to bow before the platform. Ah Chuen B'alam was the last to enter, and for once, he did not try to draw attention to himself. As discreetly as possible, he slipped onto a cushion to the right of the old priest. They were only waiting for master Pek to begin. A ripple of impatience ran through the assembly. The noble Eighteen Puma demonstrated his disgust by a disdainful pursing of his lips. The other attendants, fretting uncomfortably, glanced at each other. They all had the same thought: how brazen of the merchant to make their lord wait in such a way! What did it mean? They all heard a hurried step, too fast for someone coming to join the Ajaw's council. Then, the muffled sound of a hasty discussion reached them. The portière shook. A frail silhouette appeared in the doorframe and stood out for an instant against the light, which accentuated the protuberance on the left shoulder. With his usual movement——a slide to the left that was turned off course at the last moment by the right hip projecting forward——Xhól advanced to the middle of the room before prostrating himself in front of the Ajaw. Stone-faced, the latter uttered only one word.

'Speak!'

Xhól lifted his forehead and began his tale.

'My lord, today, I got up early. I wanted to advantage of the fact that the town was still sleepy after yesterday's celebration. I began to work on the new mural for the small temple. Work was going well. Then, the city began to wake up. That was when I decided to go into the forest, to the cave of bats. I wanted a little peace. I wanted to meditate. I am still undecided about how to represent the Cauac monster in my next painting. I wanted to get closer to his ancestral home, in the hope of seeing a dream, a vision—'

An impatient gesture from the Ajaw brought him back to his story.

'I reached the pond. There, I noticed a dark, indistinct mass laying in the silt. I drew closer and recognised the shape of a body. At first, I thought that one of the revellers had taken a wrong turn on his way home last night and had collapsed there, drunk. I got closer, to drag whoever it was onto dry ground. On turning the body over, I realised that it was master Pek. I ran back to alert you as fast as my leg allowed me. He is dead,' he ended by way of explanation.

The last sentence threw the members of the council into consternation. While the courtiers whispered among themselves, Thirteen Jaguar surveyed their faces. Consternation, yes, but not on everyone, he thought. At first the Ajaw remained silent, deep in thought. He then arose, and all fell silent. Impassive, the Ajaw asked Xhól whether he knew what had killed the merchant. The young man replied that, no, he had been too surprised; he had only thought of raising the alarm. The Ajaw then turned towards the ever straight-backed silhouette of the old priest.

'Go! Take care of the body, and come back to tell me what happened as soon as possible. I want to know if he died on his own... or if he received any help,' he ordered. 'Today's council is over. Leave me!' added the Ajaw to the others. 'Except you,' he ended, turning towards Eighteen Puma. 'I have an assignment for you.'

At these words, the courtiers rose hastily and took their leave, one after another, allowing the high priest who had seized Xhól by the arm to go first. Groups quickly began to congregate on the central plaza, spreading the news.

Thirteen Jaguar had requisitioned three guards along the way. Holding Xhól's shoulder in a vice-like grip, he walked towards the pond at a fast pace. He soon had to slow down when he noticed that Xhól could not keep up with his long, heron-like strides and was twisting and turning in every direction. He finally let go of the boy's arm.

'Well, my boy, you may as well tell me everything in detail before we arrive, he said with a wry smile.' 'First, why did you want to go to the cave? Your current painting shows the homage of the vanquished, not the Cauac monster. Tell me the truth; I demand it!'

Xhól caught his breath and first tried to regain a more regular walking pace. He glanced furtively at the priest and wondered what to think. Up until now, the old man had appeared to be quite benevolent towards him. A rarity in Dos Pilas, despite all his talent as a painter and sculptor, thought Xhól bitterly. He was an intelligent man, probably the most intelligent man in the whole city. It would be difficult to fool him. He told him everything: his desire to be alone, his sense of well-being while working on the side panel of the small temple in the deserted town, his increasing malaise as he watched the city wake up, and how his ankles, knees and hip had really started to hurt. When he had seen fat Ix Cuat coming—the sure end to all peace and quiet—it had been the last straw. But he had walked slowly because there was no hurry, and he had nobody to drag him along. Therefore, it had taken him some time to get to the pond. A thin smile appeared on the old man's face.

'Are you sure you have told me everything? You didn't meet anybody on the way?'

'No, nobody then.'

'Ah, "then". And before you went to the cave?'

'Yes, I saw someone before,' Xhól replied hesitantly. How subtle this man was. How dangerous, too. One word had been enough enough for the priest to catch him out.

'Well then, who was it?'

Xhól had to admit his surprise at seeing One Hunter on the path to the cave while the city was still asleep. He had kept on painting, but yes, he had noticed him.

'And when you reached the pond?' continued the priest.

'Well, it was still quite dark under the trees; I couldn't see properly at first. I first wondered whether some beast had been attacked when it had come to drink. But it seemed unlikely to me that a jaguar would come this close to the city.'

'Yes,' replied the priest. 'Jaguars don't come this close anymore. They have learned to distrust men. Nowadays, one must venture deep into the forest to find them. And even then, it is a very lucky hunter who manages to flush one out. What did you do at that point?'

'I drew closer, and I realised it was a man. Frankly, at first, I thought it was a drunkard, and the only question I asked myself was whether he had not drowned after stumbling in the high grass.'

'Yes, that is possible,' replied the priest, 'and perhaps that is how it happened. Except that Pek drank little at the feast; he was much more concerned with eating and watching his wife. He was rather quiet, in fact, after the first cries of surprise from his family. I don't believe he was inebriated. Anyway, let's go and see.'

The little group arrived at the edge of the pond. The body of the merchant, half turned over by Xhól, formed a dark mass in the mud of the bank. The old man bent over the body, then asked the warriors who had come with them to pull him from the shore and to lay him out on the hard earth of the trail. There, a ray of sunshine reached the ground through a gap in the trees, and he was able to examine the body. A still vigorous man, thought the priest; a man who could have lived for many more years… if not for another man's intervention.

Because one thing was for sure—this man had not drowned. None of the usual signs, he decided: no bloated stomach, no swelling. Besides, there was not enough water for that where the painter had found him, right at the edge of the reeds. No, this man had died of something else. Of what?

He asked the guards for a little water. They went to draw it from the pond using large leaves, and he began to clean the dead man's face. The priest wanted to determine his expression. What was written there? Fear? No, not fear, decided the priest. Anger? Perhaps. His neck bore no marks. Neither did his torso. He had not been struck. Not on the front of the body in any case. The old man asked the guards to turn the body over onto its belly. Then, impatient at feeling them behind him while he knelt beside the corpse, he ordered them to cut down branches in order to build a stretcher to carry back the body. Once the men had moved away, he continued his examination without appearing to notice the presence of Xhól, who had knelt down on the other side of the body.

'Seeing as you're here, my boy,' he said brusquely, 'lift up his hair while I examine his neck and back more closely.'

Xhól obeyed him. He grasped the sticky, mud-caked mane of hair and held it at the top of the head. The priest let out a satisfied exclamation.

'Ah, now here's something interesting!'

Xhól looked to where the old priest's finger was pointing: a slight wound on the left shoulder close to the neck. The cut was fresh, barely more than a scratch.

'But how could that have caused his death? The wound is not deep.' asked the young man in disbelief.

'A good question, my boy', replied the priest. 'As is "Why was he here last night?" He had just returned from a long trip. He was to attend the council this morning. Why did this man not go home to rest? What could have brought him here in the middle of the night? But as to your first question, the only way to try to find an answer is by looking! Looking where you found him.'

Xhól went back to the shore of the pond, to the place where the grass still bore the imprint of the merchant's body. At first glance, there was nothing of interest. He squatted down and began to feel the high grass with his hands. He was going to get cut to ribbons by these reeds and thorns, he thought, annoyed. How could he go on painting? The old priest, as if he had read his thoughts, encouraged him.

'Take heart, my boy. In any case, I don't think that you'll be painting much over the next few days.'

Resigned, Xhól moved on, further and further from the place where the merchant's body had flattened the grass. Three elbow thrusts away, he felt something hard under his hand and cried out.

'Stop. Don't touch it!' shouted the old priest.

Thirteen Jaguar knelt down in the tall grass and parted the blades with his long fingers. He unearthed a small-sized, polished pebble that had been sharpened around the edges. The priest ordered Xhól to go and fetch him a still-green leaf of maize.

It took Xhól a few minutes to go back to a group of huts and their vegetable gardens and return with the requested item. He held out the thick, almost woody leaf to the priest who used it to pick up the stone gently and rolled it up as a precautionary measure. Now it looked like a tamale*, thought Xhól. But why take such precautions for a simple stone?

At that moment, the three warriors returned with a stretcher. Following the priest's orders, they lifted the corpse and placed it on the bed of branches, doing their best to arrange the long, black hair along the sides of the face. Two of them took hold of the stretcher, lifted it off the ground, and began to walk. The old man spoke to the remaining warrior, commanding him to get ahead, inform the family, and return with two other bearers to relieve his companions.

The warrior took off like a shot after bowing from the waist up, one hand on his shoulder. Xhól walked in silence beside the stretcher, not daring to ask the priest what he intended to do or whether he should stay or, on the contrary, slip away. But he wanted to stay! If it were indeed murder, how would it be handled? As far as he remembered, there had never been a case of murder. The worst they had to deal with was the occasional theft, and once a hunter had been wounded by mistake during a beat.

---

* Tamales: corn pastries filled with vegetables, meat or chicken and steamed in boiling water after being wrapped in maize leaves. Still common fare nowadays in Mexico, Guatemala, and other countries of Central America.

But this—the cold-blooded murder of a man who had just returned home from a long journey and who, furthermore, was a close confidant of their lord—was something else altogether. What would happen if they ever found the murderer?

After a few minutes of silence, he dared to ask the question aloud.

The priest startled and cast Xhól a piercing look.

'Yes, very true. You are too young to remember the ways of Tikal. We have lived in peace until now. In any case amongst ourselves. Well, my boy, it's quite simple. I am going to report to the Ajaw, who will decide either to pursue the investigation himself—though I don't believe that he will have the time for that while he is busy regaining control of the city—or to entrust it to another judge. Me, for example,' he added with a wry smile. 'If I discover a culprit, given Pek's status, I will not deliver the sentence alone but will defer it to the Ajaw. Although there will not be much hesitation on the subject. If the crime is proven and the assassin discovered, death will be his fate.'

'Without any recourse?' asked Xhól.

'No. The murderer, if there is one, should not expect any pity. It will not even be possible for the merchant's family to forgive and keep the murderer as a slave; that is only permitted for less serious matters. It remains to be seen whether there has been a murder... and to prove it. That is what I have to think about: how did Pek die? And above all, who would want to kill him? Now, let me think, my boy!'

Xhól made no objection and returned to his own thoughts. Had he been right to mention the presence of One Hunter? They had never associated. Mostly because that was what everyone expected of them... and even as a child, Xhól did not want to do what everyone expected of him. No, too easy, the cripples together. Since that distant morning when he had heard the healer say to his mother that he would live, though it might have been better had the fever taken him, he had made a rule of disappointing expectations. Contrary to all expectations, the fever had not taken him. Contrary to all expectations, he would not hide inside their hut. Contrary to all expectations, he would not behave like an invalid. He had gone back to playing with the other children, except with this other self. Him, he had always kept at a distance.

Master Pek's brother had done the same, had not tried to get close to him. He too, in his own way, had not wanted to 'accept'. He had become a hunter, perhaps the most surprising of all occupations with his half-paralysed body. He had even changed his name to reflect this choice. And in a short time, he had become highly skilled with a sling. It was he who brought back the most precious skins and plumages. All these years, they had avoided each other. They had both set themselves apart, each in his own way—the two most solitary men in town, but in opposite directions. One threw himself into his paintings and his sculptures, forgetful of the hubbub of conversations, bartering and arguments that were the daily fodder of those who worked at the Ajaw's palace. The other fled from all noise, all conversation, inside the huge forest, far from the well-tended gardens and scattered dwellings the city was made of. Still, they were brothers, each the undisputed master in his field, the best in the city. This is what protected them from sarcasm. They were also the only two of their age who had not yet taken a wife... and the only ones nobody would question as to why. Yes, they were so alike, brothers in illness if not by birth, and he, Xhól, did not want his words to bring any trouble to One Hunter.

The procession headed slowly towards the central plaza. In the end, thought Xhól, they had made it without anyone coming to take over from the stretcher-bearers. It was surprising that the news did not cause more agitation! As if his thoughts had brought to life what he dreaded most, a long scream came at that very moment from around the last bend in the path before the plaza; a woman's cry, a lamentation that was picked up by a chorus of wailing voices. All of the women in Dos Pilas must have joined in! Although the woman who was now master Pek's widow was the first to run towards the stretcher and throw herself onto it, tearing her hair out and scratching her face as is customary for a widow who has just learned of her husband's death. The rest of the town followed the woman. After the widow, the loudest of these was fat Ix Cuat who had such a high-pitched voice that it was impossible not to recognise it out of a hundred, even on the busiest market.

Xhól moved away from the stretcher. There was nothing left for him to do there. His role had ended. And he did not like crowds. He moved further back, leaving the women and the onlookers to gather around the stretcher. The voice of Thirteen Jaguar rose above the tumult.

'Silence, women! Move back! Let us through!'

Only the widow continued to moan while getting up slowly, obedient despite everything. Who, indeed, would have dreamed of disobeying the oldest, the most redoubtable of the priests? She walked beside the stretcher, lowering her eyes, her hair spread over her shoulders and chest. A woman who could still be beautiful when she wanted to, thought Xhól. Except she did not want to very often. Even before her husband's departure, she did not make much of an effort. And now she would probably make even less of one. He wondered what she felt behind the façade of grief. As he was contemplating her, he noticed the piercing look she cast in the direction of the priest from under her lowered eyelids. What could that mean? That she would not feel great grief at the death of a brutal, strict husband, always raging, always reproaching her for being barren, that was only normal. Was there more to it than that? Concern, perhaps? Did she suspect something? Had she too noticed the early disappearance of the brother-in-law, who lived in a tiny shed he had built for himself in the family enclosure? It was said that the two of them were on good terms, their heads bowed under the same yoke of a difficult husband and brother.

The crowd, now reduced to silence, followed Thirteen Jaguar and the stretcher that had been taken up by two young boys. They were heading for the central plaza, despite master Pek's enclosure being further south. Xhól wondered what the old man's intention was when he saw him take the direction of the small observatory temple. The old priest had the stretcher lifted onto the platform. There, he ordered the bearers to leave it at the entrance of the room erected on the top of the building. The people below gazed at it aghast. Why not leave the body to the family and let them take care of it before burying it beneath their own platform? Was it not what everybody aspired to: to join one's ancestors and remain among those of one's lineage?

The old man turned around and made a single, imperious gesture, understood by all. In a few seconds, the plaza was once again deserted. Xhól went back to his mural on the side of the building and observed from the corner of his eye the priest Puk—a novice barely out of adolescence—who brought bowls of steaming water and piles of cloths at the high priest's bidding, narrowly avoiding falling flat on his face as he jumped down the steps two by two in his eagerness to please. Then, came the priest Ah Chuen B'alam, wheezing his way up the steps to the platform, pushing out his big stomach. Xhól could not help hearing Thirteen Jaguar entrust the care of the novices to his second in command and gazed at Ah Chuen B'alam as the man left with a wide, satisfied smile on his face.

Alone now, the high priest was relentlessly pacing up and down the platform. Each time Thirteen Jaguar reached the northern corner that overlooked the panel on which Xhól was working, the latter waited, head bent, holding his breath, until the shadow of the priest moved away again. The young painter tried desperately to apply himself to his task, without any success. Sensing the old man's constant movement above his head set his nerves on edge. Hearing him come closer, take a sharp turn on reaching the edge of the platform, and move away to the other edge in this unnatural midday silence was more than he could stand. If things went on like this, he would take advantage of the old man's next journey towards the southern edge to slip away. He snapped out of his thoughts on noticing the complete silence that now enveloped him. He stiffened, head still down. It took him a few seconds to understand—the footsteps had stopped.

Would he dare straighten his shoulders, hunched over the hem of the robes of one of his characters and raise his eyes towards the platform? He did not need to decide; the high priest did it for him.

'Go get me a rabbit. Now!'

'A rabbit?'

'Yes. Alive! Buy it in my name.'

CHAPTER 3

AN EXPERIMENT

XHÓL GOT UP, STEADYING himself against the wall,
then crossed the central plaza in a diagonal line.
Who had rabbits, live rabbits? Who would agree to
sell one to him? And in exchange for what? He then
remembered that one of fat Ix Cuat's female rabbits
had just had a litter: she might let him have one.
He set off along the path running between the
temple and the house of the warriors, and went
past the noble Eighteen Puma's homestead with its
various well-ordered huts around a square slightly

smaller than the central plaza. Two more gardens to go and he would arrive at the young woman's home. In fact, he could already hear her shouting at a slave. He reached the garden fence. Like everyone, she grew there the chiles*, frijoles**, onions and corn the household lived upon. This year, fat Ix Cuat had also begun to raise rabbits after her son had brought her a pregnant female half-strangled by one of his snares. At the first words from Xhól, the young woman's double chin shook with indignation.

'What? You want one of my rabbits? After all the trouble I go through keeping them, feeding them; you want me to give one to you, midget!'

True, he was no match for her, thought Xhól as he faced this mountain of flesh quivering with exasperation; he had not even had time to finish his sentence. His only option was to let her run out of steam: she would have to stop to breath at some point, wouldn't she? Yes, at last there was a pause in the flow of words that allowed him to get the two vital words in: 'Thirteen Jaguar.' Fat Ix Cuat drew another breath and started off again with renewed vigour. Why had he wasted her time pretending that this rabbit was for him when it was for the noble priest? Did he think she had time to waste? Still talking, she headed towards the hutch of tightly knit branches where she kept the female rabbit, rummaged inside after opening the door and pulled out a young rabbit with large, frightened eyes,

---

* Chiles: bell peppers.
** Frijoles: black beans. Still the staple food, along with corn, in many parts of Mexico and Guatemala.

brown all over its body except for the pure white of the tail and the tips of its ears.

'Will this one do?'

'I suppose so.'

'You suppose so?'

'Yes, the priest did not tell me why he wanted a rabbit, just that he wanted it alive.'

'Well then, I'll tie its feet together, and you can take it to him.'

'The price?'

'Whatever the noble priest would care to give me in salt or cocoa suits me,' she answered with an evasive gesture of the hand.

Xhól left, gently cupping the warm ball of fur in his two hands. The animal's heart was pounding. Yet, it remained still in his palm, not even trying to escape. Xhól felt surprisingly good handling so much softness. It was nothing like the pelt of a dead animal. Here was palpitating life that warmed his heart strangely. He returned to the central plaza, wondering what Thirteen Jaguar had in mind. At least it gave him an excuse to stay around. And he did want to stay around. After climbing the stairs, something that he always found difficult, Xhól stood on the platform. The old priest had his back to him, and was bent over the corpse.

Thirteen Jaguar, still examining the wound between the shoulder and the neck, wondered. Such a slight scratch could not be the cause of death. Then, what was it? Here, under the bright sunshine, he could better see the merchant's face: the features were relaxed, not marred by his usual suspicious frown. On the contrary, he seemed peaceful, happy even, as if he had just had a vision. Which was not like him at all! Yes, the merchant looked like those young priests who still considered only the pleasant side of visions, without seeking to use them to contact the spirits and fulfil their role through them.

This gave him an idea. Yes, the visions were pleasant at first, when one did not overstep the mark. However, in his youth, had he not seen the terrible power of the draught when it was concentrated? His old master was not against experiments. He had carried out several ones on prisoners marked out for sacrifice. He just wanted them to remain calm when they would be placed on the altar. Indeed, after a while, they did calm down—and die before the execution took place; a death that seemed pleasant, without torment. Who here in Dos Pilas could know that?

The first thing to do was to check whether his hypothesis was correct, using the rabbit that he had asked the young painter for. An intelligent lad, thought Thirteen Jaguar as he observed the stunted figure appear at the top of the steps. A good painter, a superb sculptor, a talented scribe... At a still very young age, he had already mastered everything he had tried his hand at. Compensation of some sort for having been left a cripple? He would have made a good candidate for the priesthood, despite his low birth and infirmity. In any case, there was no harm in keeping him around. He was getting old, thought

Thirteen Jaguar with a sigh, and even a cripple like this boy could be of use to him.

Xhól came forward until he was no more than a step away from the priest.

'The rabbit, my lord. What do you want to do with it?' he added with passionate curiosity.

'Do you want to see?'

'Yes!'

'Why does it interest you so much?' the old man asked, throwing him a piercing look over his shoulder.

'Well, my lord, it's curious——'

'Curious?'

'Yes. He has no deep wound. He doesn't appear to have been sick. He didn't drown, and knowing master Pek, he probably remained sober during the party. I am sure that he wanted to prepare for the council. So, what did he die of?'

'That's a good question,' agreed the old man. 'And we are going to try to answer it.'

'Yes, my lord,' replied Xhól, who was wondering how long his luck would hold before he would be sent back to his mural.

'Well, we are going to try an experiment. Hold the rabbit tight but without hurting it.'

While Xhól was once again contemplating the little ball of trembling fur in his palm, the old man picked up the wrapping made with the leaf of maize. He carefully untied it, taking care not to touch the stone directly.

'A long time ago,' he said, 'I saw how a man could be killed with as slight a cut as the one on Master Pek's back.'

'In Tikal?' asked Xhól.

'Yes, in Tikal. When I was still a member of their college of priests.'

'I'd like to see Tikal one day,' blurted out Xhól.

'Do not wish for that, my boy. Considering how things have changed, if ever you find yourself in Tikal, you would probably play the part of the subject of my master's experiment. You see this stone? If it were a simple stone for the sling—for monkey or bird hunting, for example—it would be completely smooth and round, wouldn't it? Examine it, though, it has been carved to make several edges. Don't touch it!' he ordered when he saw that Xhól was about to pick it up and examine it from every angle. 'See how I am holding it in this leaf of maize? If you want to take it, do the same thing and do not let it touch your skin directly.'

'Why, my lord?'

'Because of this,' replied the old man, taking the right hind leg of the rabbit and cutting the taut skin of the upper limb. 'You see the cut is slight; it is barely bleeding.'

'Indeed, my lord.'

'Left to it, you would think that this rabbit will soon go back to running, eating, living its ordinary rabbit life up until the day it is caught by something stronger than itself, wouldn't you?'

'Yes.'

'Well, no!'

Horrified, Xhól felt the body between his hands become limper and limper; the huge eyes were now closed. The racing heart from earlier now slowed down to a barely perceptible beat. And then, stopped.

'Less than one minute for this rabbit to die,' said the priest, with grim satisfaction. 'Obviously, for a man of Pek's corpulence, it took longer. Once the wound was made, there was nothing to do but wait. He must have felt surprised at the time of the shot, and wondered what had happened. Then, he probably didn't heed it any further. Meanwhile, the poison was doing it work. Oh, his death was neither violent nor painful. He must have collapsed, lain down where he was near the pond, and gone to sleep. As simple as that.'

'But, my lord—'

'Yes?' the priest asked.

'He was found with his head in the water.'

'Indeed. What are you thinking?'

'Somebody came and pushed his head into the water after master Pek lost consciousness. Did they want us to believe that he drowned?'

'Maybe. In which case, it was a foolish hope, foolish on the part of someone who had used such a poison. That gives us several ideas, doesn't it? First, the murderer must have known quite a bit about the poison because he waited at the edge of the clearing for Pek to collapse, to give the crime the appearance of an accident. And that he does not know what a drowned man looks like. In any case, it is certainly murder, and premeditated at that. The Ajaw must know. Even if we do not yet know the 'who' nor the 'why.'

'What is this poison?' asked Xhól.

The old man looked at him thoughtfully.

'I'm not sure I am going to teach you that in detail. You see, we priests regularly enter into contact with the spirits. Do you know how we do that?'

'Vaguely.'

'It is better that you do not know the precise way because such things are not for you. So, we take herbs that we mix with copal heated in a brazier. We also take other substances, including this one, but at a very low dose. It comes from the back of a Bufo toad: you hold the toad and you force it to secrete a sort of whitish milk. It does it naturally when it is angry. You collect this milk, and you can then make from it a substance that gives men visions. Someone who knew that also knew that there is a way to concentrate this substance, which creates visions and transforms it into poison. And I will certainly not tell you how to do that. I don't want you set to destroying everyone who dares to laugh at your limp!'

'My lord!' said Xhól with a look of reproach.

'Let's just say that there are certain things it is better to be ignorant of—unless we make a priest of you one day,' ended the old man with a broad smile.

The Ajaw listened to Thirteen Jaguar in silence. He had cleared the reception chamber, sending away all the servants and dignitaries present upon the priest's arrival. This time, he stood up, facing

Thirteen Jaguar, arms folded, head tilted slightly to one side while the old man talked.

'Are you sure?' asked the Ajaw.

'Yes. After the experiment I just carried out, I am no longer in any doubt.'

'But who would dare? And why?'

'Why? That is perhaps the question that can be answered most easily, don't you think? Pek left a long time ago, supposedly to bring back jade, but there were rumours—'

'Rumours!'

'My lord, the only way for something to remain a secret is if just one person is entrusted with that secret. As soon as it is shared, there is little hope that it will remain secret for long. That does not mean that the entire city knew what the merchant's real mission was,' the old priest hurried to add when he saw his sovereign's lips curl in anger. 'Simply that we, the nobles and the priests, had more or less understood that he was on a diplomatic mission, even if we did not know exactly what it was.'

'And so your understanding is that he was silenced before he could tell me anything?'

'Yes. It is quite telling, by the way.'

'Telling?'

'With respect to the place where he was found. What was he doing there at that hour? In the opposite direction to his home? Unless he had an appointment.'

'An appointment?'

'To prepare for this morning's meeting, perhaps.'

'To prepare the lies that he would tell me?'

'Or the half-truths. Half-truths are always more efficient, more powerful.'

'Yes, I see what you mean. But then,' exclaimed the Ajaw, 'Why kill him if he was expected to play a part? Who did it, in your opinion? My cousin?'

'The very noble Eighteen Puma? Perhaps. He may well have wanted to influence this morning's audience. But I cannot see him killing the merchant, especially not in that way.'

'Do you believe that my cousin is so noble of heart that he would have recoiled at stabbing someone in the back?'

'Oh, no, it is simpler than that: it required a good deal of knowledge to prepare this poison. I do not believe him to have the necessary skill.'

'You are the first to dare say plainly that my cousin is an imbecile.'

'I do not know that he is an imbecile; a good warrior certainly, but off the battlefield…'

'An accomplice, then?'

'If there is an accomplice, it would have to be somebody with a lot of knowledge.'

'A priest?'

'Perhaps.'

'That would be serious!'

'Indeed, lord. Serious.'

'Can you imagine if we had to sentence a priest to death? The effect would be appalling. And yet, there is no other way. I do not want to and cannot forgive.'

'We are not at that stage yet, my lord. We have no proof. What intrigues me is the weapon used, and the presence of One Hunter in the vicinity of the pond this morning. I will first follow that trail. One Hunter, yes, he should know something about poisons,' murmured the old man.

'Do as you like, but find the culprit. And fast!'

The Ajaw strode out of the audience chamber, leaving the old man to his reflections on the difficulty of the task that lay ahead of him.

Abandoned by the old priest on the platform of the little temple, still holding the now dead rabbit in one hand, Xhól wondered what to do next. First, leave this terrace on which he felt too visible, too exposed to curious gazes. Next, get rid of the rabbit's body in a way that would not harm anybody. Bury it? No, that would appear too strange. Burn it, then? Yes, that would be the simplest. He went down slowly, holding onto the stones forming a handrail to the flight of stairs to counterbalance the movement of his left leg.

He had reached the level of the central plaza when he discovered to his disappointment that he had indeed been observed from a distance. 'Oh no, not her!' Xhól thought. But yes, here she was. This time, she came to meet him. There was no way he could avoid her. She had chosen the worst possible moment. He had no desire to look ridiculous to her and to see a smile of scorn appear once again on her lips. She had learned that smile quickly, he thought, remembering the scene from the day before with bitterness. But no, today she came to him as joyful and as carefree as before, before the exile.

'Ah, Xhól, at last! So, tell me everything! I know that you have tagged along behind the high priest this whole morning. I watched everything from afar. What is happening?' demanded Six Sky.

Her eyes shone; for her, this was all a joke. Xhól looked at her in silence, pondering what to reveal and what to keep to himself. The priest had given him no orders on the subject. After all, she was the daughter of the Ajaw, wasn't she? Six Sky then broke off from her carefree chatter.

'Oh, I understand, you're scared? Scared of the grand lady from yesterday?' she remarked.

He looked at her without answering.

'Well, come on, we're not going to stand here in full view of everyone. Join me at the secret place in two minutes.'

The 'secret place,' he thought with joy. Did that mean that the noble lady was giving way to the little girl once again, to the child he knew from before the flight of the royal family to Calakmul? Yes, he was going to go to the secret place, too fine a phrase to designate a mere nook at the back of the palace, an open-air courtyard too small for use as a storage space or workshop. Nobody went there except the two of them, where she could escape the watchful eyes of her retinue and he that of his master. He could not recall how long they had been doing it. Yesterday, he had believed that they would never use the secret place again. Six Sky was already there when he bent to get through the low door.

'So, tell me!'

There it was, her usual impatience.

'And why are you wandering around with a dead rabbit?' she added in a great burst of laughter.

He blushed and wondered again at how good she was at making him feel like a fool. She had always had that gift. And yet, he had never resented her for it. He did not resent her this time either and told her the full story. Now she was serious, sitting on a stone, listening without interruption. She just gave him a long, hard look when he mentioned his desire to be alone, without interrupting him. She then stared at the dead rabbit with disgust.

'What are you going to do with that?'

'I was thinking of burning it.'

'Yes, that must be the best way. Tell me, you don't mind about yesterday?' she added.

'Mind? Why would I mind that you are what you have to be?'

'You think that is what I will have to become?' she asked him, with unexpected seriousness.

' "Have to"? Aren't you happy about the future that awaits you?'

'Yes,' she began with enthusiasm. 'Sometimes yes and sometimes no,' she ended, vexed. 'Oh, it's too complicated to explain!' she cried, and with a furious look she dashed out.

Xhól watched her disappear, taken aback. What did she mean by that? He had always thought that she enjoyed her rank, her future. Even when she was very young, she had played the grand lady with the other girls from the palace. It was only with him that she was a little different and, even then, only in the hiding place. Another question to wonder about, he thought joylessly, perhaps less easy to answer than the priest's. But for now, he must get rid of that rabbit, he thought, contemplating the ball of fur that now disgusted him, too.

The ugly job over, Xhól returned to his mural. First, because that was where everyone expected to see him and where the priest would come to find him if he wanted to claim his services again. And then, because he wanted to think. He had noticed that if he stayed still, sitting in front of a painting, his paintbrush in hand, he became as though invisible. He might not make two strokes of colour in an hour; it mattered little. For those watching him, he was 'painting' and nobody dared disturb him.

Xhól was again facing his mural when he saw the group arrive. At the head walked Thirteen Jaguar with long strides, as was his wont, his long, white hair standing out in the sunlight. The three warriors who had brought master Pek on the stretcher followed a few steps behind. Between them was a fourth man, One Hunter, who too struggled to keep pace with his bad leg. Oh no! thought Xhól, not One Hunter! The two young men had time to exchange a long look before the prisoner was forced to climb onto the platform. If there was one time when he did not want to follow the priest's investigation it was now, decided Xhól, trying to absorb himself in his painting again, or at least to appear to do so. At that very moment, the old man's head was outlined against the perfectly blue sky. From above the edge of the platform, Thirteen Jaguar ordered Xhól to come up and join them. There was no escaping it, Xhól thought with resignation. On arriving at the top of the stairs, he could not refrain from looking sideways at One Hunter. Today, One Hunter was the prey, and he knew it. His hunted look took them in one after another, searching for the weak spot that would allow him to take flight. Yes, at that moment, One Hunter's mind was bent on running away, thought Xhól, but did that make him guilty? No, as intelligent as Thirteen Jaguar was, he did not understand. He did not understand that for One Hunter, as for Xhól, the game was always over before it even began; that whatever they were accused of, they would always be guilty in the eyes of the inhabitants of Dos Pilas—guilty of being. In this hostile city, their salvation was their invisibility.

And the high priest had just irretrievably torn One Hunter's invisibility apart by dragging him between three guards through the centre of the city in broad daylight. There would not be a single soul who would not know about it before the day's end. Even those who lived further way in the peripheral enclosures would hear about it quickly. His life would become unbearable. And One Hunter already realised that, with his lowered head, his sloping shoulders, his resigned mask that seemed to declare his guilt. Yes, One Hunter knew that he was guilty, but only of being different. And Thirteen Jaguar, only thinking of finding the assassin, did not see that, thought Xhól bitterly. If there was only one person here who could still believe in One Hunter's innocence, it was Xhól. This is what gave him the courage to answer the priest's first question and to tell once again, looking One Hunter straight in the eye, how he had seen him coming back from the pond in the early morning.

'Yes, I was surprised to see someone, but One Hunter was not hiding and did not seem embarrassed to see me,' he added without being prompted.

Thirteen Jaguar threw him a piercing look.

'Thank you, my boy. And now, to you,' he said, turning towards One Hunter. 'What were you doing over there so early in the morning after the celebration?'

'I am a hunter,' replied the young man. 'I get up early every day. I wanted to check some tracks near the pond. I was wondering whether, despite the proximity to the town, a deer hadn't come there to drink in recent days.'

'And you didn't see anything?' the old priest asked him.

'No, in fact, I didn't go that far.'

'Why not?'

At these words, One Hunter became troubled.

'I changed my mind.'

'Changed your mind? As simple as that?'

'Yes, as simple as that.'

'Or is it that you met someone "as simple as that"?'

'I did not meet anybody.'

'No? Not even to lend this to someone?' asked the priest holding the sharpened stone carefully wrapped in one of the folds of his tunic. 'Is this not the kind of stone that you use for your sling?'

The young man, surprised, disconcerted, did not know what to answer and took refuge in silence. Xhól begged him with a look. Why would he act like this? Did he not see that he was digging himself deeper and deeper? Yes, he saw it, and he chose to do it. The priest could not get anything more out of him. Furious, he ordered that One Hunter be kept under guard in one of the rooms of the house of the warriors. Xhól's heart tightened when he saw One Hunter leave the platform between two guards. Why would he not defend himself? Left alone with the priest, Xhól did not dare be the first one to break the silence.

'You don't seem happy with this interrogation?'

Thirteen Jaguar's voice broke his train of thought.

'I am not here to be happy, or not, my lord.' Xhól answered in haste. 'I am but a painter.'

'A painter with sharp eyes. So, tell me: why do you think that he did not do it?'

'Well, why would he? Master Pek was his brother, wasn't he?'

'A brother who, it is said, never showed much generosity towards him since he survived his illness.'

'Perhaps, but is it enough to kill the man?'

'And what if he had been paid?'

'By whom?'

'By someone who arranged to meet the merchant in that deserted place in the hope of convincing him to say whatever it was they wanted him to say at the council this morning. By someone who, in the end, had an interest in silencing the merchant. Because that someone realised that Pek would not say what they wanted to hear said to the Council—'

'Someone who, even before the meeting had begun, had planned how it would end!' exclaimed Xhól, incredulous.

'Yes, if only because Pek might threaten to tell the Ajaw about the meeting. That would have been enough to disgrace or even cause the death of the person in question.'

'And who would that person be, my lord?'

'Somebody quite high up. Somebody with ambition. Somebody who vies for the Ajaw's place.'

'The noble Eighteen Puma?'

'For example,' replied the priest with a hand gesture that may have meant 'him, or another.'

'In any case, it cannot be the noble Eighteen Puma,' answered Xhól with confidence.

'Ah? Why not?'

'For at least two reasons, my lord. In the first place, the noble Eighteen Puma may certainly have been stupid—or arrogant—enough to try to buy master Pek off. On the same principle, he would never have anticipated the need to kill him, as the idea that the merchant might betray him would never enter his mind.'

'Well reasoned,' answered the priest in an approving tone. 'And the second reason?'

'The second reason is that the noble Eighteen Puma doesn't like cripples,' continued Xhól in a calm voice. 'Whenever he sees me from afar, he tries for the cruellest jokes he can find in his empty head. I must say that they rarely hit the mark; he hasn't the knack. What is spot on every time, is the way he looks at me. It speaks volumes about the contempt he has for me, a cripple who will never be seen in combat, and who was allowed to live out of pity. And from what I know, he acts in the same way with One Hunter. I even heard him say once that he didn't amount to much as a hunter, using as he does nothing but a sling. I know that One Hunter would never accept an offer from him, that he despises him, that he will always despise him.'

'Ah, you know that?'

'Yes, I need only look into my own heart to see it.'

This was the moment chosen by master Pek's wife—no, his widow now—followed by her brothers, her father, her uncle and all her family, to return onto the central plaza. She had not dared come back alone and had gathered her family together, sending for them one after another. The little group headed towards the platform where the body had been set down and from which it had not been moved yet.

She began to cry and to tear at her face again, supported and encouraged by her mother. And yet, thought Xhól once again, as he still could not get over the surprise that he felt at the young woman's behaviour, this death was no tragedy for her. Hadn't master Pek threatened to repudiate her because she had still not borne him a child after three years of marriage? Didn't everybody know that he regularly beat her? After his departure, she had at first been silent, shaky. She had become more confident as the days went by. She had put on weight, too. She had blossomed during the man's absence. The more time that went by, the longer the merchant was awaited, the more she shone. It was obvious. What a blow it must have been for her to see master Pek coming back and, with him, the spectre of her past life! However, she was now crying, tearing her hair out, lamenting and howling like any self-respecting widow. Was it enough for her that it was the 'done thing' for her to cry over a profoundly selfish being who only cared about himself, who considered his wife and brother to be no better than dogs?

The little group arrived at the foot of the platform, not daring to go up without permission.

The high priest went to the top of the stairs and looked down at them.

'What do you want?'

'Most noble lord,' began the oldest of the men, not without hesitation, 'My daughter, who is lamenting the death of her husband as she should, would like to take him to his rightful place with his family so that she can honour him. Is it not normal that he be buried under the family house, as were his ancestors? We do not know why he was carried here. Although it is a great honour for him,' he ended with a deep bow.

'Your wish is granted,' replied the priest after a minute of reflection. 'Take him away!'

The father designated two of his sons to go up onto the platform with him, bowed as he passed before the high priest, stopped at the stretcher, and looked at the man who had been his daughter's husband for three years. The two boys, uncomfortable at finding themselves in full view, quickly grabbed the stretcher and went down as fast as they could. As might be expected, the crowd was growing by the minute. Half the town was now gathered, drawn by the cries of mourning.

Nothing less could be expected after such an extraordinary event. Perhaps the assassin was there, among the people examining the body? Not that people were not used to seeing corpses in Dos Pilas... but a corpse that was dead without apparent reason, that had never happened. Nobody dared to talk out loud. But yes, Xhól could already hear the gossip circulating in low tones. Why not follow them? He might catch a look, a word, a gesture to put him on the scent. The priest's question still remained unanswered: 'Who?' Who had killed master Pek?

Xhól followed the group, amidst the screams of the women and the whispered comments of the men.

He watched closely: what was out of tune? Who wore an expression that they should not be wearing? On leaving the central plaza, the improvised convoy took a path between the palace of the Ajaw and the sculpted staircase. The procession followed a narrow trail, winding between enclosures until it finally arrived at master Pek's imposing homestead.

The main building stood on a platform two feet high. Within the enclosure, there was also a tiny hut on a smaller, lower, and more recent platform; this was the one that One Hunter had built for himself. On the death of their father, he had neither wanted to move away from the family enclosure nor wanted to live with a brother who had become a master. He had thus chosen a half measure, as far as possible from the main residence but still on the family plot. At the back, there were huts for the slaves, surrounded by plantations. Theirs was a household of ten to feed, even without children.

Master Pek, unlike his wife, had no family left alive, apart from the brother he despised and who would never marry. It had thus been vital for him to beget an heir; an heir who would continue to pay homage to their ancestors—and to him as well after his own death. Who would now take charge of that? By right, the inheritance was to go to the brother, and the childless wife would be returned to her family. But if One Hunter was accused of murder, sentenced, executed: who would inherit? Xhól would have to ask Thirteen Jaguar.

Now, he was back to thinking about the culprit: 'Who'? If one put aside the old priest's notion of a political plot, one had to admit that the only person who seemed to have a motive of some sort was indeed One Hunter. Except that, One Hunter had no desire to become a merchant, to handle so much land, or to watch over the slaves. What One Hunter wanted more than anything was to be left alone in the forest, to hunt in the way that suited him, without feeling looks of commiseration—or contempt—weighing upon him. But why had he remained silent when Thirteen Jaguar had presented him with the faceted pebble? His thoughts were going round in circles, realised Xhól with a stab of frustration. He usually thought better than that!

Yes, and usually he thought better than that because he could think out loud with Six Sky; Six Sky, who always asked the right question; Six Sky who always had the right word to take him further, further than his own thoughts dared to go; Six Sky who would dare anything! Wasn't she the one who had asked him once whether the underworld really existed? The daughter of the Ajaw! Luckily, they had been alone then. He had taken the trouble to explain to the little girl, giggling with impish pleasure, that she had to be careful, and especially not to say anything of the sort in front of others. Not even in the secret place; they might be overheard.

'Well,' she had answered with a shrug, 'what if we are?'

'It wouldn't do us any good,' he had answered, with as stern a voice as he could muster.

She hadn't needed to be told twice and had never brought up the dangerous subject again.

After all these years, it was still a delight to remember how it felt thinking out loud with her. Anyway, this was not the time for thinking, but for observing! And observing with his full attention. Yes, the widow was overdoing it, even if it was only for the sake of the neighbours. And were her father and her brothers not behaving a little over the top, too? That was easy to understand; there was the possibility of an inheritance to be claimed, even though women did not usually inherit from their husbands. Everybody had seen the guards when they had come to get One Hunter. If he were to die, there would be nobody except the widow to claim the inheritance. Well, her father would do it in her name. The Boloms were making a stand: the father, the son, the uncle; all were there, and not just to comfort their daughter, sister, or niece. A daughter, sister, or niece whom they had not hesitated to leave to her fate when that fate involved a husband as brutal as he may have been. In fact, their greatest fear before the merchant's departure on his big journey had been that his wife would be returned to them. Repudiation would have embarrassed them. What would they have done with the young woman? Who would have wanted a barren woman?

The more he thought about it, the more the whole family thing left him cold. Yes, there were the ancestors to venerate and commemorate, but that was for elder sons, thought Xhól with cynicism, those who inherit and who want to pass on their lineage to their children. None of that concerned him or One Hunter. Truth be told, he wasn't far from asking himself the same questions about the underworld as the young Six Sky had voiced in the past. But he would speak of that to no one. He knew how dangerous it was to be different. He was already too different. He would keep his doubts to himself.

Right now, he'd better stop thinking and work at making others forget his difference and blend with the crowd. He'd better mingle, ask questions, appear to interest himself in what was, without a doubt, the biggest event in the city for a long time; an event that outshone the erection of the stela or the return of the Ajaw. Because, in the end, everyone knew what the erection of a stela looked like, and the Ajaw's return had been expected by everybody. But a suspicious death!

Xhól realised with a shock that many were, in fact, enjoying themselves. They relished telling how they had seen the brother go between two guards, or that they were there when the stretcher came back, or what they had heard the high priest say, or what they said they had heard him say. In fact, gossip was buzzing now that the convoy had at a safe distance from the central plaza and the priests, all tongues merrily wagging. While the widow continued to shout in the middle of a group of women, Xhól heard one of the young warriors who had been wondering about Six Sky's future the day before wonder about the widow: was she worth it? Would there be an interest in marrying her, even at the risk of not having a child? As a matter of fact, it was maybe because of her husband starving her or the constant blows he dealt her that she had been prevented from conceiving, as these last months everybody had noticed that she seemed better, that she was filling out. Yes, but would the new husband get the inheritance? It was against all tradition.

'My friend, I wouldn't rush into it,' replied Shield of Jade. 'Father Bolom is there, and he will grasp at whatever chance may throw at him. And One Hunter is not dead yet. Perhaps they are only asking him to provide information about his brother?'

'In that case, do you think they needed three guards to ask him? They would just have sent a servant or a young priest to summon him to the temple.'

Xhól moved away from them to step between other groups, lend an ear to other comments, other rumours. He focused on the old women, the old women who had offered to help the widow prepare the body, the old women who, bent with age, did not do much anymore; a little cooking, minding their grand-children... and keeping an eye on their neighbours from dawn to dusk. This time, he reaped a better harvest.

'Do you believe that One Hunter killed him?' asked an old woman to another one, even more shrivelled than herself.

The latter appeared shocked at such an open question.

'And yet, they were getting on so well since master Pek left,' insisted the first one as she motioned towards the widow with her chin.

'Oh, that,' replied the second one, 'You know what I've always said: him, maybe, but her, no. She doesn't give a cocoa bean for him. She finds him useful, yes. She appreciates that there is a man on the property to keep the other ones at a distance. And she keeps him at the same distance.'

'So there is nobody,' answered the first tiny old woman, disappointed.

'Well, I didn't say that.'

'What are you thinking?'

'She often goes to the temple, doesn't she?'

Xhól pricked up his ears; this was getting interesting. Too interesting. On noticing that he was close enough to hear them, the two old women gave him a nasty look that made him move around the crowd once again. However, he caught a last whisper.

'Another of those not destined to live!'

'Yes, you are right. Every time I see him, I protect myself from the evil eye; you never know. Didn't he go to the gates of the underworld and back as a child? He scares me.'

Xhól heard these last words with perfect clarity but did not trouble himself to turn around and shame them in silence. 'It would only make things worse,' he thought bitterly.

CHAPTER 4
THE LADY OF ITZÁN

AWAY FROM THE CONFUSION, away from the noise, the lady of Itzán was musing. She was musing about the exile they had endured after the pitiful rout against Tikal five years before. Five years of exile, five years of having to accept the ceremonious and somehow scornful hospitality of lord Yuknoom, their suzerain. Had her husband done well to severe the alliance with Tikal, to become the vassal of Calakmul?

He had explained his reasons to her many times—as though to better convince himself. Better to be the vassal of a distant suzerain than that of a close-at-hand, dominating brother. And, of course, he hadn't had a choice. After being taken prisoner by Calakmul, his only option had been to change alliance or be sacrificed. But the result had been perpetual war for all those years since, culminating five years before with the routing of their army, forcing them to flee. Flee! Them! She had done it to keep her sons safe, to give them a chance to reign one day, but it was with rage in her heart. And the people were beginning to tire of these wars. In fact, during their five years of absence, the commoners had survived quite well under the yoke of Tikal's administrator. The change of rule had concerned them little. The final thorn in her heart was that they owed their return to power to the attack led by Calakmul and the generosity of lord Yuknoom. It was all too much for her injured pride.

The lady lay on the couch on which she always took her rest during the hottest hours of the afternoon, reflecting on what help she might bring to that husband of hers who was so in need of assistance and yet so set against all aid. When the light took a golden hue, when the shadows grew longer and the palace came back to life, she sent her young servant for Thirteen Jaguar. He arrived quickly, showing no signs of drowsiness, despite his age. She invited him to take a seat on some cushions opposite her, had some refreshments brought for him, and then dismissed the young girl.

They had known each other for a long time, she thought as she inspected the thin yet straight-backed figure, the wrinkled skin of the face, the white hair, the scrawny wrists, and the still strong hands. They appreciated each other too. In their respective spheres, they had each done their best for the city, and they each knew that they could count on the other to support their separate efforts.

When she imparted her proposal to the priest, he looked at her with approval. Yes, it was a propitious moment. But he didn't wish to make it a public ceremony, didn't wish to convene the college of priests or her retinue. Just the three of them: she, the Ajaw, and himself.

She cast a glance full of curiosity at him.

'Do you have a particular reason for that?'

'Yes. What is kept secret is always regarded with more fear.'

'More fear?'

'Those who hear about it will wonder whether it is in connection with the death of the merchant.'

'Oh that,' she said with a disdainful wave of the hand.

'Yes, that may seem a trifle to you, but it is murder, and the first cold-blooded one ever committed in this city. I do not want to let it go unpunished, whatever our feelings about Pek.'

'And how do you expect people to talk if you keep the sacrifice a secret?'

'Well, if there is one thing that I have learned in this palace, and I have held the office of priest for more than two katuns now, it is that nothing is ever secret! It will only make the tongues wag even more.

'And you want that?'

'To make them wag? Yes. If there is somebody who should be worried about the result of the divination, it will serve my purpose.'

'That was not my goal when I thought of the ceremony.'

'Who knows, perhaps the spirits will answer your question too,' he answered with a smile. 'We will meet again at dawn, in the seers' room,' finished the old man, getting up with difficulty.

Thirteen Jaguar left the lady's apartments and stopped for a moment to consider the sight of the women's court. In this part of the palace, one could also find her women's dormitory, the bedroom of the Ajaw's daughter, and those of her sons until such time as the boys would join the house of warriors. The two fiery boys were chasing each other in the middle of the courtyard, forgetful of everything except their game. And their game was war. Yes, thought Thirteen Jaguar, it was high time for those boys to be handed over to the warriors, if only to learn that there is a difference between training and fighting for real!

When he saw the elder hammer the younger one with heavy blows and heard him repeat over and over 'you weren't born here; you weren't born here; you're not from Dos Pilas; I'm your lord' with an alarming fury, he stepped in. As a matter of fact, he appeared to be the only one to be alarmed.

The women going through the courtyard paid no attention to the scene. Did it happen too often? Seeing that the nose of little Itzamnaaj K'awill, who was bearing the beating without complaint, was bleeding, the old man went over to the warring pair. On seeing him, Itzamnaaj B'alam, the eldest, stopped hitting for an instant. The little one chose that moment to slip away with a supple movement and get back up. He watched his older brother calmly, as though none of this concerned him, and said to him:

'Never forget that a combat can change at any moment. As long as it is not over, victory is never sure. If you had not let down your guard, I would not have been able to get off so easily. You are the one who gave me the opportunity.'

At these words, Itzamnaaj B'alam, mad with rage, would have thrown himself upon his younger brother once again, had the priest not seized his arm and checked his movement.

'Young man, are you not ashamed of the lack of control you are displaying?' asked the high priest in a stern voice.

'Why should I be ashamed?' raged the boy. 'I am his elder. He owes me obedience. I will be his lord one day, and he dares teach me a lesson! He well deserves that I punish him.'

'Young man, you might become his lord one day, indeed. Though death could as easily seize you before that day comes and render all ambition vain. Even if you were to rule over us someday, where did you get the idea that an ajaw does not listen to the opinions of others? Have you not seen your father summon his council countless times? Do you think that he does not pay attention to the wise words of the elders when they are admitted to a private audience? Your brother gave you good advice. Here is mine: listen to him! As it will be good to listen to the advice that is given to you in the future. You may well become our ajaw some day, but if you do not behave any better than you did just now, you will not survive long. Worse still, this city, for which you will be responsible, will not survive either.'

The scolded boy did not dare answer back; the high priest was not an easy man. The boy, silent, chin tucked in, eyes lowered, continued to sway from one foot to the other, held fast in the steady grip of the old man. He was looking for a way to get out of this mess without losing face. The opportunity was granted to him by the lady of Itzán. She appeared at that moment in the doorway of her apartment and, sizing up the scene with one look, called to him.

'Son, I want to see your sister. Could you bring her to me?'

The boy, only too happy to be given a pretext to get away, accepted and ran off at top speed.

'A good son,' muttered the lady to no one in particular, before turning heel and returning to her apartment.

If there was a subject on which they did not agree, that was the one, thought Thirteen Jaguar. The lady had always had a distinct preference for her elder son, despite him being such a bad-tempered boy.

Thirteen Jaguar then turned towards the younger son, little Itzamnaaj K'awill, keeping still at his side. He took him by the shoulder, gently this time, and led him to the shade of a patio to have a good look at him: how old was this boy? Five? No, six. Yes, he was born in Calakmul—in exile—and perhaps it was for this reason that the lady did not like him. He was a reminder of a humiliating time. No matter, this boy was astonishing for his age; perhaps he should watch over him more. Itzamnaaj K'awill looked at him calmly, without fear, and wiped the blood that ran from his nose.

He made him sit down and asked a servant for some cloth and refreshments for the two of them.

'Does this often happen?' he asked while sponging with delicate fingers the child's forehead.

'What?' asked the boy, playing innocent.

'Come on, my boy, don't try and think you can outwit me,' replied the priest.

A mischievous smile appeared on the child's bloodied face.

'All the time!'

'Who steps in then?'

'As a rule, nobody. Unless Six Sky is around, and then she scolds him. If Mother is there, then it's more likely that I will catch it. But at least he stops in front of her.'

'And what do you think about that?' asked the priest.

'That if he carries on like this, I don't see him become our ajaw.'

At this answer, the old man took a long, hard look at him.

'Why?'

'Because an ajaw must display restraint and wisdom. Did you not say so yourself?'

'Yes, and I am an old priest.'

'And I am only a child. Don't you think that I didn't learn anything in Calakmul? I observed the court. And the lord Yuknoom, too. Now, there is a ruler of men! My father, too, is a ruler. And yet... don't you think I don't know what it means to him to be the vassal of lord Yuknoom? Because I am the youngest and no one bothers with me, I take note. And I soon realised what was happening. It has been the same since our return. Do you think I haven't noticed that the joy was at best doubtful? That there have been whispers? The fools! They speak freely in front of me because I am small and little; if they knew what I think, what I see, what I know. I know that Tikal will never leave us in peace. I know that we are at war, and this one is not a game. Don't you think that the occasional desire of Itzamnaaj B'alam to prove himself the strongest pales in comparison?'

Deep in thought, Thirteen Jaguar left the women's courtyard. What should he do? Was there in fact anything to be done? Should he suggest to the Ajaw that his elder son was now old enough to join the young warriors? Itzamnaaj B'alam would use it as a renewed opportunity to proclaim his superiority over his brother. Should he ask then that he join the novices for a while? That was an option. But then they would have to put up with his bullying and his arrogance. He didn't want that for his pupils! As for suggesting to the Ajaw that it might be worthwhile to reconsider the order of his succession, that was asking for trouble; the lady of Itzán would oppose it with all her might.

This made him think that he had been away from the college and the temple far too long. How was Ah Chuen B'alam getting on with the novices since he had entrusted him with them in the morning? He strode towards the main temple, one of the first monuments to have been erected on the central plaza, along with the ball game court. It was not yet finished, nor would it be during his lifetime. The structure had already been erected. A sturdy base layer of pebbles supported a three-tiered pyramid, narrowing towards the summit, the last tier still wide enough to hold three small rooms dedicated to the most important and most secret ceremonies and the education of the novices.

He climbed the staircase on the northern side of the pyramid with difficulty. He couldn't but own that he was finding it more and more difficult to climb these steps. The joints in his knees were playing tricks on him. Old age. He could no longer ignore it. Perhaps one of these days he would no longer be able to make it to the top. What then? Would he have to surrender his place to Ah Chuen B'alam? He could already hear the man's castigating voice even though he had only passed the shelf marking the first tier of the pyramid. He made another effort and continued onto the second level. There, he sat for a moment, paused for breath, and massaged his left knee, which was causing him considerable pain. He could not help but smile on hearing the demands made by Ah Chuen B'alam and the answers from the novices: they were taking a roguish pleasure in driving him mad. And yet, he thought, checking himself, These youngsters do need teaching. There were only four of them at the moment. What would it be like if their number increased? If the city survived, there would be more of them. It was enough to hear the end of the lesson—a recitation of the proper way to conduct a crowning ceremony—for him to realise one thing: the novices hated Ah Chuen B'alam. Worse still, they were transferring that hatred onto what he was trying to teach them. With Thirteen Jaguar, they were curious about everything—sometimes too much!—eager to learn, to perform well. Now, all he could hear were sighs of irritation and comments intended to push the priest over the edge. He had to make it stop! Straight away! Not to lend a helping hand to Ah Chuen B'alam, whom he would gladly have left to sink in any mire of his own making, but to set things right with these boys. They needed to learn, and to learn to respect their elders. He stood up and covered the last flight of stairs with a firm step. He finally reached the third platform and headed towards the room on the left where the lesson was taking place.

Thirteen Jaguar stopped by the doorway. His

barely visible shadow, stretched obliquely by the setting sun on his right, did not give him away. It was the sudden immobility of his second-in-command that made the novices heads turn. Young Puk was the first to rise and awkwardly offered his own seat to the old man. He sat down without saying a word and cast a stern glance at each of the four youths. There was no need for a long speech, he thought with satisfaction, they had already got the message. He bade them rise with a motion of the hand.

'Your studies are over for today,' he said. 'You will come back first thing tomorrow and show noble Ah Chuen B'alam that he has not been wasting his time teaching you. Those who will not be able to repeat the ritual correctly will be punished.' He added in a rough voice, 'Now, leave us!'

Ah Chuen B'alam seized the opportunity to scold them.

'That is what undisciplined novices expose themselves to,' he uttered, his lips pursed.

Thirteen Jaguar waited for the boys to rush down the pyramid, and then spoke.

'When I entrusted you with them today, I expected that you would make them obey you, not that I would have to come and restore order afterwards. It is time you learned how to control them, especially if you want to replace me. Do not forget that no decision has been made about that yet.' He got up and added to his second-in-command, left speechless by the unexpected reproach.

'You will perform the observation of Venus that

I had intended to conduct tonight; I am too tired after this day of investigation.'

He left the room without paying attention to the venomous look that Ah Chuen B'alam shot at him.

Xhól had gone back to his mural, which he had made little progress on since the morning. He checked that the paint had dried properly, without any changes in hue. This might sometimes happen when the colours had been poorly blended. He put away his tools in one of the temple rooms. He had hoped to see the old priest again before the end of the day, but one of the temple servants told him that Thirteen Jaguar had gone to the lady of Itzán, who had summoned him. Xhól left with regret, crossed the central plaza towards the south, and went home. Or rather to his sister and her husband's home.

With some satisfaction, he thought that, even if his situation was not dissimilar to that of One Hunter, a cripple, still single, living with a sibling... The comparison ended there. His sister, thought Xhól with relief, had a good husband. They conducted their business together in harmony. She had her weaving; he had his pottery. Their enclosure was the only place in the city where he, Xhól, was accepted and appreciated. Their enclosure was the only place in the city where he felt a little affection. Upon entering the plot, two young boys and a slender girl hurried towards him shouting loudly.

'Uncle Xhól, why have you been gone so long?' asked the elder of his nephews.

Meanwhile, the youngest climbed up his good leg, urging Xhól to take him in his arms. Only little Itzel, once she reached him, hung back a little, silent. 'How she reminds me of Six Sky at her age!' thought Xhól with a pang. He disentangled himself and took her in his arms to wish her good evening. As the two boys were not willing to let him go, he decided to sit down where they were, in the shade of the zapote. He began to tell them a story, the little girl still in his arms, the boys sitting in front of him.

This was the story of a curse, a curse that avenging spirits had cast upon a brave hunter who had made the mistake of being too good at his art for their liking. The two spirits in question—neither great nor important gods, but gods nevertheless—were angry to see a man who handled a sling better than they did. The mean spirits had thus decided to take vengeance on him, although not openly. They used a bird as a messenger to help them draw the brave hunter into a trap. The bird was superb: its feathers of the handsomest yellow and the brightest blue that the hunter had ever seen. As soon as the hunter spotted it at the top of a ceiba, he knew that he must have that bird and offer the feathers to his lord, who happened to want a new headdress.

The brave hunter checked his sling and his stones. Then he set off and began to glide like a snake between the fallen tree trunks. He drew closer without a sound, carefully prepared his sling, then began to whirl it around... but the bird flew away! Disappointed, the brave hunter watched the

93

magnificent bird disappear, but hope returned to his heart when he saw it land on another branch, fifty paces away. Again he manoeuvred to approach the bird, taking even more precautions than the first time to move forward in the silence that was the hallmark of his skill.

The younger of his nephews began to crawl in the grass and to circle the tree against which Xhól was resting.

'Like this, uncle?' he asked, appearing above his left shoulder to surprise him.

'Yes, my boy. Something like that, although the brave hunter was even more skilful than you are.'

At these words, which made the children laugh, Xhól went on.

'Nothing would do it. Whenever the brave hunter found himself once again at the right distance to reach the bird with his sling, the bird would fly away again. Guess where to?'

'To another tree fifty paces away,' replied a soft little voice from within the crook of his shoulder.

'Yes, you understand, my little Itzel,' answered Xhól with satisfaction. 'In this way, the divine bird, for it was a divine bird, fulfilled its mission, which was to take the brave hunter far away from the city, far from all assistance. The brave hunter, intent on pursuing the magnificent bird, didn't notice; his ardent desire to catch it only growing with the chase. Each time he got close to the bird, ready to launch the fatal shot, he discovered a new detail, a new shade of colour that made the bird even more precious, more desirable. And that was how the brave hunter found himself at dusk in a place utterly unknown to him; he who knew the forest so well that he could, without hesitation, find his path in the densest thickets. And then, night fell.'

'As it is falling now,' added a laughing voice.

'Good evening, sister,' said Xhól with a smile.

No, the peaceful happiness of Ix Naah had nothing in common with the fearful attitude of master Pek's widow, thought Xhól, considering the stout young woman with a serene face, as though lit from within. And yet Ix Naah's had not been the best match out of the two.

The young woman beheld the group assembled under the shade of the tree with a bright smile. Itzel escaped from Xhól's arms to throw herself upon her mother and pull on the hem of her tunic. Ix Naah tousled her hair and took her in her arms. The little girl clung on, hanging onto her mother's neck with her arms and to her waist with her skinny legs in a ferocious manner that she had not used with Xhól. The story was already forgotten. Ix Naah, still carrying the little girl, headed for the house and looked back to announce that supper was ready. The end of the story would have to wait.

At the end of the meal, Xhól gave in. The day had been long and rich in incidents. He was exhausted. He went to bed in the hut that he called home and lay down with satisfaction. Images from the day, fleeting, jumbled, passed before his eyes. Just as he fell asleep, an idea emerged from the edge of his consciousness: what had the poison been stored in? Before he could think of an answer, he fell asleep.

CHAPTER 5

FAINTING SPELL

THE SUN HAD NOT yet risen. The lady of Itzán was already wide awake, lying on her bed in the dark, thinking. How much time did she have left to live? How much time to raise her sons as best she could, to marry Six Sky, who even though she was not her own daughter, represented a heavy responsibility? How much time to do her best so that the city would last for at least a few more years, at least for one generation, that of Itzamnaaj B'alam? The rumours of war were growing louder and louder. According to their spies, they should expect an attack at any time. But spies were foreseeing attacks all the time. And, sometimes, an attack indeed came, she thought with a weary smile. The burden felt so heavy. So many duties, so many obligations, so many risks. Would it never end? To get the answer to that question she did not, in fact, need this morning's ceremony.

She knew the answer already: no, there would never be an end to it. The rivalries between cities would last forever: forever starting again, forever fed on the victory of this one and the defeat of that one. Each time, there was a new throw of the dice to find out which city would dominate the others and which would be vanquished.

Tikal, Dos Pilas, Calakmul, faraway Teotihuacán, Cancuén, Yaxchilan, and Seibal. Even Caracol or Copan, which were not in their direct network of alliances. They were all at war. The victory of one or the defeat of another brought their share of consequences for Dos Pilas, like ripples spreading across the pond after a stone is thrown into it. The stone may have been thrown far away, but ripples would always reach Dos Pilas sooner or later.

Nothing was certain in this world. And maybe that was how it should be. After having tasted for many long years the bitterness of uncertainty, those who became old—or sick as herself—could then pass on without fear, even if the heaven promised to warriors killed in combat or to women dying in childbirth was not to be theirs. Too late for her, that one, thought the lady with a wry smile creasing the corners of her mouth with fine lines. But there was still time to perform her duty today, she thought, throwing off with a determined gesture the light blanket that she liked to use on even the warmest of nights.

She straightened herself and dressed in the dark. She had sent the servants away the night before, to avoid disturbance this morning. She left her room and headed for the sacrifice room. In one hour, the sun would rise. Until then, she would have time to pray the spirits for their favour.

Thirteen Jaguar too had woken up early. He had got up and had ascended the first platform of the great pyramid. He did not want to meet Ah Chuen B'alam whom he had left on duty at the small observation temple. For a while, he contemplated the late night stars. He too wondered what the lady's sacrifice would bring: these things never turned out as planned. As a thin pink line began to appear and tint the eastern sky, he headed for the palace and the small room dedicated to sacrifices by the royal family. The brazier had been prepared the night before by a servant. He kindled it and quickly obtained a few red embers. Then, he poured in some copal. He wanted everything to be ready when the Ajaw and the lady arrived.

She was the first to raise the curtain masking the door and watched him tending the fire with approval. She drew closer to the priest without saying a word.

She watched him prepare several trays with the stingray bone, the string of thorns and some strips of paper. A slight breeze made the brazier flicker, telling them that a third person had now raised the curtain to join them in the small room. The Ajaw came in and sat opposite his wife without saying a word. She thanked him for this with a look.

In the dark room, the spice-laden smoke from the incense brought the memory of previous sacrifices to her mind. The lady of Itzán felt a familiar change take place within her. Already, she no longer thought about her shoulders made painful by arthritis; already the presence of her husband and the priest seemed distant; already the state of trance began to make itself felt. 'Good,' said the lady to herself. 'May this trance be like the last one that announced our return to Dos Pilas! May this trance be like the one in which I saw the birth of my second son!' The upper half of her body gently began to sway forwards and backwards.

Thirteen Jaguar presented her with the first tray upon which he had reverently placed the stingray bone pared to a sharp point. She took it with a distracted air and used it to reopen the hole in her tongue. As her last sacrifice dated from a few month back, the wound had since healed over. Without hesitation, she pierced her tongue. As she removed the stingray bone, she noted with satisfaction the bright red blood coating it. She threw the bone onto the tray with a quick movement. The priest nodded with approval and presented a second tray to her, with the string of thorns that she could now slip through the hole that had been reopened. As she picked it up, he carefully cleansed the blood from the stingray bone with some strips of paper and threw the sullied strips into a basket. The self-sacrifice continued. The wrinkled hand now took the string.

Beholding her, the priest told himself that the lady was not so old. In any case, she was much younger than he—she might have been his daughter. But she had aged before her time, which did not prevent her from carrying out the duties demanded by her rank. He was suddenly jolted back to the moment when he saw the lady thread with determination one end of the string through the hole that she had just reopened and adroitly take the other end of it in her other hand. She slowly slid the string through from top to bottom. She paused to take one by one the strips of paper that the priest held out to her, soak them with the blood now flowing from the wound, and then throw each soiled strip onto the tray. She then resumed the downward movement, passed another thorn through, took another strip of paper, all the while rocking more and more violently. When the string was completely threaded through the hole and the tray laden with pieces of bright red paper, the priest transferred the strips to the basket.

Thirteen Jaguar glanced across at the lady of Itzán. Would she endure the whole ceremony? Her shoulders were alarmingly hunched. When he began to throw the pieces of paper onto the thick layer of embers, she drew closer to the brazier. Immobile, she stared at the sacred smoke, following its furls, losing herself in their contemplation, forgetful of the presence of her husband and the priest who was throwing the strips of paper onto the brazier. The Ajaw drew closer and stared at the smoke. But he will have no vision, thought Thirteen Jaguar. He has not sacrificed his blood.

The lady of Itzán began to murmur a few unintelligible words. She is seeing, the priest said to himself in exultation. Once again she is seeing. The lady had been famed for her abilities as a seer from a very young age. The monotonous chant filled the small room that was lit only by the brazier. The lady, her back straight, was oscillating forwards and backwards. Her movements became faster and faster. Then, the trance started. She began to pour out a stream of words, too fast for the two men to catch. She is seeing,' said Thirteen Jaguar to himself, but what? The lady became more and more agitated, up until the moment when she placed her right hand upon her heart and collapsed.

Thirteen Jaguar leapt forward. His first gesture was to move the lady away from the brazier. Then, he laid her on the floor with the help of the Ajaw. Next, the priest placed a cushion under her head. He couldn't see anything in the darkness. In a loud voice, he commanded the servants posted outside to hurry in. As soon as the curtain quivered, he asked the first one to lift it open and not stand in the doorway like that. He wanted to see! The face of the lady was grey, her eyes closed. She held her left arm with her right hand and rolled onto her side in search of a less painful position.

Thirteen Jaguar grasped her wrist, checked for a pulse and found none. Feeling a hand touching her, the lady opened her eyes and stared at the high priest. She seemed not to see him, as though she were still in the middle of a vision.

'War. War is coming,' said the lady in a husky, rasping voice.

Thirteen Jaguar paid no heed to the warning and asked her to explain what she was feeling. She could talk about her vision later, but for now he wanted to know which remedy would be most appropriate for her pain.

'Oh,' answered the lady. 'That will not be needed. I have already had such a fainting fit; I will not die from it. Not this time,' she added with a weary smile. 'It is the same, every time. I feel as though there is a great emptiness in my arms, in my head, my legs. If I am standing, I fall; if I am sitting, too, but I fall less far. Next comes the sensation of being stabbed in the back with a dagger. Pain seizes my left arm. My heart beats wildly. And then—'

'And then?'

'And then it goes away, as quickly as it came.'

'How many of these fits have you already had?'

'A few.'

'You should have spoken to me sooner. I can give you something that will help you.'

'Is that necessary?' she asked, looking him straight in the eye.

The lady of Itzán, assisted by her women, left for her apartments. She only needed some rest, she had said after detailing her vision. Her vision! Now alone in the sacrifice room, Thirteen Jaguar and the Ajaw were considering it.

'An army corps from Tikal on its way. Do you believe it?' asked Thirteen Jaguar.

The Ajaw stared at him.

'Yes. I can now tell you that the merchant's mission was to sound out certain nobles from Tikal on neutral ground. He was to take advantage of his halts on the road to meet with an emissary of Nuun B'alam, one of the principal lieutenants of that dog, Nuun Ujol Chaak. I ought to be on the throne instead of him! It was my right on the death of our father. But no, they chose him! I wanted to sound them out, one last time. The merchant did not have time to tell us anything precise. However, when he returned, I couldn't help but notice that he looked dejected. No, I do not think that he succeeded. So you see that is why I sent Eighteen Puma with a reconnaissance battalion yesterday. I want to know what is going on.'

CHAPTER 6

SIX SKY

THE LADY OF ITZÁN was back in her apartments. She ordered her maids to leave her alone. Lying on her bed, she closed her eyes. Oh yes, it hurt now! Especially since the trance had passed. But was it not her duty? Were sacrifices not the duty of every member of the royal family? Shouldn't she set an example to her sons? Which reminded her that while her elder son was heading in the right direction, she was not as happy with the younger one. And even less so with the girl that her husband had had from his previous wife and who had become her responsibility. Six Sky had always disconcerted her. Too easily did she thwart the closest supervision to go wandering about with those below her rank. How many times had she tried to make her see reason, the lady sighed. How many times had she—in vain—reminded the child of the duties of her birth, the restraint that she should now begin to exercise, the position that she should hold during ceremonies? How many times should the girl have to be reminded of the skills she needed to acquire to hold her rank, the marriage she was bound to make some day to strengthen Dos Pilas's alliances, and the duties of her new position, starting with providing her husband with an heir?

What a disappointment, this girl was, thought the lady of Itzán with a sigh. A girl, to begin with. And what a girl! An untamed animal, accepting no rules, no discipline, no duties. How many times had she embarrassed them in Calakmul? At each prank that came to his attention, the lord Yuknoom would smile and compliment her about the girl's spirited nature, but she saw how their inability to keep her in check amused him. The women of his house would not dare to behave in this way, implied the mocking eyes of the lord Yuknoom.

Only the day before yesterday, at the dedicatory ceremony, had she begun to conduct herself in a proper way, finally conscious of the part she had to play and of her rank, it had seemed. Would it last?

In fact, she had hardly seen her since. At their last meal, the young girl wore the satisfied smile that indicated she had done exactly as she pleased... such as seeing that crippled boy. She could not understand what attracted the daughter of the Ajaw to such an insignificant being. It was dangerous for her, dangerous for him, dangerous for the city if this business caused her to neglect her duties. The girl was growing, was no longer a child, thought the lady with renewed energy. Her father may have let her do as she pleased, in an incomprehensible display of weakness, but she would put a stop to it... and fast. Worse still, Six Sky had not yet come to inquire after her, though everyone in the palace should by now be aware of her fainting spell. If she wasn't here, that meant she was out, wandering again. She could no longer put up with such a behaviour! With an imperious wave of her hand, the lady motioned her young servant to come to her.

'Go and look for the lady Six Sky. At once!' Do not dare come back without her!'

At that very moment, Six Sky herself entered the room.

The lady of Itzán raised herself slightly and watched the girl over. What was there to be read on that young face? Guilt and excitement, yes. She didn't know what the girl had been up to this morning— she would never own up—but that would have to change, thought the lady lying back on her bed, while the young girl came to kneel at her side, not daring to speak first.

107

Six Sky had never felt comfortable with the lady, even though she had never attempted to pretend to be her mother. Oh, it wasn't so much that she had strong memories the lady of B'ulu, her mother! Just that Six Sky often wondered whether her mother, who had died in childbirth when she was only five, would have behaved like the lady. Incessant questions that created a barrier between them and made her resist the lady and her attempts at closeness: she couldn't help it.

'You were not at the palace this morning.'

It was neither a question nor an accusation; just a simple statement of fact.

'No, mother.'

'I will not speak long. I am tired after this morning's ceremony. Didn't you hear about my fainting earlier on?'

'Yes, mother, the women just told me about it.'

'From today, I want you near me, all the time, or within the palace grounds at least. You can only go out if two of my women go with you and only for as long as is strictly necessary. Do you understand me?'

'Yes, mother,' replied Six Sky, in a cheerless voice.

Yes, she understood!

'I do not have much time left. I want to devote it to completing your education. It is time you thought about marriage.'

'To whom, mother?'

'We do not know, yet. We shall see. Pek was supposed to bring us some messages, partly on this subject. He did not. But we have considered possibilities other than the distant north. Closer might be a good thing. In any case, I want no more disobedience, no more disappearing, no more hiding. I only want to see the noble lady Six Sky, daughter of the Ajaw. Do you hear me?

'Yes, mother,' replied Six Sky in an even tone.

The lady of Itzán gave her a piercing look. Too much resignation, too few tears, too little pleading; the girl was up to something.

'You will begin right away. Bring your weaving tools here, to this room. You will only work in my presence from now on.'

'But mother, will that not tire you too much?'

'In any case, it will tire me less than wondering where you are. It is time for you to join the world of women and to keep within its boundaries. We cannot risk a scene the day a diplomatic delegation arrives. You should be ready at all times. Look at your dress! How dirty it is! Go and wash yourself, get changed, and don't let me see you again until you are decently attired, like a young lady conscious of her rank.'

Six Sky lowered her eyes to hide the spark in them. She got up and prepared to leave the room. The orders of the noble lady of Itzán had been heard. Her two oldest maids, who had come with her to Dos Pilas at the time of her marriage, followed in Six Sky's footsteps. It may have been under the pretext of serving her, but Six Sky understood: the surveillance had begun, and it would be constant from now on. How boring! she said to herself while one of the maids brought her a basin filled with fresh water and the other helped her remove her mud-spattered clothes. It had been such fun to go with Xhól to the pond where master Pek had been discovered. She had not understood at first what he had had in mind when he asked her to stay by the edge of the pond while he moved around the clearing. She had protested when she had felt the first stone hit her in the back. Then he had explained it all to her: the stone was small and light, so it would not hurt her, but he wanted to visualise where the killer must have been positioned for the body to fall the way it did. And so, each time she had felt the stone hit her, she had pretended to be affected and had collapsed on the spot. Sometimes more to the left, sometimes more to the right. And then there had been 'the right one' the one time when he had said with satisfaction:

'That's it! The killer was standing over here!'

At these words, she had stood up, laughing, and rushed to join him under the first trees, away from the well-trodden paths. And there she had seen the flattened grass, as though a man had been standing there for several hours, pacing forwards and backwards, even lying down at one point. And then she had seen Xhól grab something in the grass. She had asked him, begged him to show her what it was, told him that it wasn't fair, after all she had done to help him. She had even tried to snatch the object out of his hands, but he had resisted all her attempts and left for the city.

On the way back, he had remained impervious, simply telling her that it was for Thirteen Jaguar. Nearing the central plaza, she had spotted the lady's maid who was looking for her, calling her from as far away as she could. She had not even had time to speak to Xhól, who had disappeared between two enclosures. They had separated in a bad mood, and now she didn't know whether she would ever be able to speak to him again, to apologise, at least.

How annoying it is to be the daughter of the Ajaw after all, she said to herself with a pout, putting on a fresh tunic; a clean one this time. The two maids couldn't help exchanging a joyless smile. It wasn't going to be easy to follow the daughter of the Ajaw's every step; they were under no illusions about that. As soon as she was ready and her hair smoothed, Six Sky grabbed a small, unfinished piece of weaving abandoned in a corner of the room and went back to the lady of Itzán.

Her two shadows followed her every step, right behind her. No, it would not be easy to part ways with them. But she would not admit defeat just yet! Now was the time to show up as an attentive weaver, an obedient daughter, and a lady conscious of her rank. She would be all of these: lady, daughter and weaver… in appearance.

Xhól went to the observatory temple with his trove held tightly in his hand. It was so small that once he closed his fist, it could no longer be seen. He felt the round shape of the phial and the rough edges of the engravings against his closed palm. With butterflies flying in his stomach, he asked to speak to the high priest. The two servants posted at the foot of the steps smugly replied that he should not count on seeing the noble Thirteen Jaguar that morning. The high priest had gone to the palace, with the Ajaw and the lady of Itzán.

Xhól decided to wait for him a few metres away, taking cover from the already fierce sun in the shade of a chicle tree. It would be hot today, once again. It was just the start of the dry season, and yet it already promised to be one of the hottest he had ever witnessed. He sat cross-legged in the shade of the tree, opened his hand, held up his prize, and turned the phial over in his hands.

It was a round, soft-clay flask, the diameter of a child's palm. It was not much thicker than the width of a thumb. It was decorated on both sides with sculptures of exquisitely fine craftsmanship. The narrow band that connected the two sides was covered in glyphs, some of which were unknown to him. And yet, he was well-read! It was admirable work and very precious altogether; the masterpiece of an artisan at the height of his craft. How he would love to be capable of doing the same! This phial showed him everything that could be done in miniature. Even though he loved painting murals and sculpting stone, it didn't prevent him from feeling a sudden desire to create objects like this one.

Who could have been so clumsy, so careless as to lose such an object, especially there? Head bent over his find, lost in contemplation, he did not hear the high priest approach.

'Well, my boy, they say you wish to talk to me?'

Xhól, started and—still sitting cross-legged—raised the phial with both hands, like an offering to the old man who towered over him.

'My lord, look what I found in the forest near the pond.'

Thirteen Jaguar seized the small bottle.

'Interesting, but let's not talk about that here in the open. Come with me!' he ordered.

Xhól got up and, as always, found it difficult to follow the old man. As always, he found it difficult to climb the steps that led to the platform. On a gesture from the priest, the servants disappeared, and Xhól felt free from their inquisitive and slightly disdainful looks. The priest now scrutinised the little phial; bringing it first close to his hooked nose, then holding it at arm's length, in an attempt to decipher the glyphs engraved on the sides.

'A beautiful object, yes. And one that comes from far away! I am sure that I have never seen the like of it in Dos Pilas before: neither at the palace nor at the homes of any of the lords who could afford it. Where does it come from? Where did you find it?'

Xhól told the old man about his idea for an experiment, keeping the name of who had played the 'body' to himself. In fact, the priest did not seem to pay much attention to this detail. He nodded his head in approval when Xhól explained how it allowed him to understand the trajectory of the stone and, as a consequence, to locate where he might find traces of the assassin. And indeed, under the first trees at the edge of the clearing, he had found the very place where the man had lain in ambush, trampled the grass in his impatience, and abandoned the little container in the tall grass.

'You didn't show this phial to anybody? Even to your associate?' asked the priest.

'No, not even to my associate.'

'But he must have been curious.'

'Yes, *he* was,' replied Xhól with a self-conscious smile. 'But I did not relent, and I brought it to you at once.'

'Good,' approved the priest. "You did well. Especially as you have just provided me with the answer to one of our questions.'

'Ah?'

'I suppose you tried to read the glyphs on the bottle?'

'Yes, but I didn't recognise them all.'

'That is understandable. Some of them are not even in use here. This phial comes from faraway Teotihuacán. What is more, the poison was stored in it.'

Xhól started.

'Do you see the two images on each side?'

'Yes,' replied Xhól, bending over the fine sculptures once again.

'On one side is the god K, easily recognisable by

114

his long muzzle, and on the other, the jaguar, lord of the underworld, the world of the dead. It is clear to me that this phial must have belonged to, or have been made for a priest, a healing priest who wanted to store a potent poison inside.'

'But why would a priest keep a deadly poison?'

'Now that may be one thing you should remain ignorant about. But know that some medicines that are beneficial in certain proportions can become deadly poisons at higher doses. So yes, sometimes we have to keep deadly poisons. But it is something that we do not talk about.'

'Does that mean that we are looking for a priest?' asked Xhól, shocked.

'Maybe. Maybe not,'replied Thirteen Jaguar. 'First, I am certain that none of my priests has ever had such an object in their possession: I would have known! I know them all since birth, saw them grow up and take over their office from their predecessors, whom I also trained. No, this has not been long in Dos Pilas. And, as we have a merchant who just returned, he may well be the one who brought it back.'

Xhól looked at the old man, frightened.

'He brought back what killed him?'

''Yes, my boy. Interesting, eh? One might almost call it divine retribution.'

'Divine retribution?'

'It is dangerous to become mixed up with intrigue. Those who do so must accept risking their own skin.'

'Intrigue?'

'Why do you think that the merchant decided to bring a precious flask of poison here, if not to sell it,' the priest asked impatiently. 'You are intelligent, my boy, but you have a lot to learn about people yet!'

Xhól left the priest, discomfited by his parting words. Well, if he still had a lot to learn about people, in any case about nobles, priests and merchants, there was at least one man he understood, and that was One Hunter. Since the day before, One Hunter had been kept apart, without any possibility of escape. He might be let in to bring the man some food; he didn't expect that the guards would stop him. Indeed, though surprised, the guards *did* allow him through. He entered the courtyard of the house of warriors where One Hunter was imprisoned. With two guards on duty at the door, there was no way he could escape from the compound in which the young warriors lived and trained. And what good would it do? Escape meant resigning himself to a solitary life in the forest, never to have any more contact with the city. Escape meant running an even greater risk; that of being captured by the enemies of Dos Pilas, and sacrificed.

Xhól found the young man crouching in the shadow of a pillar, immobile, staring with worrying intensity at a meagre tuft of grass that had survived the constant coming and going. Xhól sat beside One Hunter who gave him a look of surprise when his visitor put down on the ground some fruit and tamales prepared by Ix Naah. Xhól was not daunted. He knew very well that he would not gain his trust so easily. But if he wanted to save him, he would have to keep on trying. Why, indeed, did he so want to save someone who had shown him no trust , no friendship; someone who had always kept him at a distance? Why? Xhól stopped for a moment to consider. Why did he care so much about the whole business when it did not concern him at all? The answer suddenly came to him as he watched One Hunter take one of the tamales with a hesitant gesture: because he knew that One Hunter was innocent. As simple as that. He knew it! It was not fair for One Hunter to be condemned for the crime of another. He could not accept it. If it truly had been master Pek who had brought back the phial, it would be yet more proof for the high priest that One Hunter had used it to douse his weapon. But he knew that if One Hunter had done it, *he* wouldn't have forgotten the phial! And *he* would have hit the head, not the shoulder blade. The shot had almost missed. And One Hunter would never have missed such an easy one! He knew that. And because he knew that, he had to find the real culprit. And to find the real culprit, he needed One Hunter's help. And One Hunter did not want to help. Why?

Turning the question over in his mind, Xhól was at a loss about what to do next. He went for simplicity: tell One Hunter everything. Tell him everything that he had seen and thought. Tell him that he didn't believe in his guilt. Tell him that it was somebody else. Tell him that the priest believed that master Pek had been killed to prevent him from talking to the council and that he, One Hunter, had been used as a scapegoat or as an accomplice. And tell him is what he did. One Hunter looked at him for a few seconds.

'Is all of this true?' he asked.

'I swear to you.'

'Then, you are convinced that it wasn't me?'

'Yes.'

'And the high priest, on the other hand, is convinced that it was somebody who wanted to prevent my brother from speaking to the council?'

'I'll say it again. Yes.'

'Why was one of my stones found near the dead body, then?'

'To make you bear the responsibility for it. You are the only one, outside of this business with the council, who could have wanted your brother to disappear forever.'

'The only one? Really? Do you want me to tell you what I feared when you showed me the stone?' let out One Hunter in a sudden outburst. 'Do you want me to tell you? Really?'

'The dam has burst,' Xhól thought jubilantly. 'The words will flow like a fountain now.' One Hunter went on without even looking at him:

'What I feared, I tell you, was that she might have done it. If you only knew how unhappy he made her, as I did! Nobody knows. Except me. Although I lived at the back of the enclosure, I often heard them, you know! I heard him, anyway. His voice, and the blows he dealt her too. And the following morning, when we would meet, she and I, near the spring, seeing her face was enough. Seeing her walk was enough. Do you know how she walked? Like me! Almost like me! And there was nothing I could do: he was my brother, she was his wife. For as long as I can remember she never had one good day in her life since she married him. Until he left.'

Xhól let him go on, wondering how long the flow of words would last.

'Then I saw her change, stand taller, become more confident, begin to laugh again. Can you imagine? Laugh. Oh, she only did it at home when we discussed the crops or managing the slaves. She started to tease me, to smile, to laugh, and it was kindly done. She is the only one who has been kind to me. And all that died out with his return. Yes, I saw the look on her face at the feast when she caught sight of him: it was death itself that she saw rising before her, her own death. That is what the terror on her face told me. After having greeted my brother in the proper way—he only replied with a joke about my limp—I hurried home. And there, I waited.

'I did not have to wait long. They returned shortly after me. The slaves put their loads down in the storeroom. Then he ordered them out, and the two of them were left alone. At first, I did not hear them. I even had the impression that she left the house for a while. Then, all hell broke loose. I couldn't understand what he was saying, shouting, in fact. I had never heard him so angry before. And the thrashing began. Yes, the thrashing, and this time she screamed. Well, not for long. No, she did not scream for long. As for me, I stayed in my hut, wondering what to do. At some point, I couldn't take any more, and I went out. Outside, I waited for a moment in the shadows. As it kept on going, I left. I didn't want to stay there. I didn't want to be forced to listen. I didn't want to meet her at the spring the next morning, limping again. So, I ran away to the forest.'

'At night,' asked Xhól, incredulous.'Without a weapon?'

'Yes, at night and without a weapon. It's easy to see that you city dwellers never go into the forest at night if you think it's dangerous!' continued One Hunter, with a contemptuous shrug of his shoulders. 'There have been no predators sighted around Dos Pilas for a long time, you know. They are scared, the predators, if you want to know! They are wise to be so, because the only predators left are men, and they keep as far away as possible from men. No, there is no danger in entering the forest at night. It is the only place where I feel at peace. I didn't want to return too early. When I got too hungry, I resigned myself to going home to eat something: it had already been daylight for quite some time. In any case, I had to go back at some point.'

'That was when I saw you on the path from the pond?'

'Yes.'

'Then you *did* pass by the pond. What did you see?'

'No, I didn't go as far as that. I cut through the woods from the place where I was to get back to the central plaza by the quickest route. I only returned to the path at the very end of it.'

'And you didn't see anything, hear anything?'

'No,' answered One Hunter. 'I didn't see anything, except a white shadow running away, perhaps a tunic, something too vague, too fleeting for me to really notice. But when they came to arrest me, when they told me that he had been found near the pond, that they had found one of my stones, I thought that it must have been my brother's wife, my brother's wife who couldn't take any more. Although I did wonder how she could have killed him, deal him such a mighty blow. But, as I didn't want to involve her, I kept quiet, and I have remained silent since.'

'Do you trust me?' asked Xhól.

'Trust you to do what?'

'Find the assassin.'

'Why would you do that?'

'Because I know it's not you.'

'You don't think that she did it?'

'You saw nothing, besides that white tunic, that could make you think it was her?'

'No.'

'She didn't say anything to you these past months that could make you believe that she would want to kill him if he ever returned?'

'No. In any case, I was not there that often.

You know, my true home is the forest. She took good care of the enclosure, and the slaves; they obeyed her orders. I wasn't there very often during the day and in the evening——'

'Yes?'

'She was careful.'

'Careful?'

'Not to give way to gossip. She did not often go out after nightfall, even to come and talk to me. Especially to come and talk to me, if you see what I mean. She was avoiding me, yes, but it was done so kindly that I accepted it. I understood.'

CHAPTER 7

ADULTERY

MASTER PEK'S WIDOW looked at him through her half shut eyes. She didn't want him to be there, realised Xhól. When he had appeared at the entrance to the garden, she had abandoned the old crones who were attending the merchant's wake to come and meet him, and had welcomed him with a few courteous words. The enclosure was well-tended, approved Xhól; the crops well-ordered, well-irrigated. Even without what the merchant's trading brought in, the family had enough to live well off the harvest. The widow herself had a reputation for the quality of her weaving. The woman still surprised him. There was something hidden behind those half-closed eyes, Xhól thought; something she didn't want him—or anybody—to discover. At the same time, she was as smooth as the surface of the pool on the bank of which her husband had been found.

He began to ask her the questions he had prepared. He had had to find a pretext. His conversation with the high priest had given him an idea. Had there not been something destined for the noble Thirteen Jaguar among the objects brought back by her husband? Thirteen Jaguar had said something to that effect to him, Xhól; he had seemed quite impatient to get hold of it, but could not leave the palace, and had thus sent Xhól instead. Quite innocently, he described the imaginary item: a small round bottle to hold one of the high priest's most valued medicines. The name did have an impact, as did the reference to the phial. The widow glared at him, then immediately withdrew deep into herself. In a flat voice, she answered that she had not looked; since her husband's body had been brought to her, he had been her first concern. The burial was to take place that afternoon, but if the noble Thirteen Jaguar was so impatient—

She bid him to follow her into the small room where the merchant stored his most precious goods. Three parcels, still unopened, lay in the centre of the room. It looked like master Pek had not had time to unpack. And yet, thought Xhól, he had taken something out of one of these parcels as soon as he arrived. Which parcel? Xhól inspected the bundles wrapped in thick cloth. Large buffers made out of the same material were inserted between each object too. The most precious ones had been swathed in thin cotton to protect them from any shocks. The widow stood there while he inspected the packages. She was not going to leave him alone. She was right to do so. This was the most precious collection of objects he had ever had occasion to admire: a jade breastplate, some convoluted vases covered with fresh paintings, pearls, ear ornaments. And a collection of small vessels of various shapes. Xhól recognised the style at once. His heart began to beat a little faster when he lifted up a small basin, and then a cup, to the light that came through the doorway. Yes, there was no doubt about it. There was no mistaking the mastery of a craftsman. This collection was from the same hand as the one who had crafted the small bottle. He straightened up with difficulty and assured the widow that there was, in fact, nothing here that fitted the description that the priest had given him. Perhaps her husband had not found what had been ordered? The noble priest would be disappointed, but she was not at fault. With these words, he moved towards the door. Once again he had the impression that a storm of emotion passed over the surface of those dark eyes, but this time it was relief.

It was now time to go and meet again with the

priest, report what One Hunter had confided to him, and admit the part that he had had him play without his knowledge with the widow. First, he went to the palace, where the priest had his lodgings. If he could find him there, he would avoid the sneers of the servants at the observatory temple. Luck was on his side, and he was immediately led to the room where the high priest worked on his writings. Seated on a cushion, Thirteen Jaguar was staring straight in front of him, his bony hands resting on his knees. The young man hesitated in the doorway and was already mumbling a few words of apology when one of the hands lifted and beckoned to him to approach. Xhól moved forward, bowed, and sat down in front of the still silent old priest. Why did he get involved in this business? he wondered as he contemplated the bright eyes of the old man. He was sticking his neck out way too far. And now, it was too late to turn back. Once in front of the priest, he couldn't for a minute consider lying to him. He told him everything: what One Hunter had said, and what he had seen at the widow's. The priest did not take his eyes off him throughout his story.

'You astound me, my boy. Why go to such lengths without being asked?'

'My lord, I don't know how to explain it to you. Each step I take, I reproach myself for it and tell myself that I am an idiot to meddle in something that is none of my concern.'

'And yet, each step is followed by another one.'

'Yes, my lord.'

'Why?'

'I cannot let this happen,' answered Xhól.

'Let what happen?'

'Let a man who is not guilty be condemned.'

'You think that he is not guilty?'

'In no way, my lord, not even an accomplice. I believe him to know nothing, and to have been led along by the nose.'

'By whom?'

'By master Pek's widow.'

'Do you then believe that there is something between them?'

'As a matter of fact, no. This is why she can lead him along by the nose. But I am convinced that the phial was among the objects master Pek brought back and, moreover, that his wife knew about it.'

'How would you try to find out more?' asked the priest, interested.

'That, my lord, will prove difficult. The problem is that if you step in, everyone will clam up. Not because they might know who the murderer is, but because they are too afraid to speak freely to you.'

'But you, you dare speak freely to me.'

'That doesn't prevent me from being afraid,' Xhól replied with a sheepish smile.

'You are afraid? And yet you keep on going?'

'Yes, my lord.'

'Why?'

'Because I believe that, deep down, you too would never let a man who is not guilty be condemned.'

'You believe that of me?'

'Yes, even if I don't know much about men,' replied Xhól, looking straight into the eyes of the old priest.

'You amaze me, painter. There is more to you than meets the eye. And you do indeed seem to be the only one here who dares speak to my face, with the exception of the lady. And you are right. Nor do I want a man to be wrongly accused. The more because if the actual culprit remains free, it will create a ferment of decadence that will grow and rot our city. You have my authorisation.'

'Your authorisation?'

'To keep on going with what you have started so well. You are right: I cannot interrogate these people myself. Not for now, at least. With you, they may open up. Therefore, keep on using my name and my influence, if that helps you in your task. On one condition.'

'Yes?'

'That you come and report to me every evening, or more often if there is anything urgent.'

'Yes, my lord.'

'You should also know that your time is limited. Our time is limited. The Ajaw wants to settle this question before leaving for the war. And that will be soon. If you find nothing by then, One Hunter will be executed, and this whole business will soon be forgotten in the turmoil of the upcoming battle. Who knows who will be victorious and whether the city shall survive this time? In any case, I want to act as if it *will* survive.'

Xhól got up and left the room. He now knew

what he had to do: keep an eye on the widow. And night was falling— His thoughts were interrupted by One Hunter, who hailed him from the portico of the house of warriors. Xhól met him with a sigh. Try as he might, he did not know how to behave with his other self. Tell him that he suspected his sister-in-law? Out of the question. At the same time, the poor wretch must be bored stiff, locked up in this courtyard, used as he was to roaming the forest all day long. Xhól headed over to the prisoner, thankful for the evening shadows. It would make things easier; the darkness would conceal his embarrassment. One Hunter gave him the impression of being at the end of his tether, at the end of his courage.

'Tell me, is there any news?'

'No.'

That was something Xhól could say without lying. He didn't have any news: some guesses perhaps, but no news.

'Don't worry,' Xhól added. 'I spoke to the high priest, to Thirteen Jaguar himself. He is now convinced of your innocence, too.'

'Convinced of my innocence?'

'Yes, at least convinced that I think you are innocent and that I may be right. But he lacks evidence. So do I. But the Ajaw wants the culprit before going to war. We will do our best.'

'And did you see her since?'

'Y-es,' Xhól faltered.

'How is she?' asked One Hunter, seizing him by the arm. 'Tell me. How is she coping with all this?'

'Well,' answered Xhól, relieved to be able to tell the truth, if not all of it. 'Don't worry too much about her.'

'How can I not worry about her!' replied One Hunter. 'Imagine! Her husband dead, even if she didn't love him, and me absent. Who is there to help her face things?'

'Don't fret about that, I say,' answered Xhól as he freed himself.

'I can't stay here any longer,' blurted out One Hunter. 'I've had enough of this cage of stone!' he exclaimed while shooting a wild look around him.

'Come now,' replied Xhól, in what he hoped was his most encouraging voice. 'Come now. You've only been at the palace these last two days. You know very well that if you did succeed in escaping, it would be an irremediable admission of your guilt. The Ajaw would no longer listen to us, not even to Thirteen Jaguar, oldest among his advisors as he may be! Not even if we found, bound, and brought the real culprit before his throne. I beg you to be patient. A little longer. At least until tomorrow night. Will you?'

'And spend another day in this courtyard, then?'

'Yes. Are you being ill-used by the guards?'

'No. I am given food and left alone most of the time. But if you knew how much I hate being surrounded by all these people! Then, there are the sideways glances they throw at me, the whispers I can hear, even if they are not directed at me. I can't stand them, those healthy people who laugh at me, who scorn me. Even the slaves do it!'

'I know,' replied Xhól, in a placating tone.

'It can't be helped. Please, I am begging you. No rash move. You promise? At least until tomorrow evening?'

'I will,' replied One Hunter, resigned.

One Hunter turned back to the ward in the house of warriors, where a straw bed had been laid out for him, identical to those of the young warriors who shared the dormitory. He lay down on the couch, curled up on the less painful of his shoulders, and sank into a restless sleep.

Night had come and Thirteen Jaguar was exhausted. The day had been a long one, and quite eventful at that. That was how he could tell that he was no longer as young as he once was. What had happened to the young Thirteen Jaguar who could withstand the three days of ceremonies and three nights of vigils leading up to a crowning without any ill effects? He was getting old; as simple as that. And yet, he still had one last thing to do before retiring for the night: see the Ajaw. Talk to him about this business, and especially, find out whether there was any news. The noble Eighteen Puma had still not returned after almost two days of absence. What could that mean? He headed towards the royal apartments. The two servants posted at the door bowed to him and let him into the room where the Ajaw was dining in the company of the lady of Itzán and his daughter. They were all silent, all lost in their own thoughts. The priest began by asking the lady how she was feeling since the morning.

'Very well, thank you.' she answered in an even

tone. 'As I told you, these spells pass quickly.'

She was not eating much, noticed the priest. Although the sacrifice was reason enough for that. The wound would be slow to heal——if it did not become infected——and would make taking any food painful for many days afterwards. The priest then turned his gaze towards the girl; she was sulking, without even trying to hide it. Why, he did not know. The Ajaw, absorbed in his thoughts had not noticed. He gave Thirteen Jaguar a curt nod and invited him to join them. Thirteen Jaguar sat down and ate, out of politeness more than hunger.

At his age, he required very little; little food and little sleep. He had a growing feeling of slowing down in a world that was moving ever faster. Paradoxically, it was since he had begun to have that feeling that others looked upon him with even more fear and more respect, like that idiot Ah Chuen B'alam when he had told him yesterday that he would be watching the novices alone over the following days. There had been pleasure in the man's smile. Fear, too. He was sure that Ah Chuen B'alam would not dream of shirking his new-found responsibilities, even if he had wanted to. It was enough to look at him in a certain way for the man to waver. And that is the man who is going to succeed me! he thought, with a sneer that curled up a corner of his mouth.

The silent meal dragged on without enthusiasm. It was very different to the feast of two nights before. Then, they all heard a commotion in the first courtyard. The noble Eighteen Puma, without even waiting for a servant to introduce him, hurried into the room.

'This time, they are upon us!' he exclaimed.

'What do you mean, cousin?' answered the Ajaw.

'Yesterday, right after you asked me to conduct a reconnaissance patrol of the enemy's movements, we left and headed for the observation post on our northern border where you had left some guards. We walked all day but didn't reach the outpost before dusk, and slept in the forest last night. This morning, a messenger from the observation post burst into our camp in the first light of dawn. In fact, we almost killed him before he could tell us his name! He was relieved to see that it was us and told us his news. The army of Tikal is on its way. One of our spies was able to observe them from under cover without being caught. There are several battalions; all their warriors according to this man. And this army is only four day's march from here! The only good point about such a large army is that it moves slowly. They need to widen the paths to go through. And they have to carry a great deal of supplies. As soon as I learned this, I decided to come back at once, to inform you in person. I left the messenger—he was exhausted—with the best part of my squadron, and only took two men with me. I commanded to those remaining behind to split and position themselves along all the possible paths in order to inform us of their exact location each morning. We do not know yet whether they will pass by the lake or through the forest. What is sure is that this time Tikal has decided to annihilate us!'

The Ajaw let him finish, then ordered him to go and take his rest.

'I want you in good shape tomorrow. But do not say anything to anyone yet.'

'It will be difficult to keep the news secret: people saw us come back, and my men are already at the house of warriors.'

The Ajaw made a gesture to signify that this was not so important, after all.

'Let the rumours fly this evening, but I want the council to meet tomorrow, at daybreak.'

Xhól was finally leaving the palace when he heard a low call. A bird was singing in the soft evening air, but the song was too regular and repeated itself three times. Six Sky! thought Xhól. She beckoned him to follow her quickly into a narrow lane that ran between two buildings. A servant might pass by at any moment and discover them. Why should she take such a risk?

'Xhól,' she whispered as though she had heard his silent question 'the hiding place is no more. I am not even sure that we will ever be able to speak to each other again. I gave my new maids the slip this time; I won't be able to do it often in the future.'

'What is going on, Six Sky?'

'The lady of Itzán has decided that it is time I became a real lady. No more leaving the palace unless I am accompanied. From now on, she wants me to spend most of my time in her chamber, under her watch. I only escaped now because the maids are busy helping her to set for the night, and I pretexted that I needed a skein I had left in my room. If I do not return soon, one of them will come looking for me. Oh, Xhól!' she uttered, distraught.

'Isn't being a lady what you ever wanted?'

'Yes, at least I thought so. But if I have to be a lady, I want to be a lady who reigns, not a prisoner!'

'Well, if that does happen, will you not be happy?'

'Perhaps. In fact, I don't know!'

'What a child you are.'

'No, I am no longer a child,' she replied, stamping her foot.

'Exactly. That is why the noble lady of Itzán is keeping you close,' retorted Xhól.

'Xhól, please don't take that tone of voice with me.'

'What tone of voice do you want me to take? One minute, you are acting like the lady who wants everybody to respect her; the next, you speak to me as you did when we were still children. You know, Six Sky, time never stops flowing. The situation has changed since your return from exile; you are no longer the child with whom I could play. That was before. Now the time has come for you to follow your path. And even if you need a little push from the lady right now, I am certain that deep down, it is what you really want.'

'Maybe with everyone else, but not with you.'

'That is not possible,' replied Xhól. 'You know as well as I do that, if not the lady of Itzán, the inquisitiveness of others will prevent us. And when you marry, you will leave forever.'

'Is that what you want?' she asked.

'It would simplify things somewhat.'

Xhól stopped talking and turned his head towards the sound of an approaching voice.

'Leave now! Return to your maids; they have discovered that you are not in your room.'

'But—'

'Obey, Six Sky. You don't want us to be discovered now! They will be here in a minute. If you leave me now, it will create a diversion, and I will be able to slip away in the dark.'

She gave him a brief glance. Then, without a word, she fled into the night. This was it, thought Xhól. It was better to end this way. Better for her, and better for him. As night had now fallen, why not begin his watch on the widow right away? His sister might worry when she didn't see him return, and the children would have to wait one more day for the rest of their story, but that could not be helped. Xhól headed for master Pek's enclosure. Everybody had gone home. The central plaza was deserted. He could hear muffled voices in the second courtyard of the palace, the house of warriors. There, the young soldiers were readying themselves for combat, stirred by the news of the forthcoming attack brought by Eighteen Puma's patrol.

Xhól moved away, walking in the shadows

between houses. He looked at the new moon. The thin waning crescent would prove useful: he would not have to worry about his shadow betraying him. Even with his crab-like gait, he would manage not to make any sound when following someone. His progress was slow as he made his way between the different enclosures. Light shone through some of the houses: not everybody took the same care in filling with mud the gaps in the walls made of palms. This part of the city was quiet. He could hear the movement of a domesticated peacock confined in a cage here, the rustling of branches in a sudden gust of wind there, or the stifled murmur of voices coming from a shed.

Among this people of artisans and farmers, the idea of the approaching war, once public, would only bring worries and woes. The stakes were too high for these people who would not have the consolation of going straight to the paradise promised to the warriors dying in battle, should the city be defeated. For them, for us all, thought Xhól, defeat meant death, slavery or desperate flight into the forest. Nothing to rejoice at.

War lured only warriors—it was their *raison d'être*. For everyone else, it was a reason to despair. Xhól began to daydream. What would life be like if peace reigned between the cities? A life where there were no more wars, no more battles? How would the warriors survive? What would a man like the noble Eighteen Puma do if he could no longer hope to go to battle, capture prisoners, and take advantage of a victory to improve his standing with the Ajaw? All his self-importance, all his haughtiness, all his disdain for the artisans, the hunters and the farmers could not hide the fact that a man like that was nothing without a war, was good for nothing, produced nothing.

Deep in thought, Xhól reached the entrance of master Pek's enclosure. There, the silence was complete. The slaves were already fast asleep in their quarters at the back of the plot. The main house was shrouded in darkness. Nothing surprising about that, thought Xhól, the widow was alone with a corpse; a corpse that would be hurriedly buried on the morrow as it had already begun to decompose with the heat. Xhól crouched in the shadow of a bush from which he commandeered a good view of the door. He sat down in the grass, anticipating his watch to be a long one. The night was still warm. Only later, in the early morning, would it become cooler and a little dew would fall upon the trees and the grass. Upon him, too, were he still there. He would wait, no matter how long it took.

Xhól shifted slightly. He could hardly feel his feet anymore. The muscles in his shoulders had become taut too. How long had it been since he had last moved? The moon had already crossed the sky and disappeared to the west, in the shadows of the forest encircling the enclosures. The night was cold now. He struggled against sleep. He must keep his mind busy. What could he think about that would keep him awake? The city? The stela he had sculpted? Actually, why had the Ajaw placed those water lilies?

And the seashells? He had been able to take a look at them while they were still intact. They were lovely. They came from the distant sea. He had never seen the sea and could only rely on the stories that some merchants had told him. The sea was infinite, limitless, save for the occasional island—a small chunk of rock completely surrounded by water, they said. Xhól tried to imagine a small chunk of land completely surrounded by water on all sides. The blue waters slowly took on a dark green hue, and the waves became treetops, frothing into the distance. The island was the city itself; an island surrounded by trees. The forest was infinite, too, and very capable of engulfing them all once again if they ever stopped clearing, planting, building.

The hours went by, slowly. Xhól followed one train of thought, clung onto it, then let go of it to jump onto another one. Could he have been mistaken? No, that wasn't possible. He didn't want to give up. Not now. Yet he had to move if he wanted to hold out. First unfold one leg, then the other. Massage the thighs, the ankles. Move his feet, a little. He got up with difficulty, leant against the trunk of one of the shrubs hiding him. He shook himself, took a few steps, returned to his watching spot. He realised that he was behaving just like the man who had waited for master Pek by the pond. By the way, they still did not know what the merchant was doing there, near the pond the previous night. What could have brought him there?

Right then, Xhól sensed some movement.

139

The door to the main building opened, noiselessly, stealthily. He saw a white figure emerge, in stark contrast to the surrounding darkness. It could only be the widow. She headed for the small hut that served as One Hunter's lodgings. What was she going to do there? It seemed to him that she was holding something in her right hand as he watched her pass ten paces away from him, but he wasn't sure. The widow went into the hut, remained there for a few minutes, then trod the narrow path again, just a few paces away from Xhól, who did not move a muscle. Was she going home? No, now she was leaving the enclosure, and—from what he could make out in the dark—she went in the direction of the central plaza.

Xhól began to follow her, soundless despite his ungainly walk. He now knew where the widow was going. In any case, he had his suspicions. He could allow her a small lead. He was not surprised to see her reach the central plaza, slip into the shadow of the temple, carefully avoid the palace, then take the infamous path to the pond. The pond, he said to himself; that was where the key to the mystery lied.

The white figure finally came to a halt at the edge of the pond, virtually at the same place where Xhól had discovered master Pek's body. The figure remained still, waiting. Xhól hid behind a tree, a ceiba with a wide trunk, almost where the assassin had hidden. He heard a noise on the path behind him. In long, assured strides someone was approaching. Xhól wondered who it could be. It was a man, tall, in good health, and used to following this path in the dark; that he could tell. Who could that man be? He had to find out, get closer, hear what the two of them would say to each other.

Xhól glided from tree to tree, then crouched, lay down in the grass, and began to crawl. He could hear the murmur of hushed voices. There was anger in the higher-pitched one, that of a woman, but he could not make out the words yet. Should he try to get even closer, at the risk of being caught? The voices grew louder. The widow was throwing caution to the wind in her growing rage, and the stranger too. It seemed to Xhól that she was reproaching him with something, or demanding something of him. And he didn't like it! The quarrel took a sudden turn for the worse. Xhól witnessed the unknown man strike the woman on the head. She collapsed in the high grass. The man bent over her and was ready to strike a second time when Xhól decided to step in.

He yelled, got up as quickly as he could, and ran towards the couple. At first, the stranger had remained rooted to the spot. As soon as he heard Xhól approaching, he stepped back, leapt into the shadow of a nearby tree, and madly flew through the forest. With his bad leg, Xhól knew that he would never catch up. He had better see to the widow. She lay there, unconscious, but still alive. She had fallen half into the water, just as her husband had in the same place. Perhaps there would have been an attempt to pass her death off as a drowning, or a suicide maybe? A suicide that someone would have found quite convenient.

Xhól's mind returned to more practical considerations: apart from dragging her to a dry place, he could do nothing for her without light or help. He didn't know how long she would remain unconscious. He didn't know whether she needed the help of a healer or not. He decided to act just like he had done for her husband. Just like for her husband, he would go and seek assistance and a stretcher. But this time he would go straight to Thirteen Jaguar. Xhól got up and set off.

There was a risk that, during Xhól's absence, the fugitive might retrace his steps and finish the job he had begun. It was a risk he would have to take. But Xhól didn't think so. The man had seemed way too frightened on hearing him shouting; so frightened that he had leapt into the darkest part of the clearing and run away. No, that man was way too frightened—of being unmasked, thought Xhól, moving as fast as he possibly could towards the palace.

It took Xhól very little time to get past the indignant objections of the servants, gain admittance to the old priest who was already awake, and explain the new development to him. Thirteen Jaguar came out with a group of torch-bearers. Although dawn was now breaking, it was still dark under the trees.

They reached the pond quickly. Master Pek's widow lay in the same position, still unconscious. The murderer had not come back to finish the job.

The high priest bent over the young woman, took her pulse, felt her forehead, arms, legs, then her stomach where he stilled his hand. Without making any comment, he stood up and ordered two servants to put her on the stretcher that he had had them bring. They returned to the central plaza as the day broke. The widow had made no movement. At the palace, the priest had her laid out in a room of the the women's court and gave orders for at least two maids of the lady to watch over her at all times. Back in his own apartments, he bade Xhól to sit down and asked that a hot beverage be prepared for the two of them.

'Why two maids?' dared Xhól once the servants were gone.

'Did you not say that she had something to do with the death of her husband?'

'Yes, but tonight she was the one who was almost killed.'

'By the murderer. And now I know why.'

'Ah?'

'Pek's widow is with child.'

'With child!'

'Yes, she must be four months pregnant.'

'While the merchant was away?'

'Exactly. Which gives us a motive. Do you know what the penalty is for adultery? For the man as well as the woman?'

'Yes,' replied Xhól reddening. 'Death.'

'What interests me now is discovering the identity of the man. That is why I have left these women with the widow, and the guards. I want her to live, at least long enough to tell us that.'

'And if she dies before?'

'That is a risk. The blow was forceful, but not deadly, I hope. Yet, it could lead to her losing the child. And the murderer may want to finish the job.'

'Here, in the palace?'

'Yes, if he is a man of a certain standing, it would not be that difficult for him.'

CHAPTER 8

WAR!

XHÓL LEFT THE HIGH priest's apartments, went through the first courtyard, and entered the house of warriors. By now, dawn had broken. He sat down against the wall facing the rising sun and observed the hustle and bustle around him. The youngest warriors were already at their training, as they would every morning. Today, it was axe-wielding in single combat. This morning there was some added tension in the air. Had scouts not returned the night before with news of an impending battle?

Tikal was once again launching an attack against them, despite their defeat of one year ago. Well, that defeat of Tikal one year ago had been against Calakmul; Calakmul, which, over the course of the last few months, had withdrawn its troops from Petexbatún to move them back around its own territory, leaving Dos Pilas dangerously exposed. So yes, perhaps Tikal thought it was a good time to attack Dos Pilas, weakened by the retreat of its ally. Did not proud Tikal have good reasons to want to remove from its side the thorn that was Dos Pilas ever since the Ajaw's shift in alliances thirty years before? Nobody knew when they would be marching against the enemy, but everybody clearly saw that there was something coming. The priests had been coming and going from the Ajaw's apartments since early morning, and the council had been summoned, once again. The oldest men had received orders to report late in the afternoon with their weapons at the ready. All this gave the exercise an unusual flavour. The young men exerted themselves under the surveillance of their masters at arms.

Xhól spotted Shield of Jade and his best friend as the two young men were training with furious energy. Even though it was just an exercise, Shield of Jade wanted to win, as always. Xhól watched him for a few minutes: he would become an excellent warrior and, most importantly, thought Xhól, he had the advantage of being a clever one. He had no doubt that this young man would, in time, become one of the Ajaw's best officers and one day join his council. If he survived the coming battle.

Xhól saw One Hunter trying to reach him, sidling along the walls of the great courtyard to keep clear of the combating pairs. He was advancing with all the speed he was capable of, his awkward gait accentuated by his haste. Out of breath, One Hunter leaned against the wall and slid down to sit beside Xhól.

'Is it true what they say? That she was almost killed, same as my brother, in the same place? That she is now guarded by the lady of Itzán's women?'

'Yes,' replied Xhól.

He gave a pitying look at his other self: should he tell him the other news? The news that the priest had just shared with him? He decided not to. One Hunter seemed upset enough already; others could handle that, later.

'Even if this should convince the Ajaw of my innocence, I didn't want it to be that way. I didn't want any harm to come to her!'

Xhól gave him a look of sympathy mingled with surprise: had he not noticed anything? No, nothing. For him, the woman was only a victim. Should he disillusion him? No, he would say nothing for now. He would keep on enquiring, without saying anything to One Hunter yet. He would take advantage of the council to go and look in One Hunter's hut to see what the widow had been up to there. Just then, he noticed the arrival of the first attendees; Thirteen

Jaguar and his second-in-command, the priest Ah Chuen B'alam who, full of his own importance, pushed aside the young warriors. Then came the generals. The last to arrive was the noble Eighteen Puma who strode through the courtyard without casting them a glance.

Thirteen Jaguar had seated himself in his usual place to the right of the Ajaw—as was only his due, him the oldest member of the council, and the high priest besides. Ah Chuen B'alam sat down below him. Thirteen Jaguar was under no illusions: that intriguer was only waiting for an opportunity to move up one rank and occupy the coveted seat, which would literally give him access to the sovereign's ear. If there was one person who wanted to impress on him that it was time to relinquish his position, to end his cycle and to disappear into the underworld, it was Ah Chuen B'alam.

When Thirteen Jaguar's wife had died the previous year, he had almost given in to the pressure, for a while. He had released his control over the college of priests for one moment. During the first days of his grief, Ah Chuen B'alam had proved useful, understanding—too useful, too understanding. It hadn't taken him long to notice the manoeuvre, and he had taken action without wasting time. His fighting spirit had overcome the sense of loss and despair he had felt at Ix Loom's passing; Ix Loom, his companion, his helpmate; Ix Loom, whom he had kept despite her being barren for many long years. And then, one day, she had become pregnant, when neither one of them believed it to be possible any longer. And what is more, she had given him a son! But now, Thirteen Jaguar said to himself with a stab of guilt, it was time to stop thinking about the past and devote himself to the present, and the present was war. He gave then his full attention to the scout who had just entered the room with the latest news.

'Yes, my lord, there is no doubt anymore.' said the man, bowing before the Ajaw. 'The whole army of Tikal is upon us. There are far too many of them for just a looting party. They have sent out all their forces. I saw them myself when they camped on the shores of the lake last night. There are so many of them that they were obliged to, for their water supply. As soon as night fell, I ran. I ran at full speed, to warn you. It took me twelve hours to cover the distance.'

'How long do you think it will take them to get here?'

'Well, my lord, that's difficult to say. If nothing stops them: two days. Perhaps a little less.'

'What do you advise?' asked the Ajaw to the council. 'Is it better to wait for them here in Dos Pilas? Or to go out and meet them? Speak! You first,' he said pointing to the oldest general sitting on his left, just opposite Thirteen Jaguar.

'There is only one course of action I can recommend, my lord: go and meet them! Let us choose the best position from which to attack. First, we will benefit from the element of surprise. Here we would be at a disadvantage as the walls are far

149

from complete. Besides, we do not have enough men to defend the city. If we attack, we will have a chance. And if we suffer defeat, it will be easier to evacuate the noble lady of Itzán and your children,' the officer concluded in a faltering voice.

The Ajaw winced.

'Let one thing be clear! This time there will be no evacuation. Neither for my family nor for anybody's. Do you hear me?'

Thirteen Jaguar approved in silence. The Ajaw could do nothing else. Politically, he would not survive a second defeat at the hands of Tikal and a second exile. His blood-line would end there. Better to die on the battlefield than face such shame. No, there would be no escape this time. The city had no other choice than to fight back and defeat the enemy, on its own.

The Ajaw stared at every man present, holding each of them under his gaze for many seconds before passing onto the next. When it was the turn of Ah Chuen B'alam, Thirteen Jaguar felt the man's resolve shake and weaken: would he dare look away? There would then be no returning to the favour of the Ajaw who could accept many faults, except cowardice. Thirteen Jaguar wondered what the Ajaw thought of his second-in-command. Whether he would accept him as a successor when the time came. In fact, the Ajaw would have no choice unless he—Thirteen Jaguar—were to remain in good health for several years, and some of his young novices were to shape well in the meantime.

Ah Chuen B'alam might well die before him, suddenly thought Thirteen Jaguar. As the words took shape in his head, they acquired a flavour of absolute truth. Was it one of those intuitions of him? It certainly felt like one. And he had never been wrong. Die of what, then? The man was cautious; he kept well out of any battles and would be the first to flee. Very few men had borne the name of jaguar* with less appropriateness than this man, full of haughtiness but afraid of everything.

There was no longer any doubt in his mind, however; his second-in-command would die before him. Quite soon, in fact. Enthralled by such a momentous revelation, the old man had not noticed how the Ajaw had moved away from Ah Chuen B'alam to turn his gaze upon him. He had not noticed that he had momentarily disconcerted his lord. On hearing the Ajaw talk to him, Thirteen Jaguar started and let his vision flee.

There was some arguing as to the best place where to lay the ambush would be; the noble Eighteen Puma stubbornly disagreeing with the other generals. That was to be expected, thought Thirteen Jaguar. If there was a man in Dos Pilas who could equal Ah Chuen B'alam in arrogance, it was the noble Eighteen Puma. Each in their own sphere could not admit of someone being smarter than themselves.

The final decision fell upon the place favoured by the other officers; a narrow valley one day's march

---

* B'alam: jaguar.

from the city. Tikal's army would have to pass that way. They would be exposed to an attack led from the top of the hills overlooking the pass. With a little luck, they could with fewer men deal a heavy blow to their enemy. Who knew? The men of Tikal might even not pursue their offensive if their losses were too great?

Thirteen Jaguar let the men of war take care of the final details: the marching order of the different battalions, the problem of the older warriors when it was uncertain as to whether they would still have the fervour needed for combat, the supplies for the few days of the campaign. In order to march more quickly, the men would carry the strict minimum. They would, therefore, need to be supplied with food and water. The only drawback of the chosen position was, indeed, the complete absence of a river or stream in the surrounding area. The departure was set for the next morning. The Ajaw concluded the audience by announcing that he would speak to the assembled warriors after the dedicatory ceremony that he would lead that very evening, assisted by the priests. Thirteen Jaguar agreed, once again. Yes, it seemed fitting to do as much as possible to motivate those who would the next day leave their city and their families, perhaps never to return.

Thirteen Jaguar felt Ah Chuen B'alam swell with pride at his side at the idea of the preeminent role his second-in-command counted on playing in front of the entire city. Yes, thought Thirteen Jaguar, the man would not want to miss such a valuable occasion. He felt a twinge of pity in his heart for such vanity in a man fated to die in such a short time. He quickly stifled the feeling when he considered that he was not sure of anything and that his intuition could well prove to be wrong this time.

Xhól took advantage of the commotion occasioned by the summoning of the council to slip away. He had things to do. He headed for the widow's enclosure. He had feared that her parents—or her slaves—would prevent him from carrying out his search. No, nobody opposed him. News of the attack against the widow had spread, causing consternation. Her relatives were probably at the palace now. As for the frightened slaves, they were gathered around their shacks, muttering about the curse that had befallen the family. There was no longer anybody to give them orders and they were not complaining about having a day off. In any case, they didn't lift a finger to stop him from entering One Hunter's cabin. They might have reacted differently if he had tried to enter the main house, but why bother about what he might be doing in a miserable hut that contained nothing more than a bed of palm leaves, a stool and a few weapons?

Xhól stood motionless in the doorway and looked around the dark, small, and barely-furnished room. Master Pek was rich, but his riches did not benefit his brother. The slaves themselves must have been better housed. Nothing apart from the weapons. Not one piece of clothing. And few places to hide anything at all. He decided that the only possibility was the bedding. He went over to it and began to rummage among the palms, to separate them and spread them out. He wanted to inspect everything. His fingers—the scars barely healed since searching among the reeds on the banks of the pond, were still painful. However, when they encountered a hard surface covered in delicate carvings, he had no doubt: he had found what he was looking for.

He returned to the palace, hiding his find. He headed for the apartments of the high priest who had not yet returned from the council. The priest's manservant suggested that he await his master's return on the patio. Xhól sat down comfortably and inspected the small rectangular phial. Like the one found in the grass near the pool, it was not large but chiselled in an exquisite manner. He could not be wrong. It was indeed the same workmanship; it came from the hand of the same craftsman. He would swear to it.

It felt good in the shade of the columns of this remote part of the palace, sheltered from the hustle and bustle of the main courtyard. A good place, a good opportunity to think, to ponder. Would the high priest be interested enough in his findings to talk to the Ajaw before the latter left for war? After all, it was only one man's life that was at stake, whilst the next day it would be the lives of hundreds. Would the Ajaw, the noble B'alaj Chan K'awill, his lord, be inclined to listen? What value did the Ajaw accord to the life of a mere commoner, a man without lineage or any other use than to bring back the handsomest feather ornaments?

On beholding Thirteen Jaguar enter the shady courtyard, Xhól hoped that he would soon receive the answers to his questions. To his dismay, the high priest was accompanied by Ah Chuen B'alam. The man was a real nuisance; impossible to speak in front of him. Thirteen Jaguar signalled to Xhól to stay where he was and went into his apartments, followed by his second-in-command. From what Xhól could catch of their conversation, it was the usual one. The priest Ah Chuen B'alam was again complaining; complaining about the fact that the Ajaw had not asked him to speak earlier at the council, relegating him after the youngest of the generals; complaining about the minor position he would finally hold during the dedicatory ceremony; complaining about the insolent attitude of the noble lord Eighteen Puma. The priest Ah Chuen B'alam was a born complainer; it was his vocation and his art. Xhól wondered how the old priest—who was not renowned for his patience, could put up with it, or with the idea that such a man would one day succeed him.

Right now, the high priest *did* seem to put up with or, rather, not to heed him. With a weary, toneless voice, Thirteen Jaguar finally dismissed the priest as soon as a slackening in the man's complaining allowed him to do so. Not to Ah Chuen B'alam's taste, thought Xhól, observing the pinched, frowning expression as the priest left. Good riddance, Xhól thought with renewed impatience as he arose and waited for the old priest to summon him. For a brief moment, Xhól hovered on the threshold, struck by the thin frame hunched up on the cushions. How old Thirteen Jaguar looked this morning! How lacking in energy! Although the priest Ah Chuen B'alam was not responsible for the old man' state, his incessant recriminations hadn't helped. No, there was more to it, thought Xhól, pained; this was total withdrawal, as though as if the vital spark had abandoned the old body. Then Xhól looked at the eyes and felt some relief. The old man may have been tired, but his strength was there, in his look, still intact.

Xhól showed him his find and explained where he had made the discovery.

'Do you think that the widow planted it in One Hunter's bed?'

'I didn't see her do it,' was Xhól's honest answer. 'And I didn't see what she had in her hand when she passed me by. But yes, I *think* she did it.'

'You are a good witness,' replied Thirteen Jaguar with a thin smile, 'exact and fair.'

The priest then uncorked the small phial and sniffed it.

'I need to test it. Judging by the smell, however, it seems to me to be the same concoction as in the other phial.'

'Why would the widow hide it in One Hunter's hut?'

'There are two possible reasons for that, my boy. The first is that she simply did not want it found in her own house.'

'And the second one?'

'The second one is a more serious matter. She wanted it found there, at his place. I fear that I may have done a great disservice to the boy when I had him brought here publicly. She must have told herself that he would make the ideal culprit.'

'Do you believe that she did it in accord with the other man?'

'That, I can't say. Not yet. For us to find out, she will have to wake up. And even then, I am not sure that she will tell us.'

'Even after he tried to kill her?'

'You know even less about women than about men, my boy.' the old man shot back with a mischievous smile.

Xhól reddened.

'Yes, even after he attempted to kill her,' the priest continued. 'First, she may keep silent because she fears him, or she is perhaps ready to sacrifice herself to save him. Even after he tried to kill her. The opposite—and this is what we should hope for One Hunter's sake—is that she tells us everything out of resentment towards a lover who has behaved treacherously to her. When she awakens, we will know.'

'What can we do while we wait for her to regain consciousness? Can't we talk to the Ajaw? Now?'

'That is what I am going to do, my boy. If the Ajaw finds the time to see me. We are going to war, remember! Tikal's army will soon be here if we let them. And the Ajaw has decided not to let them.

157

We are going to pour all our forces into a counter-attack and leave the city defenceless for the duration of the battle. Before the new moon reaches first quarter, we may all be gone: you, me, One Hunter, master Pek's widow, Dos Pilas even. This time, the future of the city itself is at stake. How much does the life of One Hunter—wrongly accused of murder as he is, fare against that?'

Xhól had his own opinion on the matter, and the high priest, who was looking at him closely, smiled.

'Come with me, my boy. We are going to find out right away how things stand!'

The old man jumped up with renewed energy and strode out of the room. As usual, Xhól was at pains to keep up with him. Once more, they entered the first courtyard. There, the hustle and bustle had reached a new fevered high. The morning training session was over, and young warriors were now gathered in an excited circle around the officers, asking questions, getting their orders. Even the servants appeared to have lost their poise. The high priest asked one of them, slightly more composed than the others, to announce his presence to the Ajaw. A few seconds later, the slave came out of the audience chamber, lifted the curtain, and invited them to enter.

Thirteen Jaguar went into the room at a brisk pace. Xhól lingered behind for an instant then followed him. Inside, the atmosphere was quite different. There was no agitation here, only the proper poise pertaining to power and majesty.

The Ajaw was throning on the platform covered in jaguar skins. His face did not betray the fact that he would soon leave for war, or that he was in a hurry to gather his troops. Impassive as ever, the Ajaw bade Thirteen Jaguar speak. Xhól sidled against the wall in the vain ambition of going unnoticed. His hope was dashed to pieces when, summoned by the Ajaw, he was forced to move to the centre of the room and speak. He then told the story of how he had watched the widow the previous evening, his suspicion that she had hidden a phial similar to the one containing the poison that had killed her husband in her brother-in-law's bedding, and finally, the attack near the pond of which she had been the victim. He delivered his tale using as few words as possible, trembling all over. He then retreated against the wall, as close as possible to the entrance.

The Ajaw had remained impassive from start to finish: no interruption, no question, no exclamation. In a way, Xhól preferred that. On the other hand, he wondered anxiously what was going through the Ajaw's mind. Did he think that he was making it all up? The cold gaze of his lord paralysed him—as it always did. He suddenly wondered whether the Ajaw behaved in the same way in private, once the show was over. Was he this cold towards his daughter, his two sons, the lady herself?

Thirteen Jaguar stepped forward to describe how he had discovered that the merchant had been poisoned, that the poison had been brought to Dos Pilas by Pek himself— this had made the Ajaw wince—and, last but not least, that his widow was with child. By another man.

The Ajaw let the high priest present his case without interruption. Once Thirteen Jaguar had finished, he arose and spoke.

'If I understand correctly, Pek himself brought back this poison, which was used in a fashion he had not foreseen. Someone must have ordered it. I want to know whom. And why. As for the rest, what do you think? Is the widow pregnant with her brother-in-law's child? In that case, he would have had two reasons to kill Pek: the inheritance and the woman.'

'If that is the case, then I don't see who could have tried to kill her last night,' retorted the high priest.

'Perhaps the one who ordered the poison wanted to make sure that there would be nobody left who knew about it?'

Xhól's heart skipped a beat: he hadn't thought of that!

'That is a possibility,' replied the priest cautiously.

'How else would you account for it?' the Ajaw asked as he rose, came down from the platform and stood, arms folded, in front of Thirteen Jaguar.

The two men faced each other. The priest, despite his age, was still the taller of the two, impressive and cold. But it was the Ajaw who exuded strength and power. The eagle and the jaguar face to face, thought Xhól; each an aspect of the sun, of power. The jaguar had the advantage over the eagle because it was he who made the decisions about life and death, while remaining respectful of the eagle's territory. No, the Ajaw would not go against the priest's opinion without thinking twice about it.

'Well,' continued the high priest. 'The lover himself could be the culprit: what could be more tempting, having eliminated the husband who must have noticed his wife's condition upon his return, to get rid of her, too? She must have demanded that this man marry her once her husband was dead, threatening to drag him into the scandal a soon-to-be-discovered pregnancy would undoubtedly have brought upon her. And you know what price he would have paid for being complicit in adultery. Especially if he is a nobleman.'

'Do you think that he is?'

'It is a possibility,' replied the priest. 'That would explain his determination to get rid of her.'

'Two explanations for one situation,' replied the Ajaw thoughtfully. 'Two explanations that could both be right. You must first find the man who ordered the poison. And the lover too, if it is not the brother. These men—or this man, if you prefer—must come under my justice. We leave on the morrow, as you know. You have until tomorrow morning to bring me the answer to these questions. I will settle the case before our departure.'

The Ajaw turned and left the room, regaining his mask of impassiveness on the threshold, a mask that had dropped for a moment in the heat of the conversation. The curtain fell back and rustled in the wake of his departure. After a moment of silent contemplation, Thirteen Jaguar and Xhól left the room too. For once the high priest walked at a slow pace, at least slow enough for Xhól to keep up with him. This time, the high priest was disoriented, uncertain. How to get to the truth if the widow did not wake up between now and tomorrow? And, most importantly, if she did wake up, how to convince her to tell that truth?

They left the palace in silence. On reaching the central plaza, the old man shook himself out of his reverie, finally noticing the hubbub around him. Servants were leaving the palace at a run to summon captains, gather food, or requisition carriers. The orders of the Ajaw were clear: each enclosure, each family had to supply enough to meet the needs of five warriors for three days.

The women began to show up, bringing their contribution in food and taking the pleasure—the only one they could get from this war—of talking themselves into more anxiety. None would cry or lament more loudly than fat Ix Cuat, noticed Xhól. Fat Ix Cuat stood with three or four other women of her age at the corner of the hieroglyphic staircase. Her piercing voice, so utterly at variance with her physical appearance—a mountain of flesh waving with indignation, bore into his ears. All of fat Ix Cuat's anguish poured out in an incessant flow of questions addressed to all and sundry, to which nobody took the trouble to answer. How dare Tikal attack their Ajaw once again? Should they flee into the forest? Who would stay to lead them? Was it fair to take along the men as carriers? Who would protect them, the women who had to remain behind?

The Ajaw had indeed given no orders about the women, the children, the elderly or the infirm. His orders only concerned the men: all of them this time. Not only the warriors, but the farmers and craftsmen too, had to leave. The latter would erect a few hasty defences before the arrival of Tikal's army and carry the necessary food and water. All the men of sound body requisitioned! They had never seen that before. Was not war only for warriors?

Fat Ix Cuat was already lamenting her husband's fate. What would become of her if something happened to him? If he were wounded? Killed? Yes, what would become of her, wondered Xhól. She, who would lose her chief whipping boy, the repository for her daily complaints? How could she replace such a precious man? The thought made him smile.

His grin faded when he recognised Ix Naah among the women. Her face was sad, drawn, and resigned at the same time. Silent, she was listening. When she spotted Xhól, she went over to him and asked him whether what they had heard was true. Would her husband have to leave, like the others? At that, Xhól realised the gravity of the situation: in three days' time, they might have all become fugitives, if they were still alive. And he—spared because of his limp—would have to find a way to protect Ix Naah and the children, to help them survive in the forest, and build a new life for them after the old one were destroyed by the war. This war was not like any other. Tikal had too much to gain from their destruction. Tikal felt too much resentment, too; resentment that went way back to before he was born, when the Ajaw—young and spirited then, had decided to switch alliances. Since that day, Tikal had never ceased to attempt to destroy them. Not only because powerful Tikal could not accept an outpost of Calakmul—the eternal enemy—in Petexbatún, which until then had been exclusively theirs.

No, what fanned the fires of this war was hatred. There was the pure, undiluted hatred of the Ajaw for the brother who had been chosen to succeed to their father, and for the members of the council of Tikal too, who had left him to stagnate in this sleepy backwater, preferring that brother as their new ruler. To his hatred, Tikal had answered in kind with theirs towards the man they now viewed as a renegade. The consequences of this hatred between brothers, between noblemen, fell upon them all; upon them all who had nothing to do with it; upon them all to whom it mattered very little of whom Dos Pilas would be the vassal and to whom tribute had to be paid, as tribute always had to be paid to someone stronger than oneself.

'Why come here?' said Xhól to the old priest.

'You are right, my boy, let's go somewhere quiet.'

Thirteen Jaguar headed towards the least crowded corner of the plaza, close to the ball court. He sat down on one of the steps and beckoned to Xhól to join him.

Xhól sat one level below and lifted his face towards the old man.

'Let's do some thinking, my boy. You heard the Ajaw: which of the two explanations do you think is the right one? A single man who ordered the poison and was the widow's lover or two different men: the one who placed the order and the lover? In the first case, one man would be responsible for everything. Otherwise, things are not so clear: the lover may have killed Pek. Or not. The lover would have had the best reason to kill the widow. Which would be impossible if One Hunter were the lover by the way, because he was held prisoner at the palace at the time of the attack against the widow.'

'It all seems very complicated to me,' advanced Xhól timidly.

'Yes, complicated. In my experience, the simplest explanation is often the right one. Thus, as we believe One Hunter to be innocent and as we know that he could not have tried to kill the widow, let's imagine that there was only one man: the lover... who is also the assassin. The widow is still unconscious, she cannot help us. What do we have that can lead us to him?'

'The phial,' replied Xhól.

'Yes, the phial that he left behind after wounding Pek, although it still contained enough poison for a second victim. What was its first destination? Why abandon it so soon?'

'The heat of the moment—'

'Why not try to recover it later, then?'

'Well, either because he thought he could get poison elsewhere or because he did not have the opportunity to go and look for the phial.'

At these words, Xhól shivered. There was someone who had not had the opportunity to go and look for it, and that someone was Six Sky, now watched over by the noble lady of Itzán. Was it possible that, contrary to what they believed up to now, there were indeed two persons involved: the lover and another one, a woman, who had ordered the poison? But to what end?

'Do you have someone in mind?' asked the old priest, who had sensed his confusion.

'No, it's not possible. It cannot be.'

'What is not possible, my boy?'

Xhól had no choice but to explain that Six Sky was the 'associate' who had come to look for the phial with him, and that she had shown herself to be very curious.

'But I'm wrong. It was just yesterday afternoon that the lady told her she could no longer go out alone. So she could have easily gone back the previous day to pick up the phial before I brought her to the pond,' he ended, relieved.

'You know the noble Six Sky well, don't you?' the priest asked him with a hard look.

'I don't think that I know her that well anymore, my lord.' Xhól answered. 'I knew her well enough before the flight of the Ajaw and his family, and their long exile. Then she was still a child, and I knew her well indeed. Everything has changed since her return.' he added after a pause. 'And I'm not sure anymore to understand what she thinks, what she wants. But why would she have wanted that poison?'

'Who knows, my boy! There are many things happening in the Ajaw's apartments that we know nothing about. But I agree with you, she could easily have recovered the phial. Thus, no, it is not her.'

'Who else, then?'

'Lord Eighteen Puma, for example. The Ajaw designated him to lead the reconnaissance mission that morning. He only returned late last night. And there was little hope of finding the phial in the dark. What is more, he might have hoped that the widow would give him the second one, without realising that she had hidden it in One Hunter's bedding.'

'But why would she do that?'

'Because she was set on getting rid of him and drawing suspicion away from her and her lover. If it is Eighteen Puma, it is understandable that he would use their assignation to try and kill her if she wanted to force him into marrying her.'

'Their assignation?'

'Yes, it is probable that the spot was their regular meeting place. It is away from the city, far from her home and far from the palace.'

'But how can it be proved if the widow does not wake up to accuse him?'

'We can begin by searching Pek's house. We may find some clue, some proof there. As for searching noble Eighteen Puma's house on the basis of nothing more than suspicion, that will not be possible.'

CHAPTER 9

THIRTEEN JAGUAR SETS A TRAP

THIRTEEN JAGUAR ROSE TO his feet and went down the steps of the ball court, leaning on the young man's shoulder this time. Together, they headed for the merchant's house, deserted by all. The slaves had disappeared, and the widow's parents were nowhere in sight. The place hadn't had a master for two days now, and it showed. The patch of peppers was already choked with weeds. Ripe fruit had not been picked, left to rot on trees. The main building no longer had the neat appearance that had struck Xhól at the time of his first visit. Master Pek had been buried in the small hours of that morning by his servants, in haste and with little ceremony. His widow had herself been injured. If she died and One Hunter could not take over, how long would it take for the place to disappear under the assault of the forest? This abandonment left them free to search the main house. Master Pek had done well: the house was built with care upon a two-foot tall platform of rocks and pebbles. Although it was only made of wood, in its shape this house resembled the homes of the noblest men of the city. Wasn't master Pek the richest of all the merchants?

At the front was the main room, used to welcome the guests. The open-air kitchen was on the left, and on the right was the storage area where master Pek kept his most precious goods that Xhól had already visited. The corridor that separated the two rooms led to the back of the house and onto a shady patio. There, two other rooms formed the left and right sides of a square: the widow's workroom and another room that the merchant kept for his private use. At the back, the couple's bedroom closed off the courtyard.

The house was handsome, solid, and well kept. The patio must have been especially pleasant during the summer months. Xhól fancied that it was here, in the shade of the light palm roof, that the widow would sit with her women and work on her weaving.

And it was as likely as not the widow who had planted a bougainvillea in the northern corner of the patio to brighten it with its mass of blood-red flowers.

After looking around the patio, Thirteen Jaguar decided to begin their search in the bedroom at the back. Wooden slats let a little light and air through. It was enough to inspect the furniture and various objects it contained: a beautifully sculpted bed frame, thin blankets of coloured cotton, some trunks with the widow's and the merchant's clothes, a few ceramic vases—less handsome than those brought back from his last journey. Thirteen Jaguar examined with particular attention a lot of small boxes holding make-up powders and ointments.

'Master Pek was not easy to live with, everyone agrees about that,' he said, replacing a box after examination. 'On the other hand, he appears to have been generous to his wife. Many women in Dos Pilas would be jealous were they to see this room. But I fear that there is nothing for us here.'

After taking a last look around, they went on to the weaving room. The old man remained there for a long time. The room was filled with pieces of cloth he unfolded one by one, before carefully folding them again. Then, there were the skeins of thread: bright reds, blues of different shades, greens; all the colours with which master Pek's widow liked to work. They searched all of the baskets, one after another.

'What are we looking for?' asked Xhól.

'The problem, my boy, is that I don't know! I don't even know if there is anything important to find, or what size it is, or what it looks like! However, this room is the one in which the widow spent the most time, her workroom, her domain. So, search my boy, search well.'

They found nothing. They went back across the patio that led to the two rooms the merchant used for storage. There was nothing suspicious there either. Xhól showed Thirteen Jaguar the bundle in which he had found the objects from the same hand as the bottles of poison. The priest looked at the collection of small clay vessels with renewed attention.

'Yes, it is how I thought,' said the old priest. 'This lot comes from faraway Tehotihuacán even if Master Pek did not need go as far. It was enough for him to meet another travelling merchant, further north, to obtain them. It was even simpler for the poison once he was in a swamp area.'

The old man looked over the bundles of goods of all sorts that crowded the shelves: the light fabrics woven in a manner unknown to the women of Dos Pilas, the ceramics with orange designs on a black background, the vases, the censers, the cups, the salt, the feathers, the precious woods that would be used by the sculptors, the jade pearls or slabs ready to be sculpted, the obsidian knives, the earrings, and the head ornaments. Master Pek knew what would please the Ajaw, and the nobles of the city who would rush to imitate him within the limits of their means. The high priest spoke again, more to himself than to his companion.

'Yes, Pek was a shrewd and prosperous merchant;

his widow would have been an excellent match. So, why try to kill her? Why would the assassin not marry her once he had got rid of the husband? It is probably not what he had in mind when he took her as a mistress, but it was an option after the merchant died. Unless, for the man in question, marrying the widow of a merchant, however rich she may be, would be a step down.'

Still thinking, Thirteen Jaguar moved from the storage room to the main room, the last they had not yet inspected.

'It is the only room in which something might still be found,' he said. 'But here, in plain sight?'

The old man cast a discouraged eye around the room: benches, a low table, a small altar dedicated to the ancestors— In haste, he headed that way and bent down to better examine the usual amulets, some food offerings, and a small cup in which copal had been burnt behind which lay a half-hidden piece of jade.

Thirteen Jaguar seized it with a cry of joy and lifted it up to better inspect it. It was definitely a fragment; the irregular break along what had been the upper edge confirmed it. But of what? In the half-light, he could not make out the thin marks that covered it. He decided that he really was getting old. His eyesight was getting worse every day! He returned to the patio. In the sunlight, he could better examine the subject of the engraving.

'Do you think it is important?' asked Xhól who had followed him.

'Perhaps.'

'Why? Isn't it something that the merchant himself brought back?'

"No, my boy. Look at the upper edge: irregular, jagged. That is the result of a recent fracture, which must have happened at the narrowest point of the whole piece because this is nothing but a fragment. Why would Pek have put a broken amulet on his altar? And do you see this scene? The Bacabs in their canoe heading towards the underworld. I am sure that the upper part of the piece must show them too, perhaps holding up the world or— Actually, I have no idea! Although it does remind me of something. Yes, I think that this is what we were looking for. By leaving it here, the widow was protecting herself. Few people would have paid attention to this altar; everybody has a similar one at home. Nobody would have been surprised at the presence of this jade except Pek himself. And Pek is dead.'

As the search of the house had turned up nothing—or so little—Thirteen Jaguar decided to try the second tactic he had considered in order to get to the truth. It was dangerous, but he was pressed for time. He returned to the palace. When he arrived at his apartments, he took from their hiding place the two phials that Xhól had given him. He put them in a box and made for the audience chamber.

From the first courtyard, he noticed the noble Eighteen Puma enter the room. It would be a good opportunity to observe his reaction. He had himself announced. The Ajaw was indeed in conference with his cousin, but, and this surprised Thirteen Jaguar, Ah Chuen B'alam was also present. What was he doing here? Shouldn't he have stayed with the novices to rehearse with them tonight's ceremony? He almost said so but restrained himself. He always preferred to settle this sort of thing in private. A reprimand in front of the Ajaw himself would only serve to embitter his second-in-command further. In any case, the most important, the most urgent, thing was to uncover the truth.

Thirteen Jaguar moved towards the Ajaw who looked at the old priest inquisitively. He set down the box on the edge of the ceremonial platform and invited the Ajaw to inspect his troves. As expected, Eighteen Puma drew closer. The man could not stand to be kept out of anything! Neither could Ah Chuen B'alam. Not such a bad thing that he knows of the discovery, thought Thirteen Jaguar. Despite all his faults, the man was a priest and could thus be trusted. The Ajaw picked up one phial and then the other.

'These are magnificent object. Where did you find them? I did not know that anyone in Dos Pilas owned anything so beautiful.'

'They are indeed magnificent objects,' replied the old priest, 'and they come from far away. Look at the craftsmanship, the engravings, and the glyphs.'

The Ajaw returned to his inspection, weighing up one flask in his left hand and the other in his right.

'One is full and the other almost empty. What

are they?'

'Poison bottles.' uttered a high-pitched voice from behind them, that of Ah Chuen B'alam.

'Always trying to ingratiate himself!' thought Thirteen Jaguar with a hint of irritation.

'Will you allow me, my lord?' asked his second-in-command, holding out a trembling hand towards the box. 'Me too, I am in admiration of their beauty. They are truly magnificent pieces indeed,' he added, making a movement as though to seize one of the two phials.

The Ajaw allowed him with a nod and continued to stare at Thirteen Jaguar, waiting for the rest of the story.

'Magnificent and dangerous,' added Thirteen Jaguar, casting a glance around.

'Dangerous?' asked the Ajaw.

'Because of their content.'

Thirteen Jaguar stopped for a moment to observe the small group gathered around the box: the Ajaw curious, well aware that something was brewing; Ah Chuen B'alam, whose hands trembled with emotion as he lifted one of the two phials, the full one; and Eighteen Puma, indifferent this time. The noble cousin of the Ajaw had a greater capacity for concealment than he expected.

The Ajaw was still waiting, impassive. Thirteen Jaguar recounted his experiment on the content of the first phial, now almost empty, found where the murderer had waited for the merchant. For the second one, he said no more than that he had found it at the merchant's house. Which was true, strictly speaking, because One Hunter's hut was located within his brother's enclosure.

The Ajaw listened to the high priest with a smile that broadened at the end of the story.

'You are telling me that he is the one who brought back the poison that would kill him? And that he had more than one phial of it? Do you think that it was the reason for the attempt on the life of his widow?'

'Perhaps.' replied Thirteen Jaguar. 'Were it known that the second bottle existed, it would have been necessary to recover it to use it as originally planned.'

'So, what we now need is for the widow to wake up and tell us who tried to kill her. It could not have been her brother-in-law because he was at the palace under my guard.'

'One of the lady's maids was to inform me when she regained consciousness. I have still not received any word, which is surprising. I am going to see her now,' replied Thirteen Jaguar.

'I will go with you,' decided the Ajaw. 'I want my conscience to be clear. We are leaving tomorrow morning, and I want to get to the bottom of this before then.'

The Ajaw and the old priest left the audience chamber and headed for the women's quarters.

'Come, you two!' called the Ajaw, turning back towards Eighteen Puma and Ah Chuen B'alam who had remained still, not knowing whether to follow or not.

The four men entered the women's courtyard, silent and deserted for once. They went to a small chamber where the widow had been removed. Inside, an old crone watched over her, singing in a low voice. The woman laid still on the bed, her eyes closed. Thirteen Jaguar stepped forward to examine her. Yes, she still appeared to be unconscious. He wondered why. What could cause such a long fainting spell? The old crone, who had stood up on seeing the Ajaw come in, stepped aside to leave her place at the head of the bed to the high priest. As she moved, she knocked over the stool next to the bed on which a jug of water and a beaker were placed. They smashed to the floor, splashing Thirteen Jaguar and the bed itself. He had just taken the widow's wrist to check her pulse when the accident occurred and felt an involuntary contraction beneath his fingers. He examined the widow and noticed the look that filtered through the half-closed eyelids. She was conscious! The high priest sent away the old crone who would not stop begging for his forgiveness. Once she had left, he turned towards the Ajaw.

'My lord, this woman is awake! She is trying to fool us. Perhaps she has heard about tomorrow's departure?'

The Ajaw stepped forward.

'Are you sure of what you are saying?'

'Yes,' replied Thirteen Jaguar. 'She gave herself away when the jug was knocked down. I felt her flinch.'

'Woman, stop pretending and look at me!' ordered the Ajaw in his most imperious voice, the one he used in his council.

Master Pek's widow, not daring to defy the Ajaw, finally opened her eyes. Terrified, she eyed the men gathered around her.

'Speak,' commanded the Ajaw. 'Tell us who you went to meet at the pond; who is it who tried to kill you?'

The widow looked at the Ajaw before lowering her eyes.

'I cannot, my lord,' she muttered in a low voice.

'You cannot? Do you think that you can play games with me? Do you think that only enemy warriors taken prisoner end up on the sacrifice altar?'

The widow cast a wild glance around and repeated once again: 'I can't.'

Her body stiffened in a fit, as though it was trying to flee despite her reason telling her otherwise. Then she fell back on the bed, defeated. The four men watched her in silence. Master Pek's widow now looked like a terrorised animal, consumed by horror. Her hands blindly seized the cotton blanket that lay on the bed and tore at it. Her mad eyes appeared not to see them anymore. Then, all of a sudden, she froze. Her hands stopped moving, still clutched. Her face softened. Her eyes closed, once again. Thirteen Jaguar drew near the motionless body.

'Now she truly is unconscious. Fear has caused

exclamations. No anger or pain, either. Only gloomy resignation. Their lord was going to war. All the men were going to war. None of them may ever return. At the same time the next day, Tikal's army might well be bearing down upon the city.

At the palace, the lady of Itzán returned at once to her apartments to remove the heavy jade ornaments which she had put on for the ceremony. Such irony, she thought, that this honour should befall her at a time when it had become of so little interest! She felt death approaching. She was now a mere shadow of the ambitious young woman who had so craved a leading role. And now that this role was hers, her body desired only one thing; the peace and quiet that were necessary to simply keep on going.

Yes, it was ironic. She would have had quite enough with the education of her sons, the palace, and Six Sky. Which reminded her that Six Sky had not yet joined her like she was supposed to. She sent one of her maids to look for her.

The young girl, who too had changed clothes for a simpler tunic, soon appeared, looking angry and sulky. This time, there was something else about her attitude. Something of a more promising nature. The lady of Itzán questioned her with a glance. Six Sky grasped the opportunity.

'Why not trust me?' She exclaimed. 'I was on my way to join you when that girl came to tell you were waiting for me.'

Insulted innocence itself, thought the lady of

Itzán with a smile.

'Let's say that it was for all the times that you didn't.'

'That's over,' Six Sky shot at her.

'Over?' asked the lady, in disbelief.

'Don't you realise that the events of these last days have made me think? Father is leaving tomorrow, and we may never see him again. But if he does return, I certainly plan to hold the same position as you one day. Well, the position that you hold now, at any rate.'

'Explain that to me, daughter,' asked the lady, settling with dignity onto the bed, which turned into a couch during the day. 'Come and sit beside me.'

'Well, yes, I want to have the same status as you,' said Six Sky with determination. 'But not for a short while, not just in a time of war, not because the men are absent. I want to matter. From day one.'

'If you become the lady of a city——'

'Then all that will be expected of me will be to provide an heir.'

'Not only, my daughter.'

'Not only, perhaps, but all the same. How many women have ever attained the position of ajaw? Tell me, how many?'

'Few, my daughter. I admit. Is that what you desire?'

'If I am to be ambitious, I might as well go all the way, don't you think?'

This girl had the knack for disconcerting her.

She was totally unpredictable. But while this state of mind lasted, it was as well to take advantage of it.

'Tell me, what are your ambitions?'

'Well, a husband, yes, because one must have one,' replied Six Sky, resigned. 'But,' she added, 'a husband who will need me more than I need him. That is what I wish for.'

'And if we found you such a husband?'

'In that case, I would marry him,' answered Six Sky raising her chin.

'Very well, my daughter. I will keep our conversation in mind. We will think about it when better days come.'

After the ceremony, Xhól, Ix Naah, her husband and the children returned to the family enclosure in silence: the adults grave and tense, the children confused and mute with astonishment. Little Itzel came to take Xhól's hand without saying a word. He closed his palm, hardened by stonework, over her infinitely soft skin. His heart tightened at the thought of all that was at stake.

At the entrance to their plot, Ix Naah tried for her normal, everyday voice to announce that she would need a little time to prepare the evening meal. She then turned to Xhól.

'Why don't you finish your story from the other evening while I take care of the meal?' she asked. 'The children were asking for it last night, and I could not tell it for the life of me.'

This caused the two boys to break their silence.

'Yes, Uncle! Tell us how it ends.'

Xhól sat down in the same spot under the zapote, resting against the thick trunk, and took Itzel in his arms.

'Do you remember how the brave hunter found himself alone in the forest, in a place unknown to him as night began to fall?'

'Yes,' chorused the two boys.

'Night was falling. The brave hunter saw the bird settle at the top of a tree, ready to spend the night there. As beautiful as ever, as unattainable as ever. He looked for a place near the tree on which the bird had settled to spend as comfortable a night as possible. That was how, as he was searching the copse, he came across the entrance to a cave. Now, it wasn't a very big cave! Not as impressive a cave as our cave of the bats, for sure. It was just a small chamber, the ground of which was covered with a thin coat of dried clay. He decided to spend the night there.'

'Now, what he didn't know was that this little cave gave access to the underworld, to the spirit kingdom, to Xibalba—and to the dwelling place of two evil spirits. They were overjoyed to see the brave hunter settle for the night at the entrance to the cave, on their threshold. The bird had succeeded in its mission. The spirits waited for the night to get old, and the brave hunter to be sound asleep.'

'They waited for the moment when the moon has already disappeared below the horizon—and the night is at its deepest, between the moon's departure and the sun's return. Now, they didn't attack the brave hunter. No, they were more intelligent, more cunning than that! They sent him a dream: a pleasant dream at first, a dream in which the brave hunter saw himself get up and decide to explore the cave which, though small, led to an underground corridor. They sent him this dream in which the brave hunter felt no fear, no trepidation, just a great deal of curiosity and a strong desire to explore the underworld.'

'What would you have seen if you had found yourselves in the cave with the brave hunter?'

The two boys were hanging onto his every word, and the thought of answering did not even cross their minds. Seeing that he had captivated them, Xhól went on.

'Lo and behold, the brave hunter, still asleep, got up and went down to the bottom of the cave, walking with wide-open eyes that did not see, in a state of trance, without even taking a torch, yet moving around without any difficulty in the darkness. Without thinking, he had picked up his sling and his stones; a gesture so deeply rooted in him that, even dead, he would not have forgotten that sling. And you see, that was what would save him.'

'How?' asked little Itzel, breathless.

'Well, child, there was one thing the spirits had forgotten.'

'They had forgotten that they had given the brave hunter the gift of seeing in the dark in his dream. And so, when he arrived at their dwelling place, a mighty chicle tree whose branches spread as far as the eye could see in the glowing twilight, the brave hunter behaved as he would have done in a normal forest. He noticed two parrots in the tree. This was one of the shapes that the spirits liked to adopt when they were not travelling the world over with their slings in their hands. Indeed, their slings hung in the lowest branches of the tree while they— in their parrot form, were stationed at the top of the tree to watch for the arrival of the brave hunter. They were thus weaponless, and this was their undoing. In his dream, the brave hunter said to himself that, if he could not have the magnificent bird, he would then make do with these, even if they were not as handsome.'

'Before the spirits could make a move and change shape, the brave hunter had loaded his sling and had begun to swirl it around. He had been so looking forward to it all day that he threw the stone even faster than usual. After the first parrot had been hit, the second one did not have the time to take cover before being struck by another stone. Because they were spirits, the hunter searched in vain for their bodies: they had disappeared into thin air before hitting the ground! The spirits themselves, shapeless, utterly powerless now, could do nothing to harm him.'

'At that very moment, the brave hunter was awakened by a ray of sunshine entering the cave and warming his face. He leapt up. Strangely enough, he only had one stone left for his sling! He left the cave and looked towards the place where the fabulous bird had spent the night. Was it still there? At this point, he saw the magnificent bird rise up, and, instead of fleeing, this time it flew in a straight line towards him. His astonishment prevented him from loading his sling, which hung still in his hand. Drawing level, the bird spoke to him.

' "You do well not to kill me, hunter. Otherwise you will never find your city again. I brought you to where no human can ever come alone. Last night, you killed the two spirits that had enslaved me to their will. You have released me. I am grateful for that, and I want to reward you. What do you want from me?" '

'After a moment of hesitation, the brave hunter told the bird that what had first attracted him was the beauty of its plumage and that he needed it as a gift for his lord. The bird considered this for an instant before answering.'

' "I will not give you all of them, but you may choose two feathers, the most beautiful ones... if you promise not to try to kill me on the way back. Yes, I will lead you back home. You will thus show me that you possess two great qualities: patience and being true to your word. Watch out! If you try to trick me, you will lose everything! In that case, there will be neither path nor feathers! You will be condemned to wander this enchanted forest to the end of time and will never see those dear to you again. What do you decide?" '

' "I promise that I will not try to kill you, oh bird," replied the brave hunter. "And to wait patiently until the end of our voyage to receive your gift." '

'They set off. It was not easy for the brave hunter, I can tell you. And you might even think that the bird took some pleasure in teasing him because, instead of flying quietly a little ahead of the brave hunter, he began to play the same game as the day before, settling in a tree, then soaring skywards in a flurry of wings as soon as the brave hunter caught up with it.'

'The brave hunter's blood boiled, his hand twitched, and every time he saw the bird soar, he wanted to swirl his sling around. How could you expect a true hunter to resist such temptation? And yet the brave hunter did resist it. After travelling the whole day long, he finally recognised familiar surroundings. Yes, here was a zapote that had been struck by lightning; over there a copse where he would often lie in ambush; then, a path that led to a distant plot. He would soon reach the city, his city.'

'This was the moment the bird chose to stop for the last time, on a branch level with the young man's eyes.'

' "Brave hunter, it said to him. Today you have shown that you are not only brave, but also patient. And that you are true to your word, even though you found it hard. As promised, I will reward you." '

'With these words, the bird disappeared in a bright cloud accompanied with a bolt of lightning, and the brave hunter was blinded for a few seconds. When his sight returned, the bird has disappeared. He discovered at his feet the bird's most beautiful feathers, a truly royal adornment. The brave hunter thanked the bird aloud, picked up the feathers, and returned to the city, glad to be able to satisfy his lord.'

'And that is the end of the story,' said Xhól, getting up.

'And the meal is ready,' added Ix Naah, who had drawn closer without being noticed.

The children——famished as they were, didn't need being told twice and rushed into the house. The two adults followed, at a slower pace on account of Xhól's bad leg.

'Thank you,' said Ix Naah.

'Thank you for what?'

'For taking their minds off things. Tonight they will dream of a magnificent bird, not of war.'

Xhól squeezed her hand without saying a word.

CHAPTER 10

ON TOO DARK A NIGHT

THE SUMMON REACHED HIM after the children had gone to bed. Ix Naah, her husband and Xhól had stayed on the doorstep to enjoy the coolness of the evening, a welcome respite after the heat of the day. They were talking in low voices about the warriors' departure on the morrow and the order given to Ix Naah's husband to join the expedition as a carrier.

The messenger was Puk, Thirteen Jaguar's favourite novice, who came to summon Xhól on the high priest's behalf. Ix Naah contemplated Xhól with a frown.

'Don't worry, sister, I will not have to leave with the warriors,' joked Xhól. 'But I might be away for most of the night: do not wait up for me.'

Thirteen Jaguar was pacing the platform of the small observatory temple to which Puk brought the young painter without adding a word.

The old priest's voice welcomed Xhól with a burst of jubilant glee.

'My boy, we have him this time!'

Xhól stared at him, surprised.

'Yes, I laid a trap for him. The widow has woken up. Well, to be precise, I put an end to her little game: she was no more unconscious than you or I! All she wanted was to avoid answering my questions, and those of the Ajaw.'

Puk had withdrawn unobtrusively and was heading for the stairs leading to the plaza when Thirteen Jaguar stopped him.

'No, stay! You too will be of use. I'm not a young man anymore, and we may need a second pair of arms to restrain him.'

Puk bowed in respectful silence. From the glint that flashed through his eyelids and the smile that he could not quite repress, Xhól supposed that he must be glad to take part in what appeared, to a young boy cloistered by the strict discipline of the novices, to be a particularly exciting expedition.

'Yes,' Thirteen Jaguar began again, 'the

widow is awake and will be able to answer my questions... tomorrow morning. I made sure that as many people as possible knew that I would not be questioning her before then and that there would be no women at her side tonight. She no longer needs them because she is fine; doesn't that make sense?' he concluded with a broad smile.

'Indeed it does make perfect sense, my lord. And—?'

'And we are going to spend the night waiting for our assassin. I will remain in the room with the widow, to whom I administered a light sedative with her evening meal. You two—'

'—We remain in the courtyard.'

'You understand me, my boy. You stay in the courtyard until you see someone enter the room. All I am asking you to do is block the doorway so that he is prevented from fleeing, in any case long enough for me to recognise him. But I think that if I do recognise him, he will not try to run.'

They came down from the platform, crossed the angle of the plaza between the two temples, and found themselves outside the entrance to the palace. They walked across the first courtyard, still lit and busy, and entered the second one which was already quiet.

For one moment, Xhól feared that One Hunter might see them. But no, One Hunter had already retired to the dormitory where he would once again spend the night as the Ajaw had not yet ordered his release. They finally reached the third courtyard, the women's quarters. Silence already reigned there. The lady of Itzán was still with the Ajaw and had given orders to her servants to keep them busy during her absence. The lady of Itzán, thought Thirteen Jaguar, knew how to manage her household; it was out of the question for her women to waste their time in idle and noisy gossip.

They approached the widow's bedroom. Thirteen Jaguar entered the room plunged in darkness. Not even a brazier had been left burning. He could barely make out the shape of the sleeping woman. Yes, this time she was asleep, he said to himself as he approached and watched her slow, regular breathing. It was all the better, and one less thing to worry about.

He left the room and gave his orders in a low voice.

'She is already asleep. You two, hide behind the patio columns. This moonless night is your best cover.'

The priest checked that the shapes of the two boys melted into the dark mass of the pillars,. Then, he went back into the widow's room. She had not moved. Thirteen Jaguar took the stool that was still at her bedside and shifted it to the corner of the entrance wall that was furthest from the door. It was the best place to avoid detection. On entering the room, the assassin would head straight for the widow and not bother to look behind. Not only did he want the assassin to come in, which would in itself be evidence, but—to remove any shadow of a doubt, he wanted him to be caught in the very act. Indeed, if it really were the man he thought, it would take nothing less to break through his arrogance. Without that, he would be undaunted and give a shoddy excuse to explain his presence. And that shoddy excuse would have to be accepted, given his rank. No, what Thirteen Jaguar needed was a clear-cut attempted murder, with witnesses, nothing less. And it might take time to get it. First, nothing could be expected before the Ajaw was done with his lieutenants. Then, the assassin would probably wait for the whole palace to be asleep.

Falling asleep was not something that he was afraid of. The only advantage of old age was that he needed less and less sleep. On the other hand, would the two boys be able to stay awake? He had faith in Xhól. The lad had shown his determination to see the truth uncovered. But Puk? Puk had that annoying habit of doing the wrong thing at the wrong time, as if he would forever be embarrassed by the bodily form he had taken at his birth. And yet, his was a brilliant mind. Their most brilliant novice, but dreadfully awkward. He would have to keep an eye on that; it would be a pity if that were to be an obstacle on his path. Already, the Ajaw had not a very high opinion of him, precisely because of his clumsiness. And yet, when Thirteen Jaguar thought about it, out of the bunch, he was the one he could best picture succeeding him—in twenty years' time. Yesterday, the boy had deliberately tried to enrage Ah Chuen B'alam—mere novice foolery—but deep down, he already knew more than that vanity-swollen goatskin. That was his trouble. An elder who knew less than oneself was already galling, but when that elder boasted of knowledge that he did not possess, a brilliant youngster could not but smoulder. And Puk was brilliant. He had been the quickest to understand the different calendars and their interlocking, and the fastest when it came to calculating the sequences of dates, the ends of cycles and the phases of Venus. That was a precious skill, one that came naturally to a boy who only needed some slight encouragement, not the vain teaching method of Ah Chuen B'alam; Ah Chuen B'alam who had him a gift for making his students do their best to enrage him. That was another problem. He could delegate certain ceremonies to his second-in-command but certainly not the teaching: the past two days had proven that.

Thirteen Jaguar suddenly sat up, casting aside his reflections on the pedagogical skills—or lack thereof—of Ah Chuen B'alam. He had heard a noise from the courtyard. No, it was just the lady of Itzán, who was retiring to her apartments. A masterly woman, thought Thirteen Jaguar; one who will not allow her physical weakness to prevent her from governing in the Ajaw's absence. It was a pity that, among her many qualities, she had that blind partiality towards her first-born son. The priest leaned back into the corner of the room, straight-backed on his seat, attentive. The sounds of the palace subsided, muffled and scarcer now. The Ajaw had dismissed his servants. The tumult of preparing for departure had given way to the quiet of the night. And the waiting began once more. Now, he could hear nothing but the calm and regular hiss of the widow's breathing.

A slight noise came from the courtyard. Had one of the two boys just betrayed his presence? No, the sound was a regular one, the sound of footsteps, subdued, stifled and slow; footsteps that were coming towards him. There he was! thought Thirteen Jaguar, exulting. The predator had become prey and did not yet know it! Now, he could make out the sound of another's breathing, near the door. Then, a hand lifted the curtain. Finally, a silhouette was outlined in the entrance. It was so dark that he could not guess who it was. The man crossed the threshold. Thirteen Jaguar remained seated, immobile, not wanting to scare away his prey at this moment, when anything could still happen. But he had not taken into account Puk's youth, and his eagerness to do the right thing. As soon as the boy had seen the shadow outlined in the doorway, he leapt upon it—and missed. The man shrugged himself free and sent the young priest flying into the corner of the doorway. Puk's head struck the edge of the stone. The boy laid there, knocked unconscious by the impact.

On seeing the young priest hurl himself forward, Xhól did likewise and—while the assassin was dealing with Puk, grabbed him from behind by the nape of the neck, holding onto anything he could. The man, in a last-ditch effort, planted his two feet wide apart firmly on the ground and twisted his body around in a sudden movement. Xhól was thrown backwards. Thirteen Jaguar hurried to help him—too late. The assassin had already disappeared into the shadows of the portico leading to the second courtyard. And, the high priest thought with a sigh, he was much too old to run after him. The guards posted at the entrance of the first courtyard arrived at a run a few moments later. Thirteen Jaguar questioned them: no, they had seen nothing on their way, nobody.

Thirteen Jaguar, bending over Puk with concern, let out short orders.

'Search the palace! Every courtyard! Every corridor!—And somebody bring me a light.'

A servant stepped in with a torch. Thirteen Jaguar commanded him to place it directly above the young priest. He examined the wound, feeling the bloody head with his old hands.

'There is a lot of blood, as with any superficial head wound, but luckily no broken bones,' he murmured.

The boy groaned under the examination.

'You took a good knock, but you have a hard head. It will be enough to sponge the wound and put a pad on it to stop the bleeding. Come on! Get up!' said the old priest.

Puk came around on hearing the half-relieved, half-exasperated voice.

'I'm sorry, master.'

'You may well be,' replied the old man, dismayed.

'You caused my plan to fail!'

'—Perhaps not completely, my lord,' came a voice from behind them.

Thirteen Jaguar turned around and saw, by the dancing light of the torch, that Xhól had got up unaided and was approaching them, his left hand held forward, two strands of leather escaping from the closed fist.

'What do you mean?'

'When I grabbed him, I tried to hang on to anything I could lay my hands on. I grasped a necklace, and I tried to strangle him with it. Well, to immobilise him; I didn't want to kill him! But the necklace wasn't strong enough. It broke when the fellow elbowed me in the stomach. I didn't let go. Look!'

Xhól spread his fingers. On the open palm, Thirteen Jaguar discovered a small jade amulet attached to two strands of leather. He seized the object and examined it by the dim light of the torch: a slim plate that bore the delicate drawing of four figures in a boat surrounded by water lilies and rushes. The bottom of the amulet showed a recent break.

The rest of the night passed without further incident. The captain of the guard reported that nobody had been found. The Ajaw, woken by all the commotion, sent for the three of them. He listened as they told the story of the failed ambush. Then, he withdrew with the old priest into his private apartment for a few minutes. When they returned to the audience chamber, he ordered the captain to summon the generals, the priests and the lady at the earliest hour for a final council before departure. He then dismissed them all. Having placed two guards in plain view at the widow's door, Thirteen Jaguar sent Puk and Xhól away.

'We all need a little sleep, for what is left of the night. You, my boy,' he said, turning to Xhól. 'Come to the Ajaw's council in the morning. We have one last card to play—thanks to you. I want you to be there.'

Xhól considered this with apprehension.

'Me? Attend the Ajaw's council?'

'Why, yes,' replied the old priest. 'You have been mixed up in all this from the outset. It is only fair that you should be there for the conclusion.'

The sun had barely risen when the old priest went back to the widow. She awoke with difficulty, surprised to see him at her side. The old man gazed at her: what would the Ajaw decide as to her fate? Death? Perhaps he could change that if she agreed to talk, to accuse the assassin. He would have to try and persuade her.

'Widow,' he said, after gazing at her for a moment. 'once more, somebody tried to kill you. Last night.'

She looked at him in silence, waiting for him to go on.

'Yes, I told the women to put a potion into your evening meal to make you sleep; that is why you heard nothing and find it so hard to wake up this morning.'

The widow put her hand on her belly.

'No, don't worry. It did not hurt your fruit.'

'You know?'

'Yes, and everyone else will know in a few months. Don't you think that it is time you stopped playing this little game with me and the Ajaw? An assassin who will not hesitate to do away with you is still on the prowl. The father of the unborn child, I suppose?'

She acquiesced with a movement of her chin, then lowered her eyes in shame.

'But that is not all. Everything leads me to believe that this man is the same man who killed your husband. We have enough evidence now.'

The widow lifted her head sharply and stared at the priest sitting beside her.

'Yes, we have evidence, and it does not point to One Hunter. By the way, I also know what you planted in your brother-in-law's cabin.'

She looked frightened.

'So you see, we know a lot, except for one thing: the name of this man. And you can give us that.'

'Won't I be executed with him if I reveal his name?'

'Let's say that things present themselves differently: if you do not tell us who he is, it is certain that you will be executed. Right away. Before the Ajaw departure to war. On the other hand, if you confess everything, I will ask the Ajaw to spare you.'

'You will never believe me,' she answered,

desperate.

'I will believe you. I can well imagine that it is difficult for you to accuse somebody of his rank.'

'Of his rank? So, you know?'

'I think so.'

'What am I going to do?'

'Attend the council.'

'I would never dare! Accuse him in public, in his presence!'

'Yes. Don't worry. I will start the tale. I only ask this of you: to confirm that what I say is true once I have said his name aloud.'

The widow seemed to hesitate, weighing up the for and against. Thirteen Jaguar, to do away with her indecision, commanded her to get up and get dressed. He would send the women to her and wanted her to be ready. The young woman, obedient this time, got up from the bed. Now that she no longer took the trouble to hide her pregnancy, her movements were a little slower, a little clumsier, and made obvious what she had successfully hidden up to now.

Thirteen Jaguar left the small chamber and asked two of the lady's servants to come and take care of the widow, and to bring her something to eat. He paced up and down the courtyard, exultant. He had Eighteen Puma this time! Wasn't he the most obvious culprit? A man of high rank, who had not hesitated to order the poison, probably to get rid of the Ajaw himself, or his sons, or all of them at once. A determined man who had always been jealous of his cousin, had always envied him his position, had tried to usurp that position during the period of exile. The council had not followed him when he had suggested that they not welcome the Ajaw on his return from Calakmul. Some had listened to him, but not enough to tip the scales in his favour. Since his cousin's restoration to power, he had had to swallow his anger, his disappointed ambitions, and his contempt. It was no surprise that he had wanted to change the order of succession. What really surprised Thirteen Jaguar was that he had thought of using poison, and incriminated himself by forgetting the phial. Indeed, whatever one might think of him, Eighteen Puma was a brave and valiant warrior in combat. But that was the point; waiting for a man and murdering him in cold blood was not combat. It was not worthy of a warrior, and that had been enough to make him lose his head. No, decidedly, Eighteen Puma was his man.

Furthermore, he was not the kind of man to marry the widow. A cousin of the Ajaw, intent on succeeding him... Such a wretched marriage would have put an end to his ambition; as would her pregnancy and their affair, were they to be revealed. The Ajaw would show no pity and seize the opportunity to get rid of him with the approval of the whole city. For a man to steal another's wife during his absence was something that nobody would look kindly upon. They would all have agreed with the Ajaw; the death sentence was a fit one for such a crime. So, yes, even without the question of the merchant's murder, he had an excellent reason to try to do away with a widow who was hanging onto him.

Master Pek's widow left her room, leaning on the shoulder of one of the women who had helped her dress. Thirteen Jaguar examined her with attention: calm and dignified, she appeared to have taken her decision. He motioned to her to follow him and headed for the audience chamber. At the door, Xhól stood waiting. The high priest entered the room. He ordered the young painter and the widow to wait in a corner——with the servants, and then took his usual seat. Xhól was relieved to be left out for the time being. He would have preferred to be anywhere else this morning! He braced himself and remembered that all of this was necessary if he wanted to save One Hunter. He felt the trembling body of the widow at his side. She would not bear this for long, thought the young painter. The entire business had better end soon.

The members of the council began to arrive, one after another; the generals in a hurry, noble Eighteen Puma as arrogant as ever and, last of all, Ah Chuen B'alam who, for once, sat down beside Thirteen Jaguar without a word. Only the Ajaw and the lady were missing. They finally arrived; the Ajaw grave, his expression severe, the lady curious. They both sat on the platform. The Ajaw had had a cushion placed beside him for his wife. He had not forgotten to take advantage of this occasion to reiterate her status as regent. He glanced over the assembly.

'You must be wondering why I summoned you so early this morning, when we held our last council last night. We have not received any news that would change our plans. From what I know, Tikal's army is still following the path we expect. No! It is to resolve a question to which I wanted to find an answer before we leave. Three days ago, the lifeless body of the merchant Pek was discovered. Without any doubt, the approaching army from Tikal has become our priority since. However, I cannot tolerate murder in this city. Pek is entitled to my justice if I can grant it to him.—And it would appear that this morning I am in a position to do so,' he said, turning towards Thirteen Jaguar.

The high priest rose and bowed before the Ajaw, who invited him to speak with a slight nod of the head.

'Yes, my lord, I am today in a position to allow you to render justice—not only to the merchant, but to his widow too—who has twice been the object of attempted murder.'

At these words, a ripple of surprise ran through the council.

'Yes, two attempts.' the old man continued. 'The second one took place last night, here in the palace, where I had had her transported to entrust her safekeeping to the women of the noble lady of Itzán,' he said, bowing slightly to the lady. 'I informed the Ajaw of the progress of my investigation. I told him how this boy—the high priest gestured at that moment towards Xhól, who felt horribly uncomfortable on seeing all eyes turn towards him—has found a phial near the pond. I tested the contents of that phial. It happened to be a deadly poison, one difficult to obtain. This explains why Pek succumbed to a superficial wound. It was enough for the poison to enter his blood to lead to his death within minutes. What is more, the bottle containing this poison clearly came from a distant location, from Tehotihuacán. Which brings me back to our merchant, who had just returned from a particularly long voyage to the north. After some research, we received confirmation that Pek himself had brought back the poison. I will spare you the details. This is what led me to ask myself why the merchant would bring back such an item. The only logical answer was that somebody had ordered it from him. Poor master Pek! Blinded by the hope of a handsome reward, he had succeeded in procuring the poison in question, in bringing it back, and delivering it to his paymaster—only to be killed by the latter a few hours after his return. And this brings us to the murder attempts against his widow. Here, I must share something with you that fills me with shame. She is with child, and it is not her husband's.'

They all turned to the widow who cowered under the weight of their avid gaze. She held onto Xhól's arm and lowered her eyes.

'Yes, she is with child by the murderer, who tried to kill her as well so that nobody would learn what I am now revealing to you. Last night, when the assassin heard me announce that I would not question the widow until this morning, he took a desperate resolution: to attack the widow this very night, inside the palace. And why wouldn't he? This high-ranking man had ordered a powerful poison. What for? That alone makes him liable to your justice, my lord. Not only did he order this poison; what is more, he used it to remove a witness— and husband, who had become too cumbersome; a crime that in itself carries the penalty of death. Furthermore, he had already tried to rid himself of the widow with the goal of covering up the scandal that would arise from his misconduct. Yes, this man had some terrible reasons to want to finish the job last night.'

Thirteen Jaguar interrupted his speech to contemplate the members of the assembly one by one. His stern gaze held each of them for a few seconds. How strange, thought the old priest, gazing at Eighteen Puma, who was perfectly calm—curious like the others, but no more than that. Could he have been mistaken? The old priest continued his tour of the room and ended it with Ah Chuen B'alam; Ah Chuen B'alam who was clutching his throat convulsively; Ah Chuen B'alam whose neck bore a black mark that could only have been made recently, a black mark left by the cord with which someone might have tried to strangle him—or by the string of a necklace that had been violently torn away.

The truth came to Thirteen Jaguar in a flash, and for a moment threw him off balance. Everything he had thought was true—applied to the wrong man. Ah Chuen B'alam had ordered the poison. Ah Chuen B'alam had had an affair with the merchant's wife. Ah Chuen B'alam had killed the merchant. In fact, it was much less surprising that he would have used such a weapon as a sling—a weapon that allowed him to remain at a distance, and that he had lost his head to the point of forgetting the phial. Ah Chuen B'alam, no more than Eighteen Puma, could not marry the widow of a mere merchant. Here was the true meaning of his intuition. Ah Chuen B'alam would soon die. Thirteen Jaguar faced his second-in-command.

'And here, now, I have the final piece of evidence to put before you! He exclaimed with an accusatory look. 'Step forward, Xhól! Come in front of the council, and tell your lord what you saw and did last night.'

Xhól came forward, limping more heavily than usual, and stood before the Ajaw.

'My lord,' he began with an unsteady voice. 'Last night, noble Thirteen Jaguar asked the priest Puk and I to position ourselves in the women's courtyard in such a way as not to be seen, with the goal of cutting off the assassin's retreat once he had entered the widow's room. It was a pitch-black, moonless night. I could only make out a silhouette in the dark. I could not say who he was—'

At these words, Ah Chuen B'alam sat up slightly, relieved.

'When Puk threw himself upon the assassin and was knocked out against the door-frame by the blow he received, I rushed up from behind to try and restrain the man. I grabbed hold of a necklace, or rather a leather string. I pulled it with all my strength, in the hope of weakening him until the guards arrived from the main courtyard. But he knocked me off too, escaping with a sudden movement. I was thrown back three steps—with the necklace in my hand. Here it is—' he declared, opening his palm with the same gesture he had used to present the amulet to Thirteen Jaguar.

The Ajaw bent over the piece of jade with interest.

'Do you swear that what you have just told us is true?'

'Yes, my lord,' replied Xhól in a firm tone, looking the Ajaw straight in the eye. '—That is what happened.'

'I will add,' said Thirteen Jaguar, 'that this amulet—and you can see it for yourself, my lord, has been broken. But not in last night's fight. We found the other part at Pek's house. Probably a gift from the lover to a woman who had asked for a token of affection, who wanted to see him wearing something of which she held a piece, a way of cementing the relationship between them, however secret. Women are like that sometimes. I did not recognise this amulet at first.'

Thirteen Jaguar turned to his second-in-command.

'Ah Chuen B'alam, isn't it true that you have already seen this amulet? Isn't it true that you first gave it to your wife before her death, many years ago?

'But even without that, my lord, is it not enough to see the mark around this man's neck? A man of high rank. A priest who knew about the existence of this poison, who knew that he could not find it here since the buffalo toads abandoned the region. A man who knew where he could find it and whom he could ask for it. A man who, in addition to including master Pek in his treason, betrayed his accomplice by stealing his wife.'

'Come forward, woman,' cried the old priest, without taking his eyes off Ah Chuen B'alam, now a silent, trembling, gelatinous mass flattened on his cushion, using his two hands to cover his neck. 'Tell us. Is he the father of the child you are carrying?'

The widow buried her face in her hands in shame and, between her tears, admitted that it was indeed he. She immediately returned to huddle in the corner of the room. The rest of the council had remained silent up to now, dumbstruck with surprise and dread. That a priest should commit murder, attempt murder, be guilty of adultery: it was beyond understanding. How should they react? Even the Ajaw was disconcerted for a moment.

The Ajaw considered Ah Chuen B'alam coldly.

'Face me up, priest, and answer our questions.'

The man sank down a little more at these words. He cast a terrified glance left and right but detected no kindliness in the eyes of those who looked back at him. He saw nothing but death written on the embarrassed faces of the members of the council; on the face of Thirteen Jaguar, imperturbable; on the face of the noble lady of Itzán, contemptuous; on the face of the Ajaw, imperious.

'Yes, my lord.'

'Why did you order the poison from the merchant?'

Ah Chuen B'alam, flustered, avoided meeting Thirteen Jaguar's eye.

'I wanted, I wanted—'

He could not go any further.

Thirteen Jaguar finished the sentence for him.

'—You wanted to get rid of me.'

'Yes,' murmured Ah Chuen B'alam.

'Why? I am old. Couldn't you have waited for me to die?'

'No, I couldn't wait any longer!' shouted Ah Chuen B'alam, in a voice that had grown stronger, more assured.

The man straightened up and went on.

'No, I couldn't wait any longer. I have been waiting for over ten years! Every day that goes by, I wait. And you, you are just as strong, as solid, as difficult, as alive as ever. After Ix Loom's death, I had hoped that you would allow me to run the college of priests. But no, after a few weeks, you were already back on your feet and, once again, you had relegated me to second place. Second place! The one I have had to settle for my whole life. My whole life, you have been first, and I have been second. I had had enough. When I heard that the merchant was heading north, I asked him to bring me back the poison. Nobody knew of it here, nobody had ever seen it work—except you. And you weren't going to talk.'

'—And had you decided to kill Pek from the outset, too?'

'No. When I gave him the order, I thought that by paying him handsomely, I could buy his silence. As time went by, I wondered whether I would not have to make him disappear too. And then... there was the other thing,' he added, uncomfortable. 'I hadn't anticipated that. But when she told me that she was pregnant, I knew that I had to get rid of Pek as soon as he would be back; she would not have the courage to hide my name from him for long. She hoped that he would not return. But that didn't suit me! I needed the poison. And she was beginning to become a burden too, asking what we would do if he never came back. And finally, he came back! At the feast, after he presented himself to you, my lord,' he said, bowing to the Ajaw, 'he sent his own wife to tell me to meet him at his home. Such irony! She took advantage of it to whisper that she would wait for me the next morning at dawn at the pond, our usual meeting place. I saw him leave the party soon after she returned to his side to tell him that I had accepted the appointment. I met him at his house. I paid the price for the poison. He only gave me one phial, saying that he would keep the other safe. Then I knew he was going to blackmail me. I left him. I left their house and hid in their garden. I hoped to talk to the woman for a moment, to find out what she would tell him about us. But she went straight past me without seeing me and entered the house before I could attract her attention. I heard their whole argument. It was when he discovered her belly that it all began. He beat her to make her tell him my name. To her credit, she stood her ground that night. She did not break down. I suppose that the thought of our appointment the next day gave her the strength to bear it. During the beating, One Hunter came out of his hut. I was scared that he would see me, and I backed into the shadow of a banana tree. But he went past at a run, fleeing into the forest. That is what gave me the idea of using a sling and stones like his—and the poison. In fact, at first I wanted to kill her, he added pointing at the widow. I knew that she would come to meet me, despite the danger. I knew that it was my last chance to silence her. It seemed to me that by using One Hunter's weapon and a little of the poison, I could kill her even if I didn't know how to use a sling very well. And I would leave the weapon there so people would think that it was he, One Hunter, who had killed her after making her pregnant and that he had wanted to silence her on his brother's return. Perhaps even Pek himself would be taken in. He was the ideal culprit: close to her, living on the same plot. But it is true that, from that moment on, I knew that I should have to kill the merchant too, to get my hand on the second bottle. I thought about it all night, turning my plan over and over, not sleeping for a single second. It could work. If she were killed by her lover, if Pek died of illness shortly after his return; who would suspect anything? And I would still have enough poison left for—'

Ah Chuen B'alam stopped, and fell into silence.

'This is how,' Thirteen Jaguar said, 'you took up your position near the pond, waiting for your victim?'

'Yes. I saw her arrive at the appointed time. But what I hadn't counted on was that her husband would follow her. I was dipping one of One Hunter's stones in the poison when he arrived. He tried to gag her and bind her. I suppose that his plan was to have the woman on one side, helpless, and to fall upon the lover as soon as that man would arrive at the meeting place. Except that, I was already there. I swirled the sling with all my strength. I didn't really know which of them I wanted to hit. In the end, it didn't matter much to me. One or other of them had to die. They hadn't seen me. From far away, I saw that he stood still after the stone's blow, and I knew that he was the one I had hit. He turned in my direction. I was afraid that he would discover me. I ran away as fast as my legs could carry me. In my haste, I did everything wrong! I kept the sling in my hand, but didn't pick up the phial that I had left on the ground while I was taking aim. I just ran and didn't look back. She was crying out, struggling. I think he was still trying to restrain her when death came and took him, without him really noticing it. I do not know what happened next. I don't think that she recognised me, and she didn't seem to suspect me. When her family came to reclaim the corpse the next day, I took advantage of it to make another appointment with her the following morning, at the pond as usual. Then, you put me in charge of the novices, and I couldn't leave the temple that day. It was impossible for me to recover the phial at the pond. The next morning, I was again unlucky: she came, but as I prepared to strangle her after knocking her out, somebody approached us. Again, I ran away.— And I had to stay with the novices for the whole day, as per your orders, sick with fear. Fear that she would wake up and talk. How ironic! For once, you had given me responsibilities; for once, I could exercise the authority that had been my dearest wish over all these years. In reality, you had tied my hands.'

There was no longer any need to ask questions, to encourage him to talk. The man was releasing himself, unburdening himself in a flood of words.

'When you showed us the two phials, it felt like I had been struck by lightning. I hadn't counted on the fact that the idiot woman—not knowing what the second bottle contained—would plant it in One Hunter's cabin. I hadn't told her anything about the poison; it was safer not to. And that was my undoing! There was only despair left in my heart, and the futile desire to make one last-ditch attempt. I could no longer hope to recover the poison, but my goal was to save my own life and silence the woman who would betray me as soon as she came round. I could think of nothing else than to silence her. So, yes, it was I last night!'

Ah Chuen B'alam gave them a defiant look

before relapsing into morose silence.

The Ajaw considered him at length before uttering his verdict.

'Do not think that I hesitate, priest! Death will be your fate. Yet, I have no desire to make the execution a public one. In fact, I have no desire for any of this to leave the room,' he continued with a stern face. 'You will at least escape this humiliation. But you will come with us. You will leave this morning. I will pretend that I am taking you because Thirteen Jaguar is too old to accompany me on this campaign. And you will not return, trust me. The simplest way would be for you to be made prisoner by Tikal,' he added with a cruel smile. 'But I cannot count on that. You will be guarded and kept under close watch— until the battle is over.'

The priest bent his head. He would not try to escape his fate. Why would he, now that his shame had been established before everyone who counted in Dos Pilas? Now that all his ambitions had been destroyed? Pride had been his only reason to live; it would be his reason to die. The lady wore a smile of satisfaction upon hearing the sentence. It suited her to not have to guard such an awkward prisoner while the warriors were about to go and leave the city defenceless. She turned to the Ajaw.

'And the woman?' she asked. 'What is your decision about her, my lord? She cheated on her husband.'

The Ajaw bade master Pek's widow come forward, in the sight of all the members of the council.

'Come, woman, present yourself to my judgement. Yes, you cheated on your husband, and you deserve death for that. Nonetheless, I will spare you because of the two attempts to kill you—and because you accused the guilty man. Then, there is the child; I see no reason why he should endure my justice. We shall see when you come to term. Beware! The day of its birth, it shall be announced that the child will not inherit. It would not be fair towards One Hunter: his brother's possessions belong to him. You will remain at the palace, among my wife's servants, until the birth of your child. She will watch over you. And now that this business is done with,' he added for everyone's attention, 'departure is in one hour.'

The Ajaw stood up to signify the end of the audience, and the members of the council arose in a hurry. With a harsh voice, the lady ordered the widow to follow her and left first, returning to the women's courtyard. Thirteen Jaguar stayed behind, allowing the generals to go ahead. He went over to the Ajaw.

'One Hunter?' he asked.

'Yes. You may tell him that he is free,' answered the Ajaw with a smile. 'And you,' he said, turning to Xhól, 'you can tell him later all that has happened and what you did to secure his freedom."

The smile faded, to be replaced by his habitual expression of severity.

'—But nobody else! With the battle that awaits

us, everyone will have forgotten about the merchant's death two days from now.——If there remain any survivors to remember Pek, I do not want his murder to become a topic of gossip. Do you understand me?'

Xhól bowed and left the room without a word.

'A clever boy,' said the Ajaw, staring at the curtain that had fallen behind Xhól. A pity he's a cripple; he would have made a good warrior.'

'——I could make a good priest out of him,' replied Thirteen Jaguar.

'So, that's what you are up to! I see you making plans already. But those plans, whatever they may be, must now be put aside for a while. We will talk about that when I return——if I return.'

Thirteen Jaguar threw him a questioning glance.

'Yes, my friend, I have made provisions for myself as well: if we win, well and good. If we lose, I have decided that there will be no running away from Tikal a second time. I am fifty years old. Once, I was vanquished and made prisoner by Calakmul. I was twenty then, you will recall. On that day, I chose life, and I accepted Yuknoom's offer to become his vassal. Five years ago came the rout against Tikal and that humiliating exile. This time, I will not be taken prisoner. This time, I will not run away from the enemy. Ah Chuen B'alam will not be the only one who does not return from the battlefield then. It will be an honourable death for us both; too honourable for him, and the only end to which I aspire, should our fate lead to defeat.'

Thirteen Jaguar considered B'alaj Chan K'awill,

ajaw of Dos Pilas; a man he had seen grow from that far-distant day on which the child had been entrusted to him after leaving the women's quarters; a man he had seen throw himself into the most foolhardy actions with all the enthusiasm of youth; a man he had seen mature, torn for many long years between his loyalty towards Tikal and that due to his new master; a man who was now at peace.

'Whatever the outcome, I know it will be the right one,' replied the old priest.

CHAPTER 11

THE DESERTED CITY

XHÓL SLIPPED OUT OF the audience chamber and wondered whether he wanted to tell One Hunter all that had happened. He wandered through the first courtyard, and stopped on the threshold of the second. Men were running in every direction, and he had to shift from one place to another to avoid them. On second thought, he decided to wait for Thirteen

Jaguar. Explaining it all would be easier with him around. After all, it was the high priest to whom the Ajaw had given the responsibility of informing One Hunter about his newfound freedom. He stood against a column, trying to make himself as small as possible.

The Ajaw, now fully engrossed by the departure, finally left the audience chamber in the company of Thirteen Jaguar.

'The men are to gather on the central plaza. At once!' the Ajaw shouted.

The rounding-up began. From a distance, Xhól saw Thirteen Jaguar invite One Hunter to come along, and he joined them. Xhól was relieved that the widow was nowhere to be seen. The entire city was now assembled on the central plaza, silent. Battalions were formed. Gathered in one corner of the plaza stood the men in charge of carrying everything that was necessary for a three-day expedition: food, water, more weapons, and tools for erecting hasty defences. A small party of scouts had already moved ahead to confirm the latest position of Tikal's army.

The Ajaw, dressed for battle with the feather headdress, the ornaments in his hair to show his rank, the obsidian axe at his side, the shield and the spear, stepped forward. He made no speech—there was no need. Once the battalions were formed, he cast an eye over his army and, with a single cry, led the march.

'Forward!'

The Ajaw was followed by his personal guard.

A little behind, there was Ah Chuen B'alam, surrounded by three warriors; Ah Chuen B'alam who was trying to keep up appearances; Ah Chuen B'alam who was trying to pretend through his attitude and tone of voice that it was an honour for him to go with the Ajaw to war.

Decidedly! thought Thirteen Jaguar, he would never change, even on the eve of his death. He had nothing but pity now for his former second-in-command, whatever the outcome of the battle. He felt pity for all the young men he saw passing before him too. Yes, if they were to die on the morrow, they would go straight to the resting place of warriors killed in combat. Was it really worth missing all these years of life that he had known? Yes, he was old; yes, he would soon die, but he would die after so many experiences. Among which, he remembered seeing many young warriors leave for battles they never returned from. He was now seized with a deep weariness. Gone were the days when seeing the Ajaw's army set forth in such a splendid order would have awoken in him nothing but pride and the hope of glory for the city. He was getting too old. Beside him, the lady of Itzán watched the army's departure unblinkingly, then returned in grand pomp to the palace, accompanied by her two sons, Six Sky and her retinue.

Thirteen Jaguar beckoned to Xhól and One Hunter and instructed them to follow him. They headed towards the observatory temple. Xhól felt relieved; at least there was no danger of meeting the widow anymore. The old priest had them climb on the platform. Two servants hurried towards the priest. Thirteen Jaguar ordered them to bring refreshments to the little room and not to disturb them—under any pretext. The explanation was a long one. The worst moment was when Xhól had to tell how the widow had tried to incriminate One Hunter by placing the second phial in his bedding. He had not taken the news of her pregnancy and the presence of a lover too badly, but that! The idea that she had wanted to incriminate him! No, he could not accept it. Xhól could not bear the wounded look on the face of his other self, now his friend. Why did he have to be so blind? Why did he have to put so much faith in her? Why did the tale of her duplicity have to cause him so much pain? This took away Xhól's joy at seeing One Hunter finally free and cleared of all suspicion. He could hardly bring himself to mention the part of the Ajaw's judgement that concerned the child and the inheritance.

'But what am I to do with my brother's possessions? I do not want to become a merchant!' replied One Hunter, overcome. 'If only, if only—'

Thirteen Jaguar contemplated him with interest.

'—If only?'

'If only I had things my way, then I would marry her. Still!' replied One Hunter, sticking his chin out. 'And I would treat the child as my own, or that of my brother... or as if we did not know whom of the two is the father.'

Xhól looked at him in distress.

'You would do that for her? After what we saw?'

'Yes!' answered One Hunter, staring at them defiantly.

Thirteen Jaguar didn't look surprised.

'We shall see, my boy, we shall see. So many things may happen before that child is born.'

The next day, Xhól woke early and lay on his bed, wondering what to do: no more probing on behalf of the high priest, no more searching, no more ambushing. One Hunter had been allowed to go back home; One Hunter who, like himself, must be wondering what to do today. But he knew what to do! —Help Ix Naah as best he could in the absence of his brother-in-law. He jumped up and went to join his sister in the outdoor kitchen where she was already busy lighting a fire.

'Are the children not yet awake?'

'No. I didn't want to wake them; better to let them sleep. Tell me, Xhól, do you think that we should prepare to flee into the forest?'

Xhól pondered the question for a while.

'I do not know. In any case, it might be good to prepare a light package with enough food to last us through three or four days. Who knows?'

Ix Naah barely looked at him, busily cooking the corn tortillas. Neither one of them were willing to talk. An unusual silence settled between them. A silence that was not only theirs. The silence surrounded them, encircled them, submerged them. What had become of everyday sounds? The sound of neighbours busy in their plots? The sound of looms clattering at the weavers'? The sound of children running from one house to another? Muted, gone, swallowed up by the war. The men had gone; the women remained alone and kept their children at home. The city seemed dead already. He wanted to shake himself, force himself, get himself busy. Waiting for waiting's sake, why not do something worthwhile in the meantime? Something to occupy his mind, something that would make him forget the world around him. He leapt up.

'Ix Naah, I can take no more. I won't last a whole day like this, waiting. I am going to the temple to work on my mural. If you need me, don't hesitate; send one of the boys to fetch me.'

Xhól went to his mural on the corner of the observatory temple, abandoned in recent days. He picked up his brushes and colours from the little room in which he had stored them. He set down his mat before the unfinished painting and set to work. A magnificent day, he thought—and a quiet one. He had never enjoyed such peace at this time of the day. He began to crush his colours, mixing them slowly, methodically. His heart was not in it this time. Usually, he experienced a sense of excitement at the start of the day's work. He wanted to begin right away, and could not wait to see the work take shape, develop, move in unexpected directions. Today? Nothing. It was his worst day ever. He felt dead inside, without courage, without desire. And yet, he persisted in mixing the colours, not heeding the voice inside whispering that it wasn't worth it; that today he would produce nothing worth it.

He decided to begin with something easy: filling in the robe of the character he had abandoned the day he had found master Pek by the side of the pond. The first strokes were hesitant, uncertain; luckily, it was the centre of the robe. He forced himself, applied himself—and the miracle occurred; the miracle of the feeling of plenitude that overcame him when he painted. He forgot about the city, the war, and the silence that surrounded him. He forgot everything to be with this character, and then the next, and then with the background water lilies. Xhól was painting.

He spent his day like this, forgetful of everything around him. The only thing that caused him to change position, to move his mat, was when the pain grew too intense. But even that faded into the background. This day of painting— which had begun so badly—was turning into a capital one. He felt in tune, carried away by the movement of the brushstrokes, the steps of the characters moving slowly forward to the rhythm of the procession, and the gentle swaying of the water lilies trembling in the breeze of an imaginary river. He did not even care about hunger when it came, and he let it go away without a second glance.

Xhól only came out of his dream at sunset, when the light took on a reddish hue that prevented him from judging colours anymore. He put down his brushes, got up, and stretched as he inspected the still-deserted central plaza. He put away his tools and turned back, famished now. He stopped short at the idea that Ix Naah had remained at home the whole day, without any opportunity to hear the news if there were any to be had. He turned off towards the palace. Perhaps he could extract some information from the guards? But no, there was nothing! The old officer who had been left in charge of protecting the lady had nothing to tell him. According to the latest news, which dated from the morning, the army had reached the point where the generals had decided to lay their ambush. Nothing more. According to the old soldier, the fight would have taken place in the afternoon at the earliest or would even be delayed until the next morning if Tikal's army were slow. There was nothing to do but wait. Wait for a messenger to arrive with the first news of the battle.

Xhól wondered how Six Sky bore the waiting and the atmosphere of death clouding the palace. He hovered, paused one moment. Should he try to see her? He decided not to. What good would it do? He had observed her during the ceremony—she had borne her rank perfectly, without even looking at him despite his being close by, thanks to Thirteen Jaguar. He had seen how her eyes had shone when the lady of Itzán had been given the regency! At that moment, he had read into her soul. She had made her choice. What good would it do to hang onto a past that was unravelling and disappearing fast?

Xhól left the palace, the unusual silence of which oppressed him. Everything oppressed him, now that he had left his painting. Even the idea of going back to his sister's oppressed him, of looking at her worried face, of facing her questioning eyes without being able to reassure her. Just then, he saw Ix Naah arrive, little Itzel in her arms, the two boys running ahead.

'Xhól! I was so worried when you didn't return home that I came here. Is there any news?'

'No,' answered the old warrior before he could say a word. 'No, and there will not be any before tomorrow morning at the earliest.'

Wait, that was all they could do. The next day, Xhól returned to his mural. As painting had proved successful to keep his worry away on the day before, he would keep on working on his fresco. It was still quiet on the central plaza. He went to fetch his tools and his mat and settled in. This time, he had barely begun crushing the colours when he noticed a man running. His heart skipped a beat: a messenger! He abandoned his painting, leapt up and ran to the man.

'My message is for the lady!' shouted the latter without stopping.

Xhól followed him, lagging behind because of his leg. When he finally reached the palace, the announcement of the arrival of a messenger had already spread throughout the women's court, the slaves' quarters and the nearby houses. In less than an hour, the entire city would be in the know. The lady of Itzán appeared in the first courtyard, accompanied by her retinue, and Six Sky. She watched the exhausted messenger who bowed before her.

'Speak! Tell us what happened'

'My lady, we are victorious!' replied the messenger. 'It all happened as planned. The men of Tikal rushed into our trap yesterday, in the early afternoon. The battle lasted for a long time, until the setting of the sun. And in the red light, the men of Tikal fled from the anger of our ajaw. Their dead warriors are now strewn across the battlefield. And we have taken prisoners too! One of Nuun Ujol Chaak's highest generals is among them. We nearly captured him too, but he managed to get away in the end.'

The lady did not bat an eyelid, her entire being erect and dignified. She did not allow either the apprehension that had gripped her at first or the relief at the good news to move her. Six Sky, at her side, shone.

'And the Ajaw?'

'Have no fear for him, my lady. Despite his bravery in combat, he has not been wounded,' answered the messenger. 'Of the nobles, there is only the priest Ah Chuen B'alam, whom our lord had decided to take with him, who fell during the fray.'

A smile of contentment appeared on the emaciated face of the lady of Itzán.

'But,' the messenger continued, 'I left so quickly that I may not know everything. The Ajaw ordered me to return to you as soon as the battle had ended and it was certain that Tikal would not come back.'

'When will they return?'

'My lady, everybody was eager to come home. I believe you can expect them tonight. In any case, most of the troops. A battalion will perhaps remain behind to take care of our wounded.'

'Excellent,' replied the lady of Itzán. She turned towards the old warrior in charge of the guard. 'Take care of this man, feed him, and let him rest.—Have the news of the victors' return announced,' she added with majesty.

Then, the lady of Itzán, accompanied by Six Sky, who had not cast a single look at her old friend, returned to the women's court. Xhól ran at top speed to announce the news to Ix Naah, who might still worry a little about her husband until she saw him safe at home. But there was no reason to fear anything anymore, thought Xhól. His brother-in-law would have remained in the rear guard—and they were victorious.

'We are victorious!' The words kept singing in his head and seemed to be taken up everywhere he went.

'We are victorious' cried the women, the children.

'We are victorious!'—and the whole city came back to life on hearing this cry that spread like a ripple on the surface of a pond.

'We are victorious!'—and that meant that they would live, that there would be no flight into the forest.

'We are victorious!'—and that meant that they

would stay in Dos Pilas, that they would continue to look after their fields and garden.

'We are victorious!'—and that meant that Tikal would attack them no more, that they would henceforth live in peace.

'We are victorious!'—and that meant that the Ajaw's prestige had grown once again, that there would be no more whispers about the past.

'We are victorious!'—and that also meant that noble Six Sky had chosen her path, and what did he care?

'We are victorious!' he cried from afar when he spotted Ix Naah.

'We are victorious!'—and her face lit up, and the two boys followed by little Itzel rushed towards him.

'We are victorious!'—and that, in the end, was what mattered most; that she and the children were safe.

CHAPTER 12

VICTORY

THE NEWS SPREAD LIKE wildfire through the city, the city that had now come back to life and was readying itself to welcome the victorious warriors. The lady had given her orders. As soon as the messenger had finished, scouts had set off to find out when the men would arrive. They had met them on the way and had come back running. To be sure, the convoy would be slower than on the way out because of the wounded, and the prisoners too, but they would be there by sundown. And so they waited, with growing impatience. The central plaza was teeming with people by the middle of the afternoon.

A platform had been hastily erected for the lady and her retinue, but she did not appear until late in the afternoon. Followed by her two sons, Six Sky, Thirteen Jaguar, and the young priests, she moved slowly through the crowd which parted in awe in front of her. She settled onto her seat, had her elder son sit beside her, checked that Six Sky and the younger one were behaving themselves, then fixed her eyes upon the road from which the victorious warriors would enter the central plaza. The mood was feverish now; the crowd was nervous. And then came a clamour: 'They are coming!' Everybody stood up, pushing, thronging along the path.

Yes, they were coming, proud despite the fatigue of the march and the battle of the day before. The cries and acclamations thundered when the Ajaw appeared, surrounded by his generals. The prisoners followed, in the first line of which a lord could be seen. Oh yes, he was a lord, that one! It could be seen in his bearing. And soon a name ran through the delighted crowd: that of one of Nuun Ujol Chaak's closest lieutenants, the celebrated Nuun B'alam, he who had caused them so much harm by leading the attack that had forced the Ajaw to flee five years earlier. They had caught him in the end!

The man was walking indifferent to everything;

to the bonds that held his arms; to the spittle and insults of the crowd that now surrounded him; he knew he was going to die. He had withdrawn into himself, to a place where nobody could reach him. The other prisoners, their heads bowed, did not display the same equanimity. Their fate was less certain. Would it be death or slavery? Which, indeed, was to be preferred? Then the victorious warriors appeared, their heads held high, followed by the men requisitioned to assist them. Their appearance prompted endless cries of joy; a mother recognised her son, a wife her husband. The ranks broke.

The Ajaw reached the platform and sat down beside the lady. He had the prisoners march before him. With undisguised satisfaction, he looked upon Nuun B'alam, stripped of his insignia of command, his hands tied. He motioned for him to be brought in front of the platform. The crowd fell silent. Four warriors surrounded the man hated by all. With a gesture of the hand, the Ajaw ordered them to make the prisoner kneel down, and suffer humiliation. The man resisted, but under the strong hand of the captain of the guards, he found himself on the ground and bowed his head before the Ajaw. The latter looked at his prisoner with sombre satisfaction, then came down from the platform and went towards the palace, followed by his family. There would be no feast tonight. The men were tired, and their families wanted them home. The proper celebration of their victory would wait.

Xhól, who had accompanied Ix Naah and the

children, was glad to see her reunited to her husband. A strange sense of isolation gripped him when he saw them embrace, assailed by the children who clamoured for their share of attention. They did not need him for the family to be whole. He remained a little behind and got lost in the crowd. When he saw the Ajaw leave the platform, his family following along with the priests, he wondered whether he would dare address Thirteen Jaguar. He had not spoken to the high priest since their conversation with One Hunter. He elbowed his way through the throng, and struggled to keep his balance among all the people who pressed him without paying heed to his bad leg. He finally came close to the old man and succeeded in catching his eye. The high priest beckoned him to come closer. The procession was now moving at a slow pace. Under the arch leading to the first courtyard of the palace, the crowd was prevented from going any further by the guards and Xhól was able to steady himself. The old priest approached him.

'Come. We need to talk.' he said with a large smile.

Xhól followed him into his apartments. The high priest settled comfortably onto one of the cushions garnishing the bench. Xhól, still standing, beheld him for a moment. Thirteen Jaguar noticed the watchful look and smiled again.

'Is there anything the matter, my boy?'

'Yes, you. You look... different.'

'—Different?'

'From two days ago. You seemed so old when the army left. And now, you give me the impression that you are back to your former self.'

'The good news, perhaps,' replied the high priest. 'The news of the victory, for starters.—And that all went well with Ah Chuen B'alam too. The Ajaw managed to tell me so despite the confusion.'

'Went well?'

'Why yes, my boy. Believe me, it was the best way. For the Ajaw—who did not want any scandal.—And for Ah Chuen B'alam too, by the way. He has thus been spared a painful, slow, humiliating death. Instead, he was granted a swift departure that will ensure him a certain posthumous glory. He would have liked that, you know. But you are still young. You have not yet had time to think at your leisure about what a good death might be. It is normal at your age to be more concerned with the life that is opening out in front of you.'

Xhól looked at him, hesitant: why had the high priest bade him come?

'Tell me, my boy, how is your mural coming along?'

'Well, my lord, I worked at it all day yesterday.'

'—And you have never thought of doing anything else than painting or sculpting?'

' "Anything else?" ' asked Xhól. 'What else could I do with this—' he went on, designating his right leg. 'I cannot do anything else. When my master took me on as an apprentice, I was glad that he accepted me. Few men in Dos Pilas would have done the same. And what I have learned with him fills me with joy. If you knew how happy I felt yesterday as soon I managed to forget about the war! So happy! No, you cannot imagine—'

'I think I can. It is the kind of feeling I get when I look at the stars, when I contemplate Chak Ek'*—'

'Perhaps,' replied Xhól.

'Have you ever thought of becoming a priest?' said the old man.

'A priest? Me?' Xhól started to laugh.

'What is so funny?' asked Thirteen Jaguar.

'I am but a humble peasant's son, my lord. How could I ever imagine becoming a priest? And anyway, I don't know much—'

'You already know how to write, well enough to sculpt in any case.'

'Yes, but I always need your help for the exact shape of the glyphs.'

'Oh, that is just a question of training.'

'Are you serious?' asked Xhól.

'Yes, very serious. I have already spoken to the Ajaw. He has agreed to it.'

'Spoken to the Ajaw?'

'Yes. Is that a problem?'

'Well, it's just that I am not so sure that I would like to become a priest. It is true there are things I would like to learn. I have always wanted to learn. But—'

'But?'

'—But I have a feeling that I would miss sculpting,

---

* Chak Ek': the planet Venus.

238

painting, all that... I get the impression that I think better with my hands, you know. Well, no, I don't suppose that you do understand,' he finished lamely.

'Perhaps I do, my boy. Listen. Here is what I suggest: from now on, you can join my lessons with the novices. And you can continue to paint and sculpt. In fact, at the moment Dos Pilas does not have anyone to replace you. And we shall see. We shall see what you prefer. Does that suit you?'

'Yes, master,' replied the young man, with a bow.

Dawn was breaking once again over Dos Pilas. Xhól said to himself that he had only two good hours of quiet before the central plaza would once again be filled with people. Everything would need to be in readiness for the feast that the Ajaw had decided to offer the city to celebrate his victory. Yes, in two hours, it would be impossible to work. He went into the little room where he stored his tools and came out with his paintbrushes, his colours and his mat. He went to the corner where he had abandoned his almost finished procession, and began to crush the colours. He had two hours of quiet left—and he wanted to make the most of them.

INDEX OF CHARACTERS

AH CHUEN B'ALAM (632-679): member of the college of priests of Dos Pilas; second-in-command to Thirteen Jaguar.

B'ALAJ CHAN K'AWILL (625-697): first ajaw of Dos Pilas; older brother and enemy of Nuun Ujol Chaak, ruler of Tikal.

ITZAMNAAJ B'ALAM (669-698): first-born son of

B'alaj Chan K'awill and the lady of Itzán, destined to become the second ajaw of Dos Pilas. Impulsive, quick to anger, he cannot stand his younger brother.

ITZAMNAAJ K'AWILL (673-726): second-born son of B'alaj Chan K'awill and the lady of Itzán; too intelligent for his own good.

ITZEL (675-767): daughter of Ix Naah and Xhól's favourite niece.

IX NAAH (653-698): Xhól's sister.

EIGHTEEN PUMA (635-698): a nobleman of Dos Pilas; cousin to the first ajaw, B'alaj Chan K'awill.

LADY OF ITZÁN (the) (636-683): second wife of B'alaj Chan K'awill.

MASTER PEK (637-679): one of the richest merchants of Dos Pilas; murdered on his return from a diplomatic and commercial mission to the far north.

MASTER PEK'S WIDOW (652-680): a young woman, unhappy in her marriage, subjected to the violence of her husband.

NUUN B'ALAM (650-682): a nobleman of Tikal; officer taken prisoner by the ajaw of Dos Pilas during the battle of 679.

NUUN UJOL CHAAK (657-682): ruler of Tikal and younger brother to B'alaj Chan K'awill of Dos Pilas; chosen by the elders of Tikal to succeed his father as ruler of Tikal, to the dismay of B'alaj Chan K'awill.

ONE HUNTER (660-705): A young hunter whose infirmity, similar to that of Xhól, has rendered him diffident; accused at one time of murdering his brother, master Pek.

PUK (663-741): a priest of Dos Pilas; novice, second-in-command to Thirteen Jaguar and Ixtecox, and, in the end, high priest.

SHIELD OF JADE (659-741): a young warrior with a bright future.

SIX SKY (664-741): daughter to B'alaj Chan K'awill, first ajaw of Dos Pilas and the lady of B'ulu, who died in childbirth; married Yax Pac of El Naranjo and became the reigning lady of the city; remained a faithful vassal of Calakmul throughout her life.

THIRTEEN JAGUAR (605-683): high priest of Dos Pilas.

XHÓL (662-761): a painter and sculptor... and a cripple. His greatest disability might well be his total incapacity to navigate throughout the court intrigues.

BIBLIOGRAPHY

Nouvelles d'Amérique centrale, 2013. To be published in English under the title *Nueva Jerusalem and Other Short Stories from Central America*, 2015.

Le secret du masque de jade (*Le Cycle de Xhól*, *Livre 2*), 2013. To be published in English under the title *The Secret of the Jade Mask (Cycle of Xhól: Book 2)*, 2015.

THE CYCLE OF XHÓL

HISTORICAL MYSTERY, ETHNIC thriller, historical fiction: the *Cycle of Xhól* is all these rolled into one.

Over one century, the *Cycle of Xhól* follows the destiny of Dos Pilas, a small Mayan city in Petén, sandwiched between the two regional superpowers, Tikal and Calakmul. Dos Pilas, and its population, endures the ebb and flow of victories and defeats, the ever-shifting alliances, the succession of rulers, and the battles won and lost.

Each novel can be read independently and offers a complete mystery in which Xhól, painter and sculptor, is the central character. Each novel is also part of the overall cycle and little by little reveals the destiny of the city and Xhól himself. The *Cycle of Xhól* will be a sixteen-book series when complete.

Book 1: *The Merchant of Death* (2014)
Book 2: *The Secret of the Jade Mask* (2015)

THE SECRET OF THE JADE MASK

JAGUAR SMOKE PAW BOWED before Yuknoom the Great, Yuknoom of Calakmul, his father, seated on the platform piled with cushions against which the old man rested with his eyes closed.

'Father, you asked for me?'

'Yes. the gods came to me last night in a dream. In my dream, I stood on a distant hill. Far away,

I could see the city, our city, our Calakmul: I could barely make out the great temple emerging from the sea of trees, and the palace too. The sky was blue, like this morning. I contemplated my city with the satisfaction of seeing it flourish when, suddenly, a maleficent cloud formed above. Lightning sprang from this cloud and struck the pyramid. Then a voice, the voice of a god, warned me, I who was watching the destruction of what I care about most in this world, powerless and terrified.

' "Beware," said the voice. "Beware of them all! They will all betray you in time. They will all join the enemy in time. All of them, I tell you; the ajaw of Dos Pilas, who has never really accepted his defeat at your hands; Ku Ix d'Uxul in the ambition of his youth; the warriors of El Naranjo too. All of them, I tell you, want to betray you. All of them will betray you in time!" '

'The lightning redoubled in intensity and set fire to the city,' Yuknoom went on. 'I could hear shouting, screaming. Then I awoke with a start. We must act. We cannot risk our city's destruction through the fault of these traitors!'

'But, Father, it was just a dream—'

682 AD, three years after the victory of Dos Pilas over Tikal, the Ajaw is invited to Calakmul for the mid-katun ceremonies by Yuknoom the Great, his overlord.

Xhól is part of the delegation. Before long, he notices the maleficent atmosphere of mistrust and folly that has overtaken Calakmul under the influence of its ageing lord.

Soon after their arrival, the jade mask representing lord Yuknoom is stolen. The latter uses the theft as a pretext to arrest the prince of Uxul, whom he suspects of treason.

Xhól is not convinced. Why steal such a precious, such a dangerous item? Why is its maker discovered stabbed in a backyard of the visitors' quarters the day after the theft?

ABOUT THE AUTHOR

CÉCILE CHABOT WAS BORN in Liège, Belgium in 1969 and attended the Lycée Léonie de Waha, a girls-only (at that time) school founded in the 19th century to prepare girls for university. There, she received a solid grounding in the sciences and modern languages.

Afterwards, she graduated from the University of Liège with a Masters degree in Law and a second degree in European Law. Whenever she could, she chose courses that satiated her hunger for history (Medieval history, History of Islam, among others) and was most fascinated by those courses on the curriculum that dealt with the origins of law and institutions (Roman law, History of Natural Law, Philosophy of Law). At university, she began spelunking (caving) on a regular basis. Cécile has had a long career in banking & finance and is an expert in banking law, intellectual property, and contract negotiation.

Over the years, she has wandered from Mexico to Colombia, where she landed by boat in Cartagena de Indias via the San Blas islands. Along the way, she visited all of Central America.

Head to http://www.cecilechabot.com for an account of how it all started—with a spelunking expedition in Guatemala… and the discovery of a cave.

The *Cycle of Xhól* is her most ambitious writing project so far. This 16-book series of historical mysteries is set in Dos Pilas, a Mayan city located in what is today the northern part of Guatemala. The cycle starts in 679 AD with book 1, *The Merchant of Death*, and will end one century later with book 16. Before committing to paper the first line of *The Merchant of Death*, Cécile already knew that the full story would take sixteen books to complete, why it would be so, and, more importantly, how it would all end. Be warned, she stubbornly refuses to reveal that conclusion before book 16 hits the shelves. She delights in locating her mysteries in a painstakingly reconstructed universe.

She is also the author of *Nouvelles d'Amérique Centrale*, a collection of short stories based on her travels where she shares the deep impressions the continent left on her soul (to be published in English in 2015 under the title *Nueva Jerusalem and Other Short Stories from Central America*).

She speaks five languages with various degrees of fluency, lives in Brussels, and will bore you to death at social events when she gets started on her pet subject (the difficulty of mastering the declination of hard and soft vowel-ending adjectives in Czech). She has no cat because languages are enough. She is deadly afraid that some day an archaeologist might read her books and write to her to point out what she got wrong.

She is quite active on Twitter (@CecileChabot) and tweets in French, English and Spanish about literature, the Mayans, Central America, her favourite reads, what delights and amuses her—and the enchanting beauty of words.

Cécile publishes an unabashedly erratic newsletter in which she hops without rhyme or reason from her explorations of the Mayan jungles to her forays in the publishing world. Subscribe at http://www.cecilechabot.com/newsletter, and she will send you a copy of her *Diary of a Caving Expedition in Guatemala* as a token of her appreciation for doing so.

ACKNOWLEDGEMENTS

THE MERCHANT OF DEATH was first published in French under the title *Le Marchand de la mort* in 2011. There were many people to thank then for helping me to complete that first edition: the French-speaking beta-readers, editor and proofreader.

As regards the English version, I would like to thank—and tell them how grateful I am for their hard work—Anna Doherty (my translator) and Joseph Kranak (my editor).

Anna was the translator I could only dream of: utterly patient, unruffled by the mind-boggling amount of track changes and "suggestions" I kept throwing at her in several waves of drafts, and as keen as I was to find the exact word or the right turn of phrase.

Joseph brought a fresh pair of eyeballs to the job when both Anna's and mine were rendered blind by the sheer number of revisions, and helped to give the last polish to the novel with his fanatical attention to detail.

Cécile Chabot
Brussels, 9 October 2014

www.ingramcontent.com/pod-product-compliance
Lightning Source LLC
Chambersburg PA
CBHW050740230626
47052CB00004BA/765